Inheritance

By Jenny Eclair

Camberwell Beauty
Having a Lovely Time
Life, Death and Vanilla Slices
Moving
Listening In
Inheritance

JENNY
ECLAIR

Inheritance

sphere

SPHERE

First published in Great Britain in 2019 by Sphere

1 3 5 7 9 10 8 6 4 2

A CIP catalogue record for this book
is available from the British Library.

Hardback ISBN 978-0-7515-6706-9
C-format ISBN 978-0-7515-6704-5

Typeset in Goudy by M Rules
Printed and bound in Great Britain by
Clays Ltd, Elcograf S.p.A.

Papers used by Sphere are from well-managed forests
and other responsible sources.

Sphere
An imprint of
Little, Brown Book Group
Carmelite House
50 Victoria Embankment
London EC4Y 0DZ

An Hachette UK Company
www.hachette.co.uk

www.littlebrown.co.uk

To my father, for giving me his knees

Acknowledgements

With thanks to Catherine Burke and Abby Parsons at Little, Brown. Also to Geof for his endless patience and all the trips to Cornwall, and to Phoebe because she understands and believes I can do it.

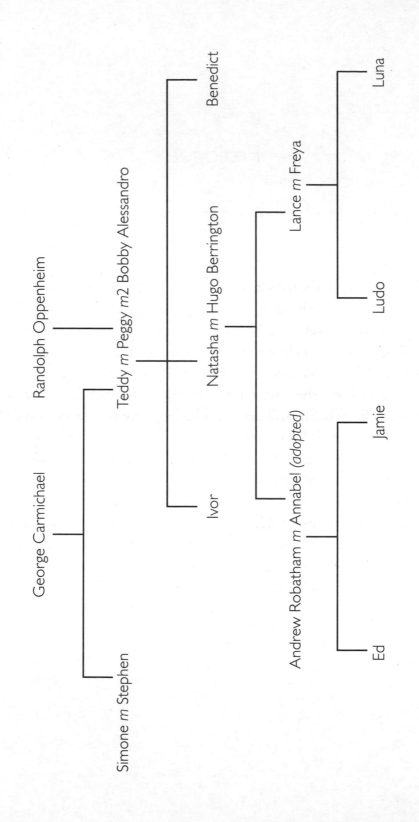

George Carmichael

Randolph Oppenheim

Simone *m* Stephen

Teddy *m* Peggy *m2* Bobby Alessandro

Ivor

Benedict

Natasha *m* Hugo Berrington

Lance *m* Freya

Ludo

Luna

Andrew Robatham *m* Annabel *(adopted)*

Ed

Jamie

Prologue

The baby lies in the half-open drawer and contemplates the cracked surface above her head. It's called a ceiling, but she has no words for anything as yet – she is three weeks old.

The baby has cradle cap and a blocked tear duct. These things are not life threatening – the baby will survive. In time she will grow and learn the names for hundreds of thousands of things, some in French. She will develop a lifelong love of baked beans on toast with grated cheese on top. She will learn to walk and run and have adventures, and she will hate going to Brownies and having her hair put in tight elastic bands.

The baby is seven and a half pounds of potential. She will go on to do all sorts of things: ride a bike, hang wallpaper, thread a needle, make casseroles, throw a pot, swear, love, laugh, cry . . . and even, one year, attempt to make her own Christmas crackers.

A world of possibilities awaits her, as long as she is found.

I

Falling (I)

Cornwall, August 2018

The pain, when it happens, is instant and surprising. It comes from nowhere, sharp, to the side of her head, her right temple, and in that split second before the sky turns black, Bel senses herself dropping and remembers watching a tower block collapsing on the television, a wrecking ball swinging.

She comes round seconds later, feeling the ground beneath her. Grass, she is lying on green grass, it prickles her back. She should get up – people will think she's drunk. You can't go to parties in the middle of the day and fall over for no reason, not when you are a woman in your mid-fifties and have been seen holding at least one glass of Pimm's.

Voices babble above her. 'Stand back, for heaven's sake.' 'Give the poor woman some breathing space.'

Oh dear, she is a 'poor woman'. She hopes she fell well; she hopes she crumpled rather than crashed.

A child is being told off in the distance. 'Ludo, what the hell?' It's Lance's voice. 'For God's sake, get her indoors.'

3

There is something impatient in her adopted brother's voice. She will be making the place look untidy – Lance and his wife Freya are very 'aesthetically aware'. She heard someone coin this phrase last night as Freya ceremoniously carried a picture-perfect fish pie to the jasmine-scented table while creamy ecclesiastical candles repeated themselves in an ancient Venetian-glass mirror.

The last thing they will want at Lance's fiftieth birthday celebration weekend is a fat middle-aged woman sprawled out on the lawn next to the tennis court.

Other voices mutter in a ragged circle around her.

'It was a stone, apparently.'

'But why was he hitting a stone with a tennis racket?'

'Because his sister wouldn't give him back the ball.'

'Just get her comfortable.'

'Where is Allan?'

'Who's Allan?'

'Her husband.'

'I think he's called Andrew. He went to get some more ice from the village, he'll be back soon. I'm sure she'll be fine.'

A man in faded red trousers leans over her, his breath reeking of garlic, and peels back her eyelids. The sensation is uncomfortable and she imagines he will have smudged the soft grey eyeshadow that Maisie forced her to apply.

'Knocked out cold, I'd say, but she's coming to. Be right as rain in a jiffy.' He commandeers a passing waitress to help him carry the woman indoors.

The man seizes her under her arms and Bel can feel her top gape away from her skirt – how embarrassing. Someone, the waitress presumably, has her by the ankles and she feels a sudden chilliness as they haul her up the shaded stone steps towards the house. So she is not completely out of it, she deduces, she can still smell the intense sweetness from the honeysuckle that clings to the grey stone wall, hear the crunch of footsteps on the gravel drive.

The waitress is gripping Bel's puffy ankles with difficulty. Bel can see through half-open eyes that she is a pretty girl with tattoos that probably made her mother cry; Japanese dragons and geisha girls run riot around her sturdy arms.

This is ridiculous, Bel thinks. The poor girl was hired to carry large white plates of intricate canapés, whirls of piped chicken mousse on tiny squares of pumpernickel, topped with dill and a sliver of cornichon, not cart heavy middle-aged matrons around. Perhaps Tattoo Girl will nick a bottle of fizz to make up for it later. It wouldn't be difficult; there are bottles cooling in plastic bins all over the place.

Bel relaxes her body: though she is not completely unconscious, playing the part will get her out of all those awkward social niceties on the lawn, and she's only too glad of an excuse to escape this party for a while.

'Where are we taking her?' the waitress asks Pink Trousers.

'They're in the blue room,' a woman's voice replies – Freya, Bel guesses. Lance's wife is in charge of that sort of thing – who gets to sleep in the main house and who gets relegated to camping in yurts. Not camping, she corrects herself, 'glamping'.

'Main house, first floor, left at the top of the main staircase and then the last door along the corridor on the right.'

Yes, that's Freya. Her foreign accent is more pronounced when she is anxious.

Not a sea view, which is a shame, but a gorgeous room none-theless. Freya has done such an amazing job. She's so clever, her children so well behaved, so beautiful, and of course Ludo didn't mean it, it was an accident. Accidents happen, though some of them have more far-reaching consequences than one can ever imagine, thinks Bel dozily, allowing herself to be transported like a sack of potatoes through the coolness of the hallway and up the broad carpeted stairs. Pink Trousers and Tattoo Girl start to puff as they round the stairs up to the first floor; as prisms of jewel-coloured light from the stained-glass window flutter across her eyelids, Bel can smell the beeswax polish ingrained into the wood of the banister rail. She knows that if she could be bothered to open her eyes she would see a large replica of a sailing boat perched on the windowsill, a relic from when the house belonged to Lance and Bel's grandmother, Peggy. Bel met her only once; an American woman with a face like an Estée Lauder death mask.

Rounding the corner on to the landing, Bel can feel the girl struggling to keep hold of her legs. Never mind, if they dropped her here she could always crawl.

'Not far now,' puffs Pink Trousers. 'Gosh, if this isn't a reminder to get down to the gym a bit more often, I don't know what is.'

Bel hopes they can't see her bra. She was going to buy a new one, but with all the other expenses of Lance's fiftieth – her outfit, Andrew's new shirt, not to mention the exorbitant gift – it went on the back burner.

'One, two, three and hups-a-daisy,' says the man, and together he and the waitress heave Bel on top of the duvet.

'Should we take her shoes off?' asks the waitress.

'Just her shoes,' replies the man. 'We don't want it to look like she's been interfered with,' and he laughs as if the idea is preposterous. The girl doesn't laugh, she gently removes Bel's all-purpose nude patent mid-heel pump, which she'd bought last summer in the Russell & Bromley sale, and Bel instinctively wriggles her toes in relief; the shoes are a tiny bit tight.

'See,' chuckles Pink Trousers, pointing to Bel's feet. 'Signs of life in the old trotters.' Now Bel wishes she'd had a pedicure. Maisie had offered to paint her toenails but went off the idea when she saw them: 'Seriously, Bel, you got some issues down there.'

The girl draws the curtains with a satisfying swish – they match the duvet, Bel had noticed this last night, making sure she complimented Freya on the detail when they went downstairs for drinks on the patio. 'Osborne and Little,' Freya had explained. 'I wanted something that reflected how the house was in its heyday, reinterpreted with a modern twist. Fresh, yes?' Honestly, the woman's English is impeccable; listening to her, you'd never guess she was from Sweden, or was it Finland? Although those children of hers are a bit of a giveaway with their Scandinavian white-blond hair and quick-to-tan complexions. Freya and Lance's children go the colour of tinned hot dogs in summer.

Poor Ludo, she hopes no one is blaming him for this – it's not as if he did it on purpose. Besides, it's a relief to take some time out of this party. It seems to have been going on for ever, what with the drive down from London, the drinks and meal last night, today's lunch and games on the lawn. If she can get out of tonight's fancy dress and barn dance by claiming to have a bit of a sore head, then brilliant. Maybe someone will bring her some supper on a tray – baked eggs, something like that?

How peculiar, she hasn't thought about baked eggs for years. Her mother's daily help used to make them for her when she was a little girl. The thought of dear Mrs Phelan, who dropped down dead with a duster in her hand ('Cleaning to the end,' her husband said proudly), makes Bel feel a bit weepy.

Honestly, she needs to stop getting so emotional about everything. Of course it doesn't help, being in this house. There is something about Kittiwake that has always managed to get under Bel's skin. Well, you were born here, she reminds herself, sinking back into cool Egyptian six-hundred thread count cotton pillows.

Bel hears the door gently close, and as sleep creeps across her subconscious she starts to dream.

Bel dreams a lot. Her dreams are complicated and in full colour. Often they don't make much sense and she has learnt not to talk about them because other people's dreams are boring, as are their holiday photos and, for the most part, their children.

7

Lying in this room with its artfully chosen soft furnishings and its walls painted Wedgwood blue, Bel dreams that she is awake and sitting upright on the bed, watching a woman paint her face in the vanity unit that sits in the alcove of the window.

The same vanity unit in the same window alcove that Bel had laid her cosmetics bag and jewellery case on last night, the one she and Andrew had instantly cluttered up with their various lotions and potions and packets of pills. But in the dream it looks different; all Bel and Andrew's possessions have been replaced by an assortment of glass jars with blue enamel lids delicately traced in silver filigree, and perfume atomisers with elaborately tasselled pumps. The room feels much darker and it sounds as if it's raining outside, though she knows that's unlikely considering that so far it's been a perfectly dry if occasionally overcast August day.

In the dream, someone has changed the curtains. Daylight is filtered dimly through a pair of green shot silk drapes, and the effect is reminiscent of an aquarium.

The woman's face in the mirror glows as white as an onion. Slowly and meticulously she powders the whiteness with another layer and particles of the powder are momentarily suspended in the air. The woman's hands are tiny and bejewelled – diamonds mostly, and an emerald as big as a thumbnail. Bel recalls seeing this ring on Freya's finger last night at dinner. 'A family heirloom,' Freya had laughed when that Lucy woman commented on it. 'For all I know, it could be paste.' It isn't; anyone with half a brain can tell the difference between the sparkling reality of a well-cut emerald and its duller counterfeit.

Even in the dream the ring shines, flashing in the mirror as the woman wields the tools of her trade, curling her eyelashes with a small, lethal-looking contraption before pencilling in her eyebrows with soft feathery strokes until they appear arched and as black as raven's wings. Kohl eyeliner is traced along the inside of her eyelids, followed by layers and layers of jet-coloured mascara, until her eyes stand out like wet pebbles on a white beach. Finally the woman reaches for a gold bullet-shaped object and reveals a crimson lipstick. Carefully she traces the contours of her mouth, making the line a little fuller than nature intended.

As she lifts her hands to remove the turban wrapped around her head, Bel is aware that the bedroom door has burst open and there is a tang of putrefaction. Something is rotting in the air, an odour as rank as decomposing fish. How strange, thinks Bel, to sense smell so strongly in a dream. Suddenly a small dark-haired boy is sobbing hysterically on the threshold of the room.

The woman's eyes flash. 'You must always knock, you know you must always knock.' Then, taking in the fact the boy is dripping brackish water onto a cream carpet, she adds, 'Jesus, Benedict, what have you been doing?'

The child is about nine years old. He is carrying a golf club and shivering uncontrollably, his clothes are sodden and stinking. 'We were playing – me, Ivor and Natasha,' he hiccups, barely able to speak for crying.

An older girl appears behind him, a plain girl with a long face and a haircut that does nothing for her, dressed in a soaking jumper and dripping woollen kilt. She says very calmly, 'It's Ivor, he fell in the pool – he's not breathing. Mummy, I think Ivor is dead.'

Behind them stands an ashen-faced young man, dressed in a butler's uniform. If her children are lying he will deny their story, but he doesn't. His eyes are wide with horror and he is speechless.

'We were only playing,' the boy repeats.

The woman's scarlet mouth twists but Bel cannot hear the howl, she can only imagine it. The woman has lost her son, and nothing will ever be the same again.

Bel weeps and even though she is still half asleep she is aware of the wetness on her cheeks. Her head throbs and for a moment she doesn't know where she is, but she can definitely smell cigarette smoke. She shivers; it's colder than it's possible to be on an afternoon in August.

Bel manoeuvres herself deeper under the duvet. She'll feel better when she wakes up, but for now . . .

Bel sleeps in the room where she was found. Even the wardrobe, where her little body was discovered swaddled in the bottom drawer, is the same. Newly restored, it gleams in the corner, its walnut sheen returned to former glory by a man in the village.

This room might have been redecorated but it is still the room where a mother heard the news that her son was dead, and where Bel's own mother stroked the swell of her stomach and wondered whether jumping out of the window might be her best option.

Beginnings, middles and ends; Peggy, Serena, Natasha and Bel. This is the room that binds them, this is how consequences work.

If Peggy's son Ivor hadn't died, then Benedict wouldn't have got the house; if Benedict hadn't inherited Kittiwake, then Serena wouldn't have run away from it; and if Serena hadn't run away, then Natasha wouldn't have . . .

It goes round in circles, but it always begins with the death of a child.

2

The Terrible Accident

Kittiwake House, Cornwall, 1950

'We were only playing,' they chorused.

'A game of water golf,' Natasha admitted later, the aim being to hit golf balls across the indoor pool without landing them in the filthy water. 'It's harder than you'd think,' Benedict chimed in, and Natasha explained that if you hit the ball too hard it bounced off the opposite wall and disappeared into the murk, but if you hit the ball too softly it dribbled over the edge. It was Natasha's job to keep score because at eleven she was good with sums, unlike the easily muddled nine-year-old Benedict. Meanwhile, Ivor, being the eldest of the three children, was in charge of the rules.

The rules decreed that whoever lost the most golf balls had to dive into the filthy water at the end of the game and retrieve as many as possible from the scuzzy depths.

'We were only playing,' they cried, and Peggy knew in that moment she would never want to wake up again.

*

The inquest came back with a verdict of accidental drowning. It didn't make sense. All her children could swim, Peggy had made sure of it, it was important, swimming could save your life.

Peggy's father, Randolph Oppenheim, had been friends with a couple who'd been on the *Titanic*. Once the ship began to sink, the husband, a strong swimmer, had stripped down to his underclothes, dived into the water and survived; his wife, a non-swimmer, weighed down by her furs and all the jewellery she could carry, did not.

How could a fit young boy, who had been swimming since he was six, drown? It didn't make sense, and yet his lungs were full of water, he had drowned. The only other remark on the pathologist's report was the description of a small egg-shaped lump on the boy's head, consistent with a bump or a knock.

Had he maybe banged his head before he fell in the water?

'No, no,' repeated her other children, 'he was fine, he was laughing, he just fell.'

'We were only playing,' the children's voices seemed to echo, over and over again.

It was all Teddy's fault. They should never have been allowed in the pool room. The water had been contaminated for months, it should have been locked and bolted, but Teddy was too distracted by his business affairs in London to sort it out. She couldn't do everything. Her husband had failed her and now Ivor, precious Ivor, her firstborn and favourite, was dead.

Back in London, with the blinds firmly drawn in the Chester Square townhouse, Peggy withdrew to her bedroom, opening what seemed like a constant stream of letters of condolence and letting them drop to the floor. She barely ate and for the first time in her life took no pleasure in her resulting weight loss.

One thing was certain, she would never set foot in Monty's Cove ever again. And if she had her way, she would torch Kittiwake House.

Her anger was like mercury. She couldn't bear to see the faces of her other children and the worst of it was that, even though she blamed Teddy, deep in her heart she knew it was her fault.

They wouldn't have been in Cornwall if it hadn't been for her, she had bought the place outright with her own money, in her own name, it was hers, hers to do whatever she liked with and she had taken her son there to die. The place had been a trap, her whole life was a screaming mistake.

Peggy Oppenheim wished she had never set eyes on Teddy Carmichael, never mind married the man, but they'd met before the war when they were young and life was fun and they fitted into each other's arms as if it were their destiny. Blame it on the dancing, thought Peggy bitterly.

In 1930, Peggy had been a twenty-year-old debutante 'doing' the London season while staying with an aunt in Pimlico. She was a glamorous young woman, with little natural beauty but a great deal of style and a hugely wealthy father, which more than made up for the fact that her nose was on the large side.

Teddy Carmichael, whom Peggy presumed was loaded due to the cut of his dinner jacket and the fact he could trace his ancestry back to King Charles II, was actually the younger son of a younger son and therefore somewhat lacking in the wallet department.

But what did that matter?

She had more than enough moolah for both of them. He was tall – which was important for Peggy, being five foot nine herself – as well as socially well-connected, beautifully mannered and, most importantly, quite apart from being utterly charming, he was brilliant on the dance floor. Together the two of them cut quite a dash as they foxtrotted and tangoed across some of London's most glittering ballrooms. No one was surprised when their engagement was announced in *The Times* in the spring of 1932.

What the announcement in *The Times* omitted to mention was that once Teddy had got down on one knee to ask Peggy to marry him and she happily agreed, he had slipped a disc getting back up. The pair had to wait until he was out of his special surgical corset before Margaret Christina Oppenheim and Edward George Christopher Carmichael could become man and wife.

By this time it was 1935. She expected to honeymoon on the Italian Riviera, but Teddy took her trout fishing in Scotland, where his back played up and Peggy was ravaged by midges, sickened by the notion of haggis and shocked by the size of her new husband's penis.

Sadly, the only place Teddy was well endowed was around the genitals. His bank balance, by contrast, was more meagre than Peggy had been led to believe. She understood his elder brother had inherited the lion's share of the family money, but surely he earned something from that job of his in the City? Yet she saw precious little of it and money soon became a bone of contention in the Carmichael household. In truth, Peggy was used to a rather more lavish lifestyle than Teddy's pockets could provide and rather than admit the severity of his financial limitations to his wife and allow her to foot the bill for any luxuries she fancied, Teddy adopted a fogey-esque horror of anything new-fangled or modern, declaring her requests for a new car, stair carpet and drapes 'vulgar'.

His wife's Americanisms had quickly begun to grate. 'How many times do I have to tell you, they're *curtains* not "drapes",' he snarled, washing down the painkillers his doctor had prescribed for his back with a glass of single malt.

She might have left him right then, had the babies not started arriving. Ivor came first in 1937, her firstborn son and heir, a golden child with a light spirit and a good nature. She had adored him on sight.

A year later came a daughter, small and sallow and so very different from pink-cheeked Ivor. They called her Natasha, but Peggy

14

was never entirely convinced by the name and she once ordered her daughter a third birthday cake from Harrods with the name Natalie piped across the top. 'Happy birthday, dear Natashalie,' sang the assembled guests.

Finally, in 1940, when Teddy had failed the army physical and been seconded to Whitehall to work in intelligence, Peggy delivered a second son, Benedict, born at Teddy's brother's farm in Norfolk where Peggy and the children had been evacuated.

Honestly, thought Peggy, lying back exhausted after a difficult thirty-six-hour labour, what was the point of a third child? This one was like yet another beige-coloured handbag. She simply didn't need it.

Three children in as many years had done for Mrs Carmichael. Thus far she had been lucky with her waistline, but there was no way she was going to risk her figure by having a fourth. So when the war ended and the family moved back to Chester Square, she did all she could to avoid another pregnancy by slathering her face with night cream and pretending to be fast asleep and snoring by the time her husband had finished his nightly ablutions.

Which came first: Peggy's unwillingness in the bedroom or Teddy's increasing reliance on drink?

Well, what else was a man supposed to do, argued Teddy. His back hurt, he couldn't sleep, his investments kept going belly-up, and to top it all, his wife lay curled up like an armour-plated armadillo in the marital bed. Whisky was the only thing that kept him warm, eased the pain and eventually knocked him out.

Peggy had expected Teddy's fortunes to pick up after the war but they didn't, and the three children played in a freezing room on the top floor with toys that Teddy and his brother had once owned: a miserable battalion of lead soldiers, entirely without paint, moth-eaten bears and a derelict-looking toy farm. Most shamefully of all, Peggy realised her daughter's stockings had been darned at the knee, 'on sir's orders' the housekeeper bleated.

15

Oblivious to the fact that Teddy was playing dangerously expensive card games at the various gentlemen's clubs in town, Mrs Carmichael came to the conclusion that her husband was mean. He had money, she was convinced of it, otherwise what was the point in him going to work every day? He simply refused to spend it.

And so, in a fit of pique, she hired a property consultant, an enthusiastic, flamboyantly dressed young man who brought lavishly illustrated brochures into her drawing room and set about choosing a second home – somewhere she would be free to play doll's houses and decorate to her heart's content.

And why not? She had her own money, she wasn't financially dependent on skinflint Teddy, her father had seen to that.

After weeks of deliberation, Peggy finally chose Monty's Cove in Cornwall, preferring its picturesque seaside location to grander shooting estates in Buckinghamshire and moated castles in Scotland.

As for the distance from London? She hadn't a clue. Peggy's geography, as befitting an American heiress, was hopeless. She may have resided in the UK since before the war, but whether Scotland was at the top or the bottom of the map, who cared? All she knew was that her adopted island was tiny, so wherever Cornwall was, it couldn't be that far away.

She fell in love with the photographs in the brochure: golden buttercup fields atop silvery cliffs overlooking a glittering blue sea. Steps carved into the cliff-face led down to a small private sandy beach complete with rock pools where her children could wander freely with buckets and spades searching for crabs.

And then there was the house, Kittiwake, a solid oblong of pale lemon stucco, smothered in wisteria and neatly boxed in at each end by square crenellated turrets. Big but not enormous, Kittiwake was described in the brochure as 'A fine Victorian coastal manor house with ten bedrooms, three bath/shower rooms and the unusual addition of a fully heated indoor swimming pool.'

'The previous owner was an American too,' explained the sales agent, and that was the clincher; if an American had owned it then there would be radiators and decent plumbing, proper shower-heads and a twentieth-century kitchen. Not that Peggy cooked, but she did eat, and the meals served in the Chester Square dining room tasted positively Victorian – brown Windsor soup, fatty grey stewed mutton and those foul diseased-looking kidneys that Teddy seemed to relish.

In Cornwall, they would have pancakes with maple syrup and peanut butter, rich ground Italian coffee and frozen orange juice. She would insist on fresh flowers on every surface – real flowers, not the hideous fake wax effigies that gathered so much dust in London – and she would collect some modern art for the walls, because passing all those dingy oil paintings of bug-eyed, bristle-faced Carmichael ancestors on the stairs every day made her jaw clench and her hands itch for an axe.

Unfortunately, Peggy's plans for the Cove were difficult to put into practice. It took so long to get there that weekend visits were impractical. As for the local shops, Peggy wondered why they bothered opening at all. Nobody stocked anything interesting or useful, everything had to be brought down from London, and what with rationing and the local workforce being so terribly slow, Peggy was almost defeated by the place.

It was easier to get to France, she realised, and as her enthusiasm for Cornwall dwindled, the house responded by sulking. Lights fused, radiators stopped working and the swimming pool developed a thick green scum.

Even the weather conspired against them. Where were the blue skies of the brochure? Every day the twin combination of wind and tide left a heavy crust of salt on the window panes and the children's toes turned blue in the rock pools.

Sadly, it wasn't only the house that was crumbling. Peggy's relationship with Teddy was disintegrating too. Over the years their marriage soured like unrefrigerated milk. Sometimes Peggy swore she could smell the failure of their union clinging to them like mildew whenever they were together, a situation that became increasingly infrequent.

They had run out of things to say, and Peggy spent more and more of her time alone in front of a mirror. Her hair was perfect, her face a flawless mask of foundation and powder, drawn-on eyebrows and lips. Looking the part calmed her nerves and she smoked elegantly through a tortoiseshell cigarette holder, drank martinis before toying with her lunch and then, most afternoons, she napped.

The accident happened early in the evening, when she was repairing her face for dinner, the drapes shut against yet another cold, wet April day.

They were spending the Easter school holidays at Kittiwake, although Teddy had disappeared back to London immediately after the bank holiday weekend, leaving her alone with the cook, the butler and her so-called mother's help – a dreary girl who suffered from nosebleeds and was forever appearing with a plug of scarlet toilet paper up each nostril. There seemed very little point in staying on; the weather was frightful and the children bored and fractious. 'Only a few more days,' she muttered to herself. Trunks were on standby, waiting to be packed. Soon the children would be returned to their various schools and she need only get up for meals.

She thought at first he was an apparition, her youngest child covered in green slime holding a golf club.

'We were playing,' he stuttered.

3

The Realisation

London, May 1950

Teddy Carmichael suspected his wife had left for good when he noticed the empty shelf in her vast mahogany wardrobe.

Peggy had taken her jewellery. The numerous leather boxes with their tiny brass keys, the salmon-pink Cartier watch case and soft suede pouch in which she kept her pearls, had all disappeared.

The witch had lied. She'd said she needed a break and had booked a liner from Southampton to New York, where her father would arrange a transfer to the Oppenheim Estate in Philadelphia. A short holiday, she said, a couple of weeks to get over everything.

He couldn't stop her. She had paid for her own ticket – first class, naturally. If his wife was going to grieve, she was going to grieve all the way back to the States and in style.

Teddy understood what she was doing. She was running away from the sorrow and the pitying looks and the endless black-edged letters of condolence – and he couldn't say he blamed her.

She left the week after they buried Ivor, that awful sunlit cherry blossom day. It should have been raining, there should have been thunder and lightning and skies the colour of steel, but the day dawned cloudless and the sun shone relentlessly. It wasn't right. Even in the chill of the grey stone church, Teddy was too hot in his thick black overcoat and his face ran with sweat and tears.

Peggy sat next to him, her features invisible save for the burning coals of her eyes and the slash of bright red lipstick behind the elaborate filigree of a black lace veil.

During the service she had stood up and sat down as requested, as if she were a wooden puppet, but afterwards, as they gathered by the side of the small grave, he could feel the uncontrollable shake of her shoulders. And as the first clod of earth fell onto their child's coffin, she moaned deep and low, a noise that sounded for all the world like it came from somewhere beyond the grave.

At that moment he reached for her black silk-clad hand, but she moved it away. He had never felt so alone in his life.

As for his other children, Peggy didn't even want them in the same funeral car. Benedict and Natasha travelled to and from the service with Teddy's brother and wife, white faces staring out of the window, their impossibly small feet climbing out of the Daimler in shiny new black shoes.

'Don't be silly, Teddy, how can anyone hold them to blame? They're children. She's being ridiculous. It was an accident,' his brother told him as they drank whisky together late into that terrible night.

It was all right for Stephen, Teddy thought bitterly, with his soft biddable wife, his four solid breathing children and his successful stud farm in Norfolk. Since the war, his brother had gone into breeding racehorses and the business was doing remarkably well. Meanwhile, Teddy was floundering. Any investment he made seemed doomed to failure, he had borrowed money against the house, his son had died and his wife had left him.

A month later, the telegram arrived confirming his suspicions. She wasn't coming back and he would be hearing from her solicitor.

The hawk-nosed bitch had not only cut him off, she'd abandoned her two surviving children. Poor Natasha and Benedict, Teddy hadn't a clue what to do with them. Thank Christ for boarding schools, he swore, as he shredded the telegram.

Over the weeks that followed the arrival of Peggy's telegram, Teddy thought about writing to his son and daughter and breaking the news about their mother, but it didn't matter how often he sat at his desk with the Carmichael crested writing paper in front of him, he couldn't for the life of him conjure up the right words. Night after night he sat there, his fountain pen dripping ink uselessly, while the ice in his Scotch made tiny catastrophic cracking noises that made his heart jump.

Everything was falling apart.

Teddy Carmichael was a coward. When the summer holidays came round, his children barely had their trunks through the front door before he sent them to stay with their cousins in the country. The alternative was unbearable, Teddy decided. Whenever the three of them were alone together in Chester Square, it felt like they were trapped in some terrible board game that was missing half its pieces.

He left it to his brother's wife Simone to tell them about Peggy. When the deed was done, she phoned to say they'd coped with it remarkably well, although Benedict had wet the bed. Like father like son, thought Teddy, blushing at the recollection of having drunk himself into a stupor of incontinence only days before.

Determined to make some positive decisions in the wake of Peggy's departure, Teddy decided to close up Kittiwake. He wasn't abandoning the place due to some silly superstition – Teddy wasn't like Peggy, he didn't have the imagination to develop any neurotic loathing of the place. Tragedy could happen anywhere. His son could have drowned in the Thames, what difference would it have made? He was gone, the boy with the glowing school reports and the ability to pluck a cricket ball from thin air was dead and all that was left of him were the things he would never grow out of.

Teddy ordered a purge of Ivor's possessions; he didn't want anything left in the house to remind him of the boy.

Some months later, when Benedict came home for a brief weekend exeat, he discovered a suitcase under his bed containing all the things Ivor had taken to Kittiwake that last Easter holiday. Rifling through it, Benedict found a ten-bob note in a pair of his brother's shorts; he shoved it into his own pocket, then shut the case and slid it as far back under the bed as possible.

Years later, when the suitcase disappeared, along with everything else from his childhood, Benedict would feel a pang of regret that the only memento he'd ever had of his brother had been frittered on sweets in the school tuck shop.

Shutting down Kittiwake was one of the few sensible financial decisions Teddy made that year. He couldn't afford to run the place and he couldn't sell it because it was in the Yankee bitch's name. So he sent word for the pool to be drained and instructed their regular cleaning woman, Brenda, to cover the furniture and wall hangings with dust sheets and promised her a generous retainer to keep an eye on things. Aside from the fact it went against the grain to allow an asset to fall into complete disrepair, Kittiwake was his children's inheritance – and it looked increasingly likely they were going to need it. In fact, at the rate things were going, it might be the only thing left for them to inherit.

With that thought in mind, Teddy poured himself a sherry. The only thing he would truly miss about Kittiwake was the wine cellar. Peggy had insisted on getting it properly stocked; in a few years' time, some of those bottles could be worth a few bob. He'd even laid down some port for Ivor's twenty-first, and the sudden realisation that this day was never going to happen made Teddy tremble uncontrollably.

4

Escaping

Somewhere in the middle of the Atlantic, May 1950

Peggy Carmichael wasn't a stupid woman. The truth about Teddy's gambling addiction had eventually dawned and she knew full well that if she left her diamonds and pearls, her rubies, emeralds and Cartier watch in Chester Square, they were likely to end up on a Knightsbridge gaming table.

Her jewels were now safely stowed in the safe of her first-class cabin on Cunard's luxurious ocean liner the *Queen Mary*, and as the ship pulled out of Southampton Harbour on its five-day voyage across the pond, Peggy wept with relief. She had escaped.

Apart from her jewellery, she was travelling light in an effort to maintain the fiction that she was only going home for a short break. In reality, she had no intention of coming back. Her marriage was dead, Teddy's touch made her skin crawl, and visions of Ivor haunted her day and night. She saw him dead, waterlogged on the side of the pool, she saw the blanket being pulled over his beautiful face as they stretchered him into the ambulance, and she saw him blue-lipped and waxy in the morgue.

But even worse, she saw him alive. Chester Square had been unbearable. She had seen him everywhere she looked, running up the stairs laughing, eating a biscuit in the conservatory, practising his batting in the back garden. It was agonising, she had to get away, she would go mad if she stayed.

What she would do once she arrived back in America, Peggy had no idea. In the meantime, the crossing was proving enough of a distraction. Not that she socialised – she preferred to keep herself to herself. Most people, observing that she dressed in black from head to toe, presumed she was recently widowed. Much to her relief, they kept a respectful distance.

She ordered her meals to be delivered to her suite, slept a great deal, had her hair set and her fingernails painted in a deep Max Factor scarlet in one of the ship's beauty salons.

A couple of days into her voyage, Peggy began to feel like a snake shedding an old skin. She wouldn't be Teddy's wife for much longer, and as for the children . . . In some respects, she wished she'd been barren. Losing a child was even more painful than giving birth to one in the first place.

The best thing to do, she decided, was to compartmentalise her life. Her children belonged to a time and a place that no longer existed. Never mind Kittiwake, she was never going back to Chester Square. England was Ivor and motherhood. In America she would be someone else. She would become the woman she might have been had she never met Teddy. The fact that she had been playing one role for the last fifteen years of her life didn't mean she couldn't play another. Philadelphia was less than a hundred miles from New York and Fifth Avenue, she could be reabsorbed into the slipstream of American society, attend the opera and charity functions, eat lobster in expensive restaurants. She would be thin and fashionable, she might even dye her hair a different colour, go darker, banish the increasing number of silver threads for ever. She would grow a new skin.

On the last night of the voyage, after a solo pitcher of frozen Margaritas and a very good fillet of hake Grenobloise, served with an irresistible potato puree, Peggy found herself pacing her quarters suffering from indigestion.

As a woman with a twenty-three-inch waist (no mean feat after three children) she didn't normally eat potato, and in this restless state she retrieved from the silk case containing her headscarves the one memento of her old life that she had brought with her: a black-and-white photograph of her three children.

Peggy had removed it from its silver frame before she left. She knew it would never sit on her dressing table next to her scent bottles and silver-backed hairbrushes again – how could she face it every day for the rest of her life? The sight of it was too painful.

The picture had been taken in a professional studio six months before the accident. Ivor, Natasha and Benedict were sitting in a row on a velvet chaise longue, for ever twelve, eleven and nine. Peggy swallowed a sob. If Ivor wasn't going to grow any older, then it didn't seem fair that the others should either.

In the photograph, Benedict wore a sailor's suit and held the yacht his maternal grandfather had sent him for his tenth birthday. Only Ivor looked directly into the camera, bright-eyed and handsome, his broad smile showing off his even white teeth; the other two looked shifty and glum in contrast. Benedict was jealously guarding the boat while Natasha stared at the floor as if wishing it would open up and swallow her whole.

Peggy examined the photograph closely and noticed for the first time that the girl's fists were clenched.

Why did it have to be Ivor?

Wiping away a tear, Peggy pulled on a coat. The night sky looked clear and it would do her good to go on deck and see the stars, walk off some of that potato.

She wished the crossing could last for ever. Being in the middle of the sea was oddly comforting. None of it felt real, there was no fixed time, no fixed place, nothing but the endless stretch of water reaching out on all sides as far as the eye could see.

It was midnight when she crept into the deserted grand salon and stared at the art deco mural on the wall. Depicting a map of the Atlantic, it featured a crystal model replica of the ship charting its steady progress across the ocean. She wished she could slow it down. Out here on the ocean, she could imagine that she was going to America to see her father and that everything back in England was as it should be; her three healthy children were happily getting on with their schooling.

She liked being in limbo. It was a relief not to be responsible for anything. On board the ship she didn't need to make any decisions beyond when and what she ate, and the food was rather good. In fact the sea air seemed to have restored her appetite; for the first time since Ivor died, she began to worry about her waistline.

The photograph still exists. It sits in a slightly battered silver frame, amongst a group of carefully curated objets d'art on the grand piano in Kittiwake's newly refurbished drawing room. Freya had to dither around for hours positioning everything to look exactly right – the framed photo, a marquetry cigar box, a Lalique glass vase, a tiny speckled blue egg and an ornate Victorian fan – but the resulting image has scored over three thousand likes on Instagram, which is the main thing.

5

Coming Undone

London, 1950–1961

The fifties were not kind to Teddy Carmichael. Every New Year he swore blind things would change and resolved to cut down on the drinking and the gambling. But every year things seemed to get worse and he couldn't help noticing the gaps that kept appearing in his life since his son died and his wife ran away.

Teddy couldn't understand what was happening. Everywhere he looked something was missing: his wife, his children, the ornamental Russian samovar in the dining room – and now some of the oil paintings that used to hang on the stairs.

At least the disappearance of the paintings would please Peggy, he sniggered to himself, stumbling past the newly exposed rectangles of Edwardian striped wallpaper that stood out vividly against their surroundings.

Peggy had disliked most of the canvases that hung in Chester Square, but she particularly hated the portraits of his ancestors, 'those deeply creepy pus-faced freaks' as she once called them.

Unfortunately, it seemed the art world agreed with her. None of the Cork Street dealers had expressed the remotest interest in those wealthy but ugly faces, so Teddy's dead relatives continued to stare at him with bog-eyed disapproval as he hauled himself nightly to his sleeping quarters.

Sometimes he wondered why he bothered with this farcical 'going to bed' routine, given that he barely slept. He might as well have laid down on the horsehair couch in his study for all the comfort his mattress gave him.

Night after night he thrashed about under the covers, attempting to do increasingly complicated sums in his head, but the figures danced and refused to add up, and the gaps between what he needed and what he had grew bigger and bigger with every month.

If he did sleep he had terrible nightmares during which he lost his teeth, enamel tumbling from his mouth leaving empty bloodied gaps in his fleshy pink gums, and it didn't take Freud to understand the reason why.

Teddy Carmichael was teetering on the edge of bankruptcy and in an effort to keep the slavering wolf from the door, he was selling off the family silver, plus anything else that could raise a few quid – china, furniture, his father's fishing tackle.

Sometimes, when he came home from his club, he thought for a moment he might have been burgled. Where on earth was that rather good little Stubbs painting, commissioned years ago by his great-grandfather, entitled *Samuel with a Gelding under an Oak Tree*?

As a small boy, it had been his favourite painting and he used to stroke the little black horse for luck before he left the house.

Sadly, some terrible tips and a disastrous day at the Cheltenham races had necessitated the painting's swift and unceremonious departure. The new owner had lifted it off the wall and given Teddy a knowing smirk as he carried it off under his arm.

It was his own fault, who else could he point the finger at? The trouble with living by yourself, he mused, was that there was never anyone else to blame.

Teddy's fateful day at Cheltenham had culminated in putting all his remaining money on a dead cert in the final race. To his horror, Moon Shadow had fallen badly in the second furlong and broken a leg. A vet was summoned to put the beast out of its misery and as he stared in disbelief at his betting slip, Teddy heard the muffled crack of the fatal shot. Weeks later, he could still hear it.

And now the Stubbs has gone.

A gee-gee to pay for the gee-gees, he giggled, trying not to slop the port he was ferrying to his bedroom. In the good old days, he'd have called for Blake his butler to see to his night-time nightcap needs, but Blake left in 1955. These days, without a butler or a wife, Teddy had to tackle his cufflinks on his own.

The trickiness of this operation, combined with the increasing morning tremor in his hands, regularly brought him to his knees, leaving him sobbing with rage on the floor of his dressing room, biting at the useless dangling shirt cuffs.

He missed Blake more than Peggy. As for Ivor, time and alcohol had dulled the pain of losing his eldest son. On one occasion, after yet another night of sweating and tossing in his bed, he awoke having completely forgotten what the boy looked like. Desperate for proof that the lad had actually existed, he'd crawled under the stairs and opened the family strongbox, rummaging through the contents until he found his eldest child's birth certificate:

Father – Edward George Christopher Carmichael; Mother – Margaret Christina Carmichael (née Oppenheim).

All ties with Peggy had been unceremoniously cut after the divorce. The legalities were left to their solicitors, but according to Cudlip and Bird of Kensington, Peggy hadn't blanched at the idea of taking over the running costs of Kittiwake.

Good job, thought Teddy, the place was nothing to do with him, although to his surprise some months later, when he discovered a spare bunch of rusting keys labelled 'Kittiwake' he found he couldn't bring himself to throw them away.

Ten years, he reminded himself. An entire decade had passed since he lost both his son and his wife, and now his two surviving children had abandoned him. Benedict, after years of being a complete nuisance at school, surprised everyone by knuckling down and clinching a place at Oxford University to study Modern Greats, whatever that was. While Natasha, now twenty-two, had miraculously transformed from a sullen, whey-faced child into a strangely delicate beauty. She had recently become Mrs Hugo Berrington and moved to Barnes, of all places.

Teddy was left to struggle on alone in a house he could no longer afford to heat or even clean properly. Natasha's wedding had financially wiped him out – he was the father of the bride and as such, tradition demanded that he paid for everything, including five bridesmaids, a wedding dress created by designer *du jour* John Bates, plus a champagne reception followed by a sit-down meal for two hundred at Claridge's.

No wonder Teddy's hair was falling out and the whisky decanter on his desk ran as dry as his savings.

He thought about asking his brother for yet another loan – Stephen had inherited a great deal more than he had – but he hadn't paid back the last lump yet and the old miser was a bit stingy when it came to handouts, so Teddy tended to rely on luck and his bookies instead.

Periodically he'd make an effort to keep away from the gaming tables, but what with the children no longer living at home and most of the staff dismissed, Teddy found the lonely chill of Chester Square too much to bear. Besides, he was incapable of cooking a half-decent meal for himself and man could not live on toast and pilchards alone.

So every night he set off for supper at his club and every night he drank too much and staggered over to the gaming tables where his run of bad luck continued to bleed his coffers dry.

Eventually his name became synonymous with ill fortune to the point where chaps he once viewed as chums refused to sit next to him in case his bad luck rubbed off on them, and a bad night on the cards was known as 'having a Teddy Carmichael'.

While the rest of the world was greeting the dawn of a new decade, Teddy had reached rock bottom and he couldn't see a way out. Things had gone so badly wrong it would be impossible to put them all right. He couldn't afford to keep up, he didn't fit in anywhere any more, he was only fifty-six years old but he was too tired to carry on. So far as he could see, there was only one solution.

6

The Telegram

Sacramento, USA, 1961

Peggy sat on the veranda in the Californian sunshine eating half a home-grown grapefruit (no sugar) for breakfast, when it struck her that Benedict had turned twenty-one the previous day. Her youngest son, who was now her eldest son – son and heir, she supposed.

She hadn't sent a card but a cheque for a hundred dollars had been signed in her accountant's office at the beginning of the month. She hoped he hadn't been expecting anything more personal and fretted momentarily over whether she should have sent him one of her father's old tie-pins.

She presumed the boy still resembled his maternal Greek grandfather rather than his chipolata-skinned father and imagined he might be quite good looking, albeit nowhere near as handsome as his elder brother. Had Ivor lived, he'd have been breaking hearts all over London by now, lining up future wives and toying with the kitchen staff.

Thinking of Ivor still brought Peggy close to tears but not like it used to, not since she had her brows lifted and the bags removed from under her eyes, a procedure which, despite taking years off her, had severely affected the mobility of her face.

Since the op, Peggy had worn a constant expression of surprise. She even looked surprised to be drinking her usual morning cup of strong black coffee as she watched the pool boy fish for stray leaves while the temperature began its glorious daily climb.

Life was good for Mrs Alessandro. She'd married her second husband, Bobby, a successful walnut farmer, seven years ago. Although he was the opposite of an English gentleman they got on well enough and had sufficient land to stable horses.

Peggy lit a cigarette and inhaled deeply. It was May; in Chester Square the cherry blossom would be out and the children attending the local prep schools would be wearing their summer uniforms, the girls in straw boaters walking in crocodile formation two by two, hand in hand.

The thought prompted an image of Natasha at six, a gap where her front teeth should be, hair in pigtails, one ribbon missing.

Time had gone so fast. Her daughter was now a married woman and, judging by the newspaper clipping her old friend Lydia Cashman had cut out and sent from the *Kensington and Chelsea Chronicle*, Natasha made a handsome bride.

She was too like her mother to be conventionally pretty, but the clever combination of an ornate hairpiece, tiara and veil served to draw one's eye away from her rather beaky nose. Peggy had to admit, even in profile, Natasha looked quite beautiful.

The groom, on the other hand, resembled any number of chinless English boys that Peggy had encountered a quarter of a century ago when she had 'done' the season in London.

Why had she chosen Teddy? Huge cock and twinkle toes aside, the man had proved himself a disappointment. Once the dancing had stopped he'd turned peevish and joyless, and the light went out of their marriage. It was easy to forget how once upon a time they had laughed together and how handsome her husband had been.

She hoped Natasha hadn't made a similarly disastrous mistake with this Hugo Berrington fellow. She kept the folded newspaper clipping tucked into the bottom of her old jewellery box, along with a certain black-and-white photograph, the one she no longer looked at.

Peggy had been invited to the wedding, which surprised her. A silver-edged card had arrived with her name on it, but not her husband's – how rude. After all, what had Bobby done to upset anyone? They hadn't even met him. No, she decided, it was no more than an empty gesture.

Natasha's idea, no doubt. In recent years the girl had taken to sending her the odd postcard. They arrived out of the blue, from England or holidays in Antibes and once from Venice. Sometimes they were simply random views of London, one featured a Beefeater at the Tower of London with a great big raven perched on top of his silly hat.

Peggy found them disconcerting. At first she thought perhaps it was an impostor pretending to be her daughter, but Natasha had always been appalling at spelling and it appeared nothing had changed. And anyway, it was somehow so typically Natasha; even when she was a child, Peggy had occasionally found her daughter's behaviour decidedly peculiar.

Citing a fear of flying and with no time to organise a boat crossing, Peggy hadn't attended the wedding but she did send a fifty-six-piece Spode Byron range dinner set to Natasha's new address in Barnes, wherever that might be.

A postcard of a London bus eventually arrived with 'Thank you, Mother' on the back, but no kisses. Natasha had always been the type to bear a grudge.

Peggy put down her cup of coffee, a squeal of bike brakes alerting her to the fact that a telegram boy had cycled right up to her breakfast table, and was handing her a telegram.

Genuinely, rather than surgically, surprised now, Peggy opened the flimsy document only to read,

TEDDY CARMICHAEL DEAD,
TOOK OWN LIFE, GUNSHOT STOP

A sudden gust of wind lifted the slip of paper and wafted it gently into the pool. Peggy watched as the boy attempted to fish it out.

Water and death, death and water. She hadn't wanted a pool but Bobby insisted. They lived in California, everyone who could afford a pool had a pool. Peggy had never set foot in it.

Peggy ground out her cigarette. It was 1961, eleven years since her family had been smashed to pieces. Surely no one would expect her to attend her ex-husband's grave? Would there even be a funeral?

Given that the man had chosen to end his life, there could be consequences. Some churches refused to bury suicides.

In any case, having cited 'fear of flying' as an excuse not to attend her own daughter's wedding six months previously, she couldn't exactly jump on a plane and turn up at a funeral. And what good would it do anyway? Her children were adults now.

Motherhood wasn't something she missed. The horror of losing Ivor had pulled the plug on her heart and drained what maternal resources she might have had. There simply wasn't enough love left over for the other two.

She was, however, dutiful, and leaving her toast untouched, Peggy went indoors and sat at her small bureau in the vast colonial drawing room of the Alessandro homestead and filled her fountain pen with violet-coloured ink.

'I'm sorry for your loss,' she wrote, 'your father's weaknesses have long cast a shadow on all our lives. Do not let his selfishness be your cross to bear.'

She didn't for a moment pause to consider her own selfishness. The fact that she had abandoned her surviving children in order

36

to create a life free from the pain of losing Ivor didn't cross her mind. To Peggy, her own actions seemed quite natural – especially now that she'd had years to justify them. But Teddy! How typical of him to take the coward's way out, he really was the most spineless creep.

She pictured him slumped in his own gore, blood splattering the wall behind him.

At least now someone would have to change the wallpaper in that gloomy little study of his.

Peggy signed and sealed the airmail letter. Let that be an end to it, she thought.

Inevitably there followed a flurry of communication between her solicitors in Florida and Cudlip and Bird in London. Some months later, when it became apparent that Chester Square and all its contents would have to be sold to cover Teddy's debts, Peggy felt a tiny prick of conscience. Her children might be adults, but they still needed a roof over their heads.

She couldn't leave them homeless – what would people think? After all, she and Bobby were well known for their charitable good works.

Hopefully, Natasha with her newly wedded status would be secure, at least as long as her marriage lasted, but how would Benedict, fresh out of university with a lower second-class degree, fend for himself?

Peggy couldn't imagine how her youngest child had managed to get into Oxford in the first place. He had never shown much academic prowess as a child, his handwriting was poor, his arithmetic worrying and his tutors despairing. He had never shone in the classroom as his older brother once had; no doubt Teddy had pulled some strings, she mused, and somehow Benedict got in, whether he deserved his place or not.

And now he was out, and since no son of hers could be allowed to live on the street, Peggy instructed her lawyer to inform Cudlip and Bird that she was prepared to spend a reasonable sum of money on a London property for her children.

The property, she stipulated, should be in Natasha and Benedict's joint names and possess at least two bedrooms, so that Benedict could live comfortably while he established some kind of career and his sister would have somewhere to stay should she ever need a bolthole.

Her only other proviso was that the property must be in a decent postcode – which in Peggy's world meant within walking distance of Harrods.

At the back of her mind, there was another solution to her children's dilemma. Kittiwake was still at her disposal. She could sell the property at Monty's Cove and use the proceeds to boost her housing offer. Natasha and Benedict could have something bigger than two bedrooms, in fact they could have quite a nice house – not on the scale of Chester Square, but a smaller version maybe?

Peggy dismissed the thought. The prospect of dealing with the dreaded place and signing papers that bore its name made her head throb. She couldn't, she wouldn't have anything to do with Kittiwake.

Hopefully, if she ignored the place, it would go away. Left to its own devices, the house would eventually crumble into a pile of rubble that would tumble off the cliff and get swallowed up by the sea. It had been years since anyone had set foot in the place – let it rot.

7

The Photoshoot

Kittiwake House, Cornwall, March 2018,
five months before the party

The journalist watches the photographer. He's been busy all morning – changing lenses, squinting at the light, bouncing around on the soles of his Converse sneakers. She has never seen him quite so enthusiastic.

It helps that the location, a stunning house perched on a glorious Cornish clifftop, is owned by a couple as good-looking as the Berringtons. Forty-nine-year-old Lance and his forty-two-year-old wife Freya are a picture editor's dream. He is dark and wolfishly handsome, while she is as blond and leggy as an Afghan hound, plus they have a couple of 'catalogue cute' little kids being adorable in the background, Ludo and Luna – natch.

At this rate there'll come a day when the name Susan is going to seem quite exotic, thinks Mel.

Nonetheless, daft names or not, this set up has all the ingredients of a glossy magazine front cover: groovy-looking family do up derelict Cornish wreck, what's not to like?

All she has to do now is interview the couple, get a bit of background, weave a story round it, give the readers something to get their teeth into.

Mel digs out her phone and checks there's sufficient battery: 89 per cent – great.

The Berringtons have agreed to conduct the interview over lunch ('I want to keep things nice and informal,' she told them, knowing that people tend to let their guard down when they're distracted by a decent meal).

There's a story here, she can smell it, and it goes beyond bricks and mortar. Mel comes from round here, she's heard stories about the place. Her stomach rumbles and the oven timer pings simultaneously. 'Lunch,' she calls.

For once they haven't had to get catering in; the lady of the house offered to do it herself. In the kitchen, Freya is setting food out on a wooden table the length of a runway. It's a photogenic spread, complete with a basket of home-baked sourdough bread. 'Lance's speciality,' Freya says. Apparently, he gets up early most days so that they can have a warm loaf for breakfast. Mel makes a mental note to include this detail, while Freya admits to making the salads and the frittata.

Each dish is worthy of its own close-up; colour bursts from every platter. 'Very Ottolenghi,' Mel murmurs, and the photographer insists on taking numerous shots before anyone can be served.

'Freya Berrington obviously takes her lifestyle very seriously,' Mel scribbles in her notebook, trying to unclench her jaw. Honestly, sometimes all this obsessive attention to detail is enough to make you puke. Mel's father has dementia and visiting his piss-sodden bungalow after jaunts like this can bring a girl crashing back down to reality before you can say 'buckwheat and rice salad with dried cherries and hazelnuts'. I mean, it's all very well, but does anyone actually give a shit?

Turns out the photographer does. He's even knocked out by the earthenware salad bowls.

Freya laughs and brushes a sweep of caramel-coloured hair out of her eyes. 'Where did I get them from? I didn't – I made them myself. That's the beauty of living somewhere like Kittiwake – you can get lost in the outbuildings. I've got a little wheel and kiln set up in one of the barns; there's a shop I stock in the village. Basically, I make things that remind me of home – I'm from Oslo, we take our food and design very seriously.'

Of course you do, dear.

Mel clicks her iPhone on to record.

'So, tell me, how long has it taken you to bring Kittiwake back to life?'

Freya and Lance are like a well-oiled machine, they speak in turns and are gushingly complimentary about each other. He is a 'gifted project manager', while she has 'an extraordinary eye for detail'; they are 'blessed'.

Mel feels a metallic bitterness at the back of her throat. Out loud she gently probes for a bit of human interest. It's all very well banging on about under-floor heating and air vents, but most readers want a bit of family background with their renovation of the month. 'You inherited it, I believe?' She looks directly at Lance, who has the grace to blush.

'Yes, from my uncle, my mother's younger brother. He, um, inherited it from his mother.'

Mel can feel her feminist hackles rise. 'The younger brother, even though he had an older sister?'

'Yes, um, it's the old-fashioned way, primogeniture. Ridiculous, I know, but in the bad old days it was the only way to keep larger estates together. Not that this is a huge estate – I mean, it's big but …' He trails off, refusing to meet her eye. They are sitting in a kitchen that could easily house her entire flat. Lance gestures to a wooden clothes pulley above their heads, 'It's not grand,' he adds, a tad defensively.

41

Mel has never seen the romance in these pulleys. In fact she can't think of anything worse than eating your breakfast while pant juice rains down from above – especially if it's your incontinent father's pant juice. But then posh people are different.

Mel has been snooping around houses in Devon and Cornwall on behalf of *Better Homes* for long enough to know how the other half fetishise their laundry. Lance might point to the ancient pulley as an example of how the house still connects with its roots, but Mel suspects that the housekeeper is instructed to arrange only attractive garments on the rack. Unsightly and intimate items of clothing will be confined to some utility room kitted out as a state-of-the-art 'laundry room and ironing station', complete with an iron that looks like one of those small motorboats millionaires use to get from their megayachts to the shore.

No doubt this lot sail too. It's something the wealthy have bred into them: the ability to swim, ride and ski – all the skills necessary to practise sports that separate them from the hoi polloi.

Sometimes, when Mel goes on these house jaunts, she steals a tiny memento. Nothing that could possibly be missed – maybe a mug or an egg cup, or a fancy soap from the bathroom (because these places always have a stash of elaborately wrapped, exotically fragranced soaps stacked up on a shelf – pomegranate and fig, the kind of thing one would never find in a supermarket).

Mel turns her attention away from her caramelised roast carrot, chickpea and feta salad with its delicious smoked paprika aftertaste for a second to grill Lance further about the origin of Kittiwake.

'There was a rumour that Kenneth Grahame based Toad Hall on the place?' She smiles innocently and he laughs in response.

'I think that was something my Uncle Benedict made up to entice visitors. He was what you might call a bit of a character. He rented it out as a small hotel for a while, back in the eighties – he was mostly living abroad by then, in France and Switzerland.

Kittiwake has had all sorts of incarnations: wedding venue, conference centre ...'

'That's why we had so much work to do,' Freya interrupts, smiling with those perfect teeth. God, she is such an incredibly healthy-looking specimen of womanhood, thinks Mel, resentfully pushing away the bread basket, knowing full well it will trigger her chronic IBS.

Freya continues, 'The people who ran Kittiwake when it was a hotel changed the name and everything. It was called The Cove back then – we've still got a stash of brochures and some headed notepaper, all terribly corporate. Fortunately, when it had its disastrous eighties makeover, they simply panelled over the original features without destroying anything. It was a complete bodge job. They carpeted over the parquet and everything – can you imagine?'

Freya pulls a funny little face as if to say, Some people have no taste whatsoever. Mel is immediately reminded of her mother's china bird collection, most of it smashed up by her father – 'Fucking chaffinch, fucking blue tit, fucking canary' – smash, smash, smash against the slate hearth of the electric fire surround.

'It's definitely had a chequered past,' adds Lance. 'As I'm sure you know, with you being a local.'

Mel finds herself nodding encouragingly, this is what she wants.

Warming to his theme, Lance continues, 'It was requisitioned by the government for a while during the Second World War, and then, before my grandmother bought it, it belonged to an American film star, fellow by the name of Ray Hammond – made a fortune out of cowboy movies and advertising cigarettes. He filmed a swashbuckler over here, fell in love with the place, bought Kittiwake and added all the mod cons. Unfortunately, the cigarette advertising backfired: within a year of doing the place up, he was dead. Lung cancer. That's when my Grandma Peggy bought it – not that I ever met her.'

Freya corrects him instantly and Mel is pleased to see a flash of annoyance cross his handsome features. 'Yes you did, at your christening,' she insists. 'There is a photo,' she tells Mel. 'On the grand piano in the entrance hall. Lance is the tiny bundle in his grandmother's arms.'

Lance picks up the thread: 'She was American, didn't actually live here after . . . um, terribly sad. She and my grandfather closed the place up, and then he, er, died.'

'Shot himself in the head,' Freya adds in a very perfunctory fashion.

'An accident, actually,' Lance insists. 'They were divorced by then, and she was living in the States. When she died, this place went to my mother's brother, her eldest son.'

'Her eldest *surviving* son,' Freya jumps in again. She is obviously a stickler for the facts.

This time Lance puts a restraining hand on his wife's arm. 'I don't think she's interested in all the gory details,' he laughs, before adding, 'But yes, Freya's right, there was an older boy who drowned.'

'Here at Kittiwake,' Freya interjects. This time Lance manages to silence her with a look.

'But to cut a long story short,' he sighs, 'after a lot of legal wrangling and boring probate stuff, the house went to her second son, Benedict, who used it for all kinds of things – parties, mostly – in his younger years. Later, as I mentioned, he turned it into a business: rented the place out as a hotel and conference centre while he lived abroad. And when he died, it came to me.'

'Us,' Freya reminds him.

'Us,' he repeats, putting his hands up in mock guilt and laughing. Then, speaking slowly and deliberately and putting great emphasis on any joint pronouns, he adds, 'And now it's *ours* . . . we can share it. We're having a big party here in August. My fiftieth.' He stresses *my* as if gallantly acknowledging that this milestone birthday is not joint, what with Freya being so much younger.

44

Lance continues, 'This party is a chance for our friends and families to get together in beautiful surroundings, eat great food, have a few drinks ...'

'My mother and my younger sister are coming over from Norway,' gushes Freya, and Lance nods along enthusiastically.

'And what about you, Lance?' probes Mel, 'Any of your family descending?'

'Well yes,' he answers, a twitch of annoyance visible in his cheek. 'My mother and my, er, older sister Bel will definitely be invited.'

'Ah, so your uncle believed in primogeniture too?' Mel observes. 'Only you mentioned you have an older sister and yet it was you who inherited Kittiwake?'

'Oh, it's a very complicated story,' says Freya, leaning forward as if poised to explain everything.

'That we don't have time for now,' warns Lance, his eyes turning cold. 'The main thing is that this August we will all be celebrating together, one big happy Kittiwake family.'

And with that he reaches forward and very firmly switches Mel's voice recorder off.

8

Blood Pressure

Clapham, London, April 2018, four months before the party

Bel is waiting to see the doctor. Her appointment is at 9.15, so she didn't have time for breakfast. Her stomach rumbles and she eyes a baby gumming at a soggy croissant.

That would be nice – an almond croissant with lots of powdery icing sugar. For a second she visualises herself snatching the pastry from the child and cramming it into her own mouth.

Suddenly Bel craves the feel of a toddler on her lap far more than the germ-riddled pastry snack. A fat lump of a child, not yet able to walk. This one is all bundled up in what looks like a hand-knitted jumper and a fleecy hat. He or she is like a parcel, wrapped up and tucked into a buggy for safekeeping.

Until recently, Bel was very much a dog person, far more likely to coo over a dachshund than a tiny dribbling human, but lately she has found herself peering into prams at newborns and getting involved in long-winded games of peep-o with two-year-old strangers while drinking coffee in Pret.

Hormones, no doubt.

You've done all that, she reminds herself. Bel has two children and not just the stretch marks to prove it – her breasts sag and her pelvic floor is shot to pieces. It's been a long time since she was able to tackle even a mini trampoline with any confidence.

Motherhood is all about sacrifice, she decides silently, picking up a tattered copy of OK! magazine and failing entirely to recognise the 'celebrity' on the cover.

The issue is a 'Bridal Special' and the unknown blonde seems to have an entire chorus line of bridesmaids behind her, all of whom seem to have identical smiling orange faces and matching bright white teeth.

Bel's wedding over thirty years ago had been small. She hadn't had a bridesmaid and Andrew didn't have a best man; instead they'd had witnesses. There'd been four of them in the register office – Bel and Andrew and their two closest friends, Liz and Barry. So much cheaper, so much simpler, though she wishes now they'd been able to afford a photographer. Smartphones might be a curse but considering they weren't around back then they have no actual record of the day. Bel has to think hard to recall what she was wearing. Late eighties, a navy velvet hairband to match her jacket and skirt, and a white pie-crust collar blouse from Laura Ashley. Andrew wore a suit from Next and a tie patterned with musical notes (which she'd hated, not that she'd said anything; he was smiling so much that as they said their vows she forgave him the tie and silently promised to choose all his accessories from that day forth).

She twists her wedding ring around her finger. They married young, she concedes. She'd been determined; once she'd found him, she couldn't wait to ditch her maiden name and become Mrs Robatham.

The baby has been called in, his name is Felix – sweet. Bel is almost faint with hunger, hopefully she'll be next. Impatiently she rifles through her voluminous handbag in case there's a forgotten snack in there, a cereal bar, a throat lozenge, even a squashed banana, but the search is literally fruitless. What she has got, however, is the morning's mail, which she'd picked up on her way out of the house. In an effort to distract herself from the increasingly embarrassing sounds emanating from her stomach, Bel picks through the small bundle. A couple of bills; a fashion catalogue aimed at women her age who look thrilled to be wearing a collarless silk shirt that comes in a variety of colours, including amethyst; a small package from ASOS for Ed's girlfriend Maisie, and a stiff white envelope addressed to Mr and Mrs A. Robatham.

Bel bristles at the inclusion of the letter A – it's old fashioned and unnecessary. Nonetheless, how novel these days to receive anything handwritten. Gleefully she rips it open to reveal a creamy gilt-edged card:

Lance Berrington has the pleasure of inviting
Annabel, Andrew, Edward, and James
to his fiftieth birthday Bacchanalian bash/August
bank holiday barn dance. Fancy dress encouraged.
Accommodation and catering provided from
Friday 24th–Sunday 26th inclusive
At Kittiwake House, Monty's Cove,
Cornwall

Bel feels her chest squeeze. She can't seem to catch her breath and she wonders if she might be about to pass out. She stuffs the post into her bag and concentrates on getting enough oxygen into her lungs. It's all right, she reminds herself, it's all right, you don't even have to go if you don't want to. But she knows that she will – after all, it's Kittiwake.

'Annabel Robatham, please.' The nurse is short and fat. She better not say anything about losing weight and exercising, thinks

48

Bel, following her vast bottom into what resembles a very untidy broom cupboard.

There is barely space for both of them to sit down. Bel takes off her coat and scarf. She can feel the heat rising from her, her body feels like a warm oven set to muffin temperature.

'So, what's the problem, Mrs Robatham?'

'Anger,' replies Bel. 'I feel furious a great deal of the time and I think one day I could hurt someone, you know? Say someone is riding a bike on the pavement, I might just push them off.'

The nurse merely nods for her to continue.

'And if I'm not angry, I'm upset. I feel so emotional a lot of the time – I have these fits of weepiness.'

Again that nod. 'And you're how old?'

'Fifty-five,' Bel responds, and she feels like adding, And I'm so middle-aged it hurts.

'Would you say you were stressed?' the nurse asks, looking surreptitiously at her watch.

Bel almost laughs, she would like to see the nurse's face if she said, Damn right I'm stressed! I'm an overweight, heavy-drinking, middle-aged hysteric, with a massive mortgage and two supposedly adult sons, neither of whom can unload a dishwasher. And if that wasn't bad enough, my eldest has moved his girlfriend in.

Bloody Maisie.

'Ow, what the hell?'

Without Bel noticing, the nurse has pushed up her shirtsleeve and wired her up to a blood-pressure monitor.

The pressure around her upper arm grows incredibly intense. If the band doesn't stop tightening, Bel's afraid it will cut off her blood supply and she will lose the use of her arm.

'Your blood pressure is very high,' the nurse tells her, and she mentions numbers that mean nothing to Bel. Andrew does all the measuring in their house, Bel still hasn't gone fully metric.

The nurse unleashes her arm and starts talking about the risks associated with high blood pressure, sudden strokes being the main concern. 'And is there any history of high blood pressure or heart problems in the family?' she enquires.

Bel hasn't a clue. 'I'm afraid I don't have any knowledge of my blood family's medical history,' she replies breezily. 'All I know for certain is that my birth mother was twenty when she died.'

The nurse raises an eyebrow. 'Gosh, that is young.'

Yes, thinks Bel, twenty is nothing these days. In fact, both her sons are older than her mother was when she passed away. 'I was adopted,' she replies vaguely, and immediately she is transported back to the room.

When Bel was a little girl and she thought about where she came from, she imagined a huge room full of newborn babies in cots. She couldn't actually hear the crying, but she could picture it. Some of the babies had their mouths wide open, all red inside like starling fledglings waiting for breakfast.

It couldn't be an actual memory – Bel had been only a few months old when she was adopted – but ever since she was little, whenever she thought about being what her parents called 'chosen', she saw the same scenario. It was like that time she went to the cinema when she was six and something went wrong with the film and the same scene kept repeating and repeating, until a big scorch mark had burnt through the screen. Even now, though she knows the scenario was entirely rooted in her childish imagination, she can still picture the scene. That room full of babies, all lined up in cots ready for their prospective parents to come and see which one they liked the look of. 'We picked you,' she can remember her mother saying, 'because you had the most beautiful blue eyes. We adored you on the spot.'

'And what happened next?' she would ask her mother when they were alone together, usually after her bath when she was on Mummy's knee, all wrapped in the big warm towel.

'We brought you home and put you in the yellow nursery that had been specially painted for you.'

Only it turned out Natasha had been lying. It had been years before Bel found out the truth. Years of assuming her real mother had died in childbirth – why else would she have been available for adoption? After all, mummies didn't give their babies away.

Back in the broom cupboard, the nurse is still talking. Apparently she is going to fit Bel with a twenty-four-hour blood-pressure monitor to check whether her readings are consistently high or whether visiting the surgery has exacerbated her stress levels. 'I'll only be a tick,' the nurse tells Bel, and exits the tiny space, presumably to fetch the blood-pressure device.

For the few minutes she is left alone, Bel wonders what it says on her medical records. She suspects they know she lies about her alcohol intake. She doesn't think she's got a problem, but she might be slightly what people call 'dependent'. Let's say it's been a long time since Bel forgot to reach into the drinks fridge for a bottle of Chardonnay on the dot of 7 p.m. – and who can blame her? It's a ritual: *The Archers* and a nice glass of chilled white wine. Andrew usually has a lager, which means there is more wine for Bel. Before she can reposition herself to peer at the screen and read her medical notes, the fat little nurse returns.

'A few more questions, then we can set this up. So, alcohol?'

Bel allows a lie to slip out of her mouth. 'The occasional glass of wine, that's all.'

'And what about exercise?' prompts the nurse, not batting an eyelid despite the fact her cornflower blue uniform is straining at the seams.

Bel fights the temptation to step out of her nice middle-aged, middle-class lady persona and say, Probably as much as you, fatty. Let's face it, neither of us could run for a bus without puking. Instead she replies, 'I do a stretch class once a week.'

51

The nurse nods. 'Maybe if you could add something a bit more cardiovascular?'

Maybe you could, replies Bel in her head while nodding in agreement.

9

In the Supermarket

Half an hour later, when Bel is in the supermarket, the cuff around her bicep buzzes into action. Immediately, she puts her basket on the floor and allows her arm to hang limply at her side, as the nurse had suggested. The cuff tightens, and she remembers how her children used to complain when she blew up their water wings until they were too tight: 'Ow hurting, Mummy, Mummy, Mummy, Mummy.'

How many times has she been called 'Mummy' in her life? Over a million, surely. Once upon a time it was the only thing she ever wanted.

She has always been maternal, she supposes. As a little girl she had loved her dolls with a passion that bordered on the obsessive, smothering them with affection. Apart from . . .

Bel has a sudden flashback. She is a little girl in a cotton flower-sprig nightie, holding a doll. A proper Tiny Tears baby doll. She called her Tina, Tiny Tears Tina, a birthday gift from Uncle Benedict. But one night, playing schools with all her toys lined up in a row at the foot of her bed, she decided she was cross with Tina and shut her in a drawer.

Standing next to the cauliflowers in the vegetable aisle, as a fully grown fifty-five-year-old woman, Bel is once again awash with the guilt and horror of this memory, recalling how she had woken in the night convinced that Tina was dead, and the ensuing desperate scrabble to open the drawer and save her.

Fortunately, Tina's mechanical eyelids had almost instantly clicked open. Relieved to find her alive, Bel climbed back into bed with the dolly tucked in beside her, apologising fervently into her little plastic ear, 'I'm sorry, I'm sorry, I'm sorry.'

Blimey, talk about Freudian! She hasn't thought about Tina for years. The double whammy of Lance's party invitation combined with the chat at the surgery must have triggered this succession of uncomfortable childhood memories. Poor Tina, she's probably in the attic somewhere, forever six months old and covered in cobwebs. Oh God, the attic – when is it ever going to get cleared out?

The monitor seems to pause before tightening again. It's pinching her arm like a Chinese burn. There's nowhere to sit down, so she stands in the aisle and waits until the tightening feeling passes, then continues filling her basket with all the things that everyone else in her house has demanded.

She has a list, a proper list written out on the back of an envelope in biro, old-school style. She cannot understand people who keep lists on their phones.

Gluten-free bagels, hummus, Cooper's thick Oxford marmalade, face-wipes for sensitive skin ('But not the anti-ageing ones, I don't need those!'). Why is she buying her son's girlfriend face-wipes and gluten-free nonsense? Since when has it become acceptable for Maisie to add things to the black chalkboard shopping list in the kitchen?

Even her handwriting annoys Bel. It's unformed, childish. And as for her spelling . . .

Bel sighs. Now is not the time to ponder Maisie's grasp of the English language. She has to think about supper. It's infuriating, never knowing how many people will be sitting at the table, or if not exactly at the table, then hanging around expecting to be fed.

She's got some neck of lamb in the freezer. If she remembers to get that out, they can have a casserole, or a tagine if she's feeling adventurous – only that would mean buying dried apricots and they're right down the other end of the supermarket. Sod it, she will do a bog-standard lamb stew. All she needs is carrots. Oh, God, she can't remember if she's got stock cubes, and they're down the far end with the dried apricots. Decisions, decisions.

She should have gone home for breakfast before attempting this. The combination of lack of food, the prospect of a family get-together and the blood-pressure monitor is making her feel slightly sick and faint. Some plain croissants lie squashed at the bottom of her basket. Life can be terribly hard, thinks Bel, wondering how much more it would take to make her cry.

Wine, she'll buy some wine. It's not on the list, but they might need a couple of emergency bottles before the van delivery this Friday. (Bel belongs to the *Sunday Times* wine club, it makes the whole 'heavy drinking' thing seem so much more acceptable, almost professional.)

The wine makes the basket unbearably heavy. She should have got a trolley. She needs fizzy water and loo rolls too, but she'll have to come back tomorrow for those. Damn and blast it, why can't Maisie buy toilet rolls? No doubt she wipes her bum with hypo-allergenic face-wipes.

At the checkout, Bel searches in her purse for her Nectar card – throughout the year, she and Andrew save up their points so they can splash out on the big Christmas shop – but she can't find the wretched thing. 'No, I'm not collecting school vouchers,' she snaps at the teenage boy behind the till, biting back the words 'you idiot', because he's clearly not; he is a perfectly pleasant young man with a job.

55

There was a time when she couldn't think of anything worse than her children working in a supermarket. Now she feels like stopping off at the information desk and asking if there are any vacancies. Ed, her eldest at twenty-six, has a part-time sort of job, but Jamie, her twenty-four-year-old, is yet to find employment of any kind.

Really, thinks Bel, I'd be happier with him sitting behind a till doing something constructive, rather than sitting around at home doing nothing.

What is it with her sons' generation? By the time she was in her mid-twenties, she and Andrew were married and had set up home in Gypsy Hill. Bel was a PA working for a small publishing house, while Andrew had a job collecting data for a pharmaceutical company in West Croydon. They used to commute in different directions from their local train station, blowing each other kisses across the platforms. We were like little adults, she thinks, remembering how she would spend her lunch hour deciding what to cook her husband for his supper back at their cosy maisonette.

It's not the Millennials' fault there's a housing crisis in London, she reminds herself, realising that the only twenty-somethings in the Robathams' social circle that live entirely independently from their parents are those with mummies and daddies wealthy enough to have bought them a flat. Well, her lads can whistle for that. Neither she nor Andrew have enough savings of their own, and the likelihood of inheriting any life-changing amounts of money any time soon are non-existent. Andrew's parents never had any, and hers . . . Bel swallows hard. All she knows is that her late father left his affairs in a terrible state and her mother now lives in what she refers to as 'reduced circumstances'.

The contents of her basket come to almost forty pounds, and as Bel has left her bags for life in the car, an unnecessary extra fifteen pence is added to the bill.

Not that it matters; fifteen pence is neither here nor there in the scheme of things. It's the amount left to pay on the mortgage that keeps her awake at night, wondering why and how they ever thought that an interest-only option was a good idea. We're never going to pay that off, she frets, heading for the exit. Not now that she only works part-time. As for Andrew, his career stalled about ten years ago. Her mother's voice echoes in her head: 'Andrew hasn't got much drive, has he?' But she pushes the memory away.

It's the uncertainty surrounding Brexit that has done for her salary, thinks Bel ruefully, wondering what would have happened had she stayed in publishing rather than jumping ship for a new venture some pals were setting up back in the mid-nineties.

Snow Nation was an agency created to recruit staff for European ski resorts, and Bel has been working at their office in Victoria since it first opened.

The owners, Jan and Marcus, have earned a fortune out of it, but the past few years have not been kind to the ski industry; rather than fight the downturn, the Leamings decided to scale down the business. As a result, Bel now works three days a week.

At first she was grateful, imagining herself spending more time in the gym and exploring new hobbies: dressmaking or maybe silver-smithing – she could have a little shed in the garden, all kitted out with whatever you need for silver-smithing . . . But with adult children to support and Andrew's move over to the NHS meaning his wages are permanently frozen, there never seems to be enough money for anything exciting or extravagant. They haven't even booked a holiday this year.

It's been ages since I've actually been skiing, thinks Bel, jealously recalling Jan's Austrian tan, with its giveaway goggle-lines, before recalling how useless her husband is on the slopes. Bless Andrew, she does love him, but he's a complete waste of a lift pass. Bel thinks fondly back to how they first met; if Andrew hadn't been such a rubbish skier, he'd never have broken his ankle and she wouldn't have had the opportunity to play her Florence Nightingale number and her life might have taken a different path. I might have married someone with a bit more drive, she muses, someone with less dandruff and a bigger pension pot.

But money isn't the only thing that keeps her awake at night. She made a list a few weeks ago of the things that worry her, and then she re-wrote the list in alphabetical order and awarded each problem a mark out of ten according to how much it upset her. Anything that causes her to hyperventilate scored a ten, while small background niggles such as needing a new mat for the hall were marked with a lowly one.

For a moment, seeing all her worries neatly written down in her lovely handwriting on the back of a handy piece of cardboard packaging that came free with a pair of tights made her feel more in control.

After a brief panic, Bel locates her car in the car park and opens the boot before realising that it's full of bin liners of stuff intended for the charity shop. Slamming down the lid, she lobs her shopping onto the back seat instead. A jar of marmalade immediately falls out of the bag and rolls under the passenger seat. Dammit, she'll dig it out later.

Bel proceeds to have her daily fight with the driver's door. It keeps sticking and she has to yank at the handle until the door flies open and almost smacks her in the teeth. She squeezes behind the wheel. The car is alphabetically third on her list and rates a worry score of seven.

She reaches for her seat belt. No . . . croissant first, if she doesn't eat right now she might black out on the way home.

As she twists her arm between the seats and reaches into her shopping, the blood-pressure monitor begins to buzz again. She holds still, thinking how ridiculous her life has become, and when the stupid thing has done its business she snatches at the bag of croissants, rips it open with her teeth and folds first one croissant, then a second and finally a third into her mouth. A blizzard of pastry flakes cascades down her coat.

Ideally, she would like to go back to bed; everything is such hard work. With one squashed croissant remaining in the packet, Bel turns the key in the ignition and for some reason, in that split second, she remembers it wasn't only the doll that she was cruel to.

Once, when Jamie was a tiny baby and Ed was in nursery, she did the same to her six-month-old child as she had to Tina.

Bel would like to deny it, but the evidence plays out in a series of undeniably accurate pictures in her head.

She is sitting on an unmade bed, Andrew has gone to work, ugly purple wallpaper is peeling off the walls and a cup of tea has formed a milky skin on her bedside table. They had not long moved into the Clapham house, so Ed must have been nearly three. He is dressed and playing with Duplo on the floor, while she has the infant Jamie in her arms and is rocking backwards and forwards, slightly too fast to be comforting the baby.

Jamie was a colicky, ungrateful baby, impolite on the bosom, greedy and dismissive. At least when Ed was suckling, he looked adoringly into her eyes, as if grateful for the nourishment. Not Jamie: he bit and tugged and spat her nipple out, as if resentful that the stuff that kept him alive had to come from her. If he did settle to feed properly, he would close his eyes tightly shut. There was no intimacy between them, she was merely a machine that produced what he needed. But mostly he cried.

In the memory, she is thirty-one years old, she has one child playing nicely on the floor and this horrible goblin baby in her arms, turning his face away from her swollen breast. She is sweating. Glancing at the alarm clock on the bedside table, she rises from the bed and walks purposefully over to a chest of drawers, the baby tucked under her arm like a swimming towel. In one swift movement she opens a drawer and rolls the baby in. She doesn't shut it completely, she closes it halfway. You can still hear him scream, so she closes the drawer a little more and the screaming is slightly muffled. Then she has a shower, gets dressed and takes Ed to nursery.

She is home within half an hour. The baby is asleep in the drawer.

He is fine.

10

Home

Bel carries her groceries into the house. The hallway is dark because of the yew tree that needs pruning in the front garden.

One day, she would like to live somewhere light, a simple wooden hut on the banks of a lake, with a private jetty. The sort of thing you regularly see in *Elle Deco*, featuring an elegant blonde in yoga pants with a cute baby on her hip. 'Skye and her family live a simple yet sophisticated lifestyle here in this idyllic isolated lakeside beauty spot . . .'

By contrast, Bel and her family live in a cramped four-bedroom house on the wrong side of Clapham Common.

It's not that small, thinks Bel crossly; the problem is that nobody ever tidies anything up or puts anything away.

The wall to the left of the front door bulges under a mound of coats; coats are piled on top of coats on top of coats. She wouldn't be surprised if, burrowing right down into the centre of all this wool, gabardine and leather, she found Ed's first anorak or the totally inappropriate velvet-collared coat that Grandtash bought Jamie when he was five. Immediately she hears Natasha saying, 'Really, darling, sometimes it's nice for children to look smart.'

What for? It wasn't as if the child was about to attend a society wedding. Her mother could be ridiculous at times. In her defence, Natasha's upbringing had been ludicrously privileged, Bel acknowledges grudgingly. No wonder she had such daft priorities, hers was a world of nannies and ponies – for a while at least, until it all disappeared.

She desperately needs to have a cull of the coats and face up to the fact that she is never going to get into that baby-blue mohair number that she bought in the Jigsaw sale three years ago. The menopause plays havoc with a woman's weight, she tells herself – though so does eating a family pack of croissants in the car, dammit.

Should get rid of that too, she reminds herself, spying Benji's lead on the hall table. The dog's been dead a good six months, but somehow she can't yet bring herself to part with his lead.

What a dreadful day that was. The vet had come over and injected the old family pet in the sitting room, and then Bel sat with Benji on her knee until the weight of the animal became somehow heavier and she knew he was dead, or 'gone to doggy heaven' as Ed's girlfriend insisted on saying in a baby voice.

No sign of Maisie, thank goodness. Mind you, the fact that her hideous fake-fur jacket wasn't hanging up with the rest of the coats didn't necessarily mean she was out. She might have draped it over a chair in the kitchen or chucked it on the living room floor. Wherever Maisie went, she seemed to leave a trail of evidence in her wake: a half-eaten bowl of cereal on the landing windowsill, a tangle of elastic hairbands around the kitchen doorknob, magenta hair dye on a beige towel in the bathroom. And it's not just her things, it's the smell of her, the sugary pong that permeates the whole house. God knows what it is, but it makes Bel's eyes water.

Sadly, Maisie's signature scent isn't strong enough to mask the whiff of dope that is drifting down from Jamie's bedroom.

Bel suppresses the urge to shout up a command to help unpack the shopping. She doesn't want to face the fact that her second son may not be dressed. You can't tell him what to do, he's twenty-four, she reminds herself, as if she hadn't been present at the birth. He'd been slow to emerge even then, eventually having to be sucked out of her using the ventouse method, a process which Andrew had described as a bit like watching someone unblock a sink. Her son's head had been like a telegraph pole for months and consequently she'd always made sure he wore a hat. Ed, her eldest child, had been the more painful, awkwardly positioned and with the largest cranial circumference the midwife had ever recorded. He was all head for a long time and very slow to sit up, possibly because the weight of the thing unbalanced him. Or maybe because he simply couldn't be bothered. Ed at twenty-six is so laid back he's practically horizontal, but at least he manages to get up and dressed. At least he has a part-time job; at least he and Maisie are saving up (in principle) for a mortgage.

Although with the wages they are currently earning this will take them the best part of a hundred years, Bel speculates bitterly, setting the blood-pressure monitor a-buzzing. And you'll be dead, she tells herself. So no point getting your knickers in a twist.

Bel leaves Maisie's face-wipes on the stairs. As Ed's live-in girl-friend, she is meant to contribute to household expenses, but she keeps forgetting and last week she left a note for the cleaner asking her to change the sheets she and Ed have soiled by taking snacks to bed with them.

Constancia had refused. 'I do not have time, Mrs Robatham, to launder sheets. I will iron, yes, but I am not a washerwoman.'

Constancia has cleaned for the Robathams since the children were small. She has a daughter, Sybille, who used to accompany her mother during school holidays and sit reading on the stairs while the boys ran around making war noises.

Sybille is only a year older than Ed, but she is already married and living with her husband in a three-bedroom townhouse in Epsom. They have a dog and are expecting a baby. Constancia is always showing Bel blurred photographs of her swollen-bellied daughter on her phone. 'She looks very happy,' Bel says, when what she means is triumphant.

Sometimes life seems like a magic trick that only some people manage to pull off, while the rest of us are whipping away the tablecloth and smashing all the crockery.

The kettle is still warm, so someone's been in the kitchen recently. Bel makes herself a cup of coffee, allowing her arm to hang limply when the machine on her arm buzzes, trying to 'take herself to her calm space' – only she can never decide if she is calmest sitting under a pine tree in Greece, or standing on a mountain filling her lungs with Alpine air. Today she conjures up a combination of both and pictures herself in a swimming costume on top of a mountain. She looks ridiculous, flabby and pink as a blancmange.

At last the cuff eases. Bel, sitting down with her cup of coffee, digs out the party invitation from her bag. So Lance is nearly fifty. Of course he is, he has always been and always will be five years younger than her. Now it's his turn to hit the big five-O, so inevitably he will be celebrating at the family seat. Correction, her adoptive family seat. Instantly she feels a metallic taste in her mouth, a familiar surge of bitterness. Lance was born with a silver spoon in his mouth, hers was only borrowed. Lance is her brother, only he wasn't adopted.

She remembers visiting her mother the day after she gave birth to him in a private room at the Portland Hospital. It was 1968. Natasha was propped up in her hospital bed with her hair freshly set and wearing a pretty floral nightie with a matching bed jacket. Her lipstick-coated smile was wider than Bel had ever seen before, it seemed to split her face in half. Daddy had brought flowers, carnations. 'Darling they're beautiful,' Natasha had laughed with her wide orange mouth.

Then the nurses brought in the baby and her mother held out her arms, her face leaking water. 'Oh, my darling baby, if you knew how long I had waited for you,' she sobbed. Then her father had knelt down by the bed and buried his face in the bedding and he'd wept too. What with the flowers and the baby and Daddy, there didn't seem to be any room for her, so she stood and waited for her mother to notice she was there.

I'm still waiting, she decides, feeling sorry for herself and reaching for the stem ginger and chocolate biscuits that had magically appeared in her shopping basket, despite not having been on any list.

August, she reminds herself. She's got plenty of time to lose a stone or so before the party and the scrutiny of her mother's exacting gaze. Natasha's superpower is the ability to guess exactly how much a person weighs as soon as they walk into a room. And I have never been elegant or thin enough, decides Bel, defiantly tucking the biscuits under her arm and heading for the stairs.

These days she sometimes takes her treats up to the bedroom for safekeeping. It seems ridiculous, hiding food from the children, but they have no idea how boring and expensive it is to have to keep replacing things, and that sometimes it isn't okay for Maisie to open a bottle of Chablis when she's having cereal for her supper, because since when did anyone suggest serving Dorset extra-nutty muesli with a crisp chilled premier cru at nine pounds a bottle?

Bel sits on the edge of her bed thinking about her mother and comfort eating. Their relationship is so complicated; on the one hand, her parents should never have adopted her, on the other . . . Bel swallows her third biscuit. You had everything you could have asked for. You had a lovely home and an expensive education, you had your own bedroom, you were taken on foreign holidays and stayed in smart hotels . . . *But, but*, nags Bel's subconscious.

Suddenly Bel is in Portugal. It is 1975, so she must have been twelve, and she's the only one of the family who's burnt. Her mother's voice is both regretful and amused: 'I always forget that Annabel doesn't have the same skin as us, poor thing.'

Her back had bubbled with huge water-filled blisters and she had to spend two days indoors to be on the safe side. But she had had plenty of books to read, and in any case she was old enough and sensible enough to be left alone while the rest of the family went down to the beach. Of course she was.

She has always been religious about sunscreen with her own children, slathering them with factor thirty even on typically miserable summer bank holiday weekends in the UK. Naturally, as soon as the boys were old enough to go off to music festivals and get sunstroke, they did.

11

Dinner

Bel has forgotten to get the neck of lamb out of the freezer, and she can't defrost the frozen lump of meat in the microwave because she chucked theirs out years ago when there was that scare about magnetrons frying children's brains. What with Jamie's GCSEs coming up, she hadn't felt like taking the risk.

They can have pasta and pesto, they haven't had that in years. When the children were little it was all they would eat – pasta and pesto and pizza. In some respects, it's a wonder they haven't got rickets.

Really, tuts Bel, you'd think I'd be more organised now I'm only working part-time. Although, if she's honest, these days she finds going to work easier than staying at home. At work she isn't constantly faced with a mountain of domestic angst, at work she doesn't need to worry about moths or the strange smell in the downstairs bathroom; all she has to do is match enthusiastic young people with available jobs in ski resorts across Europe.

Snow Nation had been a brainwave of Jan and Marcus's, which is a bit galling considering Jan and Bel were chalet maids together back in the eighties. Thanks to its success Jan and Marcus mostly spend their weekends at their barn conversion in the Cotswolds, while their pre-Raphaelite daughter Minky is a published poet and competent flute player. Bel takes a deep breath. She has to stop doing this, she has to stop comparing herself and her family to everyone else.

Jan tells her she should take up meditation, but the last time Bel tried to sit cross-legged on the floor and empty her mind she got cramp in her left calf and found herself rolling around the carpet howling like a wolf.

Instead, she decides to spiralise some carrots and make an interesting salad to bring the dish up to twenty-first-century standards. Yotam Ottolenghi has a lot to answer for, thinks Bel, as she googles 'interesting Moroccan carrot salad'.

She could make her own pasta – she has a machine, yet another household gift from Andrew. Come birthdays or Christmas, her husband never strays further than the kitchen department in Peter Jones' basement, when he need only ride the escalator up a couple of floors to find himself in a world of luxury smellies.

Bel loves a scented bath. Expensive bath oils are one of her few extravagances. It comes from being brought up in a home where her mother insisted on all soaps being triple-milled and French. Bel has sensitive skin; anything cheap brings her out in a rash. She has to be very careful what she uses, for example, the bath bombs Maisie bought her for her birthday set her vagina on fire, she might as well have rubbed her genitalia with chilli powder.

Posh soaps and scented drawer liners, her mother made such an effort to keep things nice. Everything on the surface had been so perfect, so ordered and yet . . .

Don't go there, she admonishes herself. Her past is a scab she has learned not to pick; it is so much less painful if she leaves it alone. Pulling herself together, Bel surveys the contents of the fridge. For a moment she thinks about making her own pesto. She has a pestle and mortar, but she hasn't got fresh basil – and anyway, she can't be bothered.

No, tonight it's dried pasta and pesto from a jar, but she will set the kitchen table and be generous about opening a decent bottle of wine. Red or white with pesto, she wonders. What would Natasha choose?

Her mother had been a stickler for doing things properly. Every evening in Claverley Avenue, where Bel grew up, her mother set the dining table with a proper cloth and matching napkins – late-fifties-style wedding gifts mostly, varying from simple Irish green linen to extravagant lace numbers. On top of the tablecloth she placed circular melamine mats, each featuring a different species of rose. Napkins were rolled into silver rings and slim red candles placed in silver candlesticks. Natasha took her table settings and flower arranging seriously, she had a book of Constance Spry designs and collected all sorts of accessories with which to exper-iment. Bel recalls a scaled-down ornamental wicker wheelbarrow containing a selection of spider plants jauntily placed on an Ercol sideboard.

That's all the rage again now, all the mid-twentieth-century stuff that only a few years ago everyone was slinging into skips.

Her blood-pressure monitor squeezes her arm so tight at this moment that she finds herself gasping. Sod the thing, she can't even have a bath tonight, the nurse had made it very clear she mustn't get it wet. What a complete drag. If Benji were alive she would take him for a walk; she doubts she's done more than three thousand steps in any one day since the poor thing was put out of his misery.

'I can't see what's so miserable about lying in front of the fire farting all day,' Jamie had sniped.

'Yeah,' Ed laughed, 'if that was the criteria for human euthanasia, Mum, you'd be well fucked.' And Maisie had laughed until she was slightly hysterical.

There are six around the dinner table this evening. It's a dreary rainy night in April; Maisie and Ed can't afford to go out, Jamie has no one to go out with, and Andrew doesn't like going out if he can help it and would be happy to spend the rest of his life eating supper off a tray in front of the television. He isn't fussy about what he eats, the only thing he doesn't like is bony fish. If she gave him baked beans and sausages for the rest of his days, he'd be quite happy. Thank goodness for Andrew, thinks Bel, allowing herself a brief moment of congratulation for having chosen a man who is so very different from her adoptive father, a man who wasn't afraid to lift his hand to either women or children, a man who was proud to call himself a disciplinarian, when in truth he'd been sadistic. In hindsight, Hugo was probably to blame for a lot of Natasha's behaviour. What's that phrase she heard on *Woman's Hour* the other day? *Coercive control.* Her father was a bully and, even though the circumstances had been traumatic, it was a relief when he died.

Andrew, by contrast, is a pussy cat in an extra-large Marks and Spencer's woollen jumper. He does need to lose some weight though, she thinks fondly, deciding that Lance's party in August will be a good diet incentive for both of them.

'Pasta and pesto,' chorus the boys, spying the ingredients out on the counter after she calls them down.

'Retro,' adds Ed, and Maisie giggles, signalling that she is in a good mood, which is a relief because when she isn't giggly she is morose and prone to weepiness. Having Maisie as a house guest for the past few months, Bel is now glad she never had a daughter. Her son's girlfriend is mercurial in her moods; everything seems to affect how she is feeling. She is allergic to an ever-changing roster of food groups, sometimes dairy, other times gluten, she won't touch sprouts and gets sulky if an avocado which looks perfectly normal in the fruit bowl turns out to have gone brown inside. Maisie takes everything personally.

Bel must walk around on eggshells, weight must never be mentioned, spots are a no-go area, and yet Maisie will sit in front of the television and systematically reduce every female to 'hag or slag'.

That's another thing – the sofa. Once upon a time when the boys were little and went to bed at a reasonable hour, Bel had the sofa all to herself. Now the sofa is full of twenty-somethings. Maisie takes one corner and arranges her legs over Ed, who sits in the middle, while Jamie takes the other corner and Bel is relegated to the second-best armchair.

How have they allowed this to happen, how come she has bred chicks who refuse to leave the nest? What will it take to get rid of them?

Obviously she knows she's not the only one currently sailing this particularly overcrowded boat. God knows, it's London, and with Brexit still ongoing no one has a clue what's happening; rents are ridiculous, mortgages impossible to get hold of and jobs that aren't badly paid and menial seem incredibly hard to come by.

Bel grates some parmesan and thinks fondly back to the eighties, how easy it was to be independent back then. You could literally walk into a job off the street, careers in journalism and advertising welcoming you with open arms and expense accounts. There were grants and schemes for people who wanted to be creative, and if you couldn't afford rent then you squatted.

Bel racks her brains but she can't recall anyone back then over the age of twenty who lived at home with their parents, not unless they had something medically wrong with them, like Brenda Ennis's poor wheelchair-bound brother, Trevor.

Parents were different back then too. They wouldn't have tolerated the smoking and drinking and soft-drug-taking that is considered the norm nowadays, not to mention the casual promiscuity and the daylight hours spent in bed, the ridiculous facial hair and sloppy 'chill-out' clothes. Bel has a sudden image of her father silently eating breakfast in a shirt and tie, her mother running in and out of the kitchen fetching him his toast, his fury if the butter

71

in the dish was too hard to spread. 'Strewth Natasha, is it too much to ask?' Her mother's instant apology and accompanying too-bright smile, the smile that gave Bel the tummy ache she could never explain to anyone.

Fortunately, before Bel gets truly maudlin, it's time to put supper on the table, and the kitchen is humming with noise and chatter and a slight whiff of BO. Jamie can be terribly shower shy.

Tonight her sons resemble giant toddlers with beards; both are wearing jogging bottoms, although neither has been jogging in years. The fleece-lined trousers – bottle green for Ed, navy for Jamie – resemble the first pull-up trousers she dressed them in for nursery. Zipless and buttonless, so they could manage trips to the bathroom more easily.

It dawns on her in that moment that her sons don't possess a single tie between them. If she dropped down dead this evening, they wouldn't have anything to wear for her funeral.

The idea of her unshaven, out-of-shape sons sitting in a church pew, wearing tracksuit bottoms and T-shirts with rude words on them makes her want to weep. She's glad that death would render her incapable of witnessing the spectacle.

In stark contrast to the boys, Maisie is wearing skin-tight burgundy pleather trousers and what looks like a pair of high-heeled wooden clogs.

Bel has been on a steep learning curve over the last six months. The world of young women is very different from that of her sons. For starters, there is a lot of obsessing over eyebrow shapes and the 'right' kind of yoga pants.

'Oh, I didn't know you did yoga,' Bel had commented – foolishly, as it turns out. Maisie doesn't like yoga, but she occasionally likes wearing trousers with a gusset that reaches her knees.

On the plus side, girls eat a lot less. Jamie and Ed eat like shire horses. They scoop whole tubs of hummus onto entire packets of pitta bread in a single sitting. There is no point in buying anything smaller than a bag of crisps the size of a pillow. Maisie on the other hand picks at food like a bird, especially in company. She is forever pushing her food around, or 'playing with it' as Bel's mother would say.

The way she uses her cutlery makes Beth wince too. She cuts everything up before discarding the knife completely and transferring her fork into her right hand and stabbing at her meal. 'Is she left-handed?' she'd asked Ed, but it turns out this is the way some people like to eat. 'And anyway,' her son had snapped, 'what's the big deal?'

I was brought up to believe that it is rude to wave your cutlery in the air, thinks Bel, and that elbows on the table are the height of bad manners.

If Natasha – or God help her, Hugo – were here tonight, neither of them would understand why a group of young adults were slouched around the kitchen table in various states of inappropriate dress. Maisie is sporting a cropped orange top, which is basically little more than a bra. A bra, at the dinner table! Jamie has a filthy baseball cap perched on top of his unwashed hair, while Ed is wearing what is commonly known as a wife-beater, which means that every time he reaches for something on the other side of the table, his gingery underarm hair brushes over the salad.

'Ed, why don't you ask someone to pass you the salt?' she snaps.

'Because I can reach it,' he responds, lifting one buttock off his chair to squeak out a fart.

Even Andrew is letting the side down. Her husband has taken off his shoes and socks because his ingrown toenail is hurting, and has sat down to dinner with bare feet. It's like a chimpanzees' tea party.

The blood-pressure monitor starts its infernal buzz the moment she lifts her fork to her lips.

'What in fuck's name is that?' asks Ed. When Bel tells him, they all snigger.

'It sounds like a vibrator,' titters Maisie, colouring slightly and glancing at Ed.

It's enough to make you puke. Bel can't see what's so clever about sex toys. She knows Ed and Maisie have a whole drawer full of silicone dildos and objects that require batteries; she found them when she went on a snooping mission and now wishes she hadn't. Fact is, thinks Bel, if you're already bored of gadget-free sex by the time you're twenty-something, then God help you by the time you reach fifty.

To change the subject, she produces the invitation she received earlier.

'Lance has invited us to his fiftieth,' she announces.

'Fiftieth what?' asks Ed, reaching for the last of the Merlot. Two bottles don't go far between six.

'Birthday, of course. His half-century.'

'I think I'll put my head in the oven when I turn fifty,' sneers Maisie, and Bel is tempted to retort, Good idea, then you'll have cooked at least one thing in your life.

But she doesn't. Maisie's thin little South London voice grates. Where did she grow up again? Croydon, wasn't it? She went to school with those girls that bullied Cicely Frayn's daughter on the bus.

'Well some people think turning fifty is worth celebrating,' Bel retorts huffily. She's sick to death of being patronised by young people.

Five years ago, Bel and Andrew went to Paris for her 'big five-O'. They spent a fortune on an expensive hotel and she started a period as soon as they arrived. It wasn't even due, she had nothing on her and it was one of those frightful clotty kinds of bleeds. She had to sit on the lavatory until Andrew managed to get some pads from the local supermarché. So that had been romantic.

'Who is Lance, anyway?' Maisie asks. She has a habit of making a question sound like an accusation, as if his very existence should be called into question.

'Lance is my . . .' and Bel pauses as she does every time she has

74

to explain. He is not her brother; they share not a shred of DNA. 'Lance is,' she starts again, 'Lance is my non-blood brother.' Maisie doesn't even blink, and Bel continues, 'I was adopted, but Lance wasn't, he was my parents' birth child.'

'I wouldn't mind adopting,' Maisie responds, turning the conversation immediately back to herself, as she so often does. 'You know, like one of them Chinese babies, cos they're so cute. Ah, a little chubby Chinese baby.'

Bel interrupts – she actually holds her hand up like a policeman – and says, 'I beg your pardon, Maisie, but I believe, for once, we were talking about me.'

There is a silence around the dinner table. She can feel her sons squirm. 'The fact is,' she continues.

'Oh, here we go,' interrupts Jamie and he mimes playing a tiny invisible violin against his plump shoulder.

Bel shoots him a withering look and takes up the thread of her story again. 'I was an abandoned baby,' she begins, pausing while Jamie proceeds to beat out the cliff-hanger sequence from the *EastEnders* theme tune.

12

The Housekeeper's Tale

Kittiwake House, Cornwall, 1963

She was wiping a damp cloth around a window frame on the land-ing when she first heard it. A cat, thought Bren, or maybe even the shriek of a mouse caught by a cat? No doubt she would stumble upon a bloodied little grey corpse soon enough – though headless mice didn't bother her, being a farmer's wife.

But then she heard it again and this time her breasts tightened, which was odd. Bren was in her fifties, it was over twenty years since she'd fed her babies, but the sound was undeniable: a baby, there was a newborn baby nearby. Bren's nipples tingled like a bloodhound's nose as she checked all the rooms along the first-floor corridor, the wail growing progressively louder with each step.

She found the baby in the mistress's old bedroom, wrapped in black velvet and tucked up in the bottom drawer of the wardrobe. It was a good job the tot was crying, otherwise Bren might have accidentally closed the drawer and left the infant to suffocate amongst the piles of rust-spotted sheets and ancient plaid blankets.

A girl (she had a quick peek to check) no more than a couple of weeks old, a tiny scrap of a thing. Not much to look at, as bald as a potato, spotty all over – milk rash, most likely. Sickly, too. Lucky to have survived, you might say.

It was the February of 1963 and the winter had been long and lethal, snowing even in Cornwall. No one had ever seen anything like it, the sea frozen into a block of ice like a science experiment.

Bren carried the baby back to the farmhouse, swaddled her in an old apple crate by the Aga, and watched as her little blue fingers turned pinker by the minute. It was as if the baby was defrosting.

Matthew went mad when he came in from the fields. 'This isn't some kind of dumping ground for waifs and strays,' he bellowed. 'It's not a depository for lost-and-found brats.'

But as Bren explained, the baby was Kittiwake lost property, and as such she was Bren's responsibility. 'There's such a thing as loyalty,' she told him. 'They trust me, I've been working up at that house for the past fifteen years, ever since the Carmichaels bought it from that actor chappy . . . '

'It's primarily a vacation home,' Peggy Carmichael had explained in her American accent, waving her bejewelled hand airily, prisms of light bouncing off her diamond-and-emerald rings. 'But when we do come down from London for holidays or the occasional weekend, I shall expect flowers in the drawing room, the fire laid and few simple provisions in the kitchen – milk, eggs, bacon, bread and so forth.'

As it transpired, the Carmichaels were accompanied by their own staff whenever they did visit. A cook, a butler and a 'mother's help' were all driven down a day or so before the family and, once they were all in situ, Bren was expected to find a girl from the village to come in and help her clean on a daily basis.

It wasn't a bad job as jobs go, better than gutting fish in the factory down the road, and it was interesting to see how the other half lived.

Peggy Carmichael had some rather outré ideas about décor and colour schemes. As for her clothes, they were ridiculously impractical for Cornwall. Heels and dimpled ostrich leather handbags on the beach, for heaven's sake, and a cartwheel-sized straw hat from Chanel that constantly blew off in the wind.

Mrs Carmichael hated the weather when it didn't match her expectations and she would stomp around in her ridiculous shoes, muttering, 'This godforsaken fucking country, it's the only goddamn place in the world where you need a sable in April.'

But it was nice to see the place being used again. And as soon as they all went back to London, Bren and her village girl got to clear out whatever was left in the big American fridge that stood like a giant stainless steel thumb in Kittiwake's otherwise traditional kitchen.

Duck pâté and whole sides of smoked salmon went into the rucksack she kept specifically for the purpose, along with half-drunk bottles of blood-red wine and fancily labelled Napoleon brandy. Once she purloined a few cigars from the silver box Teddy Carmichael kept in his study, but Matthew pronounced them filthy, threw them on the fire and went back to his tin of tobacco.

Then came that fateful Easter holiday when the boy died. Ivor, the eldest son and heir, the sweetest and politest of the three Carmichael children. She'd heard the bells of the ambulance that April morning and stood on the steps of the farmhouse watching the drama unfurl from a distance, had seen the butler carrying out the child's body. Peggy's screams had carried on the wind, eerily similar to the screeching of the birds that wheeled around the cliffs below the house. She could never hear them again without thinking of poor Peggy Carmichael.

The woman may have had an armload of Cartier bracelets and rubies the size of blood clots that clipped to her ears, but her boy was dead, her best boy.

Bren couldn't imagine how the woman felt. She had two

children of her own, strapping things around the same ages as the surviving Carmichael children, but twice the size of Natasha and Benedict.

Oh, those poor little mites. They had witnessed the accident, actually seen what happened with their own eyes.

The butler told her this when she ventured up the day after the family went back to London. It was the first time she had ever seen him unshaven, his eyes wild and his shirt collarless.

Blake had stayed behind to deal with the aftermath of the tragedy, and as soon as the police investigation was done he was to arrange the packing up of anything that been left in the house. He would need help – Madam's clothes, he despaired, her underwear, he didn't feel it would be right if he were to touch such items.

So while Blake took charge of Teddy's possessions, Bren and Abigail from the village packed up Peggy's and the children's clothes into various monogrammed leather suitcases. There was something macabre about picking up dead Ivor's belongings. What was one meant to do with his dirty pants and socks? Bren found herself weeping over his pyjamas. They were almost brand new and still smelt of boy.

She would have taken them for her lad Robert, but Robbie, despite being two years younger, was already a good deal bigger than Master Ivor had been.

As compensation, she took a few satin hair ribbons for her daughter Sally, who, at twelve, was just a few months older than little miss sour puss Natasha, and Abigail took an unopened Airfix kit for her nephew. No point Bren taking it; Robert was useless at that sort of thing. His hands were already too big and clumsy, he was destined to end up on the farm with his dad.

The packing operation took all day and once the car was fully loaded, the leftover trunks were taken up to the attics for safekeeping. When it was all done, Bren and Abigail sat in the kitchen with poor Blake, who was still the colour of a bleached dishcloth after his ordeal, and listened as he recalled bringing the dead child up from the bottom of the pool, the saturated weight of him, the horror of it.

While Blake wept, Abigail made a pile of ham and mustard sandwiches, which they washed down with a particularly good single malt. She was quite drunk by the time she got back to the farmhouse down the road.

Matthew was furious with her. 'State of you, woman!' he ranted, refusing to be placated by the mother-of-pearl cufflinks she had swiped from Teddy Carmichael's dressing room.

'When am I ever going to wear cufflinks?' he sneered. 'I'd only lose 'em up a cow's backside.' So she put them by for Robbie on the off-chance that he would turn into more of a gent than his dad, but even as she hid them in the airing cupboard, she knew it was a futile gesture.

It was in all the papers, the locals and the nationals. Bren and Abigail had ghoulishly pored over reports of the 'Tragic drowning of young Carmichael heir'.

'Ivor George Bartholomew Michael,' breathed Abigail. 'How come posh types need so many middle names?'

The results of the inquest were published a few weeks later. Ivor's death had been accidental – well, of course it had.

Bren wasn't expecting to hear anything more from the Carmichaels after that. She expected the place to be sold, preferably to someone who would still require her services, but several months after Ivor's death, she received a letter from Teddy Carmichael. The notepaper was headed with the eagle and wolf of his family crest, his handwriting a series of black ink loops.

A consignment of dustsheets was being sent to Kittiwake, he would like Bren to oversee the draping of the furniture and paintings.

The pool was to be professionally drained and Kittiwake was to be locked up for the foreseeable future. He would appreciate Bren accessing the premises on a weekly basis to air the place and check for any signs of physical deterioration, damp, dry rot, vermin and suchlike. Maybe her husband could accompany her?

Why? she pondered, does he think I'm scared of ghosts? Poor little Ivor, he wouldn't have said boo to a goose, not without saying 'Excuse me and I beg your pardon.' Not like the other lad, Benedict. That one was a bit of a monkey in Bren's opinion – still, rather a monkey than a misery guts. Obviously, Bren felt sorry for Natasha, what with having lost her brother like that, but she had never taken to the girl. She'd once taken Sally up to the house because Abigail had been poorly and young Sally was more than capable of running a Ewbank round and beating a hearth rug.

It was the first time Sally had met the Carmichael children. Ivor had shaken her hand and said what a pleasure it was, Benedict threw a ping-pong ball at her, which Sally threw right back, but Natasha had looked straight through her, as if the girl simply didn't exist.

So, for over ten years, while the house was uninhabited, Bren went up once a week, gave the place a good sniff, opened a few win- dows, checked the empty kitchen shelves for mouse droppings and the carpets for weevils. Sometimes Sally went with her and peeked under the dustsheets at Peggy's peculiar collection of modern art and begged Bren to open the door to the pool room – her mother had the key. 'Just this once,' Bren told her daughter. 'Then don't ever ask me again.'

It was dank in there, like a fish tank left to rot. The aquamarine ceramic tiles had begun to crack, but it was difficult to see the extent of the deterioration because the windows were too filthy to let in any daylight and all the electric bulbs had long since blown.

Sally clambered down the rusting iron steps and hopscotched across the bottom of the dried-out pool. 'Imagine, Mum, it isn't even very deep.'

Bren ordered her out. After all, she was hopping on little Ivor's

81

grave. 'Oh look,' crowed her daughter, reaching down. Sally stood back up and held out her hand, 'a golf ball.'

Bren received a cheque from Mr Carmichael every quarter. In the autumn of 1953 she wrote to him saying that she thought the roof needed repairing and asking whether she should have the garden seen to. Kittiwake was starting to resemble something out of a fairy tale. The ivy grew thick and beneath its branches windowpanes began to crack and the wooden shutters splintered and peeled.

But Bren didn't hear back from Teddy and eventually, after two of his cheques bounced, she received a letter from Mr Carmichael's solicitor saying the property was no longer any concern of Mr E. Carmichael's, and that all future correspondence concerning Monty's Cove should be directed to its legal owner, one Margaret Carmichael, currently residing in the United States of America.

The address of a legal firm in Florida was enclosed and it took a few minutes for Bren to realise that Margaret meant Peggy. From then on, the money for Kittiwake's basic upkeep came from its mistress.

Peggy's signature on the cheques was small and cramped, as if an ant had taken possession of an expensive bottle of purple ink. As the years rolled by, the money kept coming, but in the summer of 1956 Bren noticed that the signature on the cheque, still in that same tiny hand, had changed from Mrs M. Carmichael to Mrs M. Alessandro.

'Must have divorced poor old Teddy and got married again,' she told Matthew, who didn't take any notice. 'I said she must have divorced Teddy and got married again,' yelled Bren. Matthew was as deaf as a post these days and she wondered whether, given the chance, she'd divorce him and go and live somewhere else. But in reality she wouldn't know where to go. So she stayed, and every Tuesday around midday she walked up the track to Kittiwake and dusted away the cobwebs. As the years rolled by, her daughter Sally got married and moved out, but Robbie stayed at home helping his dad out on the farm and one day she pawned the cufflinks so they could buy a new tractor. She always felt bad about that, they weren't hers to pawn, she should have given them back to Mr Teddy, but he had died in tragic circumstances. Apparently a gun had gone off while he was cleaning it and blown away the top of his head. 'Accident, my foot,' spat Matthew gruffly. 'That man knew exactly what he was doing.'

It wasn't long after that that Master Benedict and his friends had started coming down to Kittiwake and . . .

Waaagh, waaagh, came the cry from the bundle by the Aga, and Bren hauled herself up to mix some formula. The infant was getting stronger and more demanding by the day.

Would the baby be any concern of Mrs Alessandro's, pondered Bren, expertly scooping up the squalling infant. Was it her duty to inform Peggy that she had a potential grandchild here at Monty's Cove?

Matthew told her not to interfere. He said that if Benedict or the mother didn't come and claim the child soon, they would have to hand her over to the authorities – he didn't want the little bastard cluttering up his kitchen.

'Poor mite,' cooed Bren, giving the baby a cuddle. What on earth was to become of her? Naughty, naughty Mr Benedict, this was all his doing.

Bren doubted Peggy knew about Benedict's jaunts down to the Cove. In fact she very much suspected that Mrs Alessandro or whatever she called herself was completely in the dark about the shenanigans that had been going on over the past couple of summers.

The whole thing had got out of hand for a while, girls running naked onto the moonlit sands, bonfires on the beach, screaming and silliness long into the night. Matthew used to go out with his shotgun and fire shots into the air, adding to the madness, warning Robbie, who was a grown man, to stay away. Not that he did. Bren knew he used to slope off there. Saw his shadow on the hill, heard the click of his bedroom door when he came in at all hours, marvelled at how he could get up at five to do the milking when he only got in at three, but she kept her trap shut, so as not to upset Matthew.

The place was a magnet for folks with nothing better to do than drink themselves silly and act the goat. Mostly they were posh types from London, their little sports cars getting stuck in in the muddy lane, shrill voices screaming with laughter and young Master Benedict in the middle of it all. What was he now, twenty-two?

Still a monkey, though. Burning furniture on the lawn at midnight, flames dancing high into the summer night sky, girls in ball gowns balancing along the perimeter of the walled garden. Anyone could have fallen, anything could have happened.

Bren had thought about writing to Mrs Alessandro on a number of occasions. Benedict might be an adult, but he was still her son, didn't his mother have a right to know what was going on? But she kept putting it off and eventually, when the weather cooled down in October, the flashy cars disappeared and Kittiwake fell back to sleep, her deserted rooms echoing in the silence, empty again.

Apart from the blonde.

Bren had nearly had a heart attack when she came across the girl one Tuesday morning in November, drifting around the place like a little pot-bellied ghost. She recognised her immediately – she was the one that didn't sound like all the others. This one sounded like a Cockney, all knocked-down beehive and slingbacks. Said her name was Serena and that she was waiting for Benedict to come back, said she wouldn't go until she saw him again, said she didn't care how long she had to wait, said she had something to tell him.

'And you must have been the something she had to tell him,' she cooed into the baby's tiny ear.

Bren felt a pang of guilt. She'd made it quite obvious to the girl before Christmas that she thought she was an interloper and that she should leave. The girl must have avoided her in the weeks leading up to her confinement, she must have hidden up in the attic in amongst the suitcases thick with dust. Had she given birth in the house all alone? Surely not, someone must have helped her . . . And then it struck her – Robbie. Her son had always been soft-hearted, he'd have come to the rescue. She'd wondered how he'd known exactly which baby formula to buy for the child once she'd taken up residence by the Aga, and the penny had finally dropped when she recalled the cardigan the child was wearing when she found her. No wonder it had seemed so familiar – she'd knitted it herself.

'Ask no questions,' she muttered to the baby, 'you'll be told no lies. And with any luck your daddy will come home soon, sweetheart.'

13

Benedict Returns to Meet the Baby

Kittiwake House, Cornwall, February 1963

'Oh, I don't think so, Bren. I mean, look at it – does it look like me? I don't think so.'

'She,' Bren told him. 'It's a she.'

Grudgingly she had to admit he was right: the baby didn't look anything like Benedict. There wasn't a single drop of Greek blood in her pallid little body. On the contrary – she was so pale there was a tinge of pale green about her, and what little hair she had was the colour of dirty straw.

It was almost March, the baby was approximately a month old and her presumed father had finally returned from the skiing trip he'd left London for the previous November.

Ridiculous, thought Bren, never mind three months, the longest she'd ever been away was for three days, and that was on her honeymoon. It was meant to be a week but they'd come home early because Matthew missed the cows.

As soon as she'd realised the master was back, Bren had walked up to Kittiwake with a basket over each arm. One contained a chicken-and-mushroom pie for Mr Benedict and a portion of his favourite bread-and-butter pudding, the other held the baby and a couple of bottles of formula.

He was delighted to see his supper, but confused by the baby.

'In a drawer? Serena's brat, you say? Well yes, she was a very rickety-rackety kind of girl, but leaving a baby in a drawer – well, that takes the biscuit, Bren.'

Bren lit him a fire in the drawing room and arranged his supper on a tray. The baby remained in her basket by the hearth while Benedict ate. Now and again he leant forward and pulled back the cover of her basket as if hoping she might have magically turned into cheese and biscuits.

Once his supper was finished, Benedict wiped around the rim of his pudding plate with his middle finger. He was a greedy man, thought Bren. Wine, women, pies – Benedict had what her husband called an appetite.

'I mean, don't get me wrong, I did sleep with the girl, but this baby?' He peered again into the basket. 'Are you quite sure it's even hers? Only, it doesn't look much like Serena either. Remember, she was the one with the golden hair.'

'That hair was dyed,' Bren reminded him. Men could be so stupid sometimes. 'She got it out of a peroxide bottle. Who knows what colour she was underneath all that bleach.'

'Yes ... but she was very pretty,' recalled Benedict, licking his lips like a wolf in a fairy tale, and Bren felt tempted to tell him how some women could create alchemy on their faces with a few cheap tricks and a steady hand with the eyeliner.

'Thing is,' he continued, 'I couldn't possibly look after it. I'm only here because I'm in hiding.' And for the next half-hour Benedict had explained to Bren in great detail how he was untangling himself from an unfortunate Alpine romance that had blossomed during some rather prolonged New Year celebrations.

An Austrian heiress, apparently. Much as he could have done

with the money, it wasn't worth the grief – the girl was insane, threatening to throw herself off a ski lift if he didn't propose, accusing him of stealing her virginity and 'besmirching her reputation'.

'Seriously,' Benedict sighed, 'it's 1963, I didn't think girls cared about having their reputations besmirched. I thought it was all the rage.'

He would sleep, as he always did, in his father's old dressing room – for a week or so until the Austrian affair blew over. 'I tell you, Bren, it's no longer a mystery how World War Two got started.' His plan was to return to London once the hoo-ha had died down.

As for the baby, he told the housekeeper not to worry. Serena would be back soon enough. 'Let's face it, Bren, mothers don't abandon their babies.'

But even as the words fell out of his mouth, a shadow of doubt crossed his face and they both knew that wasn't always true.

So Bren walked back down the track with both baskets, one containing the empty pie plate and pudding Pyrex and the other containing the baby, and when she got home Matthew yelled that if that brat woke him one more time in the night, he was going to put her in a sack and chuck her off the clifftop. But they both knew he didn't mean it, not really.

Every day for the next fortnight, while Mr Benedict lay low, Bren walked up to Kittiwake with a basket of dinner for the master. And every day she took the baby with her.

What else could she do? Matthew wasn't going to look after it, neither was her lad Robbie. As for Sally, she was a married woman now, expecting her own baby and furious that this little impostor should have landed first.

'I can't leave her on her own at the farmhouse,' she told Benedict. 'The cat could sit on her face, a lump of coal could jump out of the fire and set the place ablaze, and God knows she doesn't deserve that.'

It wasn't long before she noticed that when she was busy in the kitchen and the baby cried in the drawing room next door, by the time she went to pick her up, Benedict had got there before her. He lifted the baby up with one hand and walked around with her pressed against his chest, singing out-of-tune pop songs.

Bren didn't suppose he knew any nursery rhymes. Peggy Carmichael hadn't seemed the type to sing 'Incy Wincy Spider' with her children.

'She likes Anthony Newley,' he told her one afternoon, and she saw him plant a kiss on the baby's bald patch. 'My sister Natasha used to get dolls for birthdays and Christmases,' he told her. 'I always was a bit jealous,' and then his nose wrinkled in sudden disgust. 'But God, Brenda, something seems to have exploded in the pants area and I'm afraid that's not my domain.' He passed the child over as quickly as if she were a rugby ball, and as Bren busied herself in the kitchen with warm water and cotton wool, he leant against the doorframe and casually informed her that he was going back to London next week, now that 'the coast was finally clear'.

'The Austrians have retreated at last! But I tell you, Bren, this business with Baby Stinky Pants and the near-miss with Fräulein Whatserface have taught me a lesson. I shall be stocking up on the prophylactics in future. We don't want any more accidents.'

Bren drove a large pin into a clean towelling nappy and told him that as soon as he left she would take the baby to the police station.

He looked instantly uncomfortable. 'Seems a bit harsh. I mean, she hasn't done anything wrong, she seems quite happy where she is.'

That was when the penny dropped and Bren realised that he expected her to keep the child down on the farm. But how could she? The baby wasn't hers to keep. 'The situation can't continue,' she snapped. 'This baby needs a name and someone to love her.'

'Annabel,' said Benedict decisively. 'Her name is Annabel.' He had no idea where the name had come from, he'd never even slept with an Annabel; maybe that what one of the reasons why he chose it.

'Lots of people want to adopt babies,' Bren told him as she put the baby back in the basket alongside an empty savoury pie plate. 'If you don't want her, then someone else will.'

Benedict looked horrified. 'But what if Serena turns up?' he asked. 'I've put some feelers out in London, made some calls, but no one's seen her so far. Mind you, not knowing her surname doesn't help. As far as I was concerned, she was Sexy Serena from Southend. Can't you hang on to Annabel for a bit longer, give me a couple of months to see if I can find her? I can pay you – bed, board and nappies.' And he peeled a wad of notes from a silver money clip in his back pocket.

Bren agreed to six weeks at twenty pounds a week. Sally's baby was due soon after that, and the extra money would buy her new grandchild everything he or she needed. After the deal was struck, she quickly made Benedict some custard to go with his apple crumble and walked Baby Annabel back to the farmhouse.

'But, Mum,' moaned Sally, who had dropped by to complain about the state of her ankles. 'What if I wanted to call my baby Annabel? Only now I can't, because that baby got it first.' And then she burst into noisy tears and only calmed down when Bren told her about the money. 'My baby will have the best of everything,' Sally crowed.

Meanwhile, back at Kittiwake, Benedict fretted about what he was going to do with the baby – not that she was his responsibility. Anyone could see the creature looked nothing like him, and as for the mother . . . Suddenly Benedict wasn't so sure he wanted Serena to have the child back, not when she clearly didn't want it. What if she dropped it or trod on it? It would be like handing a car over to a drunk driver. The woman simply wasn't responsible enough.

For a moment he stopped and thought about his own mother,

Peggy, whom he hadn't seen since she ran away to America and whom he had come to regard as emotionally deep-frozen. It was as if, the moment Ivor died, her heart had instantly iced over.

Although he supposed he loved her, as he got older Benedict liked her less and less. And as he contemplated the Serena situation he realised that here was further proof not all mothers were worthy of their children.

And then it struck him – how deeply unfair it was that Serena had given birth to a baby she didn't want, when his poor old sister Natasha, who desperately wanted a baby, kept losing them.

What was the word? A miscarriage. It was that all right: a miscarriage of justice. Serena didn't deserve the baby, but Natasha did and it was as simple as that.

Benedict went upstairs and started packing. He would talk to Natasha's husband Hugo. If he played his cards right, there might be a way of wriggling out of what may or may not be his responsibility, without losing sight of the baby completely. Keep it in the family and all that.

Benedict began whistling tunelessly. The first thing he was going to do when he got back to London was visit Peter Jones. Annabel needed a pram, one of those modern ones with a box thing you could detach from the wheels and put in the back of the car – a carry cot, that was the article. She couldn't be carried around in a wicker shopping basket for much longer. Oh, and a teddy, all babies needed a teddy.

Third Time Unlucky

Barnes, London, January 1963

Natasha sat down on the sofa, reached for a magazine and put her feet up on the Moroccan leather pouffe that Hugo hated so much.

She had been instructed to rest in the afternoons, which seemed ridiculous considering she was only twenty-five. Sitting with her feet up reading *Good Housekeeping* bought for her on subscription by Hugo's mother made her feel like a fifty-something matron. Like Hugo's mother, in fact.

But she was expecting again, and woe betide her if anything went wrong this time. 'Third time lucky,' she muttered under her breath.

Her husband adored her when she was pregnant, and it wasn't as if getting pregnant was remotely difficult – it was staying pregnant that was the problem.

'Some women experience what we call spotting,' the doctor said when it first happened, 'but quite often it goes away on its own accord.'

Only it didn't. The bleeding didn't stop, it got worse, and no one could explain why. She spent a night in hospital having what they called a D and C, although no one told her what that actually meant.

'Sometimes it's hereditary,' her GP explained when she went back for a check-up some weeks later. But that didn't make sense, her mother had three children in quick succession and no doubt could have had more if she hadn't chosen to sleep apart from her husband.

Hugo took her to see a man in Harley Street for a second opinion. 'Sometimes there's something wrong with the baby,' Mr Jeffries the specialist informed them.

'Then it's a jolly good job you lost it,' Hugo announced. 'We don't want any little retards in the nursery, darling. Mother Nature knows best.'

'And sometimes it's down to bad luck,' Jeffries had shrugged sympathetically three months later when it happened for a second time, and then he'd checked his watch, stood up and shaken Hugo's hand. 'I'm so sorry old chap.'

There was a photograph of Mr Jeffries on his desk with his wife and three sons. Natasha had to fight the temptation to pick it up and throw it at the wall.

Later that night, after a silent supper, a whisky-fuelled Hugo reached into his side of the wardrobe and took out a bamboo stick; some sort of African fly whisk, she remembered thinking, before he raised it above his head and ... Even though it hurt, the beating felt like a relief. This was her punishment, she had deserved it and now it was over.

In the morning when Hugo apologised and went to work, she pressed the little grey bruises and the ache of them was somehow comforting. 'It's your fault, you silly bitch. It must be,' she told herself in the mirror before carefully choosing something with long sleeves from her wardrobe.

He had slapped her once or twice since, but not with the stick, merely with his open hand, for doing silly things: speaking out of turn, contradicting him, giving him horrible liver for his tea.

But it'd been ages since anything like that had happened. Ever since Mr Jeffries confirmed this pregnancy, Hugo had treated her like a Christmas bauble, a shiny precious thing that must be treated with utter gentleness. He made sure her baths weren't too hot and that she ate plenty of protein. 'Chicken, fish, eggs,' he intoned as he undid her nightdress and cupped her swelling breasts. 'Good girl,' he muttered, as he thumbed her nipples and kissed her on the lips.

He wouldn't make love to her. They had been advised not to, to be on the safe side, but because a man had needs, he liked her to take him in her mouth. As his wife, it was the least she could do for him. So he made her do it on the kitchen floor, after breakfast and before she did the dishes.

'Come on, darling,' he coaxed, pushing her down by her shoulders. The lino was hard under her knees, ideally she would have liked some sort of padded mat. Afterwards, while Hugo went whistling off to the office, Natasha had to make a dash for the bathroom. Fellating one's husband certainly didn't help with the morning sickness.

Even with her feet up, Natasha felt hot and uncomfortable. Her stomach tightened and she regretted finishing off some leftover mackerel pâté at lunchtime. Why had she done that? It had smelt like cat food, had it gone off? Natasha stroked her belly as if to soothe it.

Soon she wouldn't be able to do the buttons up on her skirt. There was a guide to pregnancy fashion in *Good Housekeeping*; it advised that large Peter Pan collars distracted from an ungainly bump and the most important thing was to keep one's wardrobe simple and fresh.

The tummy ache was getting worse, but as long as she took it easy she'd be fine. Mrs Phelan would be here at three to run the Hoover round the house, and in the meantime she could get up and change the water in the vase of hot-house chrysanthemums Hugo brought home the other day; if she added a spoonful of sugar they might last another couple of days.

Natasha loved fresh flowers. In summer, the garden in Claverley Avenue was bursting with roses. Her mother loved fresh flowers too. Maybe it was time she wrote to Peggy again?

It was Hugo who had originally suggested she write to her mother. When they first got engaged she told him all about her parents' divorce and her mother's second marriage to the Alessandro fellow. He said that 'it was good to keep some line of communication going' and even if her mother hadn't made it to the wedding, there was no reason why she should be permanently excluded from their lives.

'He's a crafty fox, is your old man,' Benedict had snorted. 'He only wants you to keep in touch because he thinks this new husband of hers is loaded. Doesn't miss a trick, old Hugo. Send the evil witch my love,' he winked.

She was beginning to feel positively awful, but rather than think about it, she sat at Hugo's writing desk in the dining room, filled a fountain pen with ink and wrote a letter to her mother.

> Hello mother, Happy 1963, Natasha here and guess what?
> I have splendid news, Hugo and I are expecting a baby.

She hadn't told her mother about any of her previous pregnancies, but she felt more confident about this one, and the act of writing down the words made her feel better. The tummy ache earlier must have been a touch of indigestion.

> Obviously it's very early days, about three months and
> I'm not showing yet, but I thought you would like to know,
> he or she will be your first grandchild.
> The weather here has been pretty dreadful, the papers

95

say its been the coldest winter on record and I'm praying that spring will come soon and I will see my first crocus. I wonder what sort of flowers you have in your garden? For some reason, I imagine cactuses like in a film.

Hugo is well and very busy and Benedict is back in the country after his skiing trip . . .

She kept the details deliberately vague. She didn't want to admit that Benedict was up to his usual tricks and had been spending time at Monty's Cove. Natasha paused for a second, her fingers curled tightly around the pen. How her brother could bear to open the place up again, she couldn't imagine. To her, Kittiwake would forever echo to the sound of her mother screaming, the panicked shouts and running footsteps of the butler, the hushed murmurs of the undertaker's men as they carried the small body out in a bag.

She had not returned in thirteen years and she couldn't for the life of her think how Benedict could bear to sleep there.

There was a throb low in her gut now, reminding her of being thirteen and starting her periods while she was away at boarding school. She hadn't known what it was: her mother had left without explaining anything – Natasha had been so frightened and ashamed of the bloodstained sheets and soiled underpants.

Over a decade later Natasha admits that it could have been worse; had it happened at home she'd have died of embarrassment. At least at school Matron came to the rescue with a brown-paper parcel. Inside the package was a cardboard box containing all the paraphernalia of womanhood: the thick towels with loops at either end, the elastic belt and fiddly safety pins. A packet of Anadin lay beside the parcel. Maybe that's what she could do with now – a couple of Anadin and a nap on the bed? She could finish the letter later. Natasha put the pen down and stood up.

*

96

Mrs Phelan called Hugo at work. She'd found Mrs Berrington when she took the Hoover upstairs. She was in the bathroom and there was a lot of blood. 'I phoned an ambulance first, Mr Berrington, and once I knew she was in safe hands I phoned you. They've taken her to Hammersmith Hospital.'

Natasha spent three nights in hospital before Hugo brought her home. For a week he couldn't have been kinder, insisting she stay in bed and paying Mrs Phelan extra to come in every day and keep an eye on her while he went to the office.

However, precisely seven days after she lost the third baby, he marched her down to the dining room where the half-written letter to her mother still lay on his desk, with the lid of the fountain pen she'd been using abandoned beside the letter, but the pen itself had fallen onto the carpet and leaked a pool of navy ink into the pale gold wool.

He held her by her hair and called her a careless bitch and then took her back upstairs to teach her a lesson. Afterwards he made her write out 'I shall never be so selfish and stupid again' a hundred times on the same Basildon Bond paper she'd been using to write to her mother. When she'd finished, he went out and didn't come home till three o'clock the next morning, sliding into bed next to her stinking of gin and something else, something sour, and then he'd wept into her hair. They were both sorry and surely that was enough.

An appointment was made to revisit the specialist, who examined Natasha intimately and once again pronounced her physically capable of carrying a child.

While she was busy putting her clothes back on behind the screen, the specialist muttered something to Hugo about her fragile mental state, her thinness and the fact that maybe she didn't want a child. He suggested that Natasha was somehow inducing her own terminations in a subconscious rejection of motherhood. Then he prescribed some antidepressants, instructed Hugo to administer them to his wife, and advised them to be patient – after all, there had been all that business with her brother. Childhood trauma could have quite an impact in adult life, he divulged. Time, patience and a few of those little white pills should make all the difference, he promised.

It was several weeks before Natasha sat down to write another letter to her mother.

> *Dear Peggy, I think I'm old enough to call you Peggy now? Mother sounds rather formal and I was never comfortable with Mom, perhaps if we'd been born and raised in America it would have sounded less peculiar? Who knows, perhaps you'd prefer Margaret? Anyway, I thought I'd keep you up to date with our news.*
>
> *I miscarried your grandchild-to-be, he or she disappeared down the lavatory like half a tin of red paint. Sorry about that, it was my unsuccessful third attempt at motherhood and I think for the time being I shall give it a rest. Hugo was terribly disappointed and terribly cross, so much so he gave me quite a beating, it's something he likes to do. Some men like playing golf, Hugo likes hitting me, but not on my face, you'll be pleased to hear. If he hit me on the face, I'd look like one of those poor women you see going into pubs with two black eyes, common types married to chaps who 'give 'er indoors what for'. Hugo isn't like that, he's not a brute, he's a gentleman who feels I need to be punished if I've done something foolish or careless, like lose a baby.*
>
> *Because that's how it feels when you lose a child, like you did something silly and it could have been avoided, if only you'd taken more care, if only, if only, if only.*
>
> *In other news, there are snowdrops in the garden.*

Natasha put the lid back carefully on the ink pen – she had learnt that lesson – and then she ripped the letter up into tiny pieces, before panicking. What on earth was she going to do now? She gathered up the fragments into her left hand like a fistful of confetti. She couldn't put them in the wastepaper basket, a crimson-fringed velvet monstrosity of a wedding gift from one of the Norfolk cousins, and she couldn't eat them. For a moment she wobbled on the brink of tears, but fortunately the pills that Hugo watched her take every morning, normally with a nice boiled egg, were a marvellous antidote to weepiness. Instead she walked to the kitchen, where she rooted in the bin under the sink for the empty tin of tomato soup that she'd had for her lunch. Natasha had a different tin of soup every day, Mrs Phelan made sure of it, they were all stacked up in her cupboard: tomato, mushroom, chicken and cream of celery, delicious with a splash of Lea and Perrins.

Humming gently to herself, she carefully deposited all the pieces of paper into the tin, hid it inside a grocery bag and then, without changing out of her house slippers, she ran to the corner of the road and disposed of the bag in a neighbour's bin.

When she got back indoors she sat on the hall carpet and couldn't stop laughing. She laughed and laughed until nothing was funny any more, and then she hauled herself upstairs and lay quite still under the bedcovers, almost as if she were dead.

15

Back at the Mews House

London, March 1963

Benedict was finally back in London. It always shocked him on returning to Belgravia that he no longer lived in a five-storey white stuccoed Georgian townhouse in Chester Square. How had he ended up living down a back street?

'A mews house,' the estate agent had insisted. 'Trust me, they'll be all the rage. Bijou living is where it's at, Benedict.' Benedict had gone to school with Clive Latham and had been happy to accept a lift in Clive's brand-new Bristol to an address in Cadogan Mews.

'Nice wheels,' Benedict had muttered enviously, sinking back into the luxurious cream leather upholstery.

'A happy twenty-first from the old man,' Clive had told Benedict, narrowly running a red light. 'It was a surprise. For a horrible moment, I thought it was going to be cufflinks, but when I opened the box, I found the car keys. Big relief.'

'Oh,' replied Benedict. 'My father shot himself through the head the night before my twenty-first. The things some dads will do to get out of buying their only surviving son a gift, eh?'

Poor Clive had looked mortified and his face went scarlet as they pulled into a small dead-end street.

Benedict had always used jokes to deflect from the reality of unpleasant situations. It wasn't that he wanted people to laugh when he told them about Teddy, it was more that he couldn't bear the feeling that he was meant to be ashamed, that there should be this code of secrecy. It reminded him of when Ivor died and no one would let him talk about it. The frustration of not being able to share his feelings had made him light matches under the bedclothes and burn small holes in the sheets, had made him want to break things.

Both deaths had been hugely shocking; his brother's because it should never have happened and his father's because not only was the man dead, but he had taken everything with him, leaving Natasha and Benedict with precisely nothing.

Cudlip and Bird, the family solicitors, spelt it out for them in black and white, or rather red and white, at an emergency meeting in the firm's offices. Copies of Teddy's overdrawn bank statements were spread out on the desk in front of them and papers showing investments gone wrong and shares sold cheap were waved under their noses.

All Teddy had left them was a mountain of debt. There were hundreds of IOUs stuffed into teapots and vases back at Chester Square, and it was only thanks to an unexpected intervention from their mother that Benedict now had somewhere to live.

'Home sweet home,' Benedict muttered as he opened his front door and glanced around the miniature house before walking the entire ten feet from the sitting-room-cum-diner into the kitchen and reaching for a bottle of cold Sancerre from the fridge.

At least he'd managed to lick the place into some kind of shape since he first moved in. Benedict had a brief flashback of sitting on the floor of his empty new home less than two years ago and staring in dismay at the only item left behind by the previous owners: a large rubber plant in an ornate wicker stand.

His own possessions at the time amounted to a record player, a tennis racket, a trunk of unironed clothes and, of course, The Farm.

Benedict looked at his windowsill – it was still there. People always laughed at it, they couldn't understand why a grown-up man-about-town had a children's toy displayed so prominently in his sitting room for everyone to see.

It was old man Cudlip's fault. He'd let slip that the Chester Square sale of goods was to be held in the house itself. 'The most sensible solution, save carting everything out. Sell everything in situ, as it were,' the solicitor had mumbled.

After that, it was only a question of finding out when the sale was to take place and, knowing there were only a handful of likely candidates, Benedict had simply phoned around a few auction houses until it turned out that the job had fallen to one of the less established names.

This information added salt to Benedict's wound. A bankruptcy sale would have been easier to swallow had it been someone from Christie's bringing down the gavel on his lost inheritance.

Nonetheless, he'd gone. Arriving early in a black raincoat and fedora pulled low, he felt like a child dressed up as a spy. Silly to have to resort to a disguise to enter one's own home.

What shocked him was that everything was ticketed; the entire contents of the whole house were up for sale. He picked up a cat-alogue and reeled as he realised that every bone china plate he'd ever eaten off, every ivory-handled knife and fork, every tablecloth and napkin was itemised.

His eyes swam as he took a seat at the back of the drawing room and watched a short fat man in a greasy waistcoat cajole strangers into buying his family history, the Victorian cast-iron beds that he and his brother and sister had slept in, his father's walnut shaving stand . . .

Oddly, it wasn't the larger, more expensive items that caused the lump in his throat, it was the smaller personal things – a set of golf clubs bought for his mother and used once. She'd hated the game, but he remembered his parents coming home and laughing about it, his mother threatening to take Teddy's head off with the five iron if he ever suggested they played again. He must have been very young, maybe five or six. It hadn't all been awful, they'd loved each other once upon a time. In between the arguments there had been periods of calm when they all had fun together, the five of them; there had been card games in the drawing room and games of hide and seek when even his father would join in. He had found him once behind a pair of curtains, trying to kiss his mother.

Taking a break from the stuffy clamour of the drawing room, Benedict had stepped out into the hallway and found himself pausing outside his father's study. He checked the handle: it was locked. No matter. Crossing the marble floor, Benedict opened the belly of the grandfather clock and, taking care not to interrupt the swing of the pendulum, reached for the duplicate key his father kept on a secret hook inside.

To his surprise, behind the spare study key hung another set of keys, unfamiliar and rusty, attached to a luggage label on which his father had written 'Kittiwake'.

The sight of Teddy's handwriting had made Benedict's heart twist and instinctively he lifted both sets of keys. The grandfather clock was lot number 364. The unfairness of it kindled a spark of indignation in Benedict. Whoever bought the clock wasn't getting access to Kittiwake as well – that still belonged to his mother. Hurriedly he pocketed the Kittiwake keys then re-crossed the hall, unlocked his father's study and slipped inside.

In hindsight, he wished he hadn't gone in. Whoever had cleaned up his father's mess had done the job hastily. Emptied of its furniture, the place had an air of desolation about it and Benedict wished he could have seen his father alive one last time, shared a drink, maybe even choked down a cigar with him, hugged each other and said goodbye. Surely his father could have given him something before he went, something that was for him alone. Even his battered old hip flask would have been better than nothing.

The room stank of Jeyes Fluid and the bottle-green painted ana-glypta wallpaper was in the process of being stripped. The dark gold velvet curtains, which had hung from a heavy fringed pelmet for as long as he could remember, had been removed. Without them, the room was lighter, light enough for Benedict to notice what looked like a series of rust spots on the dado rail behind where his father's desk should have been. For some reason he found himself licking his finger and rubbing at one of these rust spots. Blood, of course; his father's blood. He had put his finger in his mouth, wondering for a split second if believing in God would help, and then he locked the study up, hung the key back on its secret hook and returned to the auction.

He still has no idea why he put in a bid for it. It was the silliest thing. Perhaps it was the taste of his dead father still fresh in his mouth and that sudden fury at the waste of it all, but he had found himself raising his hand and bidding for something no one else wanted. It was such an absurd item, such an inconsequential thing, but in the heartbeat of the moment, the thought of anyone else having it incensed him.

A small titter and a scattering of applause met his successful bid. 'To the man in the hat at the back, one toy farm, beasts included.'

The paint had worn thin on some of the animals. Ivor had liked the horses best, Natasha's favourites were the chickens. As for Benedict, wandering over to the windowsill, his hand closed proprietorially around a fat pink metal pig. 'Hello, Georgie Porgie,' he muttered, surprised to find that tears were rolling out of his eyes.

Benedict wiped his face with his sleeve. He needed to concentrate, he couldn't wallow in the past when he needed to sort out

104

the future. What the hell was he going to do with Baby Annabel? If Bren took her to the police she would disappear into some orphanage and he might never see her again. And the fact was, the child could be his. She could be as entitled to these metal animals as he was.

So far, the trail for Serena had reached a dead end. There had been sightings all over the country – Suki Cunningham was sure she'd seen her at Adam Fairfax's wedding in Wiltshire, Billy Southern swore blind he'd seen her getting out of a cab in Edinburgh, while Evie Pinner was convinced she was working as a clippie on the number 9 bus. But there was nothing concrete, no trail he could follow. The girl obviously didn't want to be found. Anyway, for all Serena knew, her child had suffocated to death in the drawer of an old wardrobe. She didn't deserve her.

Natasha, on the other hand … Benedict knew that Hugo was worried about her, the doctor had given her some pills. She'd been having some odd moods, crying on the floor of the empty nursery, refusing to get out of bed and generally being 'out of sorts'. Too much time on her hands, Hugo imparted. She needed something to occupy her. Well, Benedict had the very thing.

Natasha could look after the baby. Annabel couldn't stay in the farmhouse with Bren for much longer. Benedict didn't know when babies started talking, but if she was his child, he didn't want her yattering on in that dreadful Cornish accent. Much better that the girl should live in Barnes. Not that Benedict was a fan of Barnes, it was a bit suburban for his tastes, but at least Claverley Avenue was a five-minute walk from the river and it had a garden. However the real clincher was that Natasha was quite possibly the girl's aunt.

Benedict was convinced it would be better for the child to be cared for by a blood relative. As for Natasha – surely taking in Annabel would be the next best thing to having a baby of her own?

By the time Benedict had finished the nice cold bottle of Sancerre and made himself some cheese on crackers, he was convinced that not only was the child his, but that Natasha and Hugo adopting her was a stroke of genius.

'One day,' he slurred slightly, running his finger over the farm on the windowsill, 'when she's older, she will come to Uncle Benedict's house and play with the animals.'

16

Natasha Gets Her Baby

London, May 1963

Natasha sat in the yellow nursery at Claverley Avenue and stared at the baby lying comatose behind the bars of her cot, a disgusting small green bubble of snot pulsing from her left nostril.

Baby Annabel? Natasha wasn't sure that she even liked the name. It hadn't been on the list of possibilities she'd chosen when she'd been expecting her own child, but then Sarah or Rupert, Victor or Juliette, Nathan or Louisa had all slipped away and at least this one was too big to fall down a plughole.

It had taken a couple of months to get the paperwork done, but considering no one else wanted her and the birth mother still hadn't been found, no one saw any reason to stall the proceedings. And now she was here, in this sunny nursery with its frieze of ducks endlessly chasing each other around the walls. Her daughter, wasn't this what she wanted? Natasha surveyed the room, surprised to see how much space a small baby could dominate. Annabel had only been in residence for a matter of weeks and already there was a changing table complete with a nappy bucket reeking of ammonia tucked underneath it, a chest of drawers filled with socks, vests, baby-gros and tiny little matinee jackets courtesy of Hugo's sister and mother.

There were muslin cloths and tubes of nappy rash cream and talcum powder and a dish to keep the nappy pins in, and then there were the nappies, the endless pile of terry towelling cloths, that had to be folded and fastened just so, around the tiny stranger's body.

Natasha liked it best when the baby was fed and dressed and she could take her out for a walk. She found it easier to feel like a proper mother when she had her hands firmly wrapped around a cream plastic pram handle and the wheels were making that confident spanking noise along the pavement. She also liked it when other mothers, women she had never met in her life, nodded and smiled as if to say, Oh you too, how lovely, welcome to the club. She was relieved that they couldn't tell she was faking it and they didn't smell the impostor in their midst.

As for the neighbours, if anyone thought it strange that Natasha Berrington should be pushing a huge 'newborn' baby around when only last month she'd been wearing figure-hugging slacks with not a trace of a bump on her, no one mentioned it.

It was 1963 and middle-class women didn't discuss childbirth publicly, it was a private thing and no one would have dreamt of peering into the Silver Cross Balmoral pram and asking Natasha, 'How many stitches and are you breastfeeding?'

Those who were more intimately acquainted with Natasha and Hugo knew the child was adopted. Some were even aware of Benedict's involvement, and none of them were remotely surprised – Benedict was such a naughty boy. There was however some speculation about who the mother could be, with rumours ranging from minor royalty to Kathy Kirby.

The baby herself was blissfully ignorant of all this gossip. And if she was surprised to find herself in this sweet-smelling buttercup-coloured place rather than the farmhouse kitchen with its smoke-stained distempered walls and the smell of damp collie sleeping next to her by the fire, she didn't show it. She slept, she fed, she puked and soiled her nappy.

Natasha occasionally found her slightly repellent. Sometimes she couldn't believe how much mess one small person could make. She thanked her lucky stars every day for Mrs Phelan the home help, who could remove a disgusting towelling cloth without gagging at the contents.

As far as Natasha could glean from 'other mothers', the nappy business was cope-able with because 'it's natural when it's one's own child doing it'. This, Natasha suspected, was the root of the problem. Annabel wasn't her own child. She was very fond of her, she was quite sure of that, she particularly adored her when she wore a certain pink bonnet with a frill around the edge, but for much of the time Natasha viewed her adopted daughter as if she were an animal escaped from the zoo, a small unpredictable hairless monkey that needed constant cleaning and changing.

Hugo, on the other hand, had taken to fatherhood quite easily. He even carried a picture of Annabel around in his wallet and didn't mind pushing the pram around the Serpentine on a Sunday afternoon.

But he refused to be inconvenienced by her. If she was whiny and tiresome, he told Natasha to remove her from the room and place her in her cot where she could cry all she liked.

'I'd better go to her, Hugo.'

'No, Natasha.'

'I think I should.'

'I said no. Babies have to know who's boss.'

And then Hugo turned the volume up on the record player, or the radio, or the television, and after two martinis, Natasha found it quite easy to forget there was such a thing as a baby in the house.

It was important to remember that she was as much a wife as a mother. And as a wife she had duties to perform. Hugo had needs too and it was her duty to keep him happy. Because if Hugo wasn't happy, he could be mean. Once, when she had left their bed to attend to the child in the middle of the night and fallen asleep in the armchair next to the cot, he poured tea from the pot over her hand while she was eating breakfast the next morning. Luckily it wasn't scalding hot, but it was a warning, and she had learnt her lesson.

The doorbell rang and Natasha staggered to her feet, hoping that the baby wouldn't wake up. It was Mrs Phelan's day off and she was on her own with the creature until Hugo came home and gave her the confidence to ignore her.

'No child ever died of crying, Natasha,' he would say. 'It's good for her lungs. But Lord knows it's boring, so shut the door and come and sit down.'

Benedict was on the doorstep. He visited quite regularly, at least once a week, and never arrived empty-handed. Thanks to her uncle, Annabel had built up quite a menagerie of soft toys in the nursery, but today's gift was a wind-up musical mobile to hang above her cot.

'I did ask the girl if they sold one that played songs from the hit parade instead of all that soppy nursery rhyme stuff, but apparently this is what they like.' And he demonstrated, by taking the mobile out of its box. As he wound it up, Natasha wondered how many times she would be able to hear 'The Teddy Bears' Picnic' before she went mad.

Benedict left the mobile on the floor and made himself comfortable on the Berringtons' new Heal's sofa. 'Nice,' he whistled appreciatively, patting the sage green bouclé wool.

'I'm not allowed to sit on it with the baby,' she laughed.

She was pleased to see him. He was wearing some new, rather fashionable Chelsea boots and a narrow pair of black-and-white checked trousers. Benedict could wear what he liked, he hadn't got a proper job like Hugo, who left the house looking weirdly like

110

his father. Her brother worked part-time for an antique dealer in Fulham, where he was employed to ingratiate his way into elderly people's houses and persuade them to part with valuable antique furniture for mere shillings. Benedict was good at his job; he'd been brought up sitting on Regency sofas under gleaming chandeliers, so it came naturally to spend his afternoons sipping Lapsang Souchong with little old ladies who once upon a time had known his grandparents and who dabbed their eyes when they mentioned his father. ('Such a good-looking man, such a tragic waste. And your mother was the American woman.' At this point they would invariably sniff, as if to say, Well, what could you expect?)

Benedict insisted on getting the baby up. He hadn't come all that way to miss out on seeing his special girl. And as she watched Annabel docile and gurgling on Benedict's knee, Natasha felt again the pang of wanting to love her more than she did.

Not that the baby showed any signs of neglect. She was a sturdy thing with stocky thighs and bracelets of fat around each wrist and she beamed with pleasure as Benedict bounced her up and down.

'Have you told Peggy?' Natasha asked.

'No,' her brother replied. 'I don't think it's anything to do with her.'

'Annabel's her granddaughter, sort of . . .'

'What do you mean "sort of"?'

'Well, you're not entirely sure, are you – you know, if . . . ?' Natasha found herself colouring, the conversation was getting too personal for comfort.

Benedict shrugged. 'It doesn't matter. Hugo is her father now and you're her mother and you're all going to live happily ever after.'

Natasha felt a twinge of discomfort.

'Only I'm not. I'm not her real mother. And I was thinking, Benedict, that I'd like to know more about her, about Annabel's real mother, because at the moment, she's a bit of a blank and I find myself imagining all sorts of things.'

Benedict refused to meet her eye and instead he talked directly to Annabel. 'Silly old Mummy. Yes, she's a daft old sausage.' Annabel chuckled and then he said, 'You've never met her. She isn't . . . maybe what you might expect? To be honest, I never knew much about her myself – ships in the night and all that. You know what it was like at Kittiwake last year, I went a bit crackers. All I can tell you is that she came from Southend. She had one of those accents, sounded like something off a market stall.'

At that moment Annabel started to cry and there was something piercing and shrill about the wail that to Natasha's ears sounded a teeny bit common. Christ, for a moment the baby sounded like a mini-fishwife.

'Anyway, the one thing I do know is that her name is Serena,' Benedict concluded.

17

Stagnating

Serena watched the clock on the far wall. Surely there was something wrong with it? She stifled a yawn and patted the back of her brand-new beehive; her hair had the texture of Shredded Wheat, peroxided and backcombed, sprayed and pinned into an immovable yellow edifice. This 'do ain't going nowhere, thought Serena. Just like me.

Another yawn threatened to crack her jaw and she wondered if she should pretend to be on her monthly and spend a few minutes in the ladies' toilets, smoking and checking out her stars in this week's *Rave* magazine.

Aged eighteen and far better looking, in her own opinion, than average, life seemed to have stalled for Serena. She should be a model or a film star or something, instead she was wearing a nylon overall and serving tinned goods and sliced bread to bad-tempered housewives in Southend's premier (and only) supermarket, Keddies.

At first it had been exciting – the pink nylon overall, complete

113

with her very own name badge ('Miss S. Tipping') gave her a sense of pride, made her feel like a grown-up, and they let you wear make-up, so obviously it was loads better than school. On the downside, operating a till was murder on your nails, so it was a good job her mum had a mate who was a part-time Avon lady and generous with her samples.

When she had first arrived on the shop floor, the till had been a novelty, sitting there like a great mechanical beast. It felt like learning to drive a car or operating a machine at the fun fair, all push-down buttons and funny noises. She still liked the way the cash drawer sprang open on command, but after that it got difficult. The machine could add up, but it didn't subtract the right amount of change she needed for her customers – she had to do that in her head. Serena often felt faint with the panic of it, blank with confusion while middle-aged women in headscarves with mouths like furious trout tutted and counted back the incorrect number of pennies she'd given them and demanded to see the manager. 'She tried to diddle me, Mr Salmon.'

Mr Salmon was a sweaty man in his fifties with a damp handshake and a bloatery whiff about him. He made Serena feel a bit sick when he took her elbow and guided her into his office for a chat.

'It's the numbers,' she admitted. 'I've never been good at sums.'

'Hmm,' responded Mr Salmon, 'let's see about that.' And he'd begun firing times tables at her. Serena felt as if she was back in Miss Beechcroft's yellow class in primary and for a moment she thought she might wet her nylons.

'I suggest you practise at home, Miss Tipping,' he sighed when she came a cropper on six times three for the fourth time. 'Maybe your father could help you out. We don't want to have to demote you to shelf-stacking, do we now?'

She could have told him, 'I haven't got a dad, I've never had a dad, I live at home with my mum and Nanna Tipping and there's not a bloke between us, three women pinching each other's hair-brushes and rattling the bathroom door in the morning, "Get out, it's my turn, you've been in there for ever."'

But she didn't. Instead she thanked Mr Salmon, who for some reason insisted on leaning against the doorframe as she left the office, and as she squeezed past him, her breasts brushed against his tie, almost dislodging it from its silver tie pin. Instantly she felt a wave of heat rising from his suit and wondered if she'd done it on purpose. 'I'll try,' she breathed into his pockmarked face, and walked away with an exaggerated sway of her hips. Behind her she heard the door to Mr Salmon's office close and the lock turn. A few seconds later, had she put a glass up against that door, she might have heard some peculiar whimpering noises.

Serena may not have been a virgin, but she still hadn't a clue how relationships worked. It seemed to run in the family. Nanna Tipping's husband, Grandfather Tommy, had been shot for desertion in the First World War. ('Bloody coward,' sneered Nanna Tipping. 'He'd run away from his own shadow that one – lily-livered all the way through, too wet to change a washer on a tap. Fine way to leave a wife and child.') Serena had once found a photograph of Tommy Tipping in her mother's underwear drawer. 'My Dad!' Ida had written on the back.

Her grandfather's face was washed out and sepia-tinted, a blond man with a woman's mouth. There was something about him that reminded Serena of some of the boys that hung around the pier, all winkle-pickers and hungry eyes. 'Nancy boys' as her grandmother called them. Well, she should know, she was obviously married to one. Serena wondered how her mother was ever conceived. Poor Grandpa Tipping, forever destined to fail in his duty to king, country, wife and unborn daughter, executed by a firing squad at dawn.

I never knew him, her mother said, a pattern that had now been firmly established. When had any of the men in this family ever stuck around to see their children grow up, Serena wondered, and why was it that the women were always left holding the baby?

Ida was vague about Serena's paternity. All she would admit was that the man in question was married and that it never should have happened. After a couple of Guinnesses, Nanna Tipping was more forthcoming. 'He was a beast and a liar and a con artist and he treated your mother like dirt. She met him at a fun fair. She was very naive – he told her she couldn't get in trouble if they did it standing up.'

Great, thought Serena. Thanks to her grandmother, she had an indelible picture of her own conception in her head, her mother's knickers muddied and trampled, lying discarded round the back of the waltzers.

Serena had made a pact with herself never to get 'in the family way', not by accident, not until someone had put a ring on her finger and they'd got a house of their own with all the things you needed to make a home. Sometimes, when the shop was quiet, Serena carried out a mental inventory of the requisite items: a Singer sewing machine (she couldn't sew but every woman should have one), a cream Pifco hairdryer, twin-tub washer, hostess trolley, a pressure cooker, deep-fat fryer, a television. Occasionally she had fleeting premonitions of her future life, a flash of a pair of red gingham kitchen curtains and a table set for two, glimpses of a pale green satin bedspread. She could even identify the pair of marabou-trimmed mules under the dreamt-up double bed as belonging to her, the future Mrs . . . ? But she could never see the man, he was always just out of view. She could picture his overcoat, catch a whiff of a cigarette, but his face eluded her.

What's to become of me, she fretted. I can't stay here in this dump of a place being snapped at by old bats and leered at by Gordon Salmon. There's got to be more to life than sitting behind a till at Keddies supermarket.

Serena decided that she would go out that night. She would

call on her friend Susie, who she used to go to school with, and they would mooch along the promenade. The upside of living in a seaside resort, even out of season, was that there was always somewhere to go: ice-cream parlours, coffee bars – some with jukeboxes – and hotels with cocktail lounges. Yes, she would have a proper drink, a gin and tonic, a vermouth, whatever. The way she was feeling at the moment, she'd tip one of Nanna T's bottles of stout down her neck, anything to take the edge off. She sniffed her fingers. They smelled metallic, of copper pennies and brass thruppences, and it made her feel sick. She had to leave this job, she had to leave this town; time was running out, she could feel it.

Serena clocked off at five, punching her card in the machine on the wall by the rear entrance and marched angrily home. One of her stilettoes had worn through to the metal beneath the rubber heel and the resulting screech of alloy against the concrete of the pavement matched her mood. She paused for a moment and, leaning on a convenient gatepost, scribbled a note for Susie in eyebrow pencil which she dropped through her letterbox. 'Mad with boredom,' she wrote. 'Meet me at Chico's at seven, don't let me down.' And off she tapped again. It was a Tuesday. Tuesday was liver and bacon with cabbage. The thought of liver made her feel sick, but at least it was better than Thursday's tripe and onions, which was her grandmother's favourite.

Bloody hell, what a way to live, the three of them cooped up in a two-bedroom house, with Nanna Tipping sleeping on the sofa downstairs. They'd had to start laying down newspaper for her in case she didn't make it to the toilet in the night. Couldn't or wouldn't, Serena often wondered. The whole place stank of piss and cat food, so you couldn't bring a man back even if you could find one, not with that stupid budgie twittering its nonsense in the corner all day long.

Mind you, the budgie wasn't the only one talking rubbish these days. Nanna Tipping was as bad, rambling on about darkies and Russians under the bed.

Serena felt a pang of envy when she compared her life with Susie's. It was all right for Susie, she'd stayed on at school, got her highers and was now at university in Bristol – studying physics. It made Serena's blood boil that plain old Susie with her horrible frizzy hair and glasses was having a better time than she was. Yes, something needed to happen and it needed to happen very soon.

18

The Man of Her Dreams?

Southend, January 1962

Serena was finding her erstwhile best friend even more annoying than usual. Susie was due to go back to university next week and she couldn't wait. On and on she droned about how brilliant it was in Bristol and how everyone was such good fun and all the different societies you could sign up for. Susie had already joined the Appreciation of Foreign Films Society, Conversational French and the Chess Club. 'Urgh, I can't think of anything more boring than chess,' snapped Serena, who had chewed her striped paper straw so hard she couldn't drink through it.

They were having brown cows – Coca-Cola with chocolate ice cream – even though 'In Bristol everyone drinks coffee.' Susie had tucked her frizzy hair under a black felt beret and she was wearing what looked like her father's sweater over a pair of slacks; apparently, this was how everyone in Bristol dressed. And she was going on about a jazz club that all the 'gang' piled down to on Wednesday nights and how it was so strange coming back to Southend where everyone was 'incredibly behind the times'.

Serena found herself getting hot with bad temper. She wasn't even sure she believed her friend, preferring to picture her crying over a one-bar fire and a mug of cocoa in a dismal female-only hall of residence, rather than twisting the night away in some groovy little backstreet beatnik joint.

Much to her frustration, this newly confident woman of the world who exhaled Turkish cigarette fumes and casually asked Serena if she had ever read any Simone de Beauvoir seemed to have completely forgotten that she was destined to play the part of the dreary sidekick while Serena took the limelight. It felt like their roles had been reversed, and as Serena swallowed back the remnants of her ice-cream soda, it tasted oddly bitter. Must be the liver she'd had for her tea.

Susie had a boyfriend. Smugness radiated from her as she imparted this information and she pulled a sympathetic face when Serena admitted she was still very much single. 'Oh dear,' said Susie, cocking her bereted head. 'Well, don't worry, I'm sure someone will turn up soon. Isn't there anyone at work?' Momentarily Serena thought about the chap with no teeth that winked at her from the wet fish counter every morning, and once more her liver-and-onion supper threatened to make a reappearance.

'Did you hear Julie Porter got engaged?' she blurted. Her own love life might be in the doldrums, but at least she could still gossip about her acquaintances.

'How bourgeois,' yawned Susie. 'See, that's the great thing about university: being at Bristol has broadened my horizons. Who wants to be Mrs Mousey Housewife with a couple of snotty-nosed kids hanging off her pinny? No thanks! Me and Jimmy are thinking of heading off to spend some time on a kibbutz when we finish university.'

Serena wasn't sure what a kibbutz was, so she changed the subject. 'Yes, well, I'm going to go and live in London.'

Susie laughed in her new sophisticated way, 'You've been saying that since you left school and I don't think you've even been on a day-trip yet. I was up for a couple of days after Christmas – Jimmy's folks live in Islington, it's ever so near the centre of everything.'

So that was why she hadn't seen her friend over the festive season, she'd been too busy gallivanting round London with her swanky boyfriend in her stupid hat.

It was 1962. The new decade was already a toddler. Serena turned nineteen in six months and had yet to achieve any of the things she imagined she'd have ticked off by now. She hadn't been abroad, or driven round Hyde Park Corner in a convertible sports car, she hadn't been to a casino or kissed an officer, no one had bought her proper jewellery or written her a song. So far she had allowed three men (one married) to make love to her; panicked about being pregnant twice; attempted fellatio several times but not really got the hang of it; had several dead-end jobs; gone from mouse to blond; and given up on false nails.

She could feel the panic rise. What if she never found anyone? What if Susie became horribly rich and successful and sent her postcards with foreign stamps from exotic locations, while she was stuck with Ida, Nanna T and the budgie for the rest of her life?

Then I shall put my head in the oven, she decided. The knowledge that she had this get-out clause gave her an odd sense of security. Everything would either be OK or she would kill herself – simple.

Oddly enough, in the not-too-distant future, when she was contemplating this latter option in all sincerity, she would realise that the only oven available was of the solid fuel variety, which rather than putting her to sleep for ever would merely set fire to her hair.

But all that was yet to come. Right now, she was sitting resentfully in a fugged-up seafront café on a cold and wet January night with her ex best friend, who suddenly jumped up, flung her arms wide open and squealed,

'You came, I didn't think you'd come, how brilliant, oh, Jimmy.'

121

The door of the café had chimed open, letting in a waft of dank seaside air, heavy with brine and rotten leaves that clashed with the scent of cigarettes and deep-fat fryer, and a man who appeared to be all beard and duffel coat and whose face Susie was currently kissing. Behind the amorous pair another man stood solemnly unwinding a long hand-knitted scarf from a neck which seemed to consist entirely of Adam's apple.

Ten minutes later, Serena was horrified to realise that even in the badly oxidised mirror hanging from a fraying string in the dimly lit customers-only lavatory, she had a pronounced brown cow moustache. She scrubbed at it somewhat uselessly with shiny Izal paper and ran something crystal and pink that she found at the bottom of her handbag around her lips.

'This is Antoine,' Susie had gushed, before Serena managed to excuse herself. 'He's a poet.' Ever since then, her heart had been beating like a cake whisk.

Serena exited the bathroom and squeezed in next to the stranger in a red vinyl booth with Susie and Jimmy opposite. She couldn't take her eyes off him. He was dressed like the conductor of an orchestra, but appeared to have been sleeping in a hedge. His shirt was ripped on the shoulder and his trousers were muddied, he rolled tobacco from a battered tin into skinny black liquorice-paper cigarettes and had the eyes of a weepy cow. She was smitten, even though he barely spoke to her. He didn't talk much at all. He looked feverish, coughed a great deal and occasionally closed his eyes as if he desperately needed to sleep.

Apparently his mother was French and he was a musician and a poet, 'currently living in Basildon', Susie announced.

Antoine closed his eyes and shuddered as if in deep pain. 'Temporarily.'

Serena was momentarily confused. Basildon? Surely he belonged in Paris, in a garret overlooking the Seine, drinking cognac and writing poems that didn't rhyme?

Later on, Susie hissed in her ear, 'He had a massive nervous breakdown at uni, so he's living with his aunt until he gets better. He's a genius, but last term he thought the secret police were after him and he burnt his passport, which means he can't go home until he's sorted it all out. Jimmy's very good with him.'

Jimmy was very good with everyone. He even pretended to be interested in Serena's job and she tried to be funny about how tedious it was to sit at a till all day and count out the correct change.

'You were always lousy at maths,' laughed Susie.

'I was rubbish at everything,' giggled Serena, conscious that Jimmy was rubbing his foot up and down her calf. Poor old Susie, she thought, pulling her leg out of mischief's way, she hasn't got a clue what lover boy Jimmy is doing under this table. Serena laughed: all of a sudden her own future seemed so much brighter than it had a few hours ago.

Things were going to change, she could feel it in her waters, and when she asked Antoine for a light she made sure she steadied the trembling match he held between his thumb and forefinger by clasping the frayed cotton cuff around his bony wrist and looking deep into the chocolate pools of his eyes.

19

The Plan

Southend, February 1962

Two weeks later, Serena was still expecting Antoine to turn up at Keddies. Sometimes, when she left work via the staff exit at the back of the building, she walked all the way round to the front of the store to see if he was waiting there.

She was well aware that the world of punching in and out and regulation exits and entrances would be a mystery to a poet like him, but as for getting the wrong supermarket, that was impossible; Keddies was Southend's one and only convenience store. Ask any local and they'd point you in the right direction.

Every day for a fortnight she made a little more effort before leaving the house.

'I can't see why you need to wear false eyelashes for work, Serena,' her mother sniped across the breakfast table. She was turning into a right dried-up old bag.

'Well you never know who might pop by,' Serena sniped back, swiping the best-looking pair of nylons off the drying rack in front of the stove. Her mother worked as a receptionist at one of the smarter hotels along the seafront, so no one ever saw her legs, and while Serena herself might spend rather too much time boxed in behind her till, she still had cause to roam the shop floor on occasion, finding out prices, fetching a new till roll from the stockroom. She couldn't go round with great big potatoes in her stockings. Besides, her mother's legs had had their day, how old was she now? Forty-something, her ankles were puffy and she was grey around the temples, poor cow.

'Oh, so who are you expecting?' chimed in Nanna T. 'King Zog of Albania? Princess Margaret, stocking up on Spam?'

Her grandmother was eating boiled eggs messily. As far as Serena could make out there were at least four of them rolling around in their shells on her plate as Nanna Tipping randomly smacked at them with a teaspoon. Why didn't she put them in egg cups? Honestly, that woman was the end.

'None of your beeswax, Nanna,' retorted Serena, knowing her grandmother would forgive her anything. She enjoyed it when Ida and Serena had words, she loved a bit of conflict, which is why her favourite pastime was watching the Saturday afternoon wrestling on the telly, gleefully shouting at the tiny flickering screen while biting the heads off jelly babies.

Three weeks after first setting eyes on Antoine, Serena had given up hope. She was eating crisps as she crossed Keddies' car park, and had very recently applied a large dollop of toothpaste onto the throbbing pimple which had emerged like Mount Vesuvius on her chin.

She was still smarting from the very public dressing down Mr Salmon had given her that afternoon, after she'd accidentally short-changed his wife (his *wife*, no less), by a whole nine pence. 'Nine pence, that's nearly an entire shilling,' Mrs Salmon kept repeating, pointing at Serena, her pale toadlike chin quivering with rage. 'And not a word of apology, Gordon, oh no, thinks too much of herself to say sorry. I ask you, I don't know what the world is coming to.'

Serena had been unceremoniously removed from till duties and sent to work shelf-stacking with all the other gormless half-wits who couldn't be trusted with loose change.

By the time she had finished for the day she was weepy with humiliation and rage. And to add insult to injury, she had snagged her mother's best nylons on a nail in the stockroom. She could spit, she seriously could.

Her mood improved the minute she spotted him leaning against a lamppost, dressed in black, his pipe-cleaner frame bent into a series of angles.

He looked like he could have been drawn with a ruler: sharp elbows, sharp knees, even his shoes were pointed. Serena could have sworn he was wearing patent leather ballroom dancing shoes, one of which trailed an untied shoelace.

'You could trip and break your neck,' she said as he fell into step with her. He seemed to have a slight limp.

'I think you should run away with me,' he responded, and the cage around her heart seemed to swing open and her spirit soared. Well, obviously she should, this was the solution and the answer to all her dreams. How many times in a girl's life did a poet and musician ask her to leave everything behind and set out on a journey into the unknown?

'Don't be daft,' she replied with her mouth, while her guts screamed, Yessss . . . finally!

She didn't take him home. She didn't want her grandmother saying peculiar things and anyway it was tripe night and the whole place would stink.

They sat on a bench overlooking the cement-coloured sand and he held her hand and told her how life could be different if they disregarded the rules. He told her that people didn't have to confine themselves to married units and that there was an alternative way of living in a shared environment with other like-minded people. For a moment she wondered whether he expected her to go with him to Israel and join a kibbutz like Susie and Jimmy, which would be tricky considering she didn't even have a passport. Then again, according to Susie, neither did he.

She needn't have worried. 'Cornwall,' he said. 'There are seals,' he said.

'But you don't even know me,' she said, and he looked into her eyes and in his beautiful husky tones he explained how that wasn't important, how as soon as they met there had been a spiritual connection and that's all that mattered. Then he slid his hand inside her coat, up her jumper, between the buttons of her blouse and, delving beneath the webbing of her bra, he pinched her nipple, kissing her as she gasped.

She could have kissed him all night. As it was, when she got home to a plate of cold tripe, the skin around her mouth was ragged and chapped. One day she might have to ask him to shave.

Same time next week, he would meet her in the car park, a friend would pick them up in a car, and they would drive to Cornwall.

'Maybe bring biscuits,' he breathed into her hair as he pinched her other nipple, slightly too hard this time, before disappearing into the mist that had rolled in from the sea and shrouded the promenade.

Serena didn't breathe a word to either her mother or her grandmother. She didn't want to hurt anyone, she would leave a note, she would even leave a forwarding address if she had one, but it was all so deliciously vague. Cornwall may as well have been Disneyland so far as Serena was concerned. To her it was a far-off fairy-tale place with magical seals, a place where smugglers once hid rum in caves – this much she remembered from school. What else? Cornish butter, they sold that in the shop, which meant there must be cows, cows and a beach, cows on the beach. Serena had a bad dream involving this combination and cried out in the night. 'It sounded like you were mooing,' her grandmother reported in the morning. 'Mooing like a cow, you silly cow,' and she laughed and did that thing she did with her false teeth, pushing them out and then sucking them back in before they could topple out of her mouth. It was disgusting.

The day after Antoine met her from work she bought a suitcase from the market in her dinner hour and hid it in the storeroom at Keddies. Every day she smuggled in a few necessities from home and added them to the case. 'You won't need much,' he had instructed her. 'Possessions only drag you down. But you might need a jumper,' he cautioned.

She packed a Fair Isle sweater and her lucky green V-neck, then over the course of the next few days, she added a cream silk blouse, a striped poplin shirt, a pink satin top, a tweed skirt and two pairs of slacks. The suitcase was bulging before she crammed in a pair of gold slingbacks – it might not be a city, but if Bristol had jazz clubs then surely Cornwall would too.

She decided to carry her underwear in a plastic bag along with a large tin of hairspray and her toiletries.

When the day finally came she woke up late and, in a last-minute panic, she put her bikini on under her clothes. One day, when it got warmer, she would want to swim with the seals.

20

Make Your Mind Up Time

Serena stood in the car park behind Keddies in the rain. She was holding her small suitcase in one hand and the plastic bag full of tangled bras and knickers in the other. She had no umbrella and soon she would be soaked right down to her bikini. She could feel her eyeliner running in small black rivers down her face but she wasn't crying, not yet.

The lamplights shone a dim sodium yellow, the place was deserted and for want of anything better to do, Serena started counting, counting cows lined up on a beach. By the time she got to a hundred, Antoine would be here. Half past five he'd said, and according to her watch it was ten to six.

Her mum had given her the little Timex when she was fifteen. Ida said she was old enough to have something nice, but it was only plate and some of the gold had worn thin. She'd left a note in her bedroom, propped up behind the alarm clock she'd never have to set for Keddies again. Her mother was working a late shift that evening and as Nanna T rarely attempted the stairs any more, Serena would be miles away by the time the note was discovered.

Dear Mum and Nan, I'm going away for a bit, I don't want you to worry, I know exactly what I'm doing, I promise.

But did she? Did she actually know what she was doing? She hadn't pictured it like this, leaving in the dark and the rain. She'd pictured him arriving on a horse, a black stallion like Black Beauty, that was the picture she'd had in her head.

'A friend's place,' he'd said. 'A big old house, with turrets and a croquet lawn.'

'Posh?'

'Yes.'

Oh God, what if it was haunted? She believed in ghosts and that sort of thing. Serena shivered in her patent boots, which were meant to be showerproof but weren't. She was so cold she almost wished she'd worn her nan's old gabardine, rather than a silly thin leatherette jacket. Trying to find some shelter from the rain, she moved closer to the wall and kept counting, only this time more slowly. She had been lied to before by mean-faced men out for one thing, but Antoine hadn't struck her as that type. Then it hit her, that Antoine might not realise he'd been lying: what if he thought he was telling the truth? Susie's big concerned face loomed up in her subconscious: '. . . he had a massive nervous breakdown'.

Bloody hell, what if she had fallen for the ramblings of a madman? What if he didn't turn up and she had to return home, and fry Spam fritters for her grandmother – because that's what she did on the nights her mother wasn't home and she had to take over: deal with the tea, keep the fire going and put fresh newspaper down in the budgie's cage.

Bring some biscuits, he'd said, and she'd bought a packet of lemon puffs during her tea break, but she'd left them in the ladies and now she was hungry and it was raining and her bones were damp with cold and fear.

If only there was some way of getting back inside the supermarket. It was so frustrating knowing that only a few feet away lay aisles and aisles of edible goods. Why hadn't she planned this better? A picnic, that's what was needed on a long car journey; a loaf of bread and some cheese would have been a good idea, maybe some sliced ham and a fruit cake. No wonder Antoine hadn't shown up, he must have realised how useless she was. A better woman would have made a shepherd's pie and put it in a container ready to heat up once they got to Cornwall. Serena had heard the married women talk in the canteen at work. 'The key to a successful relationship,' Big Joyce from the cut meats counter said, 'is gravy. Sex and gravy, that's all men want. And the occasional pork pie.'

God, she'd have killed for a pork pie.

A car swung round the corner, spraying Serena with filthy water as it splashed through a puddle before screeching to a halt in the middle of the empty car park.

Soaked now to the eyebrows, Serena approached the vehicle with caution. It was a Mini. Good job he'd told her that a small suitcase would have to suffice. She peered into the driver's window, where a fat ginger-haired man sat stuffed like kapok into a tweed overcoat behind the steering wheel.

The driver wound down his window and a snub-nosed girl with a face full of freckles leaned over his shoulder from the back seat and fumed into his ear, 'I bloody told you, you can't trust him as far as you can throw him – the girl's here, but he's not, and if you think she's having the front seat while I die of claustrophobia in the back, you've got another think coming.'

And with that the girl manoeuvred herself into the front of the car and climbed out of the passenger door.

'Well, get in,' she instructed Serena, tipping the seat forward and gesturing into the back of the Mini. Seeing Serena hesitate, the girl put her hands on her hips and barked, 'If you're coming, get in, because we can't hang around here like cheese at fourpence, it's perishing out.'

As Serena dutifully climbed into the back seat she noticed that Miss Bossy Boots 1962 was wrapped up in a big sheepskin coat. Maybe she could ask to borrow it, until her things dried out.

'I'm Karl,' the driver announced. 'With a K.'

The passenger door slammed shut.

'And I'm Sandy,' added the freckly one. She would be quite attractive if she smiled, thought Serena, but Sandy's mouth was firmly set in disapproving mode as she lit a Peter Stuyvesant without offering anyone else one and proceeded to tear Antoine to shreds. 'I do hope you weren't expecting to be an item,' she threw over her shoulder at Serena. 'Antoine doesn't do relationships, hasn't got enough space in his head what all the other voices. Anyway, we can't wait for him, bloody car's been overheating since Chelmsford, if we don't keep going we'll never make it.'

Serena looked at her watch. She could still get out, they could drop her at the next set of lights. If the signal turned red, she would simply demand that she wanted to get out, there was still time to get home before her mother read the note, there was still time to fry Spam fritters and get the chip pan out, she could change into clean dry pyjamas, the flannelette ones she hadn't been able to squeeze into her bloody silly little suitcase.

Sometimes, by the time she got home, her nan had already peeled two big potatoes and all Serena had to do was cut them into chips with the crinkle chip cutter and drop them into boiling fat, open a tin of peas, butter a couple of slices of white bread, fetch the ketchup and Bob's your uncle. She might even be able to return the suitcase to the market.

By tomorrow she could be back at Keddies, ignoring the winking boy on wet fish and putting her pools money in.

Oh God, what if her syndicate won the blinking pools and she hadn't put her subs in? That would take the bloody biscuit that would. Yes, she would get out at the lights round the corner. She would simply inform the two strangers that she had changed her mind and wanted to go home for her tea.

Only the car didn't stop because the lights were on green, the moment was lost and in that split second, as the car sailed through the lights, Serena decided to hell with it, she was eighteen years old and it was time she had an adventure. She could always come back. There was bound to be a train she could catch. As for money, she had plenty, what with cashing in her post office savings and her Christmas work bonus, plus the fiver she'd found in Bronwen Jackson's coat pocket that time when the cloakrooms had been empty. Poor Bronwen had cried her eyes out. 'A fiver,' she sobbed, 'a whole blinking fiver!' They'd all had to open their handbags for Mr Salmon to inspect. As if she'd have put the fiver in her purse – it was tucked under her foot; Salmon would never have the nerve to ask them to remove their nylons.

And then there was the till money, all the sixpences she'd been stashing away for months now. Her mental arithmetic was admittedly poor, but there were perks to being notoriously bad at your job, and those perks came in the shape of pilfered coins, loads of them – plus the occasional note when she dared.

The money was all safely stashed in a pink nylon quilted toilet bag that her mother bought her for Christmas. Ida had filled it with bath cubes and a pumice stone for making her feet all dainty in the bath. Serena had left her nan the pumice stone on the side of the bath. Ida usually managed to push her mother up the stairs once a week for a proper soak and a hair wash.

'You're quiet,' snapped Sandy. 'Don't tell me you wish you weren't coming, cos we're not taking you back now. And by the way, there's petrol money to take into consideration.'

'I've got cash,' responded Serena.

'Oh good,' replied Sandy, 'because Karl and I are brassic. So what do you say we pull over for fish and chips before we get too far off the beaten track?' And with that Karl tugged down hard on the steering wheel and the car came to a halt outside the Tasty Friar on the edge of town. 'Come on then,' Sandy demanded, reaching round and holding out her hand to Serena. 'Cough up. The least you can do to say thanks for the lift is buy supper – we'll talk about the petrol money later.'

Silently Serena handed over a crumpled pound note. Greedy bitch better not order any extras. 'I'll just have some of your chips,' she muttered, and Sandy flounced off with a 'suit yourself' and a warning to Karl not to cut the engine.

Left alone together in the tiny car, Serena tried to think of something she could say to the mass of bundled-up stranger in the driver's seat, but it was Karl who broke the silence.

'So, have you been before?' he asked.

'No,' she replied.

'I go for the birds,' he told her. 'Nests and eggs, that sort of thing. I'm interested, you know, in ornithology.' His bug eyes met hers in the rear-view mirror. 'Sea birds in particular.'

'Like seagulls?' she ventured. 'I'm always terrified one's going to shit on my head. I mean, I know it's meant to be good luck, but it's not really, is it, not when you've had your hair done.' And she laughed to show that she was joking and that she was a good sport, but he dropped his gaze and stared through the window at the fogged-up door of the fish-and-chip shop until Sandy reappeared with a bundle of newspaper parcels and a man by her side.

'Look who I found dithering over the pickled eggs,' she announced.

It was Antoine.

Sandy opened the passenger door and instantly the small car was flooded with damp air and the tangy scent of malt vinegar. Tipping the front seat forward, she gave Antoine a slight push and the next thing Serena knew, his face was inches from hers. He was almost close enough to kiss her, but he didn't. He didn't even look at her, he simply folded up his body as if it were an Anglepoise lamp and settled himself on the seat beside her, his duffel bag and her small suitcase separating their two bodies.

Beneath the fish and chips, Serena detected a sour whiff of BO. Antoine was sweating, his face was covered in a film of perspiration, he didn't look very well and by the time the lights of Southend Pier had faded behind them he was fast asleep, a pickled egg clutched in his hand.

21

A New Life

Cornwall, late February 1962

Serena had been at Kittiwake for several weeks before it finally stopped raining. She and Antoine had formed a kind of uneasy truce: sometimes he slept with her and she would wake up and stare at his face in the moonlight, staggered by his beauty. His head was like a newborn foal, he was perfect but untamed. Sometimes he let her stroke him for hours; sometimes he avoided her, hiding round corners, slinking away like a cat.

She had got used to him, or rather she had got used to everything being different from what she'd expected. Not that she'd known what to expect; any information she'd gleaned about Kittiwake before arriving had mostly been picked up during the interminable drive down from Southend, eavesdropping on Sandy and Karl's conversation while pretending to be as fast asleep as Antoine.

According to Karl, Monty's Cove, where the house stood, belonged to a man called Benedict Carmichael. 'Actually,' Sandy had interrupted, 'it belongs to his mother. I know someone who went to his sister Natasha's wedding – very la-di-da, by all accounts. She's good looking – big nose, mind – married Hugo Berrington.'

'Otherwise known as the shit,' Karl had replied. 'Don't know him myself, but a stinking reputation by all accounts.'

From what Serena could gather, Karl knew Benedict because his father had been the Carmichael family's wine merchant, 'before they lost all their money'. Karl had sighed at this point and rubbed his ginger whiskers. 'All rather tragic. Mind you, they've still got a pretty decent cellar at Kittiwake, though at the rate Benedict's going through it . . .'

Sandy had laughed. 'He went out with a mate of my cousin's for a while, girl called Lulu Harrison. Said she had a hangover for six months, called it off before she got permanent liver damage. Everyone says he's an absolute sweetie though.'

'Oh, he is,' Karl nodded, 'tremendous fun, and he's incredibly generous. I mean, who else would open his doors to . . . well, you know.' And even though Serena had her eyes screwed tightly shut, she was perfectly aware of their mutual glance at the rear-view mirror.

'He's a bit fragile again, it seems,' Sandy had whispered, obviously referring to the gently snoring Antoine.

'Oh, a complete crackpot,' Karl had whispered back, and they both laughed rather meanly, Serena thought, before she finally allowed herself to fall as deeply asleep as her back seat travelling companion.

Looking back on that journey, Serena can't believe how naive she was. She'd had absolutely no idea what she was letting herself in for. Even now, Monty's Cove still took her breath away, the sheer size of it, the isolation, the fact that on days when the sea mist comes down the entire place was enveloped in a thick fog and one couldn't imagine ever seeing the sea again.

The house itself was magnificent, with its thorny overgrown rose gardens and Sleeping Beauty turrets – but she was constantly bewildered by the maze of wood-panelled corridors and endless dilapidated rooms, where ornate wallpaper drooped from the walls and plaster flaked like pastry from the ceilings.

Everything was falling to pieces and it was impossible to find a dry towel. Damp pervaded every inch of the place, through cracks in the window panes and missing tiles on the roof. When it rained heavily they had to rush around placing buckets and saucepans under the leaks, until the entire top floor resonated with the sound of water dripping onto metal, plink-plink, and the stair carpet grew thick with mould.

For the first time in her life, Serena had chilblains. Her beehive had collapsed into two beige curtains that hung limply either side of a badly cut fringe, but whenever she caught sight of herself in some fly-spotted mirror she could still convince herself that she was the prettiest girl in Monty's Cove, though she did have stiff competition from an Italian girl who would be a complete ringer for Sophia Loren if she didn't have such a dramatic squint.

Poor Giulia, her left eye resembled a ball bearing ricocheting around a pinball table – one could never be sure where it might shoot next.

Once Serena had noticed this defect, she was able to relax. Yes, Giulia had arguably better legs, but seriously, that eye? Poor cow.

As for bossy Sandy, despite having a mass of coppery ringlets and an incredible bosom, she was too sour to be properly attractive, continually barking orders at Karl and treating him like a dog on a leash. Fortunately for Serena, the fourth female member of what Antoine referred to as 'the coven' couldn't compete in the looks department. Rhiannon was a plain creature from the Welsh Valleys, an emotionally fraught young woman who disapproved of most things, particularly the eating of meat. The mere sight of a rasher of bacon, rare enough at Kittiwake, would cause her to hyperventilate. 'Just leave it on the side of your plate,' Serena once snapped, turning for a second into her own mother.

Rhiannon's reaction to this comment had been to cry until she retched. 'You have no idea,' she informed Serena, 'what it's like to see animals being slaughtered.'

Serena had to admit she didn't. In fact, when she thought about it, a lot of meat she'd eaten at home had arrived fresh from Keddies in a tin. Corned beef had been a big favourite, served most Sunday afternoons with beetroot, tomato, lettuce and salad cream. Ida brought the tea into the sitting room on a trolley and they usually had jelly after. Nanna T liked it with tinned mandarins and carnation milk.

Serena pushed the memory firmly away. She wasn't homesick, it was more that this new chapter of her life wasn't quite as exciting as she'd hoped. She was also starving half the time. The kitchen range was temperamental, there were no shops within walking distance, Karl's car was forever letting them down, and if they hadn't received deliveries of groceries from a neighbouring farm every week they'd have starved. Thank goodness, then, for Robbie, the monosyllabic local farmhand who came every Tuesday morning to drop off hessian sacks of vegetables – soil-caked potatoes, worm-riddled cabbages and frost-bitten carrots – that could be turned into stews and soups. Milk and eggs were left daily at the end of the drive by a van and the kitchen pantry was well stocked with what looked like endless sacks of lentils and something Rhiannon identified as pearl barley. There was also plenty of sugar, salt and flour, which Rhiannon mixed with her precious supplies of yeast and managed to transform, like a disappointing magic trick, into large flat sullen loaves of bread.

She also insisted on making porridge. The sight of that big pot of grey slurry bubbling like a geyser of mud on the stove never failed to have Serena craving some bright pink Bird's Angel Delight. Everything in Kittiwake tasted of the earth and Rhiannon insisted that the few remaining jars of preserves and pickles be used sparingly until summer came and they could make some more. Why would you want more, thought Serena, as she struggled to taste the difference between the jars labelled plum jam and those labelled plum chutney. Sometimes she dreamed about Keddies, the shelves of scarlet jam, jars of bright yellow piccalilli, the brightly coloured tins of biscuits.

She missed sweets too, she missed the pick-and-mix counter and the tangy peppermint sweetness of seaside rock, she missed Nanna's crumpled paper bag of cola cubes tucked down the side of her armchair and Ida's secret stash of Pontefract cakes which she hid from her mother in her sewing basket. Did they miss her?

Sometimes she wondered why she stayed. Pride, mostly. The food was awful, the weather atrocious and Antoine was a lousy lover, physically clumsy and emotionally cold.

She was also rather sick of the fact that he refused to bathe. He might be beautiful in his starving Parisian artist in a garret way, but he didn't half pong. The man was also domestically selfish, refusing to lift a finger around the huge house, opting instead to wander off to find his 'muse' or sit for hours playing the hideously out-of-tune piano in the entrance hall. He said he was composing – decomposing, more like, thought Serena, removing yet another pair of his socks from under her pillow. Why did he do that?

She only persisted with him because there was no one else to fancy. Karl was round-shouldered and covered in a pelt of orange hair like something in a zoo; his whole body was slightly out of proportion, with a pair of surprisingly short bandy legs attached like an afterthought to his oversized torso.

Far more physically impressive was Gervaise, a slim dark imp of a man with exquisitely chiselled features, who danced like a dream, made delicious sponge cakes and was hiding from his father for something he did in London that had made Papa very angry indeed.

Serena couldn't imagine Gervaise being guilty of anything too awful. What on earth had he done?

'Offered a copper a blow job in some toilets off the Old Kent Road,' Karl explained.

'His father was livid,' added Sandy. 'Couldn't understand what on earth Gervaise was doing down the Old Kent Road.'

Apart from Gervaise the homosexual and Karl, whom Sandy kept her beady eye on in case he should look too long in the wrong direction, there was only Robbie the dishy farmhand, who was too shy to even look at her. Not that she'd be interested if he did; she hadn't run away from stacking shelves in a supermarket to be a farmer's wife. She pictured herself barefoot on a cold flagstone floor with a carving knife, cutting the tails off mice, and shuddered. No thanks.

February was a blur of freezing fog days followed by black ice nights and Kittiwake seemed suspended in time, as if waiting for things to get better, the weather to improve, someone to tune that bloody piano, for Rhiannon to bake an edible loaf.

In the meantime, Serena picked cobwebs off damp crime thrillers and prowled around, idly opening random doors and finding odd relics of the past: a leather button from an overcoat, a chair belonging to a doll's house, a scrap of hair ribbon and a collection of cigarette cards featuring famous cricketers.

Nothing of any worth had been left at Kittiwake. Following the accidental drowning of young Master Ivor, all the good silver, glassware and furniture was removed and put into storage in London, only to be sold when Teddy Carmichael ran headlong into financial difficulties. All that was left in the house was the second-rate, moth-eaten and uncared for.

Garden furniture had been brought inside to fill some of the essential gaps, a billiard table took pride of place in the dining room, and on the rare occasion a decent meal with meat and wine was served, they dished it up on the ripped green baize. In the hallway, a long-broken grandfather clock stood silent enough for one to almost hear the woodworm gorge their way through its mahogany guts.

Over a decade of neglect had taken its toll on Kittiwake. Pipes had burst and floorboards rotted. Serena slept in a bedroom off the top corridor. The rose-print wallpaper was faded and scuffed, Peggy's grand chrome deco bed was long gone. She slept on a mattress on the floor with or without Antoine and kept half an eye open for mice. Her belongings were stashed away in a vast mahogany wardrobe, which she wished she could padlock.

Giulia, in particular, didn't believe in privacy or indeed ownership, and couldn't be trusted. She would wander from bedroom to bedroom, helping herself to anything she fancied. Not that Serena wasn't guilty of some casual pilfering herself. On one occasion, imprisoned by the weather and bored by the radio, she'd joined Giulia and climbed a rickety ladder into the loft where they discovered a stash of travel trunks under the eaves. The locks were shut fast with rust, but they'd hacked at them with knives and chisels until they could be prised open.

The largest case contained a collection of fur coats packed tight and reeking of camphor. Mink, rabbit, beaver, leopard and the dearest little white fox fur shrug, which the girls fought over until Serena gave up her claim on the leopard skin, which Giulia took to wearing as a dressing gown.

Predictably, Rhiannon had been sickened by their haul – until the temperature dropped below freezing, at which point with great reluctance she gave in to the practicality of a floor-length beaver-skin coat with pockets big enough to house hot-water bottles.

One of the other trunks had contained items designed to be worn on a summer cruise; many had labels bearing the names from some of the world's leading couture houses. Serena had spent hours trying on flared palazzo pants and beautifully cut linen jackets with impossibly nipped-in waists. It brought back memories of primary school and playing with a dressing-up box in the corner of her classroom with her friend Susie, trying on cloaks made from curtains, and old ladies' quilted bed jackets. Clearly, she hadn't grown out of the thrill of playing dress-up, if only there was something to dress up for.

With a sigh of despair, Serena went down for her pearl barley and potato soup supper that night in a beaded twenties cloche hat.

22

The Prodigal Returns

Cornwall, March 1962

The telegram arrived on Wednesday. It was addressed to Gervaise, and simply stated 'Friday night. Kill the fatted calf.'

'So that means Benedict's coming down?' queried Antoine. He looked anxious, his eyes were bloodshot and he couldn't stop coughing.

'Yes, Benedict's coming,' shrieked Gervaise. 'At last we are going to have some fun. And about time, it's been too, too dull here without him.'

And he skipped off to the cellar to bring up some fizz and a few bottles of decent red.

'I could do my vegetable gratin,' ventured Rhiannon.

'*Che palle*,' snapped Giulia. 'Are you deaf or *stupido*? Benedict is coming – and we shall have meat.'

The next day Karl and Sandy managed to bump-start the Mini and set off to fetch provisions from Penzance. Donations were required and Serena wondered why she was handing over her cash.

'Who are these people anyway?'

'Benedict and his sister own this place and the land all around,' Giulia reminded her. 'This is his house – well, it will be when his *madre* dies.'

Serena was puzzled. 'Then where's he been all this time?'

'He have a place in London, this is family holiday home.'

'But no one ever comes here. I mean, it's not set up for families.'

'Because the place is unlucky, a child die here. Who knows?' shrugged Giulia. 'Anyway, I am having bath, I must shave legs.'

Karl and Sandy returned with bags of salted peanuts, prawns and chickens, frozen peas and brandy snaps, thick double cream, lemons and olives. Serena had never tasted an olive before. Intrigued, she put one in her mouth and instantly spat it out.

'What are you doing?' queried Gervaise. 'You only spit out the pit. Honestly, where did you go to school?'

'It's the filthiest thing I have ever put in my mouth,' Serena spluttered.

Gervaise smirked. 'Then you have never been down the Old Kent Road.' And he waltzed off to share Giulia's bath, as he often did.

The first time Serena walked in on them, naked and semi-submerged in exotically scented water, she had been shocked. The bathroom was candlelit and they were both smoking. Gervaise was reading a book of poems by Byron – more for effect than any great literary thirst, she decided.

There was a lot of this kind of behaviour going on at Kittiwake, a sort of bohemian posturing – particularly from Giulia, who would slink around like a polecat, climbing into any bed she felt like. She'd even tried to slide in next to Serena once, but Serena had immediately switched on the overhead light and asked her what the hell she was playing at. To which Giulia rolled her eyes even more dramatically than usual and flounced out muttering curses in Italian.

145

She thinks I'm suburban, Serena realised. And indeed she was; a small-town girl who had worked variously in a cinema, hair salon, shoe shop and supermarket, she had never been abroad or eaten a croissant (or a prawn, for that matter) and she certainly wouldn't have a clue as to what a girl was meant to do with another girl under the bedclothes. And nor did she want to know, she told herself indignantly. However, try as she might, she couldn't forget the sight of Giulia's coffee-coloured nipples peeping out of the bath water, how extraordinarily large they were. Serena's own nipples were very much smaller and the pale pink of English rosebuds.

She recalled a girl at school who'd had a reputation for eyeing up the other girls when they got changed for PE, blatantly checking out the contents of their white cotton Playtex bras. Miriam Perkins was a couple of years older than Serena and everyone called her names behind her back. Some years later she joined the police force and no one was very surprised when she set up home in a bungalow with two Alsatians and a woman called Mrs Shenley, who was supposed to be a widow.

'Widow, my foot,' Nanna spat. 'More queers than you can shake a stick at round here.'

By Friday morning, Serena had come down with Antoine's cold. She felt awful and at five o'clock in the afternoon she retired, shivering, back into bed. Back at Allam Street, her mother would have been bringing her tinned tomato soup and Jacob's crackers on the Eiffel Tower tray with the wicker handles. Serena ached with both illness and a sudden desire to see Ida – poor old put-upon Ida, stuck at home with nutty old Nanna and a dead-end job.

And that's precisely why you have done this, she reminded herself. You ran away so that you wouldn't end up like your mum. And she drifted off into a confused and sweaty sleep, dreaming of playing topless bingo with Miriam Perkins, Giulia and Mrs Shenley.

146

She woke up at around ten o'clock in the evening to the sound of laughter and the chink of glass. For a while she hovered at the top of the stairs, listening in and peering over the banister rail into the hall where a heap of strange coats and alien luggage had been discarded. Who were these invaders, she wondered, even though she herself was an interloper, a cuckoo in this freezing nest. The temptation to go down and join them was overwhelming; there would be a fire in the dining room, and food and drink. She hadn't eaten all day and having sweated off her fever she was starving, so she threw an Aran sweater over her silk nightie (yet another attic find), pulled on a pair of long woollen socks that Rhiannon had knitted and made her way downstairs.

Even with her poor blocked ears, the decibel level increased with every step: jazz music and voices, people talking over each other, guffaws and shrieks. How many of them were there? In the hall, candles guttered in the icy draught and the grandfather clock with its hands forever stuck at twenty to four seemed to give her a disapproving look as she tentatively opened the heavy oak door to the dining room.

Strange men in evening dress sprawled around a long central dining table on mismatched chairs. Even Karl was wearing a bow tie, his collared shirt looking chokingly tight around his throat.

Further round the table, which at second glance she realised was both the kitchen and billiard tables shoved together and covered in a white bedsheet, she spotted Gervaise and Giulia. They were sitting side by side, chiffon scarves tied in bows around their necks, faces elaborately painted, kohl-rimmed eyes, rouged cheeks and crimson lips, each with a matching beauty spot, the show-offs.

Ashtrays brimmed with cigarette butts and even through her cold Serena could smell the acrid scent of cigar smoke. The room was a blue haze of smoke and candlelight, the bedsheet tablecloth was splattered with red wine and an unfamiliar woman was spitting olive pits expertly into her delicate hand, a diamond bracelet

147

sparkling around her tiny wrist, while a body in ornate black lace lay slumped on the window seat, asleep or possibly unconscious?

The carcasses of three chickens lay splintered in the middle of the table, picked clean of meat and surrounded by empty vegetable dishes. The only untouched food was a plate of celery piped with creamed pearl barley and sprinkled with paprika – Rhiannon's vegetarian contribution, Serena guessed, as she edged around the door and crept silently into the room. No one noticed her apart from a chocolate brown Labrador who emerged from under the table and proceeded to waddle over and sniff at her crotch. It was as though the animal knew she wasn't wearing knickers and she could feel the dampness of its nose through the flimsy fabric of her night-dress. She pushed the thing away with her knee and he growled.

'Well, look who it is,' slurred Gervaise. 'Little Miss Southend-on-Sea.' She felt instantly cheap, like a novelty gewgaw hanging off one of the stalls along the seafront.

'The shop girl,' brayed the olive-spitting woman – opening her hand and discarding the pits onto the carpet. 'Benji, stop sniffing the poor girl's vagina.' Serena had never heard anyone say 'vagina' in public before and she blushed deeply on the other girl's behalf.

Frozen with self-consciousness, Serena noticed a young man strutting towards her from the far end of the dining table, clutching an oversized bottle of champagne. There was something about him, an energy, a life force, that drew her towards him like a magnet. He was slightly shorter than average, dark-haired and tanned, and there were creases around his eyes. He looked as though someone had recently told him a very good joke.

'I'm Benedict,' he said, expertly shoving the dog aside and hand-ing her a brimming glass of bubbling pale gold liquid. And as he grinned, Serena wondered whether she'd ever seen a grown man with dimples before.

Across the room, Antoine smouldered and coughed over his filthy liquorice roll-ups. Later he came to her room and made phlegmy love to her; both of them were running a temperature and their love-making was slick with the sweat of sickness rather than passion. He must have a bath tomorrow, thought Serena, before he abruptly withdrew and collapsed on top of her. She hadn't come, but he had, she could feel the cold slime of his sperm as it spread under her buttocks. Surely someone must be able to get hold of condoms, even in this godforsaken place. 'You did – you know – in time . . . didn't you?' she asked.

'Of course,' he gasped, and then he proceeded to cough all over her until she was tempted to creep off down the corridor and crawl into bed with Giulia.

23

Japes

Cornwall, April–September 1962

Benedict's presence lit up Kittiwake. The place came alive when he was around. It helped that for the entire duration of his visit the sun shone and Monty's Cove finally revealed herself in her true sparkling-sea-and-golden-gorse-covered glory.

With Antoine confined to bed on the master's orders – 'I'm not having that consumptive maniac infecting the rest of us. Tell him if he gets out of bed, I'll shoot him' – Serena, who was still rather pink around the nose, was free to observe the Carmichael party at close quarters for the rest of the weekend.

For some reason, Benedict included her in all their activities: the walk down to the private beach, complete with hip flasks and a box of Belgian chocolates; the three-hour lunch on Saturday that morphed into evening cocktails followed by the first curry Serena had ever eaten, cooked by the first Indian man she had ever met. 'Bloody good cricketer and all,' confided Benedict, spilling prawn biryani down his front. He dabbed it off with his napkin, 'See, that's the joy of a paisley shirt, you can throw as much food down it as you like and everyone thinks it's part of the pattern,' and he re-filled Serena's wine glass to the brim, yet again.

After dinner she was drunk and found herself telling wildly exaggerated stories about working in Keddies, doing impressions of Mr Salmon's wife, and revelling in the ensuing laughter. 'I've never met a till girl before,' Benedict's friend Lucinda told her. 'And I've never met an Honourable before,' Serena quipped and everyone laughed some more.

Before she went to bed, Benedict made her a hot toddy: whisky, honey and lemon. It was the kindest thing anyone had done for her since she ran away from home.

'It's what Blake always did for my father,' he told her.

'Who's Blake?' she asked.

'Our old butler.'

Of course.

In the morning, Serena was hungover. By the time she ventured downstairs, all the Honourables and cricketing curry chefs were packing up to leave. At 3 p.m., a procession of brightly coloured sports cars, horns blaring, weaved their way out of the rusting iron gates at the end of the drive.

Back at the house, those with nowhere better to go huddled on the front step and waved somewhat forlornly as the storm clouds gathered above Kittiwake's peeling yellow façade.

He reappeared in late spring, when the weather began to truly warm up and the blue of the sky and the blue of the sea reminded Serena of being a little girl and painting pictures of the seaside.

Gervaise had found a large box of watercolours; there were three different blues in the box, he told her, 'cobalt, ultramarine and cerulean'. Serena was learning all kinds of things, all the colours of blue, what the word canapé meant, and how to mix a decent vodka martini.

She began to realise that her background was as exotic and mysterious to society types as theirs was to her. OK, she'd never tasted lobster before, but how many of them had eaten jellied eels or pie and mash?

Occasionally Benedict brought a girlfriend down, but as far as Serena could tell, it was never the same one. They all sounded alike and were uniformly beautiful with exquisite clothes, but Kittiwake held limited appeal for them. It wasn't London, the wind was vicious, the plumbing awful and so many glasses broken that most of the crystal had been replaced by Green Shield Stamp tumblers courtesy of the petrol station down the road.

'I haven't a clue what I'm going to do with the place, the roof is in shreds,' Benedict once confided in her. They were smoking outside on the terrace, a full moon suspended over the sea like a golden coin. 'Can't your sister help?' she asked, but he ground his cigarette under his glossy leather boot and said, 'She hates the place. It's all a bit complicated,' and went indoors, leaving her to shiver on her own.

Benedict's birthday was the first weekend in May. He would be twenty-two. By all accounts, his twenty-first had been a huge week-long celebration which annihilated the wine cellar and resulted in one suicide attempt, a broken leg and the ceremonial burning of a stuffed grizzly bear down on the beach. There'd been reports of gunshots being fired, and the local constabulary had turned up on the doorstep.

This year Benedict had decided to keep the gathering down to a manageable thirty or so guests, with a buffet supper, drinks and dancing.

'He's mellowing,' complained Gervaise.

'He's growing up,' snapped Sandy. 'Benedict's had a shitty time of it, what with his cow of a mother and losing his brother and his father shooting himself. Maybe it's time he settled down, no one can party ad infinitum.'

Serena couldn't imagine losing a father or a sibling, but then she'd never had either. As for what 'ad infinitum' meant, she hadn't a clue.

Rhiannon looked horrified at the idea of Benedict settling down. 'But what if he wants to move back here, what will happen to us?'

'Well none of us can stay here for ever,' Sandy replied, slowly and carefully, as if explaining something to a small child. 'We all know this is a temporary arrangement, it could end like—' And she clicked her fingers and stared long and hard at Karl.

Only then did it dawn on Serena that Sandy wanted Karl to make an honest woman of her. Well, good luck with that, mate, she thought, as Rhiannon headed off in tears, followed, very much to everyone's surprise, by Karl.

Benedict arrived for his birthday weekend with a ciné camera. 'It shoots colour film,' he professed proudly, 'my sister and her husband bought it for me.' He immediately set off on a tour of Kittiwake, going from room to room with the camera attached to his face, instructing his guests to 'do something marvellous'. Serena turned a perfect cartwheel on the landing – she'd completely forgotten that she could – and Benedict was so delighted he made her do it again and again until she felt quite dizzy and collapsed laughing on the floor.

'Will you help me record the party tonight?' he asked Karl. 'Only I'm aiming to be completely sloshed by nine and I don't want to drop the thing.'

Karl blushed with pleasure at being singled out as Kittiwake's official ciné-photographer and spent the rest of the afternoon earnestly reading the instruction manual, something Benedict would never have the patience to do, conscientiously learning how to load the camera, turn the reels over and pull in and out of focus. Presumably he was hoping that, if he did a good job tonight, Benedict might lend him the equipment to record some of the nesting birds on the cliffs below Kittiwake that summer.

'Is your sister coming?' Serena asked Benedict as they pushed the furniture back against the walls in the main sitting room and rolled up various threadbare rugs.

His face clouded over. 'No, she's not a hundred per cent, she's . . . um, women's problems,' he mumbled vaguely before adding, 'Anyway, as you know, she loathes Kittiwake, I'm not sure I could trust her not to burn it down.'

Serena thought Natasha sounded a bit crazy, but she didn't say so. Instead she headed off to the kitchen where even sulky Antoine was joining in, helping to make 'the world's most powerful punch'. He was in his element, his pallid cheeks were flushed with excitement. 'I had a mate at uni,' he told them, 'a medical chap, who used to put a splash of ether into the mix – people would be passing out all over the place.'

Serena was getting bored of Antoine. He was always ill, he was very smelly and he was forever disappearing off to write stupid poetry, usually when there was something more boring but essential to do around the house. None of the men helped out domestically, not if they could help it. Karl would occasionally wash up when Sandy told him to, but Antoine and Gervaise were hopeless and the house had become even filthier when Karl and Sandy, citing their socialist principles, banned Brenda the cleaner from entering the premises. At least, with Benedict visiting more frequently, Brenda had been reinstated, much to Serena's relief. Without Bren, the place threatened to be a bit of a health hazard. True to form, as Serena looked on in horror, Antoine began decanting his punch into a rusty old tin bathtub someone had found in one of the outhouses.

Having decided to avoid Antoine's concoction and drink wine instead, Serena went in search of a bottle. There was a certain red, the one with the old-fashioned writing on the label, a Château Latour 1949, that she'd become rather partial to. Given the chance, she'd have it on her cornflakes.

154

The mood that night was giddy. Cars had been arriving all day and by 10 p.m. the house was heaving. A Fortnum's chocolate cake had been reduced to crumbs on the billiard table. At Benedict's request, the rest of the buffet was more children's tea party than sophisticated supper spread, with thickly buttered triangles of bread sprinkled with hundreds and thousands, paper plates of iced party rings and a potato hedgehog covered in tinfoil and studded with sausages on sticks. Serena was in her element – not a lentil or clove of garlic in sight.

The record player was set to full volume and a big bowl of red jelly quivered to the beat. Sometimes the stylus jumped when someone danced too close, the needle skipping abruptly from one track to the middle of another, which for some reason was the funniest thing anyone had ever heard.

And there in the background was Karl, circling the party-goers like a hairy ginger shark with the Kodak ciné camera firmly clamped to his left eye. All night long he filmed everything, capturing the night for ever on celluloid, including the moment Benedict's eyes met Serena's and together the two of them disappeared from the party.

Inevitably, by the time the film was developed in London several weeks later life at Monty's Cove had already moved on. In the middle of June, the car, Karl and Rhiannon disappeared and no one twigged what had happened until Serena found a note propped up against the toaster. Signed by them both, it apologised for hurting anyone's feelings, while explaining that their love for each other was insurmountable and that they had gone to Wales to get married.

Apart from Sandy, no one was that fussed. Losing the car was a much bigger blow than losing either Rhiannon or Karl, and at least no one would have to eat Rhiannon's porridge ever again.

Sandy, however, was inconsolable. She began spending entire days down at the beach, trying to pluck up the courage to drown herself, but as she explained to Serena, 'It's almost impossible when you're a strong swimmer.' In the end, she removed the stones from her anorak pockets, packed her cases and headed back to Oxford to enrol on a teacher-training course. When she left, she hugged Serena and swore she'd see her again, but Serena knew she wouldn't. Kittiwake was falling apart, everyone was leaving and Benedict, rather than risk an unreliable English summer on the Cornish coast, had opted to take a holiday on Cap Ferrat. And who could blame him, the weather was predictably awful and by the beginning of August, after ten days of solid rain, Giulia and Gervaise had bailed out too, having received an invitation to spend some time with Giulia's uncle in Padua. Typically, on her departure, Giulia took Serena's hairbrush and her second-best set of eyelashes, which upset Serena so much she felt sick – so sick that she actually vomited into the umbrella stand in the hall.

As for Antoine, he had departed the morning after Benedict's twenty-second birthday party, leaving Serena with a pillowcase full of poetry written in green ink, charting the demise of their relationship and describing her as a shop girl who pretended to be a mermaid. He had used a lot of swear words in his poetry. One verse simply read 'fucking whore', over and over again.

It was the first time she had ever slept alone at Kittiwake, and with the house echoingly empty, even her favourite red wine didn't help her relax. In fact, after sampling a few bottles from the cellar it seemed like the whole lot had gone off and she poured bottle after bottle down the sink, gagging at its vinegary stench.

Once the weather got colder, Serena lit the fire with Antoine's poems and watched with satisfaction as the green-ink scrawl turned to flames. She would have to move on soon, but where and when and how, she hadn't got a clue. Tomorrow, she told herself, I'll decide tomorrow.

As autumn turned to winter she realised she could no longer fit into the trousers that once upon a time she had run away in, and the voice of doubt in her head became a nagging certainty. Serena looked down at the convex swell of her belly. If she thought she couldn't go home before, she certainly couldn't now. She couldn't go anywhere. She would have to wait here until Benedict came back. After all, this was his fault, wasn't it?

24

The Invitation

Île de Ré, France, April 2018

Natasha stares at the envelope for a while. The handwriting is familiar but she cannot for the life of her . . . think.

She doesn't get much mail these days, people have become very lazy about pen and paper. She remembers sitting at the writing desk at Claverley Avenue with a whole heap of envelopes in front of her, licking stamps for what seemed like hours; she and Hugo used to have such a long Christmas card list that it would take her an entire day to work her way alphabetically through their social circle.

A is for the Abbots, June and Bernard – she still has the red leather-bound address book old Mr Blatt presented her with when she left his luxury goods shop. 'To Natasha with the beautiful hands,' he wrote.

So many names in that address book are crossed out now that she finds it depressing. Judging by the number of horizontal ink lines, it's quite obvious she knows more people who are dead than alive. And that includes her husband – dead, disgraced Hugo, who left her with very little money and very little choice but to run away to France and leave the past behind.

Everything changes, she reminds herself. You don't have to lick stamps any more, and never mind letters, people barely bother with postcards these days. And then she thinks about the ones she used to send her mother in America and how seldom Peggy replied.

The desk at Claverley Avenue released a particular smell when you opened the lid and inside there were lots of cubbyholes for pens and paper clips and a special space where the cheque book slotted in just so, the special little hole for the bottle of . . . Without warning she is reminded of a terrible deep blue stain on a pale gold carpet and her eyes fill with tears. 'Don't cry over spilt ink,' she mutters under her breath.

These days she has a computer, a laptop that she can carry from room to room, although she normally leaves it on the kitchen table, the lid firmly shut. She will be eighty at the end of the year and technology has for the most part advanced without her.

She can, however, send emails, although she has to prepare herself beforehand; sit down with a cup of peppermint tea and check the handwritten notes at the back of her diary under the heading 'How to send an email'. Her son bought her the machine, it's an Apple Mac. 'That's the best kind,' he told her, and she believes him. Lance knows about that sort of thing.

Now, where was she? Oh yes, the envelope. It's an invitation, that much is obvious. She used to get a lot of those when she was younger, back in the days when people still sent invitations to weddings and christenings and special birthdays and anniversaries. It was one of the reasons why one had a mantelpiece: to display one's invitations.

It was easier not to go wrong when there were rules, thinks Natasha, remembering a carved oak mantelpiece with a silver candlestick at either end. In the spring she filled those candlesticks with forsythia or daffodils.

159

It's spring now in France, which is nice but not the same as in London. The flowers are different and it doesn't smell the same.

These days Natasha lives on the tiny Île de Ré off the west coast of France, home of the hollyhock and the donkeys in pyjamas. Her house is so small that sometimes she dreams there is another staircase which leads off to a series of rooms she hadn't known existed. When she wakes up from this dream, she feels as though she is trapped in a cave. There really should be another staircase, how come she has ended up in this poky house on this funny island? Where did all the money go? It seemed to dissolve overnight. Of course her husband Hugo had lied to her for years about their finances and much more besides. Though whether he'd actually been guilty of any real crime had never been proved and at least moving here meant she could escape the shame of all that gossip and speculation.

The envelope is addressed to Natasha Berrington. Why don't widows return to their maiden names, she wonders. The surname Berrington has little to do with her now; Hugo was so long ago, all that charm and fury reduced to a gravestone in the Brompton Cemetery, a black marble slab engraved with his name, his date of birth and the date of his death. Nothing else had seemed appropriate; she couldn't exactly ask the stonemason to add 'loving husband and father, sorely missed'. Natasha laughs and wonders if anyone has ever had the guts to ask for an inscription that reads 'good riddance'.

She slides a lacquered red fingernail under the flap of the envelope. La Flotte might be a small town, but French women are religious about their looks and Natasha visits a beauty salon once a week. She is lucky, she has enough money for such things – she has seen other women her age who cannot afford the luxury of grooming and they look like peasants.

Mind you, even women with money refuse to bother these days. Every year there is a relentless tide of middle-class British women who flood the island with their loud voices and creased linen smock dresses, yelling commands and desperately looking for some shade, their plump shoulders turning the colour of raspberries.

Natasha has a small vine-covered courtyard at the back of her house, where she dips a fresh croissant into hot chocolate for her breakfast. Has she had breakfast today? The problem with getting forgetful is that one runs the risk of getting fat. Eating two breakfasts would be lethal. She used to be so good at not eating; undoubtedly the cigarettes helped. But she's given up, nearly – Natasha allows herself a slim menthol cigarette from the packet of ten she keeps by the back door.

She's seventy-nine – who cares if she gets cancer now? She sits under her vine and studies the embossed card.

A party at Kittiwake to celebrate her son's fiftieth birthday, a 'Bacchanalian bash', no less. She will ignore the instruction about fancy dress, at her age she doesn't need to bother with that sort of nonsense. It was different when she was younger; she remembers going to a party dressed as a gypsy, her face darkened with gravy browning. That was back in the seventies when one was allowed to . . . what is the phrase? 'Culturally misappropriate'.

Natasha inhales. Her son Lance is fifty. How odd that a tiny baby should have become a middle-aged man.

She will go, of course she will go. After all, this could be the last chance she has of seeing them all together, her family – what is left of them.

Natasha makes herself remember everyone by name. Her son Lance and his wife Freya, their children, Ludo and Luna, their cousins, Edward and James, and their father . . . Here she draws a blank; she cannot for the life of her remember the name of Bel's husband. Ah, Bel, the daughter that never truly was her daughter, the thorn that is Bel – argumentative, difficult Bel, the adopted one.

How had that even happened? Not so much as a visit from anyone in authority to make sure they were suitable parents, and

161

both she and Hugo smoked. It would never have been allowed these days.

It was all Benedict's idea, and for some reason Hugo went along with it. She doesn't recall having much say in the matter. Before she knew it, the paperwork was rubber-stamped and she was holding the child in her arms. She wishes Benedict could be at Lance's party, but sadly he can't – her younger brother is dead. He turned into a fat lothario, riddled with gout – the 'Podgy Playboy', as Hugo once called him – and succumbed to a massive heart attack about four years ago. In fact, that was the last time she'd been back in England, for her brother's funeral. So many people from all walks of life crowded into the church that day. She misses him terribly.

He was at the centre of so much of her life, the only one that knew almost everything. How odd that he is no longer here. Of late Natasha has become acutely conscious that she has outlived not only her husband but both of her brothers. She is the last of the Carmichaels, apart from some cousins, the Norfolk Carmichaels, now decrepit in various nursing homes and sheltered accommodation around Hunstanton.

Natasha shivers. At least she has her independence, she can still clean and cook for herself. At least she doesn't have to put up with strangers touching her body.

She will go to this party, though she would much rather the festivities weren't being held at Kittiwake – she has always hated the place, but the simple fact is, she loves Lance more than she loathes Kittiwake. Besides, she feels instinctively it will be the last time she will make this journey.

She will fly direct to Exeter and then take a taxi to Monty's Cove; extravagant but practical. If she flew to London, she would have to stay with Bel in that grubby house in Clapham and feign an interest in those lumpy boy-men that are supposed to be her grandsons. She visited the place when she was in London for Benedict's funeral, sleeping in a bedroom that smelt of boy – the younger one was away at university, so she had his bed. Bel had prattled on about clean sheets, but Natasha could still detect a whiff of testosterone on the pillows, and it turned her stomach. Everything about the place made her feel queasy: the waddling, breathless dog, Bel's filthy fridge, the husband, whatever his name is, walking around with bare feet. Men's feet are so disgusting, shudders Natasha, grateful again for the perks of early widowhood.

She decides to email Lance with her plans. She will ask him to book her flights, and she will plot something splendid to wear for the party; possibly white slacks with a fabulous blouse and maybe a hat. People will marvel at 'how good she is for her age' and while she is there, she will soak in enough memories of Lance to last her a good long while. She will even learn to use the camera on the iPhone he bought her. And then she will come home.

She doesn't expect any dramas. All the big dramas are over; now that she's in her eightieth year, it's time for some peace and quiet. Nothing can possibly happen that would surprise her any more.

She resolves to email her son before she forgets. Checking her 'how to' guide first, she clicks on the requisite icons and begins,

```
Dear Lance,
Thank you for the invitation. How ageing
to have a fifty-year-old son, I shall keep
very quiet about it in the village . . .
```

Natasha pauses. She doesn't know anyone in the village and despite having moved to the island more than twenty years ago she still only has a smattering of schoolgirl French, anything more complicated than a shopping list and she's very quickly out of her depth.

In some respects, this has suited her very well. It stops people getting too close and asking personal questions. '*Je ne comprend pas*,' she shrugs, and eventually they give up.

No one needs to know very much about her. To her

acquaintances, she is Madame Berrington, and Madame Natasha to her hairdresser; as for the other ex-pats, she waves, she exchanges village gossip, but she mostly retreats behind the dove-grey painted front door and is grateful to have left her past behind.

```
I will let you know exactly when I
shall need my tickets booked and look
forward to spending a wonderful three
nights with you.
```

Natasha's hand hovers over the keyboard. She learnt to type in Kensington in the fifties. Her mother had paid for her to attend a secretarial course after she finished school. Young ladies were beginning to enter the workplace. Not that she ever worked as a secretary; her brief stint in the world of work was in retail, selling gloves and purses in Blatts' leather goods shop on Sloane Street. Fortunately, she had got married before anyone realised that she was actually working out of necessity as much as 'fun'.

Natasha looks down at the liver spots on the backs of her hands. How strange to think that once upon a time she'd been employed principally because they were so beautiful. Her slim fingers, now twisted with arthritis, had once slipped so easily into a size eight glove and looked so elegant holding an expensive ladies' purse.

In fact, her hands had been so lovely that she'd even earned some money modelling cuticle cream and a certain brand of ladies' watch.

But Hugo had put a stop to it. 'Thin end of the wedge,' he'd said. 'It'll start with the hands, next thing you know, they'll be wanting your legs for suspender belts and no wife of mine is going to be snapped up to the thigh by some Johnny-come-lately photographer.'

This was not long after Antony Armstrong-Jones had married Princess Margaret and, as Hugo said, he wouldn't trust him as far as he could throw him – and Hugo would know . . .

Natasha reaches for another cigarette.

I hope Freya and the children are well,
please tell them I'm very excited to be
seeing you all in August.
With very much love, as ever xx

Mother, Natasha, Mummy, Ma, she can't decide, so she doesn't bother, the email address is enough of a giveaway.

Natasha presses the little paper-aeroplane button and then props the invitation safely between her silver candlesticks on the sideboard in her sitting room. She doesn't have a mantelpiece in the cottage – there are so many things she used to have that she doesn't have any more: a mantelpiece, a husband, a mother and a father, two brothers, a car, a daily cleaning lady, a television, a garage ... The list grows longer and longer until she's too hungry to think any more and she decides she will walk to the local market and buy some ripe tomatoes, big ones, and slice them for her lunch and eat them in her courtyard with plenty of salt and black pepper, and then she will spend the afternoon thinking about what she should give her son to celebrate his fiftieth birthday. What can she buy him, what more does he need?

He has everything. Health, wealth and happiness, he has a beautiful wife and bright-eyed children, he has a career and status and now he has Kittiwake too.

Poor Bel. Natasha wonders how her daughter feels about Lance being named the sole beneficiary of Monty's Cove in their uncle's will back in 2014. It wasn't as if Benedict and Lance had been particularly close, whereas Benedict and Bel ...

Natasha swallows hard. He had loved her, loved her unconditionally, he had stepped in and fought her corner when no one else did, he had been her port in a storm, her safe place to run. Poor Bel and poor Benedict, it must have been hard on them both. Things might have been different if Lance hadn't been born ...

But Lance had been born, and that had changed everything.

165

25

Baby Lance Is Born

London, 1968

Annabel was nearly five when her mother stopped lifting her out of the bath. Her father appeared in the bathroom one evening, shooed her mother off the wooden stool with the cork lid where Natasha sat in readiness with a towel, and told Annabel she was a big girl now and that she could get in and out of the bath by herself, because she wasn't a stupid or a lazy girl, was she? And anyway, Daddy didn't have time for any of this nonsense so she must put on her own pyjamas and go straight to bed without disturbing Mummy, because Mummy needed lots of rest.

So Annabel started getting out of the bath by herself but she couldn't dry herself properly and her pyjamas got all caught up in the bits where Mummy usually put the nice powder. Annabel couldn't reach the nice powder and every night her pyjamas were all twisted and damp.

Natasha was resting a lot. Mrs Phelan said it was on 'Doctor's orders', and that Annabel mustn't do anything 'silly' like jump on the bed. Instead she should play quietly and not be a nuisance.

So she practised walking on tiptoes, which she learnt at her ballet class, and she listened at doors and once she crept into the pantry and ate biscuits, lots of them, one after the other, until the tin was empty. Mrs Phelan had shrugged her shoulders and said, 'To be sure, there's a great big mouse in the house. I've a good mind to put poison on the biscuits.' So the next time Annabel crept into the pantry, she took a chair so that she could reach the cake tin, and ate cake instead.

One night when she was listening at her parents' bedroom door she overheard her mother say, 'Do you think Annabel's getting a bit fat?' And her father said, 'That makes two of you,' and her mother laughed, at which point Annabel realised that she had accidentally squeezed the cake she was holding in her hand and had to lick the squashed chocolate sponge off her fingers.

A few weeks after Annabel started getting in and out of the bath like a big girl on her own, Hugo decided it was time to tell her about 'the new arrival'.

'And while we're at it, we might as well tell her about . . . you know what,' he informed Natasha.

'Darling, is that strictly necessary?' Natasha queried. 'Having a baby brother or sister is already quite a lot to take in, without that stuff on top.'

But Hugo insisted and one evening after tea, Annabel stood on the cream hearth rug and heard the carriage clock chime six times as her father told her that some little boys and girls didn't live with their real mummies and daddies because of 'circumstances', but that many of these children were lucky enough to find happy homes, where they were looked after by mummies and daddies who, because they didn't think they could have a baby of their own, took in someone else's.

'Like borrowing?' she interrupted.

Sometimes Annabel went to the library with Mrs Phelan, who borrowed cowboy stories for Mr Phelan and romantic fiction, whatever that was, for herself, and books for Annabel because she was already starting to put letters together and form words, even though Mrs Phelan said her lad couldn't manage that until he was a big boy of seven, God bless him.

'Not quite like borrowing,' replied Mummy. 'Because you don't get given back.'

'Unless you're very naughty,' joked Daddy, but he wasn't smiling when he said it and for a moment she saw herself being slotted back on a wooden shelf, waiting for the next set of parents to 'borrow her'.

'So we adopted you when you were a little baby,' he went on, 'which means that legally you are our responsibility.'

'Because you're very special,' her mother added, and her eyes were shining.

'Yes, all of that,' her father continued. 'But the thing is, now we're having our own proper baby and very soon you will have a little brother.'

'Or sister,' her mother muttered nervously, her hands fluttering over her stomach as if to reassure herself the miracle Humpty Dumpty lump was still there. Hugo had already been to his mother's house in Buckinghamshire to get his old train set out of the garage.

After the 'little chat', Annabel returned to the nursery and played 'adopted babies' with her toys, choosing which one she wanted to take home most, Teddy or Suki the doll. But it wasn't a very good game because Annabel was a bit confused about the rules of adoption. She had a lot of questions that needed answering, but because she was under strict instructions not to bother her mother, she asked Mrs Phelan instead.

Mrs Phelan felt for the cross around her neck and after a lot of humming and hawing, told her about orphanages and unwanted babies.

When Bel asked why a baby should be unwanted, Mrs Phelan said she was too little to understand, but that sometimes mummies died because childbirth was a difficult and dangerous thing and that it was very sad. Then she went on to explain that sometimes big girls did silly things out of wedlock and as a punishment God took their baby off them and made sure it went to a decent God-fearing home where the poor wee innocent wouldn't be brought up in sin, and that Annabel should thank her lucky stars.

So Annabel tried to be grateful and wondered if her real mummy was dead or silly. In the end she decided she was probably dead, because, according to Daddy, Annabel was always doing silly things and a baby had never come out. So no, her real mother had to be dead. She must have died doing the difficult and dangerous child-birth thing, poor dead Mummy.

Annabel never once considered her real father's role in all this baby business. It wasn't at all clear to her what daddies did, apart from go out to work every day, then come home and be strict and make Mummy cry and smoke cigars and drink something that smelled funny called whisky. It was the mummies that mattered, it was the mummies that grew the babies in their tummies and looked after them when they came out all red and screaming.

Annabel knew this because she watched it happen with her very own eyes. She watched Mummy get big and fat with the baby inside, she even saw Mummy's belly move when the baby kicked, which made Mummy laugh even though if Annabel kicked her she would be angry.

She was taken to meet the baby the day after he was born, all red and wrinkled and small like a shrivelled party balloon.

The baby came home to live at Claverley Avenue. He was a boy like Daddy had said and Mummy got lots of flowers and cards from her friends. One of the cards had a picture of a bird called a stork on the front, carrying the baby in its beak, and Mrs Phelan told her that it was the stork who brought babies home after they were found behind a mulberry bush, which confused Annabel because she knew that the baby had come home from the hospital in Daddy's car.

169

The baby's birth was announced in *The Times* newspaper: 'To Hugo and Natasha Berrington, a much longed-for son, Lance Christopher Ivor Berrington.' Natasha ordered several spare copies of the paper and sent a cutting from one of them to her mother, who lived a long way away in America and whom Annabel had never met. 'But she's my grandma too?' Annabel had asked.

Even though Lance was only a tiny baby, he already had a box of special things that Mummy kept under her bed: the plastic name tag he'd worn in hospital, a card with his recorded head circumference, length and birth weight, his first booties, and a withered carnation from the bouquet Hugo had bought her the day she'd delivered his son.

'Do I have a special baby box?' Annabel asked, but apparently because she was adopted she didn't. So she made one of her own; she even cut a hank of blond hair off one of her dollies, and put it in a matchbox and pretended it was her real mummy's hair. Poor dead Mummy.

Annabel wasn't sure how she felt about Baby Lance. His face was all creased up like a goblin and now that he'd come home and would be living there permanently, Annabel had had to change bedrooms because 'big girls don't sleep in nurseries'. But neither did Lance. At the moment he slept in something called a 'basin' in Mummy and Daddy's bedroom so that Mummy could get up and feed him in the night. It's not fair, thought Annabel. How come that baby got night-time snacks when she wasn't even allowed to take a biscuit up to bed?

Annabel's new bedroom was called a 'box room in the attic'. It was bit gloomy, 'But we can always decorate it,' her mother told her.

'First things first,' Hugo said. 'My son's nursery has to take priority.'

'A son is a boy baby,' Natasha explained to Annabel while she was changing Lance on his special plastic mat. 'And all baby boys have willies.' Annabel watched Lance's willy, a terrible blue-veined worm that lay twitching between his chubby white legs. Once, when Mummy was changing his nappy, some wee-wee came out of the terrible worm and Mummy laughed even though it nearly got her in the eye. It seemed the kicking, weeing baby could get away with anything.

The nursery had to be decorated 'pronto' because Lance was a son and a boy and Daddy didn't want him sleeping in a yellow room in case it turned him into something called 'a sissy'.

Once the yellow walls had been repainted pale blue and the frieze of silly geese replaced by jaunty sailing boats, Annabel asked if her room could be painted too, but Hugo said Annabel had to learn that she couldn't expect to click her fingers and get what she wanted.

Annabel didn't understand what her father was talking about. Try as she might, she couldn't click her fingers. And as for getting what she wanted, all she wanted was for Baby Lance to go back to wherever he came from, so that she could sleep in the nursery again and be near Mummy and Daddy, not stuck all the way up the horrible dark stairs in a room with a window that was too high up to see out of.

Sometimes Annabel was so frightened of the night-time that she crept down the scary stairs and sat on the landing below, listening to everyone else breathe in their sleep.

26

Lance's Christening

London, February 1969

A christening was to be held for Baby Lance with a service in church, followed by a 'buffet lunch' at Claverley Avenue. It was 'high time' Hugo said, Lance was six months old now and had three teeth.

For days before the event the kitchen was out of bounds while Mrs Phelan 'slaved' over vol-au-vent cases, rice salads and trifle sponges. A cake had been ordered from a special patisserie and arrived in a red-and-white-striped box tied up in gold ribbon like a precious hat.

The entire house smelled of beeswax and carpet shampoo. Everything had to be 'spick and span', her mother told Annabel, because there was going to be a very special visitor, Grandma Peggy was coming 'all the way from America for Lance's special day'. Her mother looked feverish, her eyes were wild and she had tied her hair back with a pair of old tights.

'Where will she sleep?' asked Annabel, hoping that the grand-mother woman would take her place in the box room and she could sleep in Mummy and Daddy's bed like Lance usually did. But it turned out Grandma Peggy was going to stay in a hotel called Claridge's because she wasn't over for long and she wanted to make sure she was 'properly comfortable', at which point Annabel could swear she saw her father roll his eyes.

On the 'very special day', Lance wore a dress which was called a robe, a froth of cream lace that emerged from a cardboard box layered with sheets and sheets of tissue paper. The robe was very old and terribly delicate, so she mustn't touch it, because it was something called a 'Berrington family heirloom'.

So she didn't touch it, she simply stood back and watched Lance be sick down it.

The christening was the first and only time Annabel ever encountered her American grandmother. Peggy was a white-faced woman with black eyebrows and red lips like the wicked witch in *Snow White*. She looked at Bel on the steps outside the church and said very quietly, 'Well hello, little cuckoo in the nest, I've heard all about you,' and then she raked her hands across the little girl's scalp and in doing so, some of Annabel's thin sand-coloured hair got tangled in the woman's diamond bracelet and had to be wrenched from the root so they could both be freed.

After the boring bit in the freezing cold church with Lance hiccupping at the font, they all returned home for 'a spot of lunch'. Annabel was wearing new pink leather shoes. She had wanted black patent in the shop but her mother shuddered and said she couldn't abide black patent and that black patent was for funerals.

Her dress was pale pink and stiff with petticoats, and beneath it she was wearing her best white nylon lace tights, which were excellent for sliding up and down the freshly polished parquet flooring in the hallway.

The pink shoes were almost exactly the same colour as the poached salmon, all set out on a silver salver on the dining room table.

Mrs Phelan had decorated the giant fish with cucumber scales and black olive eyes, and Annabel could tell that she was as proud as punch of her handiwork, even though some of the cucumber scales had fallen off.

The housekeeper was wearing a black dress with a starched white pinny over it; it was her job to slice up the fish and serve the salads. She kept her head down and concentrated on the task and barely looked at Annabel, who wondered why Mrs Phelan's hands were shaking so much.

It was all a bit boring. Lance had fallen asleep, 'the little angel', and the grown-ups stood around talking. The ladies, still in their fancy hats, were all gathered in one room, trying not to drop food on the pristine carpets and sipping from champagne flutes. While the men stood together near the drinks table, occasionally laughing and clapping each other on the back.

There were no games or balloons but there were presents, a big pile of them on the hall table, all for Lance.

Annabel took a plate of potato salad. She didn't like the look of the pink fish and she wasn't allowed pudding yet, because that was 'rude and greedy, Annabel'.

She wished she had someone to play with, but no other children had been invited, because her parents 'didn't want any silliness in the church'.

In fact, her father said she was only allowed to attend 'on sufferance' because she was Lance's sister and 'woe betide' her if she did anything naughty. He said 'woe betide' quite a lot, and when he said it, Annabel knew that she should be quiet or hide.

She felt shy all of a sudden and, seizing her moment when no one was watching, she slipped under the buffet table and picked at the potato salad with her fingers. Sitting cross-legged hidden away behind the heavily starched tablecloth, she heard snippets of conversation.

'So pleased for dear Natasha, it's been such a long wait, poor thing.'

'Have you seen the mother?'

'Yes, simply terrifying, and very like Wallis Simpson.'

'Going back to America first thing in the morning. Says she can't bear to be in England, too many memories.'

'Yes, well, it must have been ghastly.'

The voices moved away and, peeping from under the cloth, Annabel recognised Uncle Benedict's shoes, brown suede and pointed, drawing near. She was tempted to reach out and tug at his trousers before disappearing under the table again. Uncle Benedict would find that sort of thing funny, he loved jokes and he laughed at everything.

He was one of Lance's godfathers. Lance had two godfathers and a godmother, which seemed quite a lot, considering Annabel didn't have any, but that's because she hadn't been christened, Mummy told her, and it wasn't likely to happen either because, 'Well, it's a bit too late, darling.'

Annabel loved Uncle Benedict. He'd brought Lance a silver rattle with an ivory bear-head handle for his christening gift, but he'd given Annabel a present too.

As soon as he'd arrived at the house he had dropped to his knees and produced a package from behind his back. It was all wrapped up in silver paper with lots of Sellotape, and once she managed to tear it open she found a small beige rabbit inside with a sad face and long ears.

The insides of the ears were lined with pink velvet, which was ideal for stroking while she sucked her thumb.

She had the rabbit with her now under the table and she reached for him as she heard the witch woman say to her uncle, 'I hear this is all your fault, Benedict.'

'I beg your pardon, Mother?'

'The girl, the fat little thing.'

'Not entirely my fault, Mother, it seemed to be a good idea at the time.'

'Really?'

'I'm very fond of her, and Natasha—'

'Doesn't need her now. Oh well, what's done is done.'

Under the table, Annabel lay down on the carpet. She felt very tired and her dress was too tight. Putting her thumb in her mouth and stroking sad rabbit's ears, she watched the woman walk away; her heels were high and shiny and black, she shouldn't have worn them to a christening.

Benedict's brown suede shoes stayed still for a second and then she heard him mutter, 'Give me strength . . . and a proper fucking drink,' as her eyelids began to droop.

27

After the Christening

Benedict left his nephew's christening as soon as decency allowed. He needed to get away from his mother, he needed a proper drink.

He headed back to the mews house that he knew he should feel grateful for and promptly finished off a bottle of Johnnie Walker.

He wished he knew how to handle the situation better. Maybe he should have arranged to meet his mother for supper at Claridge's, attempted a proper adult conversation with the woman, allowed her to tell her side of the story before she flew back to the States, listened to her and tried to understand.

But as soon as he'd seen her at the christening, his immediate instinct was to scream, 'You abandoned me when I was ten years old and I had lost my brother.'

Benedict felt again the hollowness of those months that followed the accident at Kittiwake and how he'd assumed that his mother would soon be coming home from her 'holiday'.

He recalled imagining her returning with exotic gifts from America, Disney toys and Hershey bars that he could hand around to his classmates, but instead it had been left to his aunt to break the news that Peggy wasn't coming home and that his parents were getting divorced.

Peggy had left him and Natasha and his father to face the misery of losing Ivor without her, and in doing so had ruined Teddy.

Benedict looked at the amber-coloured liquid in his glass. His father had always been a drinker, but once his mother left he didn't stop. Now Teddy was dead and Peggy was at least partly to blame. She might be his mother but she was a bitch and Benedict was suddenly consumed with sorrow and rage at everything that had happened.

He was also angry with his sister, who'd been so delighted that their mother had deigned to cross the ocean for her precious son's christening. The way she'd smiled beatifically throughout the ordeal, oblivious to Peggy's objectionable behaviour, infuriated him. And he recalled the sour grimace on their mother's face and her shudder of distaste when she tasted her first sip of champagne at Claverley Avenue. The way she had refused anything from the buffet, apart from the tiniest portion of salmon, and how she'd looked at Mrs Phelan as if the housekeeper were offering her dog shit rather than a spoonful of Waldorf salad, a dish which Benedict knew had been made specifically in her honour.

She did look incredible, he supposed, in a fitted pink crêpe knee-length dress with a black-and-white houndstooth bouclé check jacket and a little black pillbox hat with matching shoes. The woman was in her late fifties and probably weighed no more than when she walked up the aisle to marry his father. But that didn't alter the fact that she wasn't very nice, he decided, as the nasty remark she'd made about Annabel being fat flitted across his increasingly inebriated subconscious. How spiteful! Yes, the child was well rounded and he knew Natasha worried about her tendency to over-eat, but she was only six. As soon as she grew a few inches, the weight would redistribute. It was puppy fat, nothing more.

Benedict couldn't help feeling a pang of guilt over poor chubby little Annabel. How could he have stood up in church and publicly promised to undertake the duties of a godparent for Baby Lance, when he had made no such public declaration for the child who might be his?

Mind you, the likelihood of him being Annabel's father seemed to shrink daily, with the girl looking less and less like him the older she got. The arrival of Baby Lance had only served to highlight this fact. At six months, Lance, in stark contrast to his adopted sister, was pure Oppenheim with his abundant dark hair and prominent nose.

Benedict decided to keep a close eye on Annabel. The little girl needed someone on her side. Never mind Baby Lance, he had a doting mother and a besotted father, whereas Annabel had . . . well, who did she have, apart from him?

Hugo, he noticed, was particularly short with her, forever barking orders at the child, telling her to pipe down and shush. It made Benedict uncomfortable. Was it his imagination or did she actually cower in front of the man? Then again, Hugo always had a mean streak. Benedict knew some chaps who'd been in the same year as Hugo at school and they were terrified of him, and he loathed the way his brother-in-law had always dismissed Annabel's mother as 'that filthy little scrubber', as if she were some two-bit King's Cross whore, when in reality she hadn't been anything of the sort.

In any case the woman was dead. She'd died tragically young in awful circumstances and still Hugo continued to call her names. It made Benedict's blood boil. What sort of man spoke ill of the dead? So what if she wasn't a virgin, so what if she slept with other men; Benedict's mind wandered back to that night when she had taken him by the hand and they had made love in a room with another man's boots by the bed, and even the smell of them hadn't put him off.

Oddly enough it wasn't the sex that Benedict remembered with such fondness, it was the laughter. She was one of the few girls he had slept with who made him laugh, in bed and out of bed. Serena had a way of making everything more fun. She was the only woman who had ever made him feel like he could actually dance. Not that she was girlfriend material, obviously, not with that accent and the way she held her knife as if it were a pen, but that didn't make her 'a filthy little scrubber'.

Benedict decided he didn't like Hugo. In fact, he'd come to the conclusion that the man was a loathsome bully, and ruthless with it. God knew what he was capable of . . .

Benedict shook his head, he had to stop letting his imagination run away like this. Just because he didn't like Hugo didn't mean to say that he was guilty of doing something awful. Anyway, he hadn't even been there that night. What was it his sister had said? Something about her father-in-law having a heart attack the night of the party and Hugo having to leave to be with him. No, he was nowhere near Mayfair the night Serena died, he wasn't even in London. Poor Serena. How awful to go to a party and die.

Benedict shook his head and told himself to stop dwelling on the past. It was over, nothing he could do to fix it. Best look to the future instead. He lifted the bottle of Johnnie Walker to refill his glass, only to find it empty. Sod it, he wasn't in the mood to stop drinking yet. So he staggered into the kitchen where he found a dusty bottle of port tucked behind the ironing board. He'd swiped it some time ago from the Kittiwake cellar, drunk half of it at Christmas and forgotten about it, Hooper's Ruby Vintage 1937, the same year his brother Ivor was born. He opened it clumsily and, swaying now, proceeded to fill a tiny port glass until the viscous liquid spilled all over the work surface. That was the trouble with port glasses, silly fiddly things. Benedict put his lips to the spillage on the countertop and slurped at it, managing to inhale most of it into his mouth. From now on, he would simply

180

swig from the bottle, much less wasteful. And he needed every drop after the day he'd had: seeing his mother, all thin and brittle in her expensive clothes, hearing himself at the font spouting all that mumbo jumbo, all those promises he had made to Baby Lance while pretending to believe in a God he knew hadn't existed since the day Ivor fell to the bottom of the pool.

Benedict's eyes began to prick and next thing he knew the tears were flowing. Stupid to cry, but that's what he was doing, crying over spilt port, a sticky red stain all down his brand-new shirt, dark and bloody. Then, with a mighty heave, Benedict began to wail. He cried harder than Baby Lance after the cold water splashed his little blackbird head. He wept for his dead father and for his drowned brother and, oddly enough, for Serena, the girl who'd fallen from the sky.

He had been there, he had held her hand as she had taken her last breath. Poor Serena, he hadn't known her very well and she had done a terrible thing in abandoning Annabel, but she was only twenty – far too young to die.

An accident, they said, those words, a horrible echo of when Ivor died. A silly, stupid, unnecessary accident and it was ridiculous to think anyone else might have been involved.

Benedict wiped his nose on his sleeve, hauled himself to his stockinged feet and staggered up the narrow stairs to bed. Hopefully things would look better in the morning. If nothing else, at least his mother would have gone by then.

As he stumbled around, tripping over his pyjamas, Benedict had no idea that he would never see Peggy alive again. Not that it would make much difference, he would never forgive his mother whether she drew breath or not. In fact, in his opinion it was incredible she had managed to live so long, considering there was scant evidence that the woman actually possessed a functioning heart.

28

At the Hairdresser's

London, May 2018, three months before the party

Bel is at the hairdresser's. She is trying a new place that offers a 25 per cent discount on a Wednesday morning, although, as the girl on reception said when she popped in to make the booking, 'It's even cheaper on a Friday morning for senior citizens.'

'But – I'm not a senior citizen,' Bel stuttered. Oh great, this was a new low.

'I wasn't saying you was,' the girl muttered defensively.

Bel resisted the temptation to correct her grammar and eventually managed to secure a cut and colour with Milo at 11.10 a.m.

Bel has never bothered with hair dye before, but last week Maisie had rather clumsily pointed out that she was going grey.

'Mostly at the back, Bel, that's why I thought I should tell you. Only I thought, well, like, what if she doesn't know? If that ever happened to me, I'd want someone to tell me, so I could do something about it before it got like really bad.' The girl had smiled sweetly at Bel as if she were doing her a favour.

So now she is sitting in a black leather chair wearing a black nylon gown which is fastened at the back like a straitjacket. 'We're not going to turn back the tide,' Milo informs her, 'so what I'm thinking is some light marmalade streaks.'

'Haha,' Bel laughs, 'I shall feel like Paddington.' Milo, who is tattooed up to his chin and has holes in his ears that you could stick pencils through, doesn't crack a smile, so she makes the mistake of trying to explain herself. 'You know, as if Paddington's marmalade had spilt under his hat.' But the blank look on his face reflecting back at her in the mirror suggests he hasn't a clue what she is talking about. Rather than make an even bigger fool of herself, she keeps quiet while Milo paints stripes of something that looks suspiciously like Agent Orange onto segments of her hair before encasing them in tinfoil 'parcels'.

Once Milo has finished, she is left to 'cook' for forty-five minutes. Having accidentally on purpose left this month's book club choice at home, she rifles through a selection of magazines on the shelf in front of her, one contains an entire double-page spread of 'spot the side-boob'. In despair, she discards the celebrity rag and picks up an interiors magazine instead.

Bel sighs. She is hot in her nylon gown and they haven't even offered her a glass of water, never mind a tea or coffee. This self-improvement lark is not only expensive, it's time-consuming and boring, and for what? For one weekend in August when God knows what the weather will do and no one will be looking at her anyway because it's Lance's big day, his chance to shine, like he always does. The whole thing is an opportunity to show off his beautiful wife and his gorgeous children and his fabulous home.

Bel flicks through her copy of *Better Homes* magazine so crossly that she almost rips the glossy paper, until she turns the page and there it is. Kittiwake, her Kittiwake, the yellow of a pale egg yolk, covered in the silver purple bloom of an ancient wisteria, its gnarled limbs running riot around the house.

Instantly she feels an odd sensation deep within her womb, a stirring, a feeling of anxiety, a sudden need to clench her bowels. Above the turrets of the house, written in a white curly font against a blue Cornish sky, are the words 'Heirs and Grace'.

Bel has always been a fast reader and without drawing breath, she quickly absorbs the first few lines:

When wine bar impresario Lance Berrington and his Norwegian interior designer wife Freya inherited Kittiwake House from Lance's maternal uncle, neither of them knew what challenges lay ahead.

'It was pretty brutal,' acknowledges Lance, and his pretty wife nods in agreement, adding, 'I don't think either of us had a clue quite how much work needed doing.'

But happily, beneath years of neglect and a ruinously leaking roof, lay the bones of one of Cornwall's finest coastal houses.

Originally built in—

Oh, spare me the history lesson, Bel thinks impatiently, I know. I know who originally built that house and who bought it from whom, and I know what happened there too. I know that if a young boy hadn't drowned there, then the house would have probably ended up in someone else's hands, rather than those of my rather smug adoptive brother.

Bel continues to skim through the article.

Approaching fifty, Berrington has the youthful looks of a man ten years younger, but there is a determined glint in his eye and one gets the impression that once Master Lance has made his mind up to do something, not much is going to stand in his way.

Talking about the two years he and his wife spent renovating the turreted ten-bedroomed mini-mansion, Lance laughs,

'It almost killed us! It was so terribly gloomy, we used to call it the mausoleum!'

'Let's just say Kittiwake has a lot of ghosts,' Freya adds, offering around a plate of home-made rhubarb strudel.

Ghosts that are both living and dead, thinks Bel. Her scalp tingles as she speed-reads the rest of the piece, but there is no mention of her, not the slightest allusion to an abandoned baby left in a drawer and adopted into the Berrington family. Why would there be? Lance has always been slightly dismissive of Bel. Even when he was a little boy, five years younger than her, she felt patronised by him, and this feeling has never gone away. As an adult, her brother has a knack for making her feel socially inferior and gauche. She's always had the impression that he doesn't think she matters – and why should he? It was obvious from the day he was born that he was the favourite.

Lance does, however, mention their mother, 'society beauty Natasha Berrington née Carmichael, who holidayed at Kittiwake as a child', but he doesn't reveal how she witnessed the death of her elder brother while visiting Kittiwake in the Easter holidays of 1950, how she saw him drown in an indoor pool even though he could swim.

Poor twelve-year-old long-dead Ivor has no part to play in this celebration of good taste. Instead the focus shifts to the exquisite design solutions of 'the talented Freya, who has made quite a name for herself on the interiors scene'. It's only towards the end of the article that the journalist jokingly refers to the 'curse of Kittiwake':

... Lance chuckles expansively and says, 'Well, as long as we can keep the old girl standing for my fiftieth later this year, then I shall be quite happy,' adding, 'Kittiwake has had her fair share of misfortune, but you know what they say: lightning

185

doesn't strike twice. Good job too, because the last time it did, we lost most of the roof.'

That was back in the eighties, thinks Bel, when Uncle Benedict was living abroad and renting the place out as a conference centre. One night during an electrical storm, a blaze had broken out at three o'clock in the morning. The small delegation of double glazing salesmen who were staying there at the time had wandered out onto the lawn debating whether the fire was a team-building exercise that had gone too far, or the real thing.

'Let's rinse you off, shall we?' says an impossibly tiny girl and Bel, feeling like a plastic-cloaked giant, allows herself to be led to the backwashes by this elf.

The girl shampoos and massages her head and Bel wishes she wouldn't. She knows she is meant to relax but her neck is killing her and now all she can think about is her first childhood memory of the house.

It wasn't long before Lance was born. Her mother was heavily pregnant and emotionally overwrought, what with Hugo being at work and Annabel on her school summer holidays, and a doctor was called who recommended complete and utter bed rest.

Normally when Mummy wasn't well Mrs Phelan looked after her and gave her jelly with sweet milk that came out of a red tin, but Mrs Phelan went to Ireland every August – it was something called tradition and there was no persuading her to change her mind.

Her father had been furious, it was all highly inconvenient and after a lot of shouting on the telephone, Bel had ended up at Kittiwake.

Daddy had driven her down and then almost instantly disappeared. Bel recalls having a suitcase, which her father had packed, and discovering that he'd forgotten to put in any underwear.

Uncle Benedict was staying at the house with a nice pretty lady, only they were in bed most of the day and Bel wondered if they had the same illness as Mummy, but the pretty lady said, 'You've got to be kidding, honey,' and Uncle Benedict laughed.

So another nice lady looked after her, only this one was quite old, like a grandma, and her name was Brenda and she did the same job at Kittiwake at Mrs Phelan did for Mummy in Claverley Avenue. She was a cook and a housekeeper, but most of the time, she sat in the kitchen drinking tea and chatting with her daughter as they podded peas at the kitchen table.

Bel was sitting on the floor by their feet; another little girl had come to play with her, they had some wooden bricks and a doll that Bel had brought down from London, which the other girl kept taking off her.

'She's the one I found in the drawer.'

'The baby . . .'

'Not such a baby now, she's a strapping thing.'

'Thanks to you.'

'That's right, love. Half-dead she was when I found her, poor little mite. If I'd not gone back into that room . . .'

'You thought it was a cat, didn't you, Mum?'

'I did, love. I thought one of the ratters had had a litter.'

'Not a kitten though, was it?'

'No, love, not a kitten. A little scrap of a thing, half-starved.'

'Not even a bottle of milk made up, nothing.'

'By the grace of God, that's what I say.'

'You brought her back to our house, kindness of your heart, Mum.'

'Well, I couldn't leave her, could I? That's the thing I can't understand: what kind of a woman leaves her own child?'

Bel was five years old at the time and had no idea the old lady had been talking about her. Half a century later, with her head bent awkwardly over a backwash, she finds herself overwhelmed with sorrow for the little girl that she used to be.

The elf is leaning over Bel and dabbing at her eyes with a tissue.

'You're not allergic, are you? Only some people find the smell of the toner a bit strong.'

Bel sniffs and blinks hard. She never did get that doll back off the other little girl.

29

Chicken Tikkagate

London, May 2018

Bel returns from the hairdresser's and flinches at her reflection in the hall mirror. The orange isn't particularly subtle; all that money to look like a parrot.

Sinking into the chair next to the console table where a threatening pile of brown envelopes awaits, she tries to suppress the flicker of temper that burns in her chest. Who is she trying to impress anyway? Andrew couldn't care less what she looks like as long as she occasionally buys sausages, the boys probably wouldn't recognise her in a crowd of middle-aged women unless she wore a name badge, and as for Lance and Freya ... How can she and Andrew compete with those two, with their glossy-magazine lifestyle and their casual glamour?

Ever since Bel received her brother's invitation, she has been questioning his motives for inviting them. They aren't close, so why should he decide to include them now? To show off, she suspects; to gloat and dangle Kittiwake under her nose.

But deep down she knows that isn't Lance's style. He has always

189

had that public schoolboy sense of entitlement. He has never needed to show off. Lance has always been oddly gracious about his good fortune, nonchalantly accepting his natural prowess at *everything* – swimming, tennis and even skiing, dammit. And now here he is, approaching fifty, playing lord of the manor and celebrating his big landmark birthday as befitting a man with a large Cornish estate. Anyway, it's not as if he can't afford to be generous. There are plenty of bedrooms, he doesn't have to worry about costs per head. Perhaps, as Andrew said, 'He probably thought it was a nice thing to do. Especially for your mum. After all, she's getting on a bit.' And her husband's right. Natasha is almost eighty – not that anyone would guess, her mother has always been remarkably well preserved and is the type of woman who gets a kick out of people presuming she is a decade younger than her years.

Come the dreaded party, Natasha will no doubt look more glamorous than I will, Bel admits ruefully, knowing that if proof were ever needed that she isn't Natasha's real daughter, one need only look in her wardrobe.

Her mother is chic, everyone says so, as befitting the daughter of Peggy Carmichael, a woman who was famously fond of the couture houses. 'But then Mama had the figure for that sort of thing,' Natasha always boasted, adding Peggy's mantra: 'Bread and potatoes, darling – you can never look good in clothes if you eat starch. Starch belongs on collars, not on the plate.'

Natasha would visibly cringe if she could see what Bel was wearing now. There are moth holes in her jumper and a marmalade stain on her trousers. 'Which is all very well if you're nipping out to walk the dog.' Her mother's voice floats all the way over from France. Only, I haven't got a dog any more, thinks Bel, fighting back the tears and feeling unsure as to what is upsetting her most: the prospect of seeing Natasha, Benji's death, or her hair, her horrible hair.

Don't be so silly, she reminds herself, running her hands through the offending 'do. It will wash out before the party. There's a few months to go yet. Plenty of time to lose at least half a stone, find something decent to wear, and if her hair still looks ridiculous, then she can always shave it off. With any luck, people will think she's having chemo and be nice to her.

Bel's reflection has the grace to look shocked at this notion. What a horrible cow she is, why would she even think that having cancer would be preferable to a few stupid marmalade stripes?

You need to get things into perspective, she admonishes herself, and then she bares her teeth in the mirror and makes a succession of ugly faces. Sometimes she hates herself and everyone else so much that it's difficult not to go round the house breaking things.

She reminds herself that there is a simple solution to all this agonising: she could politely decline the invitation, citing some fictional holiday, apologies and all that. Even better, they could actually book a real holiday and not even have to lie. She can go online this afternoon, see what's available (self-catering obviously, hotels are far too expensive for the four of them).

But all of a sudden she feels exhausted at the prospect. Does she honestly want to waste money on yet another lousy holiday let, somewhere miles down a dirt track with the boys bored and muti-nous and rather too big for a domestic back garden swimming pool? The last one three years ago in Mallorca had been a nightmare. She and Andrew spent most of the week in the supermercado buying cases of beer for their sons, who started drinking as soon as they finished breakfast and didn't stop until they belligerently fell into bed. And who could blame them, when the sleeping accommoda-tion had comprised two bedrooms rather than the advertised three, with the second bedroom a kiddie-sized bunk bed and a big box of toys in the corner? No wonder they'd drunkenly regressed into a fetid knot of constant boozy bickering.

So it's decided: they will go to Lance's party. Even if she has to pay the boys, they will go, put up a united front. Show Lance, Freya and her mother that they are a happy functioning foursome. And with this in mind, Bel boots up the old Dell laptop in the kitchen and fires off a delighted-sounding email to her brother.

```
Dear Lance -
```

No, far too formal.

```
Hey Lance, just got home from the
hairdresser's (fighting the tide of
grey, haha) where I spotted the article
featuring you and Kittiwake, in amongst
the celebrity-Botox-and-filler mags! I have
to say, the photos are phenomenal. Freya
is so talented, the place looks almost
habitable, haha, can't wait to see it in
the bricks and mortar, so to speak.
What a great idea to host your fiftieth
down there, no doubt Natasha will be very
excited at the prospect. As are we! Yup,
that's right, I wanted to confirm that we
can all come and we simply can't wait. Till
August then.
All our love to all of you
Bel xxx
```

Three kisses looks as if she's trying a bit too hard, Bel decides, and edits them down to one.

Feeling a little bit calmer for having finally RSVP'd, she digs the purloined copy of *Better Homes* out of her bag and leaves it on the kitchen table, so that she and Andrew can have a good laugh about it later, and comforts herself with the thought that Andrew probably won't even notice her hair, never mind say anything mean about it. He's not like the husbands of some of her friends who make nasty comments about their weight or wrinkles. Mind you, she acknowledges, it's not like Andrew's in any great shape either; his legs are spindly, his shoulders slope and his belly is as round as a football.

We've turned into each other's matching slipper, Bel admits to herself. There's precious little passion but we'd be lost without each other. Once again she feels a rush of gratitude towards her husband. If it wasn't for him, she wouldn't have everything she had craved since childhood, her own house and her own garden, complete with her own birdhouse hanging off her own apple tree, not to mention her own children – not that they are children any more. What has time done with those pink-cheeked boys, she wonders. Glancing at the school photograph on the kitchen windowsill featuring her sons in their regulation green sweaters, their hair slicked down by some unknown hand, it strikes her that if either of her sons had been abducted as children only to turn up some fifteen years later, she probably wouldn't recognise them. She'd still be searching for the sweetness and freckled snub noses of their primary school years.

Placing a coffee pod into the espresso machine and trying to ignore the fact that someone has left several jars lidless on the counter, Bel digs around in the cupboards for some ibuprofen. Her head is killing her. She attempts a few neck and shoulder stretches; if she had any sense, she'd roll out her mat in the living room and pull up a nice relaxing restorative yoga session on YouTube, but she can't be bothered, a handful of pills will have to suffice. Someone has put an empty blister pack of tablets back into the ibuprofen box and Bel feels her jaw clench in irritation. How can she keep track of things if people keep being so stupid and selfish? It happens all the time, millimetres of orange juice and single rashers of bacon are shoved back in the fridge, mere scrapings of Marmite returned to the cupboard. Why?

Hunger isn't helping her foul mood. The hairdresser took so long she missed her lunch and now it's gone three o'clock. Feverishly she pulls the lid off the cheese Tupperware and angrily eats the only remnant of cheese that has been left in the box, its rind mottled with green. Sod it, she refuses to go out again – restocking the cheese and the ibuprofen can wait. There's plenty of stuff in the fridge and freezer for a simple stir-fry tonight, though she'll have to do rice as there aren't any noodles. Bel hates cooking rice. Midway through her fifties she still hasn't mastered the art of making it light and fluffy. Last time she cooked rice, Jamie commented that it had the same consistency as a wet nappy.

Maybe he'd like to make it himself, thinks Bel, cramming a handful of crackers from the tin into her mouth and hauling herself upstairs. Her head throbs and the light is painful to her eyes. If she's not careful, she's going to develop a migraine. It crosses her mind that the worst things for a migraine are coffee and cheese, but it's too late to worry about that now. Sleep is the answer, if she gets a good few hours in a darkened room, with any luck she'll dodge a full-blown attack.

Closing the curtains against the spring sunshine, Bel slides into bed fully dressed. Some days really aren't worth the effort, but before she can close her eyes there is a shout from downstairs. Ed or Jamie, she can't tell, and she doesn't care.

'I've got a migraine,' she shouts from under the duvet. There is no response, no 'Can I get you a cup of tea?' Only the distant flush of a toilet.

At least that's something they all mastered eventually, she sighs, recalling the time when Ed developed a phobia about using the flush and she was forever encountering a toilet bowl of cheerful yellow urine, occasionally studded with little brown turds. Christ, her children have always been quite repulsive.

Bel finally closes her eyes, falls into a deep sleep and dreams of waking up in Kittiwake in a set of children's bunk beds.

Three hours later she wakes in real life to the sound of the doorbell. It's still light outside but it's nearly 8 p.m., and the smell of an Indian takeaway wafts upstairs. Of course they haven't cooked. Cooking an evening meal would involve making decisions, taking responsibility, finding pans, chopping boards and knives; it would require getting off arses to slice, dice and set the table.

If there were any biscuits left under the bed she would stage a protest and stay in her room, but hunger drives her downstairs. Hopefully they will have ordered her favourite chicken tikka masala, with pilau rice and a Peshwari naan. She hopes there is a jar of mango chutney in the cupboard, the stuff from the takeaway is thin and vinegary. All of a sudden she is ravenous – what a brilliant idea, a takeaway in front of the telly.

Andrew is at the door, handing over twenty-pound notes. As he turns around with a grease-spotted brown paper bag in each hand, guilt crosses his face at the sight of her.

'What are you doing up? I thought you were asleep, we weren't going to disturb you.'

She decides to be cheerful. 'Looks like there's plenty to go round,' she replies, smiling as if to say, See how pleasant I can be, how accommodating I am?

No one has got plates or cutlery out and there is only a tiny teaspoon of the good mango chutney left. Bel immediately goes into domestic mode, counting plates, laying out serving spoons and unpacking the cartons. There is a tinfoil tray with a cardboard lid labelled 'ch tikk mass' in black marker pen. At least someone's chosen her favourite.

Andrew calls the boys in and they pile through, immediately snatching at the food, karate-chopping poppadoms so that they splinter all over the work surface and clumsily spooning rice in the vague direction of a plate. Good job Constancia will be clearing up the mess tomorrow, thinks Bel. She waits until Ed and Jamie have taken what they want and disappeared back into the living room before helping herself, only to find the carton of chicken tikka

195

masala has vanished. 'That was Maisie's choice,' Andrew explains. 'It was all she wanted.'

Bel can't help herself. She marches into the sitting room and seizes the carton from Maisie's hands before she can pile the whole lot into Ed's Beatrix Potter christening dish, which she has taken to using 'because it's so cute'. Silly bitch.

'I think there's enough to share,' she tells the girl, then marches back into the kitchen where Andrew is sitting nervously at the table. She pours half a bottle of white wine into a large brandy glass that she has snatched from the cupboard, and she's still trembling with fury when Ed comes in to tell her that stealing food from his girlfriend is the behaviour of a 'madwoman'. It's all she can do not to pick up the Chardonnay bottle and swing it at his head.

'Oh, fuck off, baldy,' she says instead, and for a moment her eldest son looks a tiny bit hurt. Good.

30

Guilt

London, May 2018

Tikkagate was a week ago and Bel is still mortified by her behaviour, occasionally experiencing flashbacks of Maisie's face as she swiped the chicken tikka carton from under her nose. The girl's instant look of confusion and hurt, the same face her sons pulled when they were little, followed by the endless fraternal round of accusations, 'He's being mean to me.'

I was mean to her, Bel confesses inwardly, forcing herself out of bed. I acted like a crackpot. Even Andrew had looked embarrassed on her behalf. Why do I keep behaving like this, she asks herself, immediately excusing herself with a list of reasons.

Because she swans about in my house, wiping her arse on my toilet paper, shagging my son and smirking at me because I don't spend forty-five minutes a day shading in my cheekbones and pouting into the mirror.

Maisie pouts constantly; whenever she passes any remotely shiny surface, her face automatically turns into what looks like a sexed-up guppy, she lowers her lids and purses her lips, whatever time of day it is and whatever she's meant to be doing.

Bel finds it incredibly off-putting, especially first thing in the morning, plus the girl needs to cover herself up a bit more. It's bad enough having Jamie and Ed coming downstairs with what look like tent poles in their jogging bottoms; there's no need for Maisie to go around exposing her genital shaving rash. A rash induced by using Bel's leg-stubble razor, no doubt. Personally, she has never dared to wield anything that lethal near her own undercarriage, which is why Bel's nether regions are as neglected as the failed vegetable patch in the back garden.

I might make it a rule that everyone needs to be fully dressed for breakfast, thinks Bel, soaping herself down in the en-suite shower and realising that the sag of her belly has finally formed an official saddle of flesh that hangs low over her pubic region.

Her mother will make some comment about this development at Lance's party, no doubt. She will say something along the lines of 'Well, a lot of women thicken around the waist in middle age, dear, which is unfortunate. I think the only solution is discipline.'

Natasha has always been stick thin, but then Bel has never seen the woman enjoy a meal in her entire life. She approaches every morsel as if the dish may have been contaminated. The thought prompts a flashback to making a lemon meringue pie in the school holidays and her mother struggling to swallow a couple of mouthfuls. 'This pastry is very heavy.'

It's been four years since she actually saw her mother in the diminutive flesh and the realisation that it was at Benedict's funeral makes Bel feel weak. She allows herself to sit on the floor and let the hot water rain down on her head. The good thing about working part-time is that she doesn't have to rush off anywhere; sometimes it's good to just sit and think, even if the memories are too sad to bear.

Benedict died in Switzerland but he was cremated in London. He was only seventy-four – not old these days, but he had burnt himself out, the fags and the foie gras had finally done for him.

Lance had called her. She was furious that he knew before she did, but he explained that Natasha had been contacted first and she had called him – obviously, any excuse to speak to the prodigal son.

Bel hadn't seen her uncle very regularly for a number of years, and she regrets that now. They emailed occasionally; Benedict had always kept abreast of technology, quite literally ... she blushes at the memory of finding a selection of Polaroid photographs back in the eighties featuring his then girlfriend wearing nothing but a feather duster.

He'd hidden them in a vase. She was a redhead – natural, apparently.

At the funeral an elderly woman with grey roots and a face that looked as though all the skin had been pulled and tucked into a seam behind her ears approached Bel and whispered, 'I loved your uncle very much. He was a generous lover and a purveyor of the fine art of cunnilingus, years before it was fashionable.'

It had taken Bel a couple of minutes to match her to the girl in the vase and as she looked around the congregation, she realised that it was full of weeping women of a certain age with elaborate hairdos wearing sheer black stockings. 'Benedict's harem,' her mother had sniffed dismissively.

Without any warning, Bel's shower begins to run cold – and no wonder, she's been sitting here for nearly an hour, trapped in the past and using up all the hot water.

Wrapping herself in one of the few towels that is free from any form of Maisie grime – hair dye, fake tan, foundation, whatever – Bel wonders what Natasha would make of Maisie, should they ever meet. She doubts her mother has encountered anyone quite like her, a girl from a broken home on an actual South London estate, a girl who cannot pronounce her aitches and mispronounces 'ask' on purpose because she thinks it makes her sound more street, when in fact it makes her sound ridiculous.

On the other hand, Natasha might admire Maisie's figure and the girl does have a certain way with clothes. The other day she walked out in a pair of red satin martial arts trousers, which Jamie had persuaded Bel to buy for him when he went through a teenage kick-boxing phase, yet another short-lived hobby paid for and abandoned.

Bel sighs and drapes the damp towel over the radiator, wishing for the millionth time they had a heated towel rail, and some new towels for that matter.

As she goes about the dreary daily faff of swallowing pills, applying deodorant and finding acceptable underwear, she wonders how much money she and Andrew would have saved if they'd ever said 'No' to their children.

No, you can't have an electric guitar; no, you don't *have to* go to Reading Festival; no, you can't have another pair of designer trainers to replace the ones you may have left on a park bench; no, you can't have a lift to Alfie's house; no, you can't have ten boys sleeping over and smearing pizza all over the walls and filling the house with noxious fumes just because it's your birthday. No, no, no, no, your girlfriend can't move in and start causing havoc with the plumbing thanks to an overabundance of non-biodegradable face-wipes being flushed down the lavatory.

Bel had had a word with her about this issue only a couple of weeks ago, citing the environment and the damage carelessly discarded face-wipes can do and how eventually they could end up twisted around the guts of sea creatures.

The girl had looked at her blankly. 'But we're nowhere near the sea.'

Bel's conscience pricks, she knows she is conjuring up horrible bitchy thoughts about Maisie to justify her appalling behaviour last week. She needs to watch herself, she is starting to look unhinged.

200

Fifteen minutes later, Bel is down in the kitchen, infuriated to find the glossy magazine featuring Kittiwake has disappeared She was sure it was in one of the piles of paper that migrates regularly from the kitchen table to the dresser and back again.

She hasn't even shown it to Andrew yet.

Not that he'd pay much attention. Andrew doesn't do jealousy, decides Bel, and it strikes her now that his vague contentment annoys her. Andrew has never been particularly dissatisfied with his lot. For example, unlike many of their friends, he has never wanted a second home. He once told Bel that he couldn't see the point of spending all weekend on the motorway only to bleed another set of radiators.

'Andrew doesn't have much drive,' her mother once said of Bel's husband, and Bel bites her lip at the memory. She'd said it right after Benedict's funeral, when she came to stay for a couple of nights. Bel had made so much effort to make her comfortable. She'd put a scented candle in Jamie's bedroom and made sure the bed linen was fresh and properly ironed. She'd even bought croissants from Marks and a selection of expensive conserves, but the only comment her mother had made before they left for the service was to object to Bel's handbag. 'Brown with a black coat, dear?' The criticism of Andrew came late that night, when Bel had taken her mother some hot milk up to help her sleep. She was sitting up in bed wearing a white cotton long-sleeved nightgown and as Bel sat down on the edge of the duvet, her mother casually came out with it and in the split second after the words left her mouth, it was all Bel could do not to throw the scalding drink in her face. Instead, she had put the mug down on the bedside table that she'd cleared especially, made her excuses and left. The tears she'd wept in the days that followed weren't only for the loss of Benedict, they were also for the loss of any chance of making things better between herself and Natasha.

A couple of years ago, Andrew had paid for Bel to attend a

two-day residential creative writing course in Holt where she had written a poem about this tricky relationship.

It was called 'Jam', and the gist of it was that to maintain a pleasant taste and consistency, any communication with her mother had to be kept entirely sterile, otherwise the resulting 'jam' of their relationship became wasp-infested and mouldy.

When she read it out to the group, she had cried and everyone had hugged her, which was both lovely and appalling at the same time.

One woman with long unwashed grey hair and a jumper made from string had hugged her that bit too long and in the end she was glad to get back to Clapham, where she hid her poem at the bottom of her underwear drawer.

'My creative streak has never been properly fulfilled,' she mutters to herself, digging around for the magazine and getting increasingly furious about it.

Eventually, after a good half-hour of fruitless searching, she finds the magazine under an egg-and-bean-stained frying pan in Ed's room. There are no plates visible, just two dirty forks. They must have eaten their meal direct from the pan then, the savages.

Bel jumps as Maisie pushes the door open. She has a towel wrapped around her body and another on her head. She has been in the family bathroom, doubtless leaving the usual great scuzzy tidemark around Constancia's freshly scrubbed tub.

Bel feels caught out and guilty. She shouldn't be sitting here on Ed's bed, it's an intrusion. Maisie looks horrified to see her. Bel quickly reaches for the moral high ground.

'I couldn't find this,' she waves the magazine at Maisie. 'It's the house,' she garbles, 'an article about Kittiwake, the house where Lance is having the party. Look—' and she shows Maisie the pale lemon house, which now has a big sticky juice ring above the front porch.

'Oh yeah, cool.' Maisie sits down next to her. She is so close Bel can see the droplets of water that cling to her bony clavicle, smell the Aesop geranium bath oil, Bel's bath oil, a gift from Jan 'and all at Snow Nation'.

Still dripping, Maisie reaches over and turns the page of the magazine. 'Is that him then, your brother?'

Maisie is stabbing a damp finger at a photograph of Lance with his wife and children, artfully posed on the lawn at Kittiwake, the sea in the distance. They are all wearing navy and white, the children are interchangeable in Breton stripes and jeans, Freya is wearing a white shirt with a navy cardi, while Lance is all in navy. It brings out the blue of his eyes. Under his arm is a healthy young black lurcher; no putrid gums and parasitic worm for this mutt, notices Bel, momentarily thinking of poor dead smelly Benji.

'Only, you don't look anything like him,' insists Maisie in her slightly nasal Croydon whine.

'No, I was adopted, remember – I told you a few weeks ago? After I was found at Kittiwake, I was adopted by the family that owned the place. It was basically a convenient solution to the situation. Things were quite different back then, I think they're much stricter now – I'm not saying they should have adopted me, but . . . ' For a moment she wants to confide in Maisie – girls are so much more sympathetic than boys, all her friends with daughters say so.

Bel feels a pang of bitterness. Neither of her sons have ever shown any interest in how she feels about being adopted. It never crosses their minds that she might have struggled with her identity growing up. By contrast they have sailed through life in a lifebuoy of her love. Even when she dislikes her children, she still loves them, she can't help it. There is a leaky valve in her heart, she cannot turn the love off – even now, when they are drowning in it.

'He's like dead fit, you know, for his age.'

'Yes, I suppose so,' Bel laughs self-consciously. 'Only, when you grow up with someone you don't see them in that kind of light and there was a bit of an age gap.'

203

'Yeah, I was thinking that. Like, how much?'

'Let me think,' says Bel. 'I was born in '63 and Lance came along in '68, so five years.'

'Oh,' Maisie looks confused, 'only he looks like loads younger.'

'Yes, well, his wife doesn't have a proper job,' snaps Bel. 'So she basically spends all day stroking his ego and looking after the kids. I reckon I'd look a damn sight younger if I didn't have to do absolutely sodding everything.' The veiled accusation is wasted on Maisie.

'It says she's an interior designer and an ex-model.'

'Yes, I think she did do some modelling. She's a perfectly sweet girl, and I'm sure she's got her work cut out – I mean, look at the size of the house. I dare say she has help, but even so. And Lance has very high standards, he likes things—'

Suddenly Maisie stands up and the towel drops away, revealing her small sinewy frame. Reaching into the top drawer of Ed's tallboy, she pulls out some underwear, and proceeds to climb into what looks like a game of cat's cradle rather than anything that could possibly contain a human backside, before coming straight out with it. 'Can I come?'

Bel pauses. Obviously, the girl means 'Please may I come?'

Maisie has the grace to colour slightly. 'Only there's room in the car and, anyway, Bel, if I don't come I don't think Ed will, and if Ed won't, I don't think Jamie will either.'

It's blackmail, thinks Bel, trying not to notice Maisie's complete lack of undercarriage hair and the swing of her breasts as she lassos them into her bra.

'I'd have to ask Lance,' she mutters, stalling for time. 'It's his party and it's meant to be for friends and family.' Maisie pouts and instantly Bel feels the familiar kick of guilt in the guts – this is precisely what she promised she wouldn't do after last week's chicken tikka episode. She backtracks quickly, 'But I don't think he'd mind.'

Why would he? He probably wouldn't even notice. Lance is popular, no doubt lots of people have been invited to his party and at least Maisie will add some glamour to the Robatham clan, as long as she doesn't open her mouth.

So . . . 'Yes, Maisie, why not.'

Maisie scrambles onto the bed and begins to bounce.

'Cool,' she squeals, 'I've never been to Cornwall. I might dress up as a mermaid. Yeah, a sexy mermaid with silver hair and seashells over my tits.'

Maisie bounces again and lands on top of the open magazine and the perfect family portrait rips across Lance's face.

'Oh shit,' she says.

31

Two Months to Go

Kittiwake, June 2018

Freya is in her element. The preparations for Lance's fiftieth are all-consuming. She has spreadsheets on her Mac concerning yurt hire and catering contracts, notebooks containing finely drawn black ink diagrams detailing exactly where in the grounds the hog roast and ice-cream van should be positioned, plus a special Pinterest board, entitled 'top secret', on which she has gathered internet images from around the globe to help her decide on a decorative theme for Lance's party. So far, authentic piñatas from Mexico and quality calico bunting vie with retro fairy lights and vegan mosquito-repelling outdoor candles.

The food and drink are sorted. The party itself will be catered by a well-known local company based in Helston. She has arranged for trestle tables to be set up in one of the open-sided barns behind the house, with accompanying hay bale seating. Welcoming drinks (Pimm's/prosecco/ginger beer) will be served on the front lawn and on the Sunday, weather permitting, there will be a stroll down to the beach for a barbecue breakfast of rare-breed organic sausage sandwiches.

For months Freya has been sourcing vintage wicker baskets from Etsy to transport all the items required for this jaunt and she's found enough red-and-white gingham fabric locally to run up forty matching napkins on her state-of-the-art sewing machine.

As for the Friday evening before the festivities proper begin, she herself will prepare a large fish pie for the 'family only' supper; after all, they're in Cornwall, it would be sacrilege not to use the bounty of the sea. She has already tipped the taciturn fishmonger off about her intentions, but she will be ensuring that the freezer is well stocked with supermarket mixed fish supplies to be on the safe side. She has factored in how many potatoes she will need for the mash and how many jars of mango chutney will be required as an accompaniment. Lance insists on mango chutney with fish pie, and as it is his birthday then mango chutney he shall have. She will do a raspberry pavlova for dessert, but will not make the meringue base herself – she is prepared to put herself out for this party but not kill herself in the process. Oh, and there will also be a cheese board, naturally, for those who would rather eat Cornish brie.

Deep down, Freya knows she is doing this as much for herself as for her husband. If all goes to plan, her Instagram will be on fire after the party and the newly refurbished house and the weekend festivities will be her interior design calling card. Obviously most of the guests are friends and family, but one or two clients will be coming, influential locals who have supported her projects in the past.

Freya has put the children into tennis club for the first two weeks of the summer holidays; much as she loves Ludo and Luna, she has a lot to do and she can't do it with those two pulling at her, needing her attention, wanting snacks and trips to the beach.

As for the birthday boy himself, Lance is spending a lot of time in Exeter. Apparently there have been staff shortages and an abusive chef scenario to deal with. Lance is the boss, sometimes he has to go and troubleshoot, but he always comes home at weekends. She doesn't really mind, everything is tidier when he isn't here and the towels in the bathroom hang in the correct formation of pale grey to charcoal on the heated towel rail.

At the moment she is concentrating on the entertainment side of things, making sure the croquet lawn has its full complement of hoops, balls and mallets, and that the designated games shed is fully stocked with tennis paraphernalia so that guests can make the most of Kittiwake's two brand-new gravel courts. In a stroke of genius, she has even ordered a selection of old-fashioned pogo sticks and space hoppers off Amazon, because she thought it might be fun to transport Lance back to his seventies childhood. Maybe they can set up some sort of race, grown-ups versus kids? Freya's mother would certainly be up for it; Mari is only in her late sixties and still a keen skier, whereas her sister Elise had nearly made it as an Olympic figure skater – when you live in Oslo, you learn to ski and skate practically before you can walk. At the thought of her own childhood, Freya is hit by a wave of homesickness. They never have proper snow in Cornwall, not since she's lived here at any rate.

She is looking forward to seeing her mother and sister. Elise is bringing her three kids, who are similar ages to Luna and Ludo, which will be fun, especially since Freya has hired a couple of local girls to do some weekend nannying. Why should the mothers get lumbered with all the kiddie care?

Lance's London nephews are a good deal older than their cousins so it's doubtful whether they'll share the littlies' excitement about collecting hens' eggs in the morning or climbing into the new sustainable wooden treehouse that Ludo and Luna received from a very generous Father Christmas last year. She can't remember exactly how old they are – she doesn't know Lance's family very well. Apart from weddings and funerals, they hardly see them.

Freya looks down at the art deco square-cut emerald-and-diamond engagement ring sparkling on her left hand, which for insurance purposes has been valued at fourteen thousand pounds. What a lucky girl she is.

She and her husband met ten years ago when Freya was employed as the maître d' in one of Lance's restaurants. She had given him some tips on styling the place and when profits rose as a direct result of Berringtons' newly acquired cool reputation, Lance asked her to marry him, pushing the small velvet box across the tablecloth so she could see his grandmother's green-eyed ring winking up at her.

Peggy's ring. Peggy had been the original mistress of Kittiwake (Lance has briefed her on the family history). His grandmother was American and had bought the house as a holiday home. But then, in a nutshell, Ivor died, Teddy shot himself, Peggy was killed falling off a horse and Kittiwake had gone to Lance's Uncle Benedict, who in turn had eventually given it to Lance.

It's a blood thing, Lance once said, adding that eventually it would go to Ludo. She had bristled at that: why not Luna? 'Because Ludo is the oldest boy,' he explained. 'They can't share it, it would end up being sold, that's the whole point behind primogeniture, and yes, it's ridiculous, but that's the way it is. Luna can have the restaurant and the flat in Exeter.'

Freya's eyes drift to over to the piano and the photograph of Lance in his grandmother's arms. If she looks very carefully her engagement ring is visible in the frill of Lance's christening gown. Almost unnoticeable at first glance is a small girl with flyaway hair, peeping out from behind Peggy and holding a toy rabbit. This is Bel, Lance's adoptive sister.

Poor Bel, Lance once said, she might have got Kittiwake if she had turned out to be Benedict's child. Apparently he'd had some kind of entanglement with the mother, but Bel wasn't his, so she didn't inherit and he got it instead.

Freya sighs contentedly. Now the place is back to its former glory, they can all celebrate together. For a second she fantasises about the whole family singing 'Happy birthday, dear Lance' and her husband looking thrilled and handsome before leaning over the cake to blow the candles out.

She has spent a long time racking her brains over what might make a suitable cake for Lance's fiftieth. It needs to be what *The Great British Bake Off* would call a 'showstopper', something with enough wow factor to make the guests gasp. And, most importantly, big enough to hold fifty candles.

She has doodled and sketched for days on end. She had thought about commissioning someone to make a cake in the form of his favourite thing but decided that a Victoria sponge Aston Martin would be vulgar and then it hit her: the cake should be in the shape of Kittiwake. Because this party isn't just to mark Lance's half-century, it's also to celebrate the restoration of the family seat.

The August bank holiday weekend will be the first opportunity for most of their friends and family to see all the back-breaking work they've put into its resurrection.

Not that they'd physically done any of the grunt stuff themselves. Lance, despite kitting himself out with a high-vis jacket and a hard hat to 'inspect the site', had stood as far away from the action as possible and barely muddied his steel-toecap boots. Instead they'd employed a team of 'great guys' – Polish, mostly – who slept in one of the barns for the duration of the building works.

Naturally, when it came to tackling Kittiwake's precious interior, the Poles weren't allowed to get their bear-like paws anywhere near Freya's £200-a-roll wallpaper. Although Freya had insisted on calling herself the 'project manager', a team of specialists from London had been entrusted with the actual job of tiling, papering and painting. Eamon, Jilly and Davide had been accommodated not in the barn but in guest bedrooms, of which Kittiwake had plenty to spare. 'The gang of three', as Lance had fondly nick-named them, had plastered, painted, gilded and glued for months while Freya sourced vintage light fittings from the internet, pored over her Colefax and Fowler samples and dithered over the virtues of ceramic tiles versus Italian marble.

The London trio have only recently departed, leaving a trail of Farrow & Ball paint fumes behind them and acres of gleaming waxed floorboards. On the day they left, Freya sat on the bottom step of the sweeping staircase and breathed in, knowing it would never be as perfect as this again.

There are still a couple of rooms that aren't properly finished, but with two months to go before the party, Freya feels quite confident that every last tile will be grouted with time to spare. And now that the house is ready, it's time to put the finishing touches to the party plans.

Freya would normally make Lance's cake herself – her strudel is unbeatable – but when it comes to cake sculpting, she is out of her depth. It's one thing to order a dinosaur-shaped cake tin for Ludo's seventh birthday and go mad with the green food dye, but a scale model of Kittiwake is beyond her.

There is a woman in the village who has won prizes at local shows – Freya shudders involuntarily, she can imagine the kind of thing – she'll give her a call this afternoon. As long as she creates the design and this woman merely executes it, surely nothing can go wrong.

Confident that everything is in hand, she spends the after-noon capturing Kittiwake in watercolour. By August, the fat cream-headed roses on the east side of the house will be in their full second bloom, and the lilac bushes planted around the foot of the house will be thick with bees. It's going to be the perfect backdrop for the party.

Freya looks at her watch. She's got time for a spot of yoga before

211

lunch. Loping into the sun-drenched living room, she unrolls her mat and sits cross-legged for a moment with her hands in prayer position as her teacher has taught her. Then she closes her eyes, and thanks the universe for giving Kittiwake to Lance, and not to Bel.

32

School Days

Lawn House, London 1969–1970

Annabel's bedroom still hadn't been decorated, but Mrs Phelan said she was a lucky girl to have her own bookcase and a special big wicker basket to keep all her toys nice and tidy – and every night she was allowed to choose three soft toys to accompany her to bed.

Rabbit was still her best toy, although sucking her thumb and stroking his ears wasn't very nice after Mrs Phelan started painting Annabel's thumbs with something called bitter aloes. Daddy had brought it home from the chemist because 'thumb-sucking is a disgusting habit, sweetheart', even though Baby Lance did it.

Baby Lance got away with a lot of things in Annabel's furious opinion; for instance, even though he was meant to sleep in his very own nursery, he still got taken into Mummy and Daddy's bed when he cried at night and sometimes he was still there in the morning, lying on Mummy's chest like a big cat.

Occasionally, when Daddy had gone to work, Annabel was allowed to climb into her parents' bed too and in these moments, before she had to get dressed and go to school, she loved her baby brother, with his special milky smell and tiny purple lips with the little blister from sucking too hard at his bottle – she loved his chubby hands and the deep dimple in his cheek, just like Uncle Benedict's. She could have stayed with Mummy and the baby like this all day; for ever, in fact.

But her mother always had one eye on the clock and eventually she would start shouting, 'Oh God, look at the time, Annabel – hurry up now, you mustn't be late for school.'

Annabel attended Lawn House in Hammersmith, a small prep school for nice girls from good homes.

Lawn House wasn't particularly academic; it promised parents that their daughters would be educated in the value of good manners, how to make an egg cosy out of felt and the practice of saying Grace before meals, preferably with eyes screwed tightly shut and small sweaty hands clasped together in what looked like religious fervour.

Annabel found school a mixed blessing. It was bad when she wanted to wee-wee and had to put her hand up in class and the teacher said, 'Honestly, Annabel, can't it wait?' but good when it was story time and you all sat on the big square of brightly coloured carpet in the corner of the classroom and listened to the teacher read from a picture book. She also quite liked lunch, especially when it was a pink custard day.

As for the uniform, Annabel found it hard work – it was too big, the green tartan kilt itched, her shirt constantly came untucked and she struggled to do up the tiny buttons on the green cardigan. Then there was the hat, a dark green beret in winter and a straw boater with a green ribbon trim in summer. School was an endless stream of things she wasn't allowed to forget or she'd get in trouble. By the end of her first year Annabel was writing herself daily reminders in the back of her jotter in what Miss Langton described as 'a very neat hand', and from then on, making lists was a habit she would never grow out of.

What she hated about school was the lonely feeling in the pit of her stomach when she thought about Mummy and Lance at home together without her.

She imagined them by the fire, eating crumpets. It seemed like the baby was never off her mother's knee; he was crawling now and putting wooden blocks on top of each other and Mummy would call him 'a very clever boy', which seemed ridiculous when Annabel was the one sitting at her desk, sucking intently at the end of one of her plaits and doing very hard sums. Plait-sucking had taken over from thumb-sucking, but nobody seemed to notice at school and at home she did it in secret, mostly in bed where she had to have the side light on so that she didn't have nightmares.

Recurring nightmares plagued her childhood: she was alone in a dark forest and, like Red Riding Hood, she had a basket over her arm. However, unlike Red Riding Hood, she was wearing her school uniform, sometimes with the boater, sometimes with the beret. In the dream she got very hungry, but when she looked in the basket it was empty and the next thing she knew she was awake in a wet bed and had to tiptoe to the bathroom to fetch a towel to cover the wetness. The only person who knew was Mrs Phelan, and she promised not to tell – she simply checked Annabel's sheets and changed them if necessary. 'What does it matter?' she said to Annabel. 'With a baby in the house there's always plenty of washing to do, an extra sheet is neither here nor there.'

Mrs Phelan was very fond of Annabel. 'Poor little mite,' she said to Mr Phelan, 'stuck at the top of the house in that dingy little bedroom.' But Mr Phelan said it wasn't any of her business and in any case, all men want a son, someone to carry on the family name.

When Annabel was seven and in the green class at Lawn House, 'a terrible thing happened', which was 'most upsetting'. Her grandmother, the American lady, died. She fell off a horse in a place

215

called Sacramento, suffered something called a catastrophic brain bleed and never regained consciousness.

Annabel gathered all the information about her grandmother's death from listening in on her mother's weepy telephone conversations. She then repeated what she could remember to Rabbit and anyone who would listen in the school playground. She told the story so often that a not-very-nice girl called Elaine Shawcross accused her of being a show-off, which Annabel has to admit was a tiny bit true.

Natasha was in pieces, even Baby Lance couldn't cheer her up. After two days of listening to her wailing, 'My mother, my mother, no, Mummy, no,' Hugo told her to get out of bed and buck her ideas up.

So she did – she booked flights to America for herself and Lance. Hugo couldn't go because he had work and Annabel couldn't go because she had school, but Lance had neither school nor work so he went with her. Benedict was going too. Natasha had twisted his arm, she told Hugo. Even though she was still very sad, Annabel heard Mummy humming as she packed her suitcase.

Annabel was horribly jealous. It was so unfair, Lance was going to go on a plane before her and he was only two.

The night before her mother, uncle and brother flew to her grandmother's funeral, Annabel was allowed to stay up and eat supper in the dining room with her parents. Mrs Phelan prepared a roast chicken with all the trimmings because, as she whispered to Annabel in the kitchen, 'Americans only eat hamburgers.'

As Hugo carved, Natasha explained to Annabel that she, Benedict and Lance would be staying in a hotel so as not to intrude on Bobby Alessandro's grief.

'Who is Bobby Alessandro?' Annabel asked, and her mother replied, 'My mother's husband,' and Hugo chipped in bitterly, 'The one with all the money.' Then Natasha started crying again and left the table.

Annabel would have liked to eat her mother's abandoned potatoes but didn't dare – her father was always telling her she ate too much – and the realisation that she was going to be left alone with him made her cry too.

'Jesus H. Christ!' growled Hugo. 'Bloody hysterical women, what's the matter with you all?' and Annabel sobbed very quietly all the way through her pudding.

The night before her mother, uncle and brother were due to return from Sacramento, Annabel dreamt that the plane carrying them home burst into flames and crashed into the sea. She was woken up by her own screaming; her bed was sodden and her father was standing at the foot of it.

Hugo turned the light on and sniffed the air suspiciously. Annabel's little box room had started smelling because the bed had been wet on too many occasions to dry out properly. Hugo, livid, stripped the bed and made her inspect the yellow ring of stale urine that now permanently stained the mattress.

'How old are you? Are you a baby?' And he fetched a rubber sheet from the nursery and told her she must lie on that – no sheets, no blankets, no clean dry pyjamas, nothing but the clammy rubber sheet, because she needed to learn a lesson and if she didn't learn that lesson he would have her put in nappies. 'Do you understand me, Annabel?'

By the time Annabel got home from school the next day her mother and Lance were home safe and sound. Natasha was very quiet about her time in Sacramento, merely saying that the weather was very good and that sadly she hadn't had time to do any shopping, apart from some duty-free purchases at the airport.

She had however managed to bring home a bag of Alessandro's Finest Walnuts.

Hugo sneered at the brightly coloured bag on the table and muttered, 'As long as that's not all we're going to get,' at which point Natasha said she was very tired and if everyone would excuse her she would like to go to bed, which was funny because it was only half past six and even Annabel normally stayed up till seven thirty.

Several weeks later Annabel woke up, mercifully dry, to the sound of banging and shouting from her parents' bedroom. Annabel's wristwatch, which had illuminated hands, told her it was quarter past midnight. Maybe they had decided to move the furniture around? Creeping onto the landing but not daring to venture any further, she leant over the banister and between the bangs and yelps she heard her father shouting, 'A fucking bag of walnuts, Natasha! And Benedict gets fucking Kittiwake.'

In the morning Mummy was wearing sunglasses, which made Baby Lance laugh and laugh, but Annabel didn't join in. She was only seven but she knew that sunglasses indoors was a very bad sign indeed and she was extra careful about going to school without making a fuss or forgetting anything.

33

Best Friends

London, 1971–1974

Annabel was eight before she secured her first proper best friend. For months she had been trying out potential candidates, slyly stealing her hand into Laura McKinnon's when they walked in a crocodile to the park, only to be rebuffed when Laura refused to share her hymn book with Annabel in assembly the next day.

It was a slow and painful process; did she have bad breath like Gail Coombe, who had trouble with her adenoids and wore something called 'grommets' in her ears? Maybe she was a bit boring like Susan Meeks, who nobody minded, but no one actually liked?

Annabel was beginning to despair when, on a never-to-be-forgotten Wednesday afternoon, Miss Mills the art teacher, who was cardboard-thin and wore her hair in a bun, told the girls about the 'exciting project' she had lined up for them today.

Annabel squirmed with pleasure and got that funny feeling near where her wee-wee hole was at the idea of this exciting project. She loved Miss Mills and even though Lydia Golding was the best at art, Annabel often got stars for her work. Gold stars were the best, then red, then green – Annabel didn't count green stars, as they were usually handed out to girls who weren't very good but had 'tried hard and improved'.

The previous week Annabel got a red star for her picture of fruit in a bowl, which Miss Mills said was 'a very confident attempt at a still life'.

'This week we are doing portraits,' Miss Mills said now, and some of the girls flapped their hands together in that silent clapping way which was all the rage that term. Miss Mills asked the class to pair up, explaining they were to sit opposite each other and concentrate very hard and use paint not pencil. 'I want you to be bold,' said Miss Mills, 'so put your smocks on and choose a partner.'

Annabel hated this bit: the moment when some girls immediately paired up, reaching and squealing for each other as if to be partnered with anyone else would be a fate worse than death. She hesitated, not sure whether to wait to be chosen or to choose someone she didn't like but who would be grateful to be picked.

Fortunately for Annabel, a couple of pupils were absent due to illness that week and as a result a friendship reshuffle was required. Miss Mills took charge of the situation. 'Susan, you go with Gail, and Annabel, I want you to partner Clare.'

And just like that Annabel found herself teamed with probably the most popular girl in the class: the badge-wearing book monitor, Clare Holbrook.

For a second Clare looked a bit put out, but she was a cheerful girl and decided what with Wendy Thomas being poorly, then at least Annabel Berrington was better than smelly Gail Coombe who made piggy noises when she breathed.

Annabel couldn't believe her luck. In her opinion, Clare Holbrook was not only the most popular but also the prettiest girl in the class; she had golden hair like a princess, a heart-shaped face and lips that were the most lip-shaped that Annabel had ever seen.

Miss Mills said something about not worrying about the portraits looking exactly like their subjects; what she wanted was for the girls to 'capture the essence of their sitter'.

Whatever that might mean, thought Annabel, taking a deep breath and carefully loading up her brush with yellow paint. Clare wore her thick blond hair in high-up bunches which brushed her shoulders, and she was a robust, pink-cheeked child whom her parents referred to as 'the milkmaid' because there was something particularly wholesome and English about her, something that conjured up a cream tea under a willow tree.

At the end of the class, Annabel was awarded a gold star for her portrait of Clare. Miss Mills said she had done an excellent job on the bunches and captured something of Clare's 'lively and mischievous spirit'. At this point, the whole class burst into spontaneous applause and while Clare simpered with pleasure at being the centre of attention, it was all Annabel could do not to punch the air and yell 'At last!'

Poor Wendy Thomas – by the time she got over a particularly nasty case of impetigo, Clare and Annabel were inseparable, forever whispering into each other's ears and giggling together in the girls' toilets. And if Annabel was upset by Clare's muddy, sour-faced portrait of a plain-looking girl with lank beige hair and a horrible nose, she never said anything.

It wasn't long before Clare invited Annabel for tea. 'Who are these people?' enquired Hugo at breakfast. Natasha mumbled something in reply about Mrs Holbrook working in the BBC costume department and Mr Holbrook being a radio drama producer.

'Well, they sound awful,' Hugo responded, dabbing at his moustache with a linen napkin. 'I don't approve of working mothers, but as long as you don't get any ideas, darling, and if Mrs Phelan doesn't mind picking her up, then I'm sure she'll be fine.' It was only after her father stood up, casually swiping one of Lance's toast soldiers and leaving the room, that Annabel realised she had been holding her breath: *Yes*, her father said *yes*.

After school the following Tuesday, Clare's au pair Magda took them back to a tall thin house off King Street in Hammersmith, where Clare lived with her older brother and sister and three moulting cats who left ginger hairs all over a burgundy velvet sofa.

Annabel had never been in a house like the Holbrooks' before. For starters, it was very untidy, with books and papers and half-eaten plates of food all over the place. Both Mr and Mrs Holbrook smoked and Clare picked a semi-crushed cigarette out of an ashtray, put it between her lips and started strutting around pretending to be a model on the catwalk while Annabel shrieked with laughter on the hairy sofa. Clare was the funniest best friend in the world.

They were allowed to have spaghetti hoops on little tables in front of the television for tea and for pudding they had Mini Rolls: 'Magda doesn't cook,' Clare informed Annabel. 'She's a bloody waste of space, but what can you do?'

Annabel was thrilled – she'd been at Clare's less than two hours and already they'd done pretend smoking and actual swearing. But best of all was going into her new friend's big sister's bedroom and trying on her clothes and playing with her make-up.

Camilla was training to be an actress at the LAMDA, explained Clare; she was seventeen, while Christopher, her brother, was thirteen and away at school. 'Good bloody riddance,' said Clare, licking around the wrapper of her Mini Roll.

After the dressing-up and the make-up, they listened to records on the record player in the living room. On the wall above the fireplace was a big painting of striped lines in singing colours. 'It's modern art,' Clare shouted. 'It's the latest thing,' and together they danced to Camilla's Rolling Stones LP.

When Mrs Phelan came to pick her up, the old woman went all tight-lipped at the sight of the make-up on Annabel's face and as soon as they got round the corner she spat on her hanky and wiped it all off.

'Your father would have a canary,' she snapped. 'Now listen,

222

young lady – if you ever want to go back to that place again, you'd better watch it.'

For the remainder of their time at Lawn House, the two girls were inseparable. Annabel even risked inviting Clare back to Claverley Avenue and was shocked to see Clare morph into a quieter, duller version of herself, asking politely if she should take her shoes off in the house (yes, of course), shaking Natasha's hand and saying, 'Very pleased to meet you, Mrs Berrington.' At teatime she washed her hands and sat nicely at the kitchen table, while Mrs Phelan bombarded her with questions about Camilla and her showbusiness lifestyle and whether or not her parents minded about the sort of company she might be keeping.

Clare adopted a very adult tone with Mrs Phelan. 'Camilla is very dedicated to her art, Mrs Phelan – there's actually quite a lot to being an actress these days, it's not just showing off, and you have to be quite clever, what with learning lines and all that.'

Sometimes Annabel and Clare made up plays and one day, when they were ten, Clare made up a play about a man and a woman booking the same hotel room during a thunderstorm and deciding after a big argument that thanks to 'adverse weather conditions' (which was an actual phrase that Clare had heard on the television news), they should share the same bed.

Annabel was a great deal more embarrassed about stripping down and getting into bed with Clare than Clare was, and she froze up rather when Clare insisted that the man she was playing was a doctor and needed to examine the woman. They then attempted some French kissing, which was something Clare had seen her sister doing on the sofa when she was meant to be babysitting. Apparently it was also called 'necking' and Camilla did it with an older boy who secretly came round to the house on his motorbike and wore a leather jacket.

Clare referred to him as the 'Filthy Herbert' and told Annabel that she was going to 'Filthy Herbert' her before sliding her tongue

223

into her mouth. The only time Annabel had tasted anything remotely similar was when she had gone on holiday to France and her father made her try snails.

After that they each inspected what lay hidden inside the other's knickers: 'It will get hairy down there,' said Clare in her best doctor's voice, 'in a few years' time. As hairy as a cat down there.' When Annabel refused to believe her, Doctor Clare reverted back to real-life Clare and explained she had seen her sister and her mother in the bath. 'We're not a locked-door kind of family,' she confessed. 'My parents think society is far too uptight about nudity.' She then tried to explain what her father's willy looked like – 'sort of like a massive uncooked sausage' – before they both got dressed and embarked on a noisy game of Kerplunk.

At going-home time, when her au pair, aka 'the nicotine fiend', came to pick her up, Clare once again morphed back into polite mode and insisted on knocking on the drawing room door and simpering, 'Thank you very much for having me, Mrs Berrington!' before skipping off down the path with fag-ash Magda.

Annabel loved Clare with all her might and all her main but she didn't want to play the 'pant-inspection' game again; she preferred Monopoly.

34

Big School and Bras

When Annabel was eleven, Hugo decided she needed to go away for the duration of her senior school education.

'London day schools are all very well,' he explained to Natasha, 'but there's a lot of new money around and the fees alone aren't keeping the riff-raff out – there are a lot of scholarship girls who are being given places merely because they're clever, regardless of where they come from, which is what I call the thin end of the wedge.'

In Hugo's opinion, Annabel was in danger of 'getting in with the wrong type' and a good old-fashioned girls' boarding school in the English countryside would ensure that her future social group was more carefully vetted.

It was 1974; just a year since women had been allowed on the Stock Exchange floor for the first time and Clare's sister had joined the chorus of *Hair* in the West End. 'Fully starkers at the end,' Clare shrieked proudly. 'Tits, fanny, the lot.'

Annabel told her mother the exciting news, leaving out the 'tits and fanny' bit, but nonetheless Natasha spoke to Hugo about it and he declared that Clare was no longer welcome in the house – the family wasn't respectable. And that was that. 'I will brook no argument,' Hugo kept repeating.

A few nights later, Annabel punched Lance in the face when she realised he'd left the lid off her Silly Putty and it had gone all dry and useless.

'That's another reason to get her out of the house,' Hugo remarked grimly, inspecting the bruise on Lance's cheek. 'She's running wild. Let's face it, darling, we've done our best, but neither of us can be sure what sort of temperament might reveal itself if we don't keep her on the straight and narrow. Boarding school is the only solution.'

Secretly, Natasha was relieved; there was a look in Annabel's eyes sometimes that made her skin crawl – a look she recognised, if only for a fleeting second, a look of sudden hurt and surprise.

Hugo spoke to his mother about suitable schools and Heather Berrington suggested Downley Manor in Hampshire, where several minor members of the royal family had learnt how to sit nicely and sew.

After passing the requisite examinations ('all pretty babyish stuff', according to Annabel, who was near the top of the class at Lawn House), a letter eventually arrived informing Hugo and Natasha that 'the applicant' had been successful.

Enclosed in the letter was a 'uniform and extras' list. Downley Manor girls wore a grey skirt with a maroon cardigan and a white shirt, a combination which her mother insisted was 'terribly chic, darling', while the extras included items such as a hockey stick, tennis racket, tuck box and name-taped pyjamas.

It seemed odd to see pyjamas on a school uniform list and her mother told her that it would be exciting sleeping in a dorm with other girls her own age, but Annabel's bottom lip kept wobbling and there was nothing she could do to stop it.

'Go and splash your face with cold water,' Natasha suggested.

During her last term at Lawn House, Annabel occasionally cried in the toilets over the 'terrible situation' that she found herself in and her supposed best friend, who had already started having sleepovers at Susan Meeks's house, kept telling her that September was ages off, and she shouldn't worry because things might change.

But September came and nothing had changed. She didn't see Clare all summer and next thing she knew her trunk was on the roof-rack of her father's car and the entire family were setting off for Downley Manor.

Hugo had to stop the car twice for Annabel to be sick – soggy cornflake-splatters all over the kerb – and they hadn't even made it on to the motorway.

After it happened for the second time, Hugo said he wasn't going to stop again and for the rest of the journey Annabel sat with the window open and a plastic bag on her knee.

When they arrived, Lance ran his toy car up and down the beige walls of her dormitory, exactly like at home; the windows were too high to see out of and because she was the last of her dorm to arrive, she got the bed by the door.

'So if a murderer comes in, you'll be first.'

This prospect hadn't occurred to her – she actually thought being nearest the loo would be quite a good thing – but that's what Belinda Gray told her on their first night, as soon as Matron put the lights out. 'You first, then Carol, then Gillian, then me last – that's if he's got any strength left to strangle anyone else.'

Annabel went home for the half-term break with great big shadows under her eyes, which her parents mistakenly attributed to working hard.

'Well done, good to see you're knuckling down,' Hugo told her.

'Darling, go easy on the marmalade,' Natasha interjected. All Annabel did that holiday was eat and sleep; she was exhausted and starving and when it was time to return to school she cried all the way back to Hampshire.

It wasn't until Annabel was thirteen and found herself sitting

227

next to an anorexic fifth-former that she knew what it was to leave the dining table at Downley Manor feeling full.

The girl was called Linda. They didn't speak, Linda simply palmed food into Annabel's waiting napkin. Potatoes and meat mostly – Linda was very good about eating her vegetables.

Puddings were messier, especially when custard was involved, but the system proved to be pretty efficient and as Linda got progressively thinner, Annabel positively bloomed.

Matron had to let her skirts out and her thighs began to chafe; the sports mistress called her 'the hefty lump' and put her in goal when they played hockey, a decision which resulted in Annabel cowering at the back of the net allowing in goal after goal.

She needed a bra but her mother hadn't bought her one, so – much to Annabel's shame – Matron wrote Natasha a letter instructing her to do so.

'Poor you,' Natasha said, 'it must be very uncomfortable. I've never been particularly encumbered.' She took Annabel to Peter Jones where she was fitted with something that looked rather surgical. Afterwards they went to the toy department and bought Lance an Action Man for 'being so good while Mummy and Annabel did something so boring'.

Annabel's new bras were the colour of Elastoplast and bore no resemblance to the flimsy satin and lace garments that her mother wore.

Every day Mrs Phelan would hand-wash Mrs Berrington's 'smalls' in a froth of Lux flakes in a special plastic bowl that was kept under the kitchen sink.

Annabel's were simply chucked in the washing machine and within a couple of weeks had turned a liverish grey.

She and Clare wrote to each other for a while, Sunday afternoon letter-writing being encouraged at Downley Manor. Once a polite note had been dispatched to her parents, usually ending with, 'Oh and love to Lance xx', she was free to write to her 'best friend in all the world'. Eschewing her fountain pen for the special multi-coloured biro that had been in her Christmas stocking, Annabel chose a different colour for each new paragraph. She tried to make her time at boarding school sound as exciting as she possibly could, but she obviously struggled because when Clare wrote back, she began her letter with 'Boarding school sounds so boring, it should be called "boring school", haha!!'

Clare's notepaper was pink with a Love Is ... cartoon in the left-hand corner featuring a nude couple cuddling and saying 'Love is ... wanting m-m-m-more', which was quite rude. Clare gossiped on about how brilliant it was to be a day girl at St Paul's and how she luvved Marc Bolan and David Bowie, proving this point by drawing hearts around both their names, and did Annabel watch *Tiswas* on Saturdays mornings? Because 'it's ever so funny'.

No, thought Annabel sadly, at Downley Manor they had Saturday-morning school, when they played sport and did their homework. They weren't allowed to watch *Top of the Pops* either, so she hadn't seen the side of Clare's sister's head 'on the telly' the previous week. (Camilla had been asked to the studio by a camera-man and she was now doing modelling as well as acting.)

Clare enclosed a Photo-Me-booth snap of herself sticking her tongue out and crossing her eyes, which made Annabel laugh but feel sad at the same time. She couldn't compete. Clare was living a life firmly rooted in London, a world of Tube trains and Top Shop, while Annabel's world had shrunk to petty squabbles in the dorm over hair bobbles and being told 'no' all the time: No, you can't wash your hair, it's not Thursday; No, you can't have posters on your walls, it will damage the paintwork ...

Instead of being allowed to tape pictures directly to the wall, each pupil had a regulation-sized wall-mounted corkboard, 'for post-cards and memorabilia or maybe even a favourite poem, girls'. To be honest, even if she had been allowed posters, Annabel wouldn't have known what to put up – she didn't have a favourite pop star, she was so out of touch.

No wonder Clare moved on without her and eventually the letters petered out.

Eventually, desperate not to have an empty corkboard, Annabel, like many others at Downley Manor that term, pinned up a sepia-tinted stanza of 'Desiderata' which began 'You are a child of the universe' – even though the last thing she felt like was 'a child of the universe'; she mostly felt lonely and slightly bored.

For all the years that Annabel was at Downley Manor she never felt close enough to anyone to confide that she was adopted.

At prep school, it had been a badge of honour, a whispered secret to tell her classmates at playtime. Being a foundling seemed like something out of fairy tale – who knew where she came from, she might even have been royalty. 'My mother died in childbirth,' she repeated over and over again into different ears, 'and no one knew what happened to my father. He may well have been eaten by bears.' From the moment Hugo first told Annabel about her 'circumstances', she'd begun to imagine the backdrop to her adoption, stitching together a scene that she went over and over so many times that it became impossible to unpick. It was like a dream which she could see in vivid detail every time she closed her eyes, and it always began in a room full of babies.

In the room a man and a woman were walking up and down between rows of cots and peering in at the contents. She could always see them quite clearly, they are Mr and Mrs Berrington, Natasha and Hugo. The lady who will become 'Mummy' and the man that one day she will call 'Daddy' – when she learns to talk, that is.

But for now, in the scenario, she was a helpless baby wrapped up like a sausage roll in a blanket that had been numbered for identification purposes. Every time Natasha looked in a cot she shook her head sorrowfully. The hat she was wearing lived on top of the wardrobe in the master bedroom, it was pink with a little stalk on the top that wobbled as she shook her head. As well as her best hat, Natasha was wearing her good cream mohair coat, and she carried a handkerchief with which she would dab at her eyes occasionally. Mummy's hankies were kept in a silk pouch with Chinese embroidery all over it, they were lace-edged and mostly monogrammed – lots of things in the house had initials on, even Bel's possessions would eventually be monogrammed AJB, Annabel Jane Berrington, but not yet. Because right now she was a tiny baby without a name, or maybe she did have a name but it was an old name and it got lost along the way. Sometimes she wondered if once upon a time she was called Mandy. Because there were entire days when she felt like a Mandy. But on that day she was nameless and numbered and swaddled like a baby-girl Jesus in a pink blanket because this was how the mummies and daddies could tell if the bundle was a girl or a boy.

A doctor checked the babies, colour-wrapped them accordingly, and placed them on a sort of conveyor belt that delivered the freshly wrapped bundles to the nursery. This was where the pink- and blue-blanketed babies waited in their cots to be chosen. At the end of the day, the ones who hadn't been chosen were collected up, washed and fed ready to be put out again for inspection the next day. If the babies grew too big for their cots, then they had to go to a place called an orphanage, which was a 'crying shame' but 'that's the way the cookie crumbles', and anyway Bel should 'count her lucky stars' because this was her special day, this was her day to be chosen.

Natasha and Hugo had reached the point where they were exhausted by looking into tiny faces. They didn't mind whether they got a boy or a girl, what was important was that as soon as their eyes met, it was love at first sight.

As Bel got a little bit older and read stories in books about other orphans, she began to weave her own details around the facts that she had been told on her adoptive mother's knee and decided that her mother must have sacrificed her own life so that she, Bel, could live.

By the time Bel was nine, she could picture the scene: the sorrowful doctor turning to a nurse and explaining, 'It's either the baby or the mother.' And the mother, Bel's birth mother, whispering, 'The baby, the baby must live.' Sometimes Bel acted it out in her bed, squirming in pretend agony with a doll between her legs, repeating, 'The baby, the baby must live.' Until she grew out of playing with dolls, hit adolescence, and began to find the whole thing embarrassing.

No one else at Downley Manor was adopted and she didn't want to be the odd one out, 'the weirdo', because in a boarding school of around four hundred girls, anything that set you apart from the norm labelled you weird.

Too tall – weird; spotty – weird; fat – weird; short – weird; hairy – weird. Anyone who was spotty and tall was double-weird, and by the same principle anyone unfortunate enough to be short, fat *and* hairy was triple-weird.

Annabel was lucky that in her year there were at least three girls who were fatter than she was, so despite being on the heavy side of normal, she was just about acceptable. But she couldn't afford to push herself over the edge of 'normal' by being a bit fat *and* adopted, so she kept her trap shut, grateful that her family, real or not, provided an alibi of extra-normal.

A lot of girls were envious of Annabel's family – after all, her father drove a Jaguar, wore a good overcoat and sounded like Prince Philip, while her mother was attractive and beautifully dressed. 'Gosh, Annabel, your mum looks like she buys all her clothes in Paris.' What came as a surprise was the fact that her trump card was Lance: 'Ah, he's such a little cutie! You must love him so much, I bet you miss him when you're here.'

232

'Yes,' she lied, but the truth was she didn't. She missed the idea of him, but the reality was that he was a nuisance; for example, he didn't have clue how to put the lid back on a felt-tip pen.

The five-year age gap between Lance and his sister never seemed to narrow. If anything, boarding school succeeded in creating an even bigger chasm between Annabel and her entire family. Not that she ever told anyone – she always pretended to be utterly delighted about going home and made a big show of not being able to stand the wait. But the truth was, the person who made the biggest fuss of her when she did go home was Mrs Phelan.

'Darling, do remember Mrs Phelan is paid to help around the house, not sit and listen to you droning on in the kitchen,' her mother had to remind her. When Annabel was older she would realise one day that her mother never knew Mrs Phelan's Christian name. It was Caitlin.

35

School Days – Periods

At Downley Manor, when the girls were fourteen, they received 'hygiene classes' rather than sex education. Once a week, a middle-aged woman in a tweed suit cycled up the gravel drive to impart biological half-truths and religious nonsense to teenagers, some of whom were more gullible than others.

There was endless talk about becoming a woman and the sanctity of marriage and the union between a husband and a wife during which 'a seed might be planted, ahem, between the woman's legs', but there was no actual scientific detail. What Annabel could have done with was some kind of map.

During these classes there was never any mention of sex and pleasure. They were, however, shown an oddly graphic film about the effects of syphilis, during which two girls fainted and three cried.

Oddly enough, despite being one of the heaviest, Annabel was almost the last in her class to begin menstruating, and was fifteen before she eventually started her first period while she was at home for the Christmas holidays. Even though the cramps were awful and the whole experience was dreadfully embarrassing, it was also a sort of relief, because at last she would be able to join in with the other girls who talked about the 'curse' and being 'on' and going to Matron for two paracetamol and a hot-water bottle.

She now understood what the little paper bags that hung on the back of the toilet door were used for, although why the lady pictured on the front of the bags wore a crinoline and a bonnet was something that would continue to puzzle her for the rest of her menstruating life.

Annabel didn't tell her mother about starting her period, but one evening Natasha came into her room holding a glass of delicious-smelling amber-coloured liquid, which she proceeded to balance carefully on Annabel's bedside table. The drink contained a maraschino cherry on a golden sword cocktail stick.

'Poor you,' she began, pulling a funny downturned mouth face. 'Mrs Phelan told me, she said she'd bought you some pads – and there's always a supply in the airing cupboard, although once you get more used to it, you might want to use tampons. A lot of young women do, and it makes going about your life so much easier.'

Annabel was mortified. Her mother had never spoken to her like this before and she suspected her lack of inhibition might have something to do with the sweet-smelling drink on the bedside table.

'Thing is, darling, I have to tell you this stuff otherwise I wouldn't be doing my job, but now you've started your monthlies, well – it means that technically you can have a baby.'

Annabel felt herself blush. She was starting to feel like she was running a very high temperature, but Natasha carried on, oblivious, gently hiccupping every now and then.

'I mean, it won't happen for years, not until you're married and everything, because you're not that kind of girl, hic, but what I'm saying is that you have to be careful. You have a bust and men, well, men can behave quite badly given the chance and, well, hic, don't give them the chance, make sure you're never alone with a man. I mean a strange man, I mean obviously you can go out for lunch with Benedict, hic.'

And then Natasha laughed so hard that for a second she almost lost her balance and fell off the edge of the bed. By the time she straightened up again, the hiccups had stopped.

'Not that having periods automatically means that you're going to get pregnant and have a baby ... God knows, the pregnancy bit is the easy bit, your real mother could have told you that, but actually carrying a baby, that's the hard bit, keeping it in, because sometimes they don't ... they don't, what do they call it? Go full term, darling, babies die before they're born and it's all very sad.'

Natasha reached for her drink. Her eyes were glazed. She'd never mentioned Annabel's real mother before and something about what she'd said made Annabel suspect they had known each other. For a few moments there was a roaring noise in Annabel's ears. Stop! she wanted to insist. What do you know about my real mother? But the words wouldn't come out of her mouth and she sat mutely while her mother carried on.

'What I'm trying to say, Annabel,' Natasha slurred, 'is that it's not fucking easy being a woman, and most men are complete shits.'

With that, her mother drained the rest of her glass, removed the cherry from the golden sword with her fingers, put it in her mouth and sucked on it like it was a gobstopper. Her cheek bulged with the thing before she swallowed it, then she reached for the glass again and knocked back the non-existent dregs.

'That's all I wanted to say – goodnight, dear.' And with that her mother staggered out of the room.

Annabel wanted to call her back: there were things she needed to know, like how many sanitary towels was it normal to use in a day, what were you supposed to do if they didn't flush away and there was no bin, how many days should it last and when does the tummy ache go away? But her mother had gone downstairs before she could get a word out. Annabel could hear her getting the ice out of the freezer and slamming the tray against the worktop with more force than usual.

Lance was in bed, Mrs Phelan had gone home and her father was yet to return from work; he was having to 'work all hours' at that time, something about a difficult case. He kept missing his supper.

An hour or so later, when the period cramping became unbearable, Annabel crept down to the bathroom where the Anadin was kept and as she crossed the landing, she heard a strange noise from downstairs: her mother was crying in the kitchen.

She would have liked to comfort her, but she didn't have a clue how and anyway this was a side of her mother she didn't recognise.

The Natasha that Annabel knew didn't stumble around in her stockinged feet, waving drinks around and talking about dead babies.

A moment later the acrid whiff of burning wafted up the stairs, followed by a metallic clatter as something crashed onto the sink unit and a hysterical high-pitched voice screamed, 'Blood and shit.'

It sounded like a stranger in the kitchen, but it was Natasha, and as her mother opened the back door and ranted into the night sky, Annabel ran back to bed, turned on her radio and fell asleep. When she woke up the next morning, the batteries in her transistor were dead and her mother's eyes were red-rimmed at the breakfast table.

It was Lance that eventually broke the silence. 'What's the grill pan doing in the back garden?' he asked.

Annabel looked to where he was pointing. Lying on the grass next to the burnt-out grill pan were two charred and blackened fillet steaks. A single magpie picked at one of them in a desultory fashion. One for sorrow, thought Annabel.

That Christmas Annabel received books and stationery, a diary, a Kiku bubble bath set, the Fleetwood Mac album *Rumours*, a lava lamp and a navy-blue pinafore dress with red heart-shaped buttons, which was actually too young for her and worn with her ever-increasing bosoms looked faintly ridiculous.

A couple of days after Christmas, Annabel was at home alone

while her parents took Lance to a pantomime. Once the coast was clear, she tried phoning Clare but there was no one in, and Annabel returned to her lonely seat in front of the *Two Ronnies Festive Special* where, much to her delight, she caught sight of Clare's sister in a comedy sketch. Camilla didn't actually say anything but it was definitely her. Annabel practised how she would casually drop this shiny golden nugget of gossip into conversation once she got back to school. 'Well, actually, my friend Clare, the one who goes to St Paul's School for Girls in London, well, her older sister, you know the one that went starkers on stage, well, she's on the telly now.'

Hugging the information like a hot-water bottle to her chest, Annabel took herself off to bed. She was seeing Uncle Benedict for lunch the next day; she could tell him about Camilla, he loved gossip. What a good job she hadn't gone to the panto, she'd have missed *The Two Ronnies* if she had. Not that she'd been invited.

'I'm fifteen,' she reminded herself. 'I don't need pantos, I have periods and breasts and everything.'

36

Benedict and Bel Go Out for Lunch

London, December 1978

Benedict and Annabel's annual Christmas lunch had been a tradition for as long as Annabel could remember. He always took her
somewhere 'jolly' before he went off skiing. Benedict loved skiing.
'Some men like golf,' he would say to Annabel, 'but they tend to
be goons.'

Benedict made Annabel laugh more than anyone she had ever
met, even Clare.

He was the only adult who genuinely seemed to care whether
she was happy. She didn't really understand it – he hadn't any
children of his own and, despite being Lance's godfather, he never
singled her brother out for any special attention. On the contrary,
he seemed to have chosen her as his 'special girl', which was both
thrilling and a bit nerve-racking.

Every time Benedict phoned Natasha to arrange a lunch date
with Annabel, she lived in dread of her mother saying, 'Oh yes,
and this time, he wants Lance to come with you.'

She couldn't bear the idea of Lance tagging along. Lunches with

Benedict were sacrosanct – he always took her somewhere slightly glamorous and didn't bat an eyelid when she ordered a milkshake *and* a pudding.

On this occasion, he was taking her to Joe Allen's, which he promised her was 'terribly trendy'. Annabel thanked her lucky stars for Benedict; now she had something else to talk about at school, probably in the girls' toilets where they would all huddle around the radiators for warmth.

'Have you ever been to Joe Allen's?' she'd ask. 'It's terribly good fun, you see quite a lot of famous people there, even at lunchtime.'

On this particular occasion, they sat two tables away from Rula Lenska. Benedict nodded at the famous redhead and silently mimed an appreciative wolf-whistle under his breath.

'My friend's sister is an actress,' a bog-eyed Annabel told him. 'Have you heard of Camilla Holbrook?'

They were eating burgers and chips at the time and Benedict choked on his burger and had to drink all his vodka and all Annabel's Coke before he could stop coughing.

Rula Lenska looked slightly annoyed.

Once Benedict recovered, he ordered a fresh round of drinks and they continued as usual to catch up on each other's news.

Annabel told him she was neither happy nor unhappy at Downley Manor, that she was pretty good at some subjects but a bit bored in others, she acknowledged that she wasn't unpopular but that she didn't have a best friend and she missed Clare, who she never saw any more because her father didn't approve of her, mostly because of her sister.

Benedict raised his eyebrow at this, but let her carry on.

This was why she liked talking to him: he never interrupted her or told her what she should think, he didn't criticise her table manners or demand she put her shoulders back – he let her be.

Sometimes he confided in her too, things she wasn't expecting to hear. Once, when she was about twelve, he told her that his own mother, Grandma Peggy, had despaired of him and that he and Natasha had had a 'perfect' older brother who died when he was twelve. He didn't tell her how, he simply said, 'His name was Ivor.'

The dead brother information shocked Annabel and she never repeated it to anyone, especially not her mother. It wasn't that it was a secret, it was more that the words were too sad to say out loud.

After he told her about Ivor, Annabel was determined to be nicer to Lance. Much as he annoyed her, she couldn't imagine life without him.

Benedict was allowed to ask her questions that no one else was. He asked her about boys and she told him that she pulled out pin-up pages of pop stars from *Jackie* magazine, but because they weren't allowed to put pictures on the walls at school she kept them in a file under her bed and put gold stars on the ones she fancied the most.

Benedict told her it sounded like a very efficient filing system and that she should come round to the mews house one day and put his girlfriends in some kind of order.

Last year Annabel made a list of Benedict's girlfriends in biro on a paper napkin. Beside each name she wrote down the hair colour and build. In the end she had had to ask for two more napkins, because the tally came to over thirty.

At this lunch, Benedict told her he was seeing a girl called Alannah who had a very charming long neck, like a swan.

'Swans mate for life,' Annabel said.

'In that case,' he replied, 'Alannah is not like a swan, she is more like a giraffe,' which made Annabel laugh until Coke came out of her nose.

They laughed a lot when they were together and Annabel noticed that, when they laughed, women looked at Benedict and smiled in the same indulgent way they smiled at babies in prams.

Her uncle was both dishy and adorable, if a tiny bit fat around the middle. 'It's the cheese,' he admitted, prodding his own gut. 'Brie is my downfall.'

His paunch didn't seem to matter. Once, when they were having lunch at the Savoy Grill, a young woman tiptoed over while her partner had gone to the gents and passed Benedict a scrap of paper with her telephone number on it. She was called Glenda.

'Remember Glenda,' Annabel reminded him and the two of them sniggered for ages, while the waiter took away their ketchup-smeared plates and handed them both a dessert menu.

But before she could choose, Benedict put his serious face on. 'And how are things at home?'

If he hadn't asked the question, she wouldn't have given it any thought, but now she did, she had to admit that her parents seemed to be shouting at each other more than normal and that her mother was sometimes weepy and too tired to get up in the morning, and when she did, her face was puffy and she had to put on a lot of make-up to look normal.

'Mummy keeps saying she's getting old,' she told Benedict. To which he replied, 'Well, that's ridiculous, she's not much older than me and I'm in the prime of my life.'

And he looked it. Benedict was enjoying life as a thirty-eight-year-old bachelor (but not of the confirmed type) who lived in a mews house in Belgravia, cleaned daily by a bad-tempered Mexican woman who loved him more than life itself. He bought his groceries from Harrods food hall but mostly ate out around Kensington and Chelsea; his social diary bulged; he dabbled in antiques but didn't have to work full-time any more because he rented out Kittiwake to a small hotel chain. In short, he managed to maintain a lifestyle that was the envy of his peers, most of whom were now saddled with neurotic wives, mouths to feed and school fees – like Hugo, in some respects.

He nodded when Annabel told him about her father working late and the rows that ensued. 'I think sometimes Daddy can be a bit mean to Mummy,' Annabel confessed.

Benedict rubbed his face with an invisible flannel and lit a cigarette, even though he normally didn't smoke until after they'd had their pudding.

'It's very important that you are kind to Natasha – I mean your mother,' he said. 'She needs our support. Sometimes when women reach forty they stop feeling attractive and start wishing they were younger.'

Annabel hadn't a clue what Benedict was talking about – why should her mother care how old she was and what she looked like? It wasn't like she had anything really horrible to worry about, like homework or school dinners.

Bored by the subject of her parents, she turned her attention to dessert.

'Can I have chocolate ice cream today, please?' she asked.

It was only when she finished her double scoop with extra whipped cream that Annabel decided there was something she wanted to ask her uncle; something her mother had mentioned that kept coming back to her, like having a drawing pin stuck in your shoe. She couldn't ignore it any longer.

'Did my mother . . . ' she began, before pausing and starting again. 'Did Natasha know my mother?'

Benedict looked slightly taken aback. 'What on earth makes you ask that?'

'Oh, just something she said. It sounded like they may have met.'

Benedict wiped his invisible flannel over his face again. 'They didn't exactly mix in the same circles, but it's not impossible.'

'Then *you* knew her?'

'I didn't say that.'

But Annabel was not stupid. 'If you say "They didn't exactly mix in the same circles",' she argued, 'then you must have known what kind of circles my mother mixed in.'

For once Benedict couldn't meet her eyes. 'That's not the point.'

Suddenly Annabel needed to know something very urgently, once and for all.

'But she is dead, isn't she, my mother – she is dead?'

'Yes,' Benedict exhaled as if he'd been holding his breath. 'Yes, your mother died when she was very young and Natasha and Hugo adopted you and I for one have been grateful every day of my life that they did.'

'Why?'

'Because you are very dear to me, young lady. Now let's finish up here and see if there's a small treat I can buy for you.'

In the end he took her to a tiny place in Soho where a man in leather trousers chopped her bunches off and gave her a long 'Purdey' bob. Annabel's hair, if unfashionably putty-coloured, was thick and took to the style immediately.

'Next time I'll put a few streaks in it for you, darlin',' the hair-dresser gushed.

Annabel could have wept with relief – not only was she going back to school after the Christmas holidays as a fully menstruating woman, she had seen a mate's sister on the telly and had lunch with Rula Lenska, but to top it all off, she had a trendy haircut as well.

That night Natasha and Hugo rowed about whether Benedict should have asked their permission before cutting Annabel's hair.

'Oh, for Christ's sake, Hugo,' was the last thing Annabel heard her mother scream before she placed a pillow over her head and willed herself to fall asleep.

37

Finances

1979

The week after Annabel turned sixteen she was summoned to see the headmistress. As she sat outside Miss Clements's room on a hard wooden chair staring at a display of dried hydrangeas on a polished console table, Annabel couldn't for the life of her imagine what she had done to merit this 'little chat', as her form teacher called it.

It couldn't be her behaviour, she wasn't particularly noisy or disruptive; in fact you could accuse her of being the opposite, considering she had a tendency to fall asleep, face-down and dribbling on the desk, when a lesson bored her.

She wondered idly if something had happened to Natasha or Hugo, or maybe even Lance? What if Lance had died, what if history had repeated itself and Lance had drowned or been run over or had a deadly allergic reaction to something?

By the time the school secretary popped her head out of the office to say that Miss Clements was ready for her, Annabel was convinced that Lance was dead. She could see herself by his tiny grave, an inconsolable Natasha wailing beside her, clutching a glass of amber-coloured liquid in her black-gloved hand.

Her eyes were already brimming as she stepped into what the sixth formers called Miss Clements's lair.

The headmistress was an elderly woman, overdue for retirement, her room was stuffy and Annabel noticed the bin was full of toffee wrappers. She sat up very straight so that whatever had happened no one could accuse her of slouching.

'Ah yes, Annabel Jane Berrington,' intoned the head. 'Let me see, yes, here we are.' She peered into a ledger. 'Termly fees . . . unpaid.' Her lips pursed with disapproval as she continued, 'Normally I would contact your parents in the first instance, but it has been brought to my attention that the fees are usually paid by a Mr Benedict Carmichael and I wanted to check with you that nothing untoward has happened to this Mr Carmichael.'

'He's my uncle,' Annabel explained. 'I saw him the other week, he had a burger and chips and was as right as rain.'

'Well, that's a relief,' smirked Miss Clements, as a cat curled itself around her swollen ankles. 'Then I shall alert your parents to the situation and let's hope it can be resolved before further action needs to be taken.'

Annabel felt herself burn bright red. 'Does anyone else know?'

'Oh, we are very discreet,' muttered Miss Clements. 'Although obviously if the fees remain unpaid, a pupil cannot stay, no matter how remarkable her academic record – and yours, I might add, does not fall into that category.' And with a wave of a puffy ringless hand, Annabel was dismissed.

Back at Claverley Avenue a few days later, Natasha held a piece of paper under Hugo's nose. She was trembling with rage and the paper shook like a leaf. 'The school fees – Benedict hasn't paid them. He always pays her school fees, it was part of the agreement. We can't afford these on top of Lance's. Why hasn't he paid them?'

Hugo knew why but he couldn't tell his wife. 'It'll be some silly oversight. I'll go and see him. You mustn't get like this, Natasha, it's not good for you.'

If only he still had some of those little white pills the doctor had given him earlier on in their marriage – whatever they were, they were like magic beans; within thirty minutes of taking one 'like a good girl', his wife had become docile and biddable. Unlike the shrewish woman in front of him now.

She was too thin these days, exactly like her mother, Peggy, had been. Natasha wasn't eating enough and her scrawniness was a turn-off. Hugo liked his women to have plump arms and fleshy hips, all the better for biting and pinching. He liked tits that filled bras. She had over-fed Lance, that was the problem. So thrilled at last to have a living child, she had let him suck the shape out of her, and now there was nothing left for him.

Hugo arranged to meet Benedict in a pub across the road from Victoria train station. It was a rough kind of place, where they were unlikely to accidentally bump into anyone they knew – a vital consideration when discussing private matters like these. The pub was all sodden beer mats and pockmarked dartboard, the kind of dive where exhausted commuters had 'one too many' before facing the long slog back to the suburbs, and office girls in sweaty nylon tops hung around hoping for another gin and orange before wobbling home alone.

Benedict arrived first. The place was heaving but he managed to find an empty corner near the gents. Every time the toilet door opened, the stench of urine was overpowering. Benedict sat with a pint in front of him and a bag of pork scratchings, trying not to breathe in.

Hugo turned up half an hour late, and bought them both fresh pints before joining Benedict in his smelly corner.

He barely managed to sit down before Benedict muttered, 'I will tell her if you don't stop it.'

Hugo wiped the foam from his mouth, 'Stop what?'

'Seeing that Holbrook girl, the actress – she's too young and you're married.'

Hugo laughed, 'Have a look around you, old chap, I don't think I'm the only one with a bit on the side.' And as if to illustrate his point, a middle-aged man sitting on the next banquette slid his hand beneath the skirt of a mousey young woman who started licking his ear and wriggling around like an electric eel.

The man had dandruff on his shoulders, and in his non-exploratory hand he held a cigarette which was in danger of burning his fingers.

'Natasha's my sister,' Benedict protested.

'I know, old boy, and she's getting into a right old paddy about the school fees.'

'I'll pay them, if you promise.'

Hugo smiled wanly. 'Thing is, Benedict old chap, in some respects the school fees might not be the only thing you owe. We took Annabel in believing she was yours, flesh and blood, so when you think about it, all these years of bed and board, shoes, holidays and suchlike – plus the girl eats like a horse – then I should say you've got off pretty damn lightly.'

Benedict put his pork scratchings down.

'Are you in trouble, Hugo?' he asked.

'Not exactly trouble,' his brother-in-law replied. 'Let's just say things are a bit tight – a couple of investments have gone AWOL, usual nonsense, and it's left me a bit short this month. So if you can clear the school fees . . . '

And with that Hugo went to the bar to get another round while Benedict watched transfixed as the wriggling eel girl lifted a wallet out of the middle-aged man's pocket, only to pass it to an even younger girl sitting on the edge of an adjacent stool.

Dandruff Shoulders wasn't the only one to get turned over that evening. By the time the two men parted company, Benedict had written a cheque to cover the school fees and lent Hugo a further seven hundred and fifty pounds.

'I wish I did know,' he told his brother-in-law as they drunkenly shook hands. 'I wish I did know if Bel is mine. I'm terribly fond of her.'

'No doubt you are, old man, but give us some credit, you couldn't have taken care of her. Besides, you've never had the slightest proof. Let's face it, you were in a pickle, she was a baby and Natasha needed a baby. Simple.'

But as Benedict weaved his way home, he decided that it was time to do what he could to find out, one way or the other. He'd read about some new technology – what was it called? DNA testing. Lord knows what it involved but he needed to find someone who could do it for him, a doctor. Harley Street would be the place. He knew a couple of chaps with practices down there. Dr Whatshisname had got him out of a bit of a hole concerning his todger not six months ago. The thing had started burning, he could barely pee it stung so much, and then a yellowy pus began to ooze from the very tip of it. Benedict had thought he was going to die. 'Die of fucking?' his doctor laughed. 'Not quite, mate, but it is syphilis and you could go mad, so let's get some of these down you.' And he prescribed Benedict a two-week course of what he referred to as 'nuclear-strength antibiotics' and advised Benedict to use a condom should he find himself in bed with girls who 'put it about a bit'.

Yes, McFarlane was the man to go to, he'd get in touch with him first thing in the morning.

38

Benedict Finds Out

McFarlane was sniffy about the idea of DNA testing.

'It's pretty new-fangled,' he told Benedict. 'I don't actually have the technology here in the surgery, there are all sorts of legal implications and the girl isn't eighteen, we'd need the consent of her adoptive parents. However,' he continued, 'there are other steps that might prove easier to take. For starters, Benedict, you came to me with an infection some months ago, which leads me to think you might have been slightly careless over the years and yet this is the only potential offspring you are aware of?'

Benedict nodded. 'I'm not really a condom kind of man, and fortunately most girls these days are on the pill.'

McFarlane smiled. 'Nowadays, yes, but back then – when was it, the early sixties? – that wasn't the case. Anyway, it won't do any harm to run a couple of basic tests before we go down the DNA route. Oh, and the other thing we need to find out is your blood group. Blood groups can be very useful when it comes to paternity cases, so we'll take a couple of samples today, blood and semen, and see what comes up.'

Ten minutes later, having taken a syringe full of blood, dark red with haemoglobin, Dr McFarlane sent Benedict away to masturbate into a plastic cup.

Fortunately, a battered copy of *Playboy* did the trick in no time. Benedict couldn't help feeling proud of how much of a sample he was able to produce.

'Nearly had to ask for another cup,' he smirked at the nurse.

McFarlane's receptionist called him ten days later and Benedict agreed to pop in to discuss the results with the doctor, though it seemed ridiculous that he couldn't be told everything over the phone and save himself a journey.

'Confidentiality,' the receptionist had retorted before putting the phone down.

A couple of hours later, Benedict was sitting opposite Dr McFarlane. To his surprise, he found that his hands were sweating like Swiss cheese as he watched the doctor open a file and scrutinise the results. He was desperate for a positive sign, a nod, a smile, but McFarlane's face was as blank as an empty Scrabble tile. Eventually, the doctor looked up at Benedict over half-moon glasses, cleared his throat and began to speak.

'There is no possible way you can be this child's father. The proof is conclusive, even without a DNA test.'

Benedict slumped back in the expensive black leather chair. 'Ooof,' he said. 'Ooof.' It was a ridiculous noise, but he couldn't seem to catch his breath. He would have liked to put his head on his knees, but he didn't want to seem overly dramatic.

McFarlane must be used to this. Breaking bad news was part of his job; people came to him with funny lumps and nagging doubts, and some would go home reassured and relieved, but others . . .

'I'm sorry.' Dr McFarlane had added a measured dose of sympathy into his tone, though not too much, because it wasn't as if Benedict was going to die, he simply wasn't a father and it wasn't as if he'd ever thought he was, not truly, not deep down.

'The fact is, old boy, you don't have any sperm.'

Benedict almost laughed; what a chump this man was, he had sperm, his sperm had very nearly spilt over the top of that plastic cup the other week, he had sperm to spare.

'That's semen,' McFarlane explained patiently. 'You ejaculate normally, no woman would ever know, but the fact is, there is no sperm in your semen, so you cannot father children. Oh, and the other peculiar thing, you have a quite a rare blood type: you're AB rhesus positive. Less than five per cent of the population share your blood group, so it's something you should know, should you ever need an emergency transfusion.'

Benedict had gone pale.

'I'm sorry, old man,' the doctor continued. 'Do you need a glass of water?'

Benedict didn't want a glass of water – he wanted something stronger. He waved away the offer, stood up on shaking legs and started backing out of the door, unable to look at another man.

'I know it's a bit of a shock,' said McFarlane, 'but it doesn't make you less of a man.' Benedict put his hand up, he was in no state to continue this conversation. 'Send me the bill,' he instructed, as if he had merely been to the garage to have his car MOT'd, and he left the building having completely forgotten his umbrella.

As he crossed Cavendish Square, his mind reeled. If only he hadn't interfered. Things had been fine. Not knowing was agony, but knowing what he knew now was even worse.

She wasn't his, there never had been any chance. Benedict began muttering angrily under his breath: 'Of course she isn't, I'm an idiot, she's nothing to do with me, absolutely nothing, zero, shit, oh, Christ.'

He found a pub at the back of Oxford Street and drank three double gin and tonics in quick succession, threw up in the gents and went home feeling lonelier than he ever had in his life. He'd always thought that one day he might settle down, marry some nice girl with wide child-bearing hips, maybe even move to Kittiwake and raise a brood down there. But not now. He couldn't marry anyone now, it wouldn't be fair . . .

And in that moment, Benedict resolved to make the most of the cards he had been dealt. There would always be girlfriends and dinner dates, and in some respects he was a lucky man, he had the mews house in London and the income from Kittiwake, he hadn't got cancer, he wouldn't die . . . though at precisely that moment, he wouldn't have minded if he did.

A week or so later, he informed Hugo that he had conclusive medical proof that he was not Annabel's father, but nonetheless he would continue paying her school fees.

'I'm still very fond of the girl,' he insisted over the phone. 'We have a bond, I can't quite explain it, but, Hugo, I don't want her to know about this. It's not as if she ever suspected anything in the first place, no one has ever hinted that I could be her father. I can still be her favourite uncle.'

But he felt demoted.

Hugo played it very cool, 'Well, what did you expect? I always said the mother was a filthy little scrubber, looks like I was right. Could have been anyone's child, but not yours. Oh well, at least now we know, though I'm not sure how Natasha's going to take it.'

Natasha didn't take it at all well. She told Hugo that she felt she had a stranger in the house, that ever since having Lance she had found it harder and harder to feel any real affection for Annabel, not when she was conscious the whole time that she wasn't her real mother. The presumed link with Benedict had been the only thing that made it possible to accept her.

Hugo wished he hadn't broken the news so late at night. Natasha had been hitting the hard stuff even harder than usual, drinking steadily since before dinner.

'It was easier when she was a baby,' Natasha slurred. 'Babies are

253

so vulnerable, you love them because they need you, but as children get older, you start to see them for who they really are, only I don't know who she is, I only met her mother once.'

Hugo raised his eyebrows, 'I didn't know you'd met her.'

Natasha laughed; a mean, metallic mirthless sound. 'Oh, don't play silly buggers with me, Hugo, we both know I was at that party. She knew who I was, and she certainly knew who you were too.'

Hugo held his hand up. 'Whoa, Natasha, I think you're getting a bit carried away. I think you need to calm down.'

Only Natasha wasn't going to calm down, she was upset and on her fifth martini, so if Hugo wanted a fight then she was more than ready to give him one.

'Oh, come off it, Hugo. Young and blond and tarty, I knew at first sight she was right up your street, what with those big tits of hers – no wonder she lost her balance.'

Hugo was silent for a second. Natasha could be startlingly venomous at times. His voice became cold and sanctimonious: 'Hold on, Natasha, let's not forget that the woman in question died that night. Yes, she may not have come from the same background as either you or I, but the fact remains she was a young woman who lost her life in a tragic accident less than a year after she gave you the child you so desperately wanted.'

At this moment, Annabel – home for the Easter holidays, unable to sleep, and listening from her usual perch on the stairs – heard a glass being hurled at the wall, and her mother yelling the words, 'But I didn't want her child! Why should I want a child whose own mother didn't want her? Whose own mother abandoned her in a drawer? I wanted my own child – adopting the baby was your idea, yours and Benedict's, and now it's backfired on the pair of you.'

There was the sound of a scuffle behind the closed door and Annabel scurried back to her room, knowing full well who would come off worst. No doubt her mother would be wearing sunglasses again in the morning.

Once she was safely under the bedclothes she tried to make sense of what she had heard. So her mother was dead, but she evidently didn't die in childbirth. She'd got it wrong all these years, there was no death-bed wish to save the baby 'at all costs'.

The truth was, she had been abandoned, her mother hadn't wanted her, it was as simple as that. The woman who gave birth to her had left her in a drawer because she wanted to go to parties rather than look after her own child. Annabel switched on her side light as if seeing clearly would help her think clearly.

As for Benedict's involvement, how come he suspected he might have been her father? If he thought that, then he must have slept with her mother.

Annabel knew about the rudiments of sex, if not how it actually worked. Occasionally she would slide her finger into her vagina and wriggle it around the small gristly knot that made her breathless. She knew that this was roughly the place where a man needed to put his penis for intercourse and possibly conception to take place. She had done the drawing of the sperm and the egg.

Benedict must have put his penis into her mother's vagina, only he wasn't her father – but she never thought he had been.

Everything she knew was wrong, no one had ever told her the truth, she had been lied to since she was a tiny baby, unwanted and given away. Why would anyone do that to a baby? Was she really so unlovable?

Why had Natasha adopted her, was it because she thought she was her brother's illegitimate baby, or was it because she didn't think she could ever have her own child? Would she even have bothered if she'd known that one day Lance would come along? Lance who had the same eyes as Natasha and Benedict?

As for her birth mother, whoever she was, it seemed the only thing she had to thank her for was a big pair of tits.

Annabel's breasts were the bane of her life. No matter how hard she tried to disguise them, strange men gawped at them on the street and attempted to grope them in crowds.

A distant memory surfaced and Annabel blushed with shame as she recalled being touched up by Father Christmas.

She'd been about thirteen when she'd accompanied Lance into the Harrods grotto and been forced by a foul-breathed Santa to sit on his knee. She had perched there, feeling stupid and not saying anything, while an elf gave Lance some stupid toy and Father Christmas touched her breasts.

Annabel switches off her bedside light. She is so furious she doesn't know what to do with herself.

39

Annabel Rebels

No one knew what was wrong with Annabel. She had never been a particularly difficult girl; bright, certainly, definitely university material, not Oxbridge, but possibly Manchester or Leeds, lots of opportunities out there for a girl like her.

Adopted, yes, the school were well aware, but that was years ago, when she was a baby – it was no excuse now. The girl was fifteen. There were other pupils in her year who had much more difficult personal circumstances to contend with: Ellen Highshore's father was brain-damaged after scaffolding fell on his head as he walked to the office two years ago; Nina Brady's mother ran off with a woman who lived three doors down, and poor Penny Clarke's mother had only recently died after a prolonged and painful struggle with cancer.

Penny shared the same dorm as Annabel, which made it all the more peculiar, but the undeniable fact remained that the letters were found in Annabel's locker. All the letters Penny's mother had sent her daughter in the last few months of her life, personal letters, full of shared memories and hope for Penny's future. Letters only a mother could write to her daughter, Penny's most treasured possessions, kept in a leather box along with some of her mother's jewellery – which strangely enough hadn't gone missing. Whoever had tampered with the leather box had ignored the cameo pendant, the topaz-and-diamond ring and the marcasite butterfly brooch, and taken only the letters.

Nobody could understand why anyone would do such a thing. Penny had not long returned to school after her mother's funeral. She had no reason to suspect that Annabel was the culprit, she thought they were friends – Annabel had found her crying and comforted her on several occasions.

But then Miss Clements ordered a locker search.

Annabel couldn't explain it either, but she didn't deny taking them – she merely hung her head and stared at her shoes in the headmistress's office.

Miss Clements 'regretfully' decided to suspend her until the end of term. She would only be allowed back into school to sit her O levels, during which time she would sleep in the San and speak with no one.

Because Hugo refused to come and fetch her, Annabel was put into a taxi and dropped off at the train station with enough money to buy a single ticket home. For a moment she thought about catching a train to anywhere but London. Her father had made it plain on the phone that she'd brought shame on the family name, and that he and Natasha were disgusted by her behaviour.

Annabel had no idea how she was going to face them, let alone how she was going to cope with living at home in that stuffy little box room, trying to revise for her exams with a ten-year-old brother charging around the place.

Lance didn't go to boarding school. Natasha refused to let him go, so he was still at his prep school in Westminster, where he showed promise on the clarinet and had private tennis lessons: 'Both musical and sporty,' Natasha crowed.

Even worse than the prospect of facing Hugo and Natasha was

the idea of having let down Mrs Phelan. Mercifully, her carriage was empty, and as Annabel sat snivelling forlornly, she realised that even if she attempted to put into words what had made her do it, no one would ever fully understand.

How could she explain that all she wanted was to know how it felt to have a mother who loved you more than anything else in the world?

That's why she had taken the letters. She hadn't intended to keep them, she only wanted to read them. She was going to put them back but Penny had returned to school earlier than anyone had expected and by the time Annabel had finished her last lesson of the day, the letters had been discovered in her locker and all hell had broken loose.

An hour later, as the train pulled into Waterloo, Annabel's face was swollen and blotchy and she was utterly confused as to what her next step should be. She didn't have any money for a taxi and was clueless about how to navigate her way from Waterloo to Barnes on foot. Anyway, what if no one was in when she got home? She didn't have a key; she pictured herself sitting on the step and waiting in abject misery, what if she needed to go to the loo?

With the prospect of facing the music getting closer, Annabel's mind flitted to other alternatives. She didn't have to go home, she could always sleep rough or give hand jobs to old men and get enough money for a hotel. Sonia Baines had demonstrated how to wank someone off only a couple of weeks before – she said the main thing was to swap hands now and again because it was very tiring.

In a state of despair, Annabel stepped down from the train only to find to her utter amazement that a familiar face was waving to her from beyond the ticket barrier. It was Benedict – Benedict had come to meet her. Annabel was thrilled and slightly embarrassed; she hadn't seen him since she found out he wasn't her father.

Her shyness soon melted away. He looked exactly the same as he always did and he was smiling, like he always did, which was odd because surely everyone in the whole wide world hated her guts at the moment.

She felt the sting of tears again and by the time he had wrapped her in his arms, she was blubbing like a baby. He said nothing, gave her his handkerchief that smelled of limes, took her case and propelled her towards the taxi rank.

'I thought we'd have some lunch at mine so you can tell me all about it.'

Back at the mews house, Benedict tied a red gingham-frilled pinny around his waist and put a pan of water on the hob. He had cooked a chicken – 'One of my exes showed me how,' he explained. 'To be honest, it's not that difficult; the most important thing is to remember to remove that disgusting plastic bag of giblets. Now, I'm afraid gravy is beyond me, so we're having it cold with new potatoes, a nice green salad and Harrods' very own home-made mayonnaise.'

He had even chopped some parsley to scatter on the new potatoes. Annabel felt tears coming again; she hadn't expected anyone to be kind to her.

Benedict reached into the fridge. 'I know you're not old enough to drink, but I'm going to have a nice glass of chilled Chablis, and even though you are in utter disgrace, young lady, you may have half a glass, to take the edge off, and then we'll decide on a course of action.'

He handed her a glass and they looked each other in the eye for the first time since she got off the train, and instantly both of them felt a great flood of relief. Benedict because he didn't feel any different about her, even though he knew categorically that she wasn't his, and Annabel because she knew that, whatever she said, he would listen, and that knowledge caused a huge weight to lift from her chest.

'OK, why don't you go upstairs, get out of that uniform, splash your face with some cold water and by the time you get down, lunch will be ready,' her uncle said.

Annabel did as she was told and once she was back in civvies with her face washed and her hair brushed, she realised that although she was still upset, she was also starving and actually looking forward to her lunch.

Benedict waggled a serving spoon at her as she came back down. 'Now, as you can imagine, Hugo and Natasha are very upset about the suspension.'

She was glad he referred to them by their Christian names and not as her parents. It was time everyone stopped pretending.

'But,' Benedict reached into a cupboard for some plates, 'as I pay the school fees, it's me who should feel pissed off.'

Benedict hacked at the chicken with a bread knife. Annabel could tell it was a bit overcooked, but she carried the salad bowl and the potatoes over to where he had arranged some cork placemats and they sat down at a small round walnut dining table squeezed between the sofa and the staircase.

During lunch, he regaled her with stories of his work and latest girlfriend, the twin vases he was convinced were Ottoman that turned out to be Woollies fakes, his latest squeeze's peculiar habit of licking his ears which made him feel both sticky and uncomfortable, and the sudden appearance of punks on the King's Road. 'Rather sweet, if you ask me – every generation needs to rebel, and I was lucky, I had the sixties, Summer of Love and all that.'

But after they washed up the dishes together in his tiny galley kitchen, he finally got serious. Once the last plate had been dried, he removed the pinny from his waist and said, 'OK, Annabel, let's thrash this out.'

He brewed a pot of tea and nodded to the sofa, but Annabel refused to sit down; she paced the small sitting room and looked at anything other than Benedict's face before she finally began to speak.

'I overheard them, Natasha and Hugo. I've always been good at sitting on the stairs and listening, I've done it ever since I was very small, and I heard them talking about you, me and my birth mother.'

Benedict's hand trembled at this and milk slopped onto the tray holding their tea. Annabel didn't stop, she continued talking in a strange emotionless monotone.

'Basically, in the space of ten minutes flat, I found out that everything I ever thought I knew was a lie. My mother didn't die in childbirth, she walked out on me, and Natasha didn't choose me because I was special, she adopted me because she didn't think she could have a child and she thought you were my father. Because if you were my father, then it meant we shared some family blood, so it wasn't like she was adopting a complete stranger – only she was, and I think she suspected as much as soon as Lance was born, I think she knew then that I didn't belong.' Annabel took a breath and carried on. 'And I know taking those letters was weird and wrong, but the thing that's completely weird is that even though Penny had lost her mum, I was still madly jealous of her, because I knew how much her mother loved her and I needed to read those letters to see how that might feel.'

Benedict was chain-smoking now, ash and stubs piling up in the bright yellow ashtray with the word RICARD printed on the side. Annabel continued to pace, picking up the odd ornament and putting it down in slightly the wrong place, rearranging the animals around the toy farm on the windowsill.

'But the thing that confused me most is you. Why you had never told me that you might have been my dad and that you knew my mum, that you knew her well enough to *sleep* with her, and that you could have described her to me and told me what she sounded like – if she was taller or shorter than me and what kind of shoes she wore.' She was holding a glass paperweight now and Benedict wondered for a moment if she was going to throw it

262

at his head. He wouldn't have blamed her – it was high time she was told the truth.

He got up and opened the cupboard under the stairs. Annabel was still tossing the paperweight from hand to hand.

'I've got something to show you,' he said, and he drew the curtains.

40

Benedict Tells What He Knows

Annabel stopped pacing and watched as Benedict switched on a table light and disappeared into the cupboard under the stairs. Seconds later, he emerged with a large attaché case in one hand and a dusty cardboard box under his arm.

As he dropped the box onto the dining table, Annabel could see that it contained reels of ciné film, stacked up on top of each other, each neatly labelled.

Frowning with concentration, Benedict rooted around and eventually dug out one of the circular tins. Across the lid in grey and white Dymo tape was a word and a date: KITTIWAKE 1962. Breathing heavily and swearing occasionally, he then lifted a projector from the attaché case and assembled it on top of the nest of tables by the sofa, positioning it so that the projector was pointing at the wall directly opposite.

Finally, with everything set, he lit yet another cigarette, patted the empty seat on the sofa next to him and told Annabel to sit down.

Reluctantly, she did as she was told and perched next to him, sitting bolt upright with her knees clamped together, staring at the blank wall.

The machine began to noisily whir, projecting a beam of light which immediately illuminated a bright white square on the wall. Grey spots flickered, followed by a random succession of upside-down numbers. Then, in faded Technicolor, the wall seethed with an indistinct blur of bodies. The picture quality was poor – Benedict fiddled with the lens on the front of the projector and the focus became a little sharper. The blur became people dancing, hair swinging, elbows jerking, and then the camera wheeled abruptly away from the dancers and over to a table crowded with bottles: wine, gin, vodka, Martini, and a large tin bath which looked like it might be full of punch, before swivelling back to the dancers again.

Apart from the mechanical whir of the projector, there was no recorded sound. Fingers silently clicked in the air and Annabel wished she knew what was playing on the invisible gramophone.

Some danced as if they were being subjected to electric shocks, others moved more slowly, eyes closed in ecstasy, while a few mooched self-consciously, staring fixedly at their own feet. Suddenly a small blonde with a lopsided bouffant and a low-cut top jiggled right in front of the camera, raised her arms in the air, threw her head back for a moment and then shimmied her beautiful face right into the camera lens.

In that single moment Annabel could see the thickness of her eyeliner, the glue of her false eyelashes, the slightly crooked teeth that flashed inside that delighted fleeting grin and then she was gone, the blondness and the smile simply vanishing, and in the space left behind there was Benedict, young and thin and hungrily following the girl with his eyes.

The older, fatter Benedict sitting next to her on the sofa coughed and stopped the tape as it tickered to a halt. He pointed at the screen and said, 'That was your mother. That was Serena.'

She made him play it at least ten times over, sitting forward now on the sofa, craning to take in every last detail of the woman, each time trying to glimpse something new.

Her earrings? Gold hoops.

The colour of her eyes? Green.

Eventually she allowed herself to laugh at young Benedict's slightly gormless expression as the object of his obvious desire dropped out of shot for the umpteenth time.

'I think I might have slept with her that night,' he admits. 'I thought you might have been mine, and I wish you were.'

She could have cried again then, but she didn't – she'd already cried enough and her face was still sore.

Benedict fetched another bottle of wine from the kitchen and offered her another small glass and then told her everything that he could remember about her mother.

'Her name was Serena – she came from Southend and she sounded like a fishwife. I had never met anyone like her; she was naughty and funny and preposterous and a bit reckless. We were never what you might call an item, but we did sleep together.'

Annabel interrupted: 'Did you know she was pregnant?'

'No,' answered Benedict. 'I went abroad for the summer, came back to London in the autumn to do spot of work – I seem to remember a letter she wrote saying she wanted to talk to me, but nothing about expecting a baby, so I forgot all about it. Then I went skiing over Christmas and the New Year, stayed out in Courchevel a bit longer than I intended, got mixed up with some nutty girl, went back to Kittiwake to hide for a while – and there you were.'

'And my mother?'

'Nowhere to be seen.'

Without realising it, Benedict had reached for her hand, and she let him.

'Brenda, the housekeeper, she looked after you. There's a farmhouse down the track, you lived there for a while, but . . .' He shrugged. 'Natasha was so miserable and kept losing all these babies

266

and you were a baby who needed a home and it seemed the ideal solution. Hugo had all the right contacts, your real mother was nowhere to be found, all I had to do was sign some papers.'

Annabel had so many questions she didn't know where to begin, so she started with the end.

'So how did she die?'

'Ah, well . . . ' And now it was Benedict's turn to get up and pace.

'We found out later that she was actually living in London, Earls Court. She'd changed her name, which made things a little tricky – called herself Renee Culpepper. Then one night she went to a party, this rather smart house, Mayfair, there was a balcony and she fell. And I was there – not when it happened, she was already lying on the pavement when I arrived, but I was able to be with her, I held her hand until the ambulance arrived, but by then she had gone.'

'And my parents were there too?'

Benedict looked shifty. 'I didn't see them, but a lot of people were there, it was one of those big society bashes. There were a lot of parties like that in the old days. By the time the police came, a lot of people had disappeared – they had reputations to worry about, wives who didn't know where they were, that sort of thing. But that doesn't alter the facts: it was a warm night, she'd been drinking, sitting out on the balcony and she lost her balance. No one actually saw what happened. It was an accident, Annabel.'

'Have you got any photographs of my mother?' Annabel demanded.

'No.'

But he had. He'd kept a newspaper cutting reporting her death, it was on the front page of the *Evening Standard*: 'Nightclub Hostess Falls to Death at Society Party'. The grainy photograph accompanying the story made her look harder and older than she was.

'What about Kittiwake? I went when I was little once, but I can't remember anything.'

'Yes.' He reached into a drawer and showed her a small battered black-and-white photograph of a large turreted house covered in some kind of foliage. On the gravel drive in front of the house was an old-fashioned car and standing next to it were five people, two adults and three children. Benedict studied the photograph as intently as Annabel before muttering, 'Everyone in that photograph is dead, except Natasha and me.'

Outside the mews house, the light faded and Benedict and Annabel sat in the dark holding hands as he told her how he and Natasha had witnessed their brother's death down at Kittiwake and how his mother didn't have enough love left over for her other children once he had gone and how his father gambled everything away and decided to end it all on the eve of Benedict's twenty-first birthday.

And then when both of them had wept some more, Benedict, who was quite drunk, phoned Natasha and – pronouncing his words very carefully – informed his sister that he had Annabel safe at Cadogan Mews and that she would be staying in Belgravia for a couple of nights until everyone calmed down. There was a short pause before Benedict raised his voice and informed Natasha, 'I couldn't give a shit what Hugo thinks – we'll speak tomorrow,' and put the phone down.

For a moment they looked at each other in appalled silence before collapsing into giggling hysterics. The next thing Annabel knew they were making toast in the kitchen before settling down in front of the television to watch *Celebrity Squares*.

Later, when Annabel said goodnight to her uncle, Benedict asked her if she'd like to visit one day.

For a moment, she looked at him, confused.

'Kittiwake – would you like to go back there one day?'

'One day,' she said. 'Yes.'

41

One Week to Go

Kittiwake, August 2018

Freya slides her egg-whites-only omelette out of the pan and onto a hand-thrown ceramic plate. She made a series of these last summer, each irregularly dipped into indigo slip before being fired and glazed. Sadly, they don't seem to be dishwasher proof but the cleaner will insist on putting them in at seventy degrees, leaving Freya to pick out the jagged fragments once the wretched thing finishes its cycle.

'Ridiculous,' she tuts to herself, everyone is so hopeless, but she can't manage the place by herself. Since she took on the role of chatelaine of Kittiwake, it has become a full-time job, and with the party looming ever closer she occasionally finds herself hating the place.

The house is voracious, it gobbles up her time and sucks huge amounts of money from the joint account. There was a moment, a glorious moment, when the refurbishment was complete and the place was perfect, but all she can see now is its gradual decline, the smudges of her children's fingerprints on the copper-clad kitchen island, a wonderful burnished metal rectangle that in certain lights sets the entire room ablaze.

What she needs is another, secret kitchen where she can prepare meals without destroying the pristine beauty of the show kitchen. An Ikea job with cheap Formica work surfaces would do.

Kittiwake requires constant attention, one daily cleaner isn't enough. There are too many staircases for a single Hoover to de-fluff, too many brass door handles for one pair of hands to polish.

As for the windows, several local cleaning companies won't touch them, their ladders aren't long enough, the turrets are too treacherous, a sudden gust of wind and a man could lose his life. Then there are the gardens; they may have been designed by a crack squad of internationally renowned landscape architects, but they need more care than a sick child. Aphids and mildew attack the roses, black-headed caterpillars have been found amongst the rapidly browning box hedges, and now she can only hope that they can get the party out of the way before the infestation turns the entire ornamental hedging into a hideous brown crisp.

Faen, she thinks, mentally swearing in Norwegian, that's all I need, a great big stinking invasion of black-headed caterpillars.

A week to go. Freya swallows her omelette uninterestedly, how boring to be forty-two and reduced to having to keep a constant eye on her figure.

It was the caesarean with Luna that did it, the puckered emergency slash across her belly that seems to have perma-nently damaged her abdominal muscle tone. Try as she might, she cannot completely firm up her scarred midriff; her bikini days are over.

Not that anyone can tell. She is otherwise lean and rangy, she has a personal trainer who comes twice a week to take her running and do weightlifting, plus she visits a neighbour's barn conversion on Tuesday mornings for an invitation-only Ashtanga yoga class.

After the class, the women drink pink prosecco and complain

270

about their husbands, who are variously too fat, dull and not rich enough.

Freya keeps quiet during these conversations. So much so, they've nicknamed her 'Smug Freya'. She's heard them discussing her: What has she got to complain about, with her big house, tennis court, sea views and studio outbuildings . . .

'How many bedrooms again, Freya?'

'Oh, it used to be ten, but one has been converted into a dressing room, so only nine now.'

'Do you have a pool?'

'No.'

'Oh!'

Lance won't – he is happy for the children to swim in the sea and in hotel pools when they go on holiday, but the one thing he will not have is their own private pool.

He's superstitious, because a child drowned here years ago, how silly. A pool would firm up her tummy. Bloody Lance, he always has to have his own way.

On paper, everything is 'theirs', but it isn't – it's his. Lance wears his sense of entitlement more lightly than some, but he is still coated in it, like a wetsuit. What else would one expect from an upper middle class, privately educated, about-to-be-fifty-year-old man?

Not that he looks fifty. 'Virile' is the word that springs to mind when she thinks about her husband; he is broad-shouldered, his hair is thick, he tans easily, he oozes charm, everyone likes him.

She tries not to worry that he spends so much time in Exeter during the week, or that sometimes he has to stay in London to meet with prospective clients – 'pressing flesh', he calls it. She's fine with all that, as long as the flesh is of the hand variety and not of the young female breast or buttock.

Freya forces her paranoia to one side. There is too much to do before next weekend to start worrying about her husband's fidelity.

She digs her notebook out of her ancient Mulberry satchel, wondering not for the first time why she hadn't simply chartered a yacht around the Greek islands to celebrate her husband's half-century. It would have been a damn sight easier and possibly a good deal cheaper than this wretched party.

Once she has her trusty notebook and pen in hand she feels better, more in control. She needs to check her to-do list, make some calls, send a few emails, stare at the three new outfits she has bought for the celebrations, and then check the BBC online weather forecast – but only the once, she mustn't get obsessive about it.

The prospect of bad weather consumes her every waking moment. After a ten-week summer heatwave (surely global warming is even more reason to have a pool installed?) August has been unsettled. It shouldn't matter, yet it does – she has visions of the weekend being a total washout with bedraggled bunting, rain-sodden hog roast and a forlorn mud-splattered ice-cream van under leaden skies. It can't, it simply can't. Freya can feel herself hyperventilating.

She closes her eyes and breathes long and deep, Kundalini yoga style, and wonders whether to take one of the tiny white pills she keeps in her sunglasses case for emergencies.

Instead, she decides to make a tour of the house, to check that the beds in the spare rooms have been made up, that the guest washrooms are adequately provided with the mini Banho soaps that she buys online from Liberty (the packaging amuses her; it's not important, but it is).

She checks the supplies of towels and lavatory rolls and makes a plan as to where everyone should sleep, dithering over who should have the smallest single bedroom and deciding it will have to be her mother rather than Lance's – Natasha takes priority, especially as this was her childhood home. Correction, second home – there was another house in Chester Square, Lance had pointed it out years ago on a trip to London, an impossibly grand Georgian number. Once upon a time, there had been even more money than there is now.

Fortunes lost and fortunes made. Lance is a good businessman, he can be hard-hearted and ruthless, no doubt a side of him inherited from his father, Hugo – the name that no one ever mentions. She knows about him, she knows that accusations were made but nothing was ever proved and she knows his death was shocking and unexpected, as shocking and unexpected as her own father's. But unlike Lance, she misses her father and she wishes more than anything he could be visiting with her mother next week.

Freya continues her tour. For the duration of the party weekend the children's playroom in the attic will be converted into a kids' dormitory. Airbeds that blow up as soon as you plug them into the wall have been ordered – simple. All the kids will pile in together, which means her sister, who is coming sans husband but bringing her new baby, can have Luna's room. Meanwhile Bel and Andrew will have the large spare at the back of the house with the en suite, which leaves the second-best spare double free for Toby and Lucy.

Toby is Lance's best friend from university. Lucy is his second wife, his first having been put out to pasture several years ago. Freya tenses again. Bloody Lucy, with her tiny girlish frame and her disgusting home-rolled cigarettes.

With all the kids sharing, the weekend nanny can have Ludo's room, which is conveniently situated at the bottom of the stairs leading up to the playroom. In an ideal world, the girl would sleep out on the landing, guarding her charges like the dog in *Peter Pan*, but Ludo's room is the next best thing.

Who else, puzzles Freya, slightly disconcerted that there are still two bedrooms to be allocated. Of course! Annabel and Andrew's children, those two fully grown hairy men. Obviously they can't be lumped in with the littlies in the playroom – she doesn't know them from Adam, there's no telling what they might get up to.

Then Freya remembers Bel's flustered phone call a few weeks ago, apologetically asking if it was all right if some girlfriend came too. 'No problem,' Freya had replied, instantly putting Bel out of her misery, her relief palpable even from several hundred miles away. What was it with that woman? She always seemed to be in a state about something.

The couple could share the twin bedroom next to the playroom on the top floor, which meant the other brother would be left with the day bed in the small single room on the half-landing.

This is Freya's favourite spot in the house: a tiny lockable hiding place with an oriel window where she can curl up in the Etsy vintage quilt that is exactly the same colour as the blue glass vase on the Victorian washstand, watching the sky and the sea merge into each other like a Rothko painting.

When this is all over and the children are back at school, Freya vows to spend more time in her studio barn; she might get some private watercolour tuition, or maybe start experimenting in oils.

How odd to have children old enough to have partners, she thinks, unable to imagine Luna and Ludo as teenagers, never mind adults. She has a vague recollection of the photograph that accompanied Bel's last Christmas card, in which the sons appeared to be doughy twenty-somethings, their beards smacking of laziness rather than Shoreditch hipster, tummies as round as babies', their father a blur on the edge of the frame, while Annabel looked – what was the word? Frantic. Poor Annabel, how odd that she should have been abandoned here, that her past is so entwined with the house, even though she doesn't truly belong.

Lance has told Freya the facts: that Bel was found in a drawer in the back bedroom and that Uncle Benedict persuaded his sister to adopt her because Natasha kept losing babies. Only she hadn't lost Lance – he had clung like a barnacle, the son and heir to everything.

Freya snaps out of her reverie; the doorbell is ringing. She has to race down the stairs; the trouble with having such a big house is that sometimes delivery people get sick of waiting and leave before you manage to get to the front door. Increasingly she is convinced it's a spite thing, a sort of 'Well, fuck you, Madame Muck, here's a sorry-you-were-out slip' and the inconvenience of a ninety-minute round trip to the sorting office.

Freya is breathless by the time she flings open the door and the postman hands her a single parcel. A quick check of the postcode confirms it's what she has been waiting for and one of the knots that has been tugging in Freya's chest immediately comes undone. Everything will be fine, everything is falling into place.

Several weeks ago, Freya had sent a precious ciné reel of Kittiwake taken back in the sixties off to a tech company to be transferred onto DVD. Finally, after an agonising wait, the tape and the original reel have arrived back safely.

Freya is relieved. She wants to project the DVD via laptop onto the bare brick walls of the barn where she plans to have the disco in the evening, but first she needs to see if the conversion has worked.

Freya attaches the Apple USB SuperDrive to her MacBook Air, inserts the DVD and wires it up to their state-of-the-art 82-inch Samsung TV.

The telly set Lance back a penny under four thousand pounds and promises HD, surround sound and dynamic crystal colour. Yet, for all that money, it has no built-in DVD player.

After a few seconds, bodies begin to dance on the screen. Freya turns the sound up, but it's been recorded without audio. In the silence, skinny young men thrust their hips in front of girls in heavy eyeliner. They could almost be Millennials, but there is something other-worldly about the people on the screen: they are strangely similar but totally different from today's youngsters.

Freya is surprised to find herself moved. These people will be old now, most of them approaching eighty, arthritic and deaf, some of them will be dead. Suddenly the DVD seems terribly sad.

Were any of you happy, she wonders, but her reverie is interrupted by a snort of laughter.

Lance is home early from Exeter, he has already helped himself to a cold beer from the drinks fridge and doubtless left the bottle-top on the counter. For a few seconds they watch the footage together, transfixed by the sight of a ridiculously pretty blonde dancing right up to the camera lens, then, as she leaves the frame, Lance points a finger at the television.

'Freeze it,' he commands. Freya obeys on instinct and Lance sits down heavily beside her. 'That's Benedict,' he says. 'He was quite a good-looking fellow back in the day, bit of a catch.'

He takes the remote off her and presses play. Benedict has stopped dancing and is gazing hungrily at something over his shoulder, then he begins to gyrate again, thumbs looped into the waistband of his purple trousers. Freya laughs, Benedict is dancing in a way that only men in the sixties ever could. 'Bit of a goer,' his nephew continues. 'Truth is, he never grew out of it, became the eternal playboy, which, by the time he hit sixty, was a bit of a joke. Remember when he came to our wedding in that safari suit?'

Freya struggles to match the man on the screen with the slightly ridiculous creature she met ten years ago. Somehow, Benedict had transformed from this snake-hipped young man into a fat grey Simon Cowell lookalike, all unbuttoned shirts and lots of grizzly grey chest hair.

Lance looks wistful. 'Sometimes, when he used to meet me from school, I could hear people laughing at him. But once you got to know him he was the most charming company, the kindest, sweetest chap. I think in the end he was a bit lonely, riddled with gout and holed up in Montreux. He never married – came close, but . . . no kids. I think that made him sad. Remember, we couldn't go to his funeral? About four years ago – we were in Corfu. If I'd known he was going to leave me Kittiwake . . . ' Lance trails off. He should have gone anyway.

Together they watch a very much alive and pouting Benedict strut around a previous incarnation of the same room they are sitting in now. He has a bottle of wine in one hand and a cigarette in the other.

It is 1962. Benedict's waist is a mere twenty-six inches, his hair grows thick around his temples and his liver is still a nice healthy pink. The beautiful blond girl reappears, takes him by the hand and leads him away from the camera.

'Saucy,' smirks Freya, wondering if she and Lance might take the opportunity of the kids being at tennis club to go upstairs and fuck each other's brains out. Let's face it, it's been a while.

42

Natasha Thinks About Packing

On the Île de Ré, Natasha packs her case and unpacks it again. The action soothes her and she mutters under her breath, 'Underwear, blouses, skirt, trousers, party outfit, cardigan, sweater, gifts, toiletry bag, shoes, nightie, dressing gown and slippers.' She tries to relax – there are still five whole days before she will have to zip the thing up.

It is five days, isn't it?

She checks her calendar, counting the five empty squares that lead from today until the square that contains the handwritten word 'Cornwall' in shaky blue biro. It's definitely five days – as long as she's got today's date right. She glances at her watch and the little number in the glass bubble confirms she has five more days.

Her passport and flight information are on the sideboard. Her passport expires next year. She doubts she will get it renewed. The photograph inside is nine years old, she hopes she will still be recognisable to the authorities; how embarrassing to be turned away from passport control because your ancient face no longer matches your ID. Natasha decides to make herself up with extra care when she travels, plenty of foundation and lots of powder on top, that's the trick, like plastering a cracked wall. Her mother's face springs to mind, the perfect white oval with the crimson lips that gradually bled into the fine lines above her fraying mouth, the same mouth that one day long ago formed a scream that didn't seem to stop for days. She still hears it sometimes, and has to turn up the radio until her heart stops jumping. Stop it, she reminds herself, stop thinking, the house won't be anything like it used to be – Lance has promised her she 'won't recognise the place'.

Natasha swallows hard and sits down, she wishes she could make do with hand luggage only, but with the weather being unpredictable and the toys she has bought for Ludo and Luna, plus the gift for the birthday boy himself, she simply can't.

Natasha likes to be properly dressed for any occasion. How she looks has always mattered to her – it pains her not to have the right coat or jacket for any occasion, the correct shoes. Hers are a dainty size four; despite her age, her feet are still elegant. Too bad her hands are lined and liver spotted . . .

A small pilot light of fury flares up in her chest as she remembers how Hugo put a stop to her hand modelling. She wouldn't have gone much further; feet and ankles yes, possibly up to the knee, she had good legs, they are still slim, possibly too slim – her appetite isn't what it was. She dreads the meals at Kittiwake. She hopes they won't mind if she leaves something on the side of her plate – 'Something for Mr Manners,' her old nanny used to say. She hopes the children like their gifts and if they don't, she hopes they are polite enough to pretend to. When Lance and Annabel were growing up, she made them write thank-you letters the week after Christmas – any later would have been rude.

Bringing up children isn't easy, she concedes, you can have all the rules under the sun, but if a child decides to go off the rails then there's not much you can do to stop them.

Memories of the rows Annabel had with Hugo echo in her head, the door-slams and yelling.

It was the ingratitude that Hugo couldn't bear – after everything they had done for the girl, to have her repay them like that, behaving so badly at such a crucial time. She was lucky Downley Manor let her sit her exams, but she never went back to the sixth form and it was as much her decision as theirs.

Natasha remembers Annabel informing Hugo and herself that she intended to take her A levels – English, French and Domestic Science – at the local technical college. She needed to make a fresh start, she insisted. Hugo had ranted, Natasha had wept, but the girl could be quite determined, her jaw set into an unattractive poke, and in the end they had caved in.

Benedict had backed the girl all the way. In private, he had told Natasha that while he might not be her father, he still counted himself as the girl's uncle and as far as he was concerned it was not in Annabel's interests to go back to an institution where the pupils were treated like fifties debutantes.

So Annabel went to college in Chiswick and on Saturdays she worked in a wine merchant's owned by a friend of Benedict's, where she earned money that she spent on clothes and records like any other teenager, a fact which made Hugo furious for some reason.

Control, she supposed. Her husband was a very controlling man and Annabel at sixteen began to confront him in a way that Natasha had never dared.

Natasha finds herself rubbing at bruises that faded many years ago. She had always borne the brunt of Hugo's cruel streak and she recalls the countless dark-grey pinch marks under her arms. His violence could be sly and unexpected: a swift kick that came out of the blue, a bite on the breast when they were fighting in bed. Her husband was always careful to keep his blows below her face, because as long as no one guessed what was going on behind closed doors, then he could keep on doing it.

His cruelty wasn't only physical. He was unfaithful, and

delighted in parading his conquests in front of her. His favourite trick involved deftly removing an unlit cigarette from an attractive woman's lips in order to light it between his own. How he would have hated the smoking ban.

The trouble with Hugo was that he was very confident of his own allure. While other men approaching middle age were already receding, combing fragile strands of Brylcreemed hair across greasy pates, Hugo's mane of thick blond hair waved back from his brow in true matinee idol fashion.

Natasha sniffs, she could always smell those other women on him. She had the nose of a bloodhound and her knowledge of the Harrods perfume department was such that she could usually identify the exact perfume his latest squeeze had doused herself in before meeting lover-boy Hugo.

It was how she had known about the little tart – not that she'd been able to identify *her* scent. Chanel it certainly wasn't.

Natasha pushes the thought away and looks again at the ordered piles of packing on the bed and repeats, 'Underwear, blouses, skirt, trousers, party outfit, cardigan, sweater, gifts, toiletry bag, shoes, nightie, dressing gown and slippers.'

She hasn't bought anything for Annabel. Should she? No, it's not her birthday. As for those sons? She will give them each a ten-pound note.

Her eyes alight on Lance's gift, sitting on top of her neatly folded pants, and she wonders again whether it's a good idea.

The dilemma of what to give her son for his fiftieth birthday had given Natasha many a sleepless night until she faced the fact that she hadn't the money to buy anything extravagant, so the obvious solution would be to give him something precious that was already in her keeping. The watch is a good make, an Omega; she thinks it might even be quite rare.

Hugo had been fussy about things like that. He was particularly choosy where shoes and watches were concerned. According to

281

Hugo, a polished lace-up and a decent timepiece were the sign of a true gentleman.

Not that he had been much of a gentleman, not in the end. The watch had been amongst her husband's personal effects in the cardboard box she had picked up from the police station the week after he died. Natasha can still recall the shock of that sequence of extraordinary events. One day she was an unhappily married woman, the next, her husband had been taken in custody charged with embezzlement, then within twenty-four hours he was dead.

A silly, pointless passing, but a convenient one nonetheless, she concludes. 'Sepsis', according to the death certificate, or blood poisoning as it was more commonly known.

Someone once told Natasha she should have sued the police over her husband's death. It was a disgrace: an innocent man, hauled from his office and dragged into Marylebone police station to be questioned over the embezzlement of thousands of pounds from the law firm where he worked.

Hugo had taken umbrage, as any gentleman would, and fought like a wild thing, protesting his innocence all the way to the police car. ('You've got to remember we were taught to box at prep school,' Benedict had commented, 'but not with the constabulary.')

As a consequence of his actions, Hugo had been held in custody for resisting arrest and knocking off a policeman's helmet. The whole situation was absurd. What a load of trumped-up nonsense, his friends bellowed. Or rather, some of them did. Others remained very quiet indeed.

At some time during the night he was taken ill in his cell, but there were delays, no one thought it was serious – inmates were always trying it on, faking seizures, pretending to pass out. By the time they got him to hospital, his appendix had burst like a rotten plum and his body was flooded with toxins. He was dead by the morning.

All charges were immediately dropped, which was a relief, but as Benedict once muttered, 'What else could they do? A dead man can't go to court.'

No one else was ever charged with the embezzlement and although several colleagues turned up for the funeral, none of them came back to the house and a great deal of sherry and fruitcake went to waste.

Hugo hadn't had many friends, Natasha recalls, but then why would he? She was his wife and even she hadn't particularly liked him.

It was only after he died that she found out he'd taken out a second mortgage on Claverley Avenue and that, rather than the comfortably off widow she had expected to be, she had been left with barely a brass farthing. It was possibly the meanest thing her husband had ever done to her, worse even than the time he broke her arm in the South of France and she had to spend the rest of her holiday with her left arm encased in plaster. It was only thanks to Benedict buying her out of her share of the mews house they co-owned that she was able to run away and start her new life in France.

Exhausted, Natasha slumps on her bed next to the empty suitcase, kicks the piles of carefully chosen clothes onto the floor and shuts her eyes.

She is the only one who knows everything.

43

Bel is Beside Herself

Bel is beside herself. The party is in less than a week and she has failed to lose more than two pounds; an outfit she bought in the Hobbs summer sale a month ago mocks her from a hanger in the wardrobe, its size-twelve label might as well read 'silly cow'.

Hoping for a miracle, she tries it on again but the thing won't go over her hips. It's a linen shift dress with sunflowers on and wrenching it off she hears the lining rip – good, it's going in the charity bag, she never wants to see it again.

Catching sight of her doughy reflection in the mirror, Bel despairs. She had meant to go to Rigby & Peller and buy a decent bra, she was going to treat herself to gel nails and new knickers, and now time is running out. She should be tanned, she should be lithe, and yet with just days to go before her brother's fiftieth birthday party she is still twelve stone of uncooked pastry.

Furious with herself and deciding that desperate times call for desperate measures, Bel throws a white waffle cotton dressing gown around her lumpy frame and sends out a frantic SOS. 'Maisie,' she bellows up the stairs, 'can you come to my bedroom? I need some advice, please.'

Bel sits down heavily on the double bed and the wretched thing has the temerity to creak. Her immediate instinct is to get an axe and chop the thing up for firewood, only she hasn't got an axe.

How can this have happened, when she has known about this weekend since April?

But deep down she knows how, because although every morning she has religiously rolled out a yoga mat and joined Adriene on YouTube for a daily workout, her virtual-reality teacher hasn't noticed that instead of downward dogging and tensing her glutes, Bel has been wandering off mid-session to make herself a cup of milky coffee with two sugars.

Maisie finally appears and slouches against the doorframe. Despite not seeming to do any exercise at all, apart from shagging Ed, she is wearing a pair of sweat pants that threaten to fall off her.

Bel explains the situation and Maisie begins to rifle through her wardrobe, pulling out anything that might have party potential and throwing it on the floor. Sadly most of these garments, Bel realises, are over a decade old, remnants from the days when she possibly could have squeezed into those navy palazzo trousers and that polka-dot shirt with the dramatic ruffle down the front.

'I don't get it,' Bel tells Maisie, 'I've been exercising like crazy and it simply hasn't worked, I think there's something wrong with my metabolism. It's so unfair, I used to be quite fit.'

Maisie looks at her as if to say, Yeah, right. Compelled to explain herself, Bel continues: 'You might not think it, but I was quite sporty once upon a time. Not at school, I hated sport at school – hockey, yuck, I was always stuck in goal, petrified the ball was going to smack me in the teeth. Awful. But later, and this might surprise you, I was rather a whizz on skis. Sometimes having a powerful thigh can be an advantage, Maisie. Anyway, I loved it. It was Benedict who first took me, my uncle,' she adds, dropping her robe and attempting but failing to wriggle into a bright yellow

285

cotton A-line skirt with big red buttons on the pockets. 'The one that used to own Kittiwake, where, you know . . .'

Maisie looks bored. Bel discards the skirt and ploughs on with her story: 'Well the thing is, Maisie, I took to skiing, turned out I had naturally good balance.' Maisie, who has seen Bel fall off her yoga mat while attempting to stand on one leg, raises an eyebrow. 'And I wasn't scared . . .' Bel pauses and sits down; even to her own ears this sounds implausible, it sounds like she's describing a completely different person, but it was true, as a young woman she had been completely fearless on the slopes.

Was it because back then I had nothing to lose, she wonders, deciding that love and motherhood are the two things guaranteed to turn a woman into a snivelling coward.

'Anyway,' she continues, 'what I'm trying to say is that I was a complete ski ninja.'

For a moment Maisie stops rummaging and asks, 'Is that why you work part-time at, thingummy, at Snow Patrol?'

'Snow Nation,' Bel corrects her, allowing herself a tiny smirk. 'I think Snow Patrol is a band!' Ha, she thinks, get me, being all cool.

'Whatever,' retorts Maisie unimpressed. 'The ski place.'

'Yes, it's the ideal job for me, because I know what people expect from the staff in these places. I mean, it's no good recruiting any old Tom, Dick or Harriet. Let's face it, there's nothing like having experienced a job to know what kind of skills are needed,' Bel replies.

Maisie is completely uninterested now. She is sitting on the floor as if the ordeal of looking through Bel's wardrobe has completely wiped her out. She's staring at her hands, picking her nail varnish off. Small glittery purple flakes fall to the carpet.

Christ, thinks Bel, why is no one in this house remotely interested in anything I have to say? Even Andrew nods off now and again when she is halfway through an anecdote: she has caught him. He needs to learn to fall asleep with his eyelids open like snakes do. She makes one last concerted effort to engage with the girl.

'Thing is, I used to work as a chalet maid.'

'What's a chalet maid?' asks Maisie. She looks genuinely confused.

Bel seizes her golden opportunity. If she plays her cards right, she could have this girl on a flight to Geneva by the middle of September; she will even provide the salopettes.

'Well, you could always sign up with Ski Nation and see for yourself. I'm sure I could get you some work experience.'

'I don't like the cold,' Maisie sniffs dismissively. 'I was only asking.'

Bel back-pedals, 'The thing about chalet-maiding is that it depends on your experience: if you don't know how to do anything, then you're relegated to cleaning and bed-making. If you can cook, though, you don't have to do any of the menial cleaning stuff, you make breakfast and supper for however many people are staying in the chalet – usually it's about eight.'

Maisie screws her face up. 'Why can't they like make their own breakfast and their own bed?'

Bel swallows back a What, like you do? Ha! and simply answers, 'Because that's what you're being paid to do.'

'Like a servant.'

'Well, I didn't see it like that. It got me away from home, it gave me independence and it's how I met Andrew. He was staying in one of the chalets and I was the maid and . . . '

'Kinky,' sniggers Maisie.

Only it hadn't been like that. Andrew had been with a group of his friends from university, a baying mob of over-entitled Hoorays, out of whom he had been the least privileged, the most grateful and by far the worst skier. Andrew was the quiet one who swept up broken glasses and helped stack the dirty plates into the dishwasher after a meal.

Inevitably he had broken his ankle on the third morning of his ten-day holiday and Bel found to her astonishment that, rather than dashing for the slopes the minute she had finished her duties, she chose to keep him company.

By the end of the week they were in love, an easy comfortable love, and two years later they were married.

Bel hauls herself back to the present. 'Yes, well, anyway, Maisie, this won't buy the baby a new bonnet.'

Maisie looks more confused than ever.

Bel gives up, she can't keep trying to explain everything. There are some things Maisie will never understand and some things she is intrinsically good at, like clothes. The other day, she had worn Ed's old school cricket jumper over a floral playsuit and had looked amazing. Somewhere in the pile of possibilities on the bedroom floor is her ideal party outfit, it has to be, otherwise she will have to go to Lance's celebration in her dressing gown.

Half an hour later, the dressing gown is looking like the only plausible solution. Nothing that Maisie picked out as having any party potential fits; sleeves get stuck halfway up her arms, buttons refuse to meet buttonholes, and any zips that Bel manages to force up immediately start creeping down. Defeat stares at them from a large pile of discarded garments on the bedroom floor.

'Don't forget it's late-night shopping on Thursday,' Maisie reminds her. 'You could always meet me after work and I could, you know ... last chance 'n all that.' And then she slinks out of the door like a cat.

Bel sits back down on the rudely creaking bed. Talking to Maisie about Snow Nation has reminded her that the last time she'd been properly thin was back in the early eighties when amphetamines had been readily available on the ski slopes where she worked. There had been lots of jokes for those in the know about where to go for the 'best white powder', and for a while she felt amazing, full of energy and a stone lighter than she'd been at school. At last, she'd found the solution and it was oh so easy. The occasional toot kept her hand out of the biscuit tin; she didn't feel all that hungry. Even when she was back in London it was easy to find supplies – not that she'd ever had a habit, not really. But then Andrew had found out and read her the riot act and said that she was doing untold damage to her heart and that he didn't want a drug addict girlfriend. She had a choice, he told her, him or the speed, and she had flushed her supply down the lavatory in front of him, pleading him not to leave her. Damn Andrew, it's his fault she's so fat.

44

Maisie's Little Secret

Maisie retires to Ed's bedroom, hoping she's not going to have nightmares after seeing her boyfriend's mother in her underwear. Seriously, who even knew knickers came in that size and shape? Closing the door with relief, she sits cross-legged on the pink fur bed throw she bought herself from TK Maxx and attempts to meditate like Russell Brand, but within a few seconds she is bored and decides to check on her party outfits.

Opening the cupboard, Maisie catches her reflection in Ed's wardrobe mirror. She automatically drops her chin, widens her eyes and pouts. Now what? Maybe she should masturbate, send Ed a selfie, see if it turns him on?

He is getting a bit lazy about sex – which reminds her, she ought to get down to the clinic and have that implant put in. Idly she kicks off her sweat pants and knickers and has a brief forage around her clitoris, but her fingers freeze at the memory of Bel in her bra and pants. What was all that hideous pubic hair about? Maisie pulls her top and bra down with the hand that isn't poking around her vagina and pulls a succession of porn faces over her naked tits. What if Jamie should walk in?

She knows he's at home. He rarely goes out. Would he try and fuck her? She shuts her eyes and briefly attempts a fantasy about Jamie fucking her in this room, his brother's bedroom, while Bel clunks around in the kitchen below.

But the fantasy does nothing for her. Jamie has bad breath, his teeth are yellow and his beard smells. At least she makes Ed put grooming oil in his.

This is hopeless, she doesn't fancy Jamie, Ed is boring and she's grown out of her secret Louis Tomlinson crush. Then she remembers – there is someone ... and she reaches under the chest of drawers to retrieve the magazine she's been hiding there for weeks and stares hard into his face. Dropping down to the floor, Maisie wedges her back against the door because the last thing she needs is Bel blundering in with a 'nice' cup of vile tea and a foul biscuit.

She had recognised him as soon as she saw the picture and her mind flips back to a night last December, before she had moved in with the Robathams.

She'd needed extra money, it was Christmas, there were parties to dress up for and presents to buy, so she had agreed to apply for some waitressing work along with a mate.

An agency had put a call out: 'good-looking personable girls needed for exclusive men-only festive celebration'.

Maisie's friend Megan had spelt it out for her. Basically the evening would involve a load of middle-aged blokes off the leash and on the lash at some posh hotel down Park Lane. Having enjoyed a civilised dinner, the gentlemen would proceed to spend the remainder of the evening getting utterly hammered and behaving like dicks.

She had walked the interview, literally – they wanted to see how she moved. After she'd sashayed up and down for a bit, they asked if she could balance a tray. When she nodded, they asked if she had a nice black outfit: heels, shirt, skirt – short, but not silly short – and tights?

Maisie must have looked confused at the suggestion she wore tights. It was December, it was freezing, obviously she would be wearing tights. 'Only, if you wear hold-ups or suspenders, they tend to get a bit over-excited,' they explained.

So she'd worn tights (70 denier), a black elasticated skirt and a black satin shirt.

The shirt was too good for waitressing and she hoped she wouldn't get gravy down it, but in the event she hadn't carried a single dirty plate. The hotel staff took care of the dinner service, while the girls who'd been employed specifically for the 'do', like herself and Megan, were purely on drinks duty.

Once the complimentary wine on the tables had been finished, it was their job to collect extra orders from the bar – spirits mostly. 'Whisky, brandy, or maybe a five-hundred-quid bottle of Grey Goose vodka, sir?'

Megan had been right about how the evening would pan out. At first it was pretty sedate, the gentlemen had eaten their beef Wellington without so much as spilling a drop of jus down their dress shirts, but after dinner when the bow ties came undone, the comic had been booed off (Maisie had seen him a few minutes later, desperately trying to exit the building via the service lift) and the raffle, featuring a fortnight on St Barts, proved which table had the most money, then things got a little wilder.

Maisie hadn't found it at all intimidating. She'd been to a school where the only sport most boys were interested in was up-skirting, and you couldn't get through registration without someone commenting on someone's tits, so it didn't bother her.

She played along, she sat on the laps of fat men and laughed when fifty-pound notes were tucked into her cleavage. She was more than equipped to deal with this kind of nonsense; in addition to a push-up bra she wore a little money belt around her waist, with a compartment for change and a compartment for tips, but by around 11 p.m. things got a little muddled, she was tired, she'd had a few sneaky drinks herself. Who cared if a few tenners meant for the change compartment of the belt went into the tips side? These blokes were loaded, she wasn't, and everyone knew what kind of game they were playing.

He was on table number 9, over in the far left-hand corner, she had to pass the table every time she went to the bar. She saw him watching her and put an extra sway into her hip action, sucked in her stomach and pushed her tits out; he was good looking in a clean-shaven telly presenter kind of way, which was fine by her.

Maisie had never had a type, she fancied people on instinct – older, younger, bald or beardy, executives or mechanics she didn't care, it varied and it just so happened that her type that night was the bloke on table 9.

By midnight, the place was carnage, men were falling over other men, some were trying to dance, others were riding around on each other's backs, one man was crying and a few had fallen asleep face down in the festive tiramisu.

The bar girls had only been employed till midnight and at ten to, pale-faced hotel staff positioned themselves in a ring around the room, poised to do a final tidy once the gentlemen decided to call it a night.

Finally the metal shutters came down on the bar and the crowd began to thin. Maisie's money belt felt satisfyingly heavy.

On stage, an exhausted-looking red-coated MC announced through an onstage microphone that 'Any more drinks would have to be purchased from the residents' bar', someone was sick into an ice bucket, balloons popped, and men began to stagger out into the night.

But one man remained in his seat, Mr Table 9. She walked past him on the way to get her coat – she and Megan were going to get an Uber back to South London – but he caught her hand and put something in it, a key card in a cardboard sleeve with the number 303 written on the front. He patted his breast pocket and she noticed that tucked in front of a cream and black spotted silk handkerchief was a matching key card, he gestured five minutes with his hand and left the table.

Who did he think he was, the prick? Maisie retrieved her coat, she could see Megan waiting outside the revolving doors at the rear exit, she only had to cross the lobby and she and her friend could go home. But she didn't, she was going to, but the lift was gold and shiny and the next thing she knew the doors were sliding open and she was pressing the button for the third floor.

She knocked lightly on 303 and he was there almost instantly. He said his name was Greg, he called her 'Amazing Maisie', said she could have whatever she liked from the minibar. She even opened a jar of jelly beans – he laughed at that, he said she was like a kid in a sweet shop, and then they had had sex all night and ever since then, it's that sex she thinks of when Ed loses his erection between her legs and turns away in a huff, it's that sex she thinks of when she is alone and horny like now, it's that sex she told a furious Megan about the next day in glorious detail and it's that sex that she remembers as being the best sex she has ever had in her life.

Maisie is being quite vocal now, if Bel hadn't popped out to the chemist to pick up some athlete's foot powder for Andrew, she might have heard and come charging up the stairs, she might have barged in without knocking, in which case, she may well have been surprised to find her son's girlfriend, in flagrante, frantically pumping the large scented candle Bel's boss had given her for her birthday in and out of her neatly shaved vagina, while the magazine article featuring her adoptive younger brother lay open and propped up against the chest of drawers.

Maisie comes and collapses, she is breathless – masturbating can be quite demanding. After a moment or two, her scented wanking candle is reunited with its holder and she readjusts her clothes. As it happens, she knows now that he wasn't called Greg at all, his name is Lance and he's going to shit himself when he sees her at the weekend.

Serve him right, thinks Maisie, remembering the shame of having to go straight into work from the Park Lane hotel the next morning. She was still wearing her smelly waitress outfit and recalls spending the entire day painting miniature Christmas scenes onto acrylic fingernails with a stinking hangover, hands shaking over countless tiny plum puddings and bearded Santa faces. She'd been sick twice in the staff toilets before lunch.

45

Jumpsuit Weather

Kittiwake, the day of the party

Freya wakes up and immediately checks the weather on her iPhone. She could open the curtains and look out of the window, but Lance is still fast asleep.

Typical, she thinks, after the hottest summer on record in over forty years England has reverted to her usual sulky self and the weather app predicts a mixture of sunshine and cloud with 30 per cent chance of rain in the afternoon. Tomorrow is the same, while Sunday doesn't bear looking at.

Freya tries not to feel bitterly disappointed. If only Lance had been born six weeks earlier, they could have held the party under blazing July skies and by now the entire weekend would be over and Instagrammed.

She tries to slow her breathing down. Today is 'family only' she reminds herself, secretly wishing it was only *her* family and that Natasha and Bel plus her mob were arriving tomorrow, along with all the other guests. Ideally, she'd like a night alone with her mother and sister, the two people, apart from Lance and the kids, that she loves most in the world. Her sister's small children are coming too and Freya smiles at the prospect of seeing them: little pug-faced Astrid, freckly Nico and baby Aksel. Freya is delighted her sister decided to have a third child, it had given her the perfect excuse to buy an overpriced but adorable wooden crib she had seen in a reclamation yard some months ago.

Once five-month-old Aksel has made use of it, she might take it downstairs and come October she can fill it with decorative gourds?

Freya pads down to the kitchen in her floral Toast pyjamas. Katie, the part-time nanny, is making pancakes with the children. Freya tries not to mind about the egg-goo mess and tugs Katie's plait playfully, although slightly harder than she intended, as she passes her by and kisses her children on top of their pink scalps. Despite their father's Mediterranean looks, her children are resolutely fair, their hair the colour of the white owl she occasionally sees in the barn.

Katie is to keep the children occupied all day, preferably out of the house, while Freya and her usual daily cleaner plus another girl from the agency do a final titivate around the house. Freya mentally runs through her to-do list: garden flowers in all the bedrooms and bathrooms, charming bunches of mismatched dahlias chosen seemingly at random, plus scented candles and boxes of long matches in all the en suites and lavatories.

The fresh fish van should be arriving at nine, followed by the yurts and porta-loos for the top field before midday, this afternoon the trestle tables will be erected for Saturday night's feast in the barn, and at 3 p.m. the gardener is coming to position the outdoor candles and fairy lights, tick, tick, tick.

She has timed this operation with military precision: she wants everything including the fish pie done by 4 p.m., giving her plenty of time to get ready to meet her guests in a smiling and relaxed fashion, despite not being able to wear the knitted lace Missoni shorts she was saving for the occasion.

Today is jumpsuit weather. Hers is a charcoal parachute silk number which she will wear artfully rolled up at the ankle and wrist to show off her tan and the children will be in nautical stripes. She likes them to look as though they belong to the seaside, just as a small piece of the seaside belongs to them.

Freya feels a sudden wave of exhaustion – all this monumental effort and some people probably won't notice any of it, because there are some people who simply don't care if there are empty toilet rolls lined up on top of the lavatory. She is thinking of Lance's sister, naturally.

Freya visited Bel's house in Clapham once and found the experience profoundly depressing.

They had been having an awkward cup of tea (served in vile mugs emblazoned with ugly pictures and stupid sayings) in the sitting room when an ugly dog had waddled to the middle of the lawn and proceeded to take a crap in front of the French windows.

No one had mentioned it but Bel must have been mortified.

The great thing about having a lurcher, decides Freya, is that even mid shit, they are elegant. Anyway, it's not Bel that she's trying to impress, it's her husband's mother, Natasha, who remains unmoved by anything other than Lance, her expression melting as soon as she sets eyes on her son. Freya considers for a second how difficult this must have been for Bel growing up. Her own mother Mari was scrupulously fair in sharing her love between Freya and Elise, dividing it as precisely as the chocolate bar she would cut in two when they came home from school.

But then she and Elise are Mari's own, they both have her eyes and Elise has her nose while Freya has the same wide smile and perfect teeth, poor Elise having drawn the DNA short straw from their father's side of the family around the mouth.

Surely the woman will have something to say about Kittiwake, surely she will marvel at its transformation, the clever colour schemes and quirky individual touches. As if for luck, Freya strokes a piece of driftwood on the windowsill. How many pieces of drift-wood had she discarded along the beach until she had found this one, the perfect combination of colour and shape, so beautifully sun-bleached and intricately knotted? She has surrounded it with an arrangement of 'interesting' striped pebbles and black-only shells.

Sometimes the children try to add to this collection with any old rubbish they pick up on their trips out and Freya has to secretly re-edit the display at night. It's like when they attempt to dress the Christmas tree and she has to redo the entire thing while they're asleep.

Outside, the pristine bunting flaps in the breeze and a gunmetal cloud crosses over the sun, but it's only momentary and as the sun reappears, Freya notices that her precious bronze kitchen island, is splattered with pancake mix and covered with a thousand tiny greasy fingerprints. Freya removes a wooden spoon from the earth-enware jar next to the cooker and bites down hard on the handle.

Please, she intones silently, let me have this one perfect weekend and I will never ask for anything else.

Eventually, Katie corrals the children into the garden and Freya can concentrate on wiping down the work surfaces. The kitchen island has its own special bucket of cloths and cleaning agents, and she finds polishing the thing somehow therapeutic.

It's Lance's actual birthday tomorrow and she has spent a fortune on his main present, but it's what he wants. He had even pointed it out in a magazine. The children have bought him a Liberty silk pocket handkerchief and some Paul Smith socks and they've both hand-painted him a card. Luna's is quite good but Ludo's makes her wince. Never mind, she will find somewhere discreet to display it. Gifts will be presented at breakfast time tomorrow over smoked salmon and scrambled eggs; fresh bagels are being delivered by van at 8 a.m. If they don't turn up, she will burn down their premises.

Freya chooses a couple of Nespresso pods for the machine. She and Lance can have coffee in bed, the calm before the storm – not that there will be a storm. She checks her weather app again. No storm, although Sunday's beach breakfast barbecue looks certain to be rained off and all her lovely wicker baskets will go to waste. If only it wasn't a bank holiday weekend, she despairs. Normally everyone would leave on the Sunday, but oh no, this is a three-day event, like a mini-festival, complete with ukulele band and fire-eaters. She is very tempted to put brandy in her coffee, but she resists.

She is going back upstairs, her husband is going to wake up to the aroma of a freshly brewed cup of coffee and then he is going to take her in his arms and – how long has it been? Putting the milk back in the fridge, Freya notices a small colourful packet tucked behind the bread bin. Who the hell has brought Angel Delight into her E-number-free kitchen? If she finds Katie has been feeding her kids with that muck she will have her fired, drawn and quartered. She drops the offending article in the bin.

The phone rings. It's Bel, who is calling to say they're setting off now and is there anything Freya wants picking up on the way, like some bread or loo rolls or something? No, she reassures Bel, she doesn't need anything picking up, everything is in hand, just bring yourselves, she adds cheerily. 'See you later.'

Freya shivers. Dammit, she might have to put the under-floor heating on.

46

The Drive Down

Bel isn't sure what she is dreading most – the drive down or seeing her mother. She has woken up with what might be cystitis but could be nerves and has been peeing every half-hour from 5 a.m. until Andrew woke up at eight. There is some of that fizzy pink powdery stuff in the bathroom cabinet that is meant to work wonders for UTIs; it's three years past its sell-by date but she knocks back the medicinal sherbet anyway.

They have agreed to leave at ten, but with two hours to go, Bel already feels anxious. Jamie, who never goes out, went out last night. In fact, come to think of it, she didn't hear him come home.

Oh God, what if he's gone missing and she has to phone the police? She'll kill him.

As for Maisie and Ed, oddly enough she can already hear them moving around above her head. Maisie was in a high state of excitement last night, the poor child has probably hardly ever seen the sea, Cornwall can be yet another new experience she can thank the Robathams for, like guinea fowl and Manchego cheese.

Sitting on the lavatory again, Bel promises to be good all weekend. She won't be catty or snide or wince on the motorway,

301

even when a big lorry overtakes and she is convinced they are all going to die.

She will do everything in her power not to annoy anyone, she wants to present a united front, a normal, healthy, happy family, with fully functioning adult children.

She wishes her sons had let her pack for them. She has told them both that jeans will be fine, she offered to buy them new shirts, but they curled their lips like cheap Elvis impersonators and rolled their eyes.

Well fuck you, she thinks, breaking her promise to be good and kind and patient before she has even wiped her bottom.

When they were little boys she would buy them cotton shorts from Mothercare and iron their little T-shirts if they were going anywhere nice. She made sure they had sensible lace-up shoes that were properly fitted by the nice lady in Peter Jones, she bought them new socks and white pants and vests and replaced them at the beginning of each new term. Her boys were well turned out and washed behind the ears, their hair smelt of anti-dandruff shampoo and she lined them up at night to make sure they cleaned their teeth properly.

She would like to do the same now, she would like to shave off their beards and flannel their necks, she would like to remove each individual blackhead from around Jamie's nose with one of those metal extractor things she has seen on the internet and she would like to burn Ed's filthy trainers and kit him out with a fun but respectable pair of suede desert boots.

As for herself, all she can do is to pull her stomach in and hope for the best, but at least thanks to Maisie she won't be wearing her dressing gown tomorrow night.

Surprisingly the girl had been as good as her word and Thursday's late-night shopping trip had been more successful than Bel anticipated. They'd met outside Top Shop directly after Maisie finished work and Bel had been slightly taken aback when Maisie had linked arms and purposefully marched her to down to Cos on Regent Street. Here, jaw set in a poke of determination, the girl had rifled through the shop with a speed and efficiency that had left Bel feeling tortoise-like by comparison, before pushing her into the changing rooms with an armload of possibilities. Twenty minutes later, Bel had been surprised to see a version of herself in the mirror that she knew 'worked'.

Nothing about the navy and white polka-dot pleated chiffon skirt had screamed 'buy me' from the rail, but teamed with a sweet square-necked, puff-sleeved, Tyrolean-style blouse that mercifully didn't require tucking in, even Maisie had given the ensemble the thumbs up.

Standing at the till, waiting to pay for her new clothes, Bel had felt a sudden warmth towards her son's girlfriend, and suggested they attempt a couple of shoe shops and the possibility of a nice girlie supper somewhere with a celebratory bottle of prosecco thrown in. But Maisie had apologised and explained that she'd accidentally booked herself in for a professional spray tan at a mate's salon in Streatham and was already running late. Which was a shame, because for a brief moment the two of them had felt a bit closer. So Bel had gone home on the Tube alone, consoling herself with the thought that at least Maisie having her tan done elsewhere had saved yet another of her towels from looking like an incontinence blanket. Silver linings and all that.

She has packed a shared suitcase for herself and Andrew, instructing him that he must be responsible for his own toilet bag and prescription drugs, as she has no room in hers.

Bel views her toilet bag with despair, then squeezes in the remaining cystitis powders. Once upon a time, she could go away for a weekend with nothing more than a razor and a few paracetamol, but those days are long gone. Now her ancient Superdrug floral zip-up contains blood-pressure medication, anti-indigestion tablets, Deep Heat in case her back gives out, multi-vitamins and, the latest addition, a tube of over-the-counter cream to prevent itchiness of the vagina – a new and troubling condition which no doubt she will have to go and speak to her GP about.

The Robathams eventually set off at 11.45 a.m. Bel is already hungry, so before getting in the car, she swipes a couple of packets of biscuits from the cupboard and the contents of the fruit bowl. That should see them through till lunch. Unfortunately, Andrew has forgotten to fill the car with petrol as she'd asked, so about half a mile from the house they stop at the local Texaco garage and to her dismay, Ed, Jamie and Maisie all troop out of the car in search of energy drinks (despite none of them having done anything more energetic than get out of bed so far this morning), Doritos (Ed), chocolate (Jamie) and cereal bars (Maisie). Instinctively she knows that none of them will offer to pay for anything and, sure enough, Andrew gets back in the car looking slightly shell-shocked with a bag of wine-gums and a couple of bottles of water, neither of which are chilled.

Bel feels the tension creep in round the back of her neck. She had intended to do some yoga before they set off, in fact she'd intended to bring her yoga mat but there wasn't enough room in the car, not after Maisie piled all her luggage in the boot.

Apparently she has packed one bag with clothes and the other with make-up and accessories, 'Wigs an' stuff,' she explained airily. Jamie and Ed have each brought a small rucksack, Jamie's seems to be mostly full of those Marvel magazines he buys from that peculiar place in Covent Garden.

It would be nice to chat, but the three passengers on the back seat have their headphones on and Andrew is concentrating on getting out of London and cursing their sat-nav system for being several years out of date.

Bel puts Radio Four on low and lets the words wash over her, so much information, so much opinion, she's not sure whether people had so many opinions back in the old days, they were too busy doing stuff to sit around and talk about it, but now everyone's an expert and everyone's got a podcast and everyone's meant to listen to what everyone else has to say and yet so much of it is nonsense.

They've been on the road for half an hour before Bel realises she's forgotten her book and it's book club next week, which she's been looking forward to, because she hasn't seen some of her friends since before the summer break and there will be a lot of catching up to do. Bel imagines herself saying, 'Well, we haven't been abroad as yet this year, but we did have a fabulous long weekend with all the family in Cornwall – yes, at Kittiwake, you might have seen the place, it's often featured in magazines, yes my brother owns it, that's right, Lance,' and at that point she could show them all a few photos on her phone. She imagines scrolling through a lot of smiling faces holding champagne flutes aloft, a flaming fiftieth birthday cake, her and her mother with their arms wrapped around each other, Lance and Andrew clapping each other on the back.

In the photoshopped images of her imagination, her sons are beardless, Andrew is standing up straight and Maisie is nowhere to be seen.

An urgent need to pee brings her sharply back to reality, she cannot and will not have cystitis this weekend, they aren't even on the motorway yet.

Fortunately, before she is forced to ask Andrew to stop, Maisie pipes up to say she is always travel-sick if she sits in the back of the car, which for some reason brings out the *Sweeney* driver in Andrew and without indicating, he swerves in front of a lorry to pull over into the forecourt of a garage on the edge of Hammersmith.

There is a huge amount of horn blaring and Bel has to virtually chew off her tongue to stop herself screeching, Jesus Christ, Andrew, you could have got us all killed! Seriously, how can anyone still be car-sick in their twenties, thinks Bel as she dutifully vacates the front seat, remembering those awful journeys back to boarding

305

school when she was young and how the fear of being sick was worse than actually being sick.

Fortunately, as if to compensate for nearly wiping out the entire Robatham family, the garage happens to have both a lavatory and a small M & S food section.

Bel nips in to use the loo and buy some emergency sandwiches, just in case.

By the time she gets back to the car, Maisie is in the front seat, having kicked off her shoes and hoisted her bare feet onto the dashboard.

Squeezing into the seat behind her, Bel can see that she has been expertly spray-tanned and her toenails look like they have been gold-leafed.

'Well, this is fun,' she attempts, but no one is listening and she leans against the door and tries to sleep. If the lock failed and sent her tumbling out onto the motorway, she has a horrible feeling that no one would even notice, never mind care.

Well, Andrew would miss her cooking, she supposes, but once he got used to filling in an Ocado order, he'd be fine. The only one that ever cared, the only one who was truly interested in her was Benedict. If only Benedict could be at the party. She misses him badly, she'd even forgive him for leaving Kittiwake to Lance, if he could be alive to forgive.

You did get the farm, she reminds herself. Once, when she'd told a friend that her uncle had left her a farm, the friend had presumed she'd meant a proper farm, with land and barns, when the reality was a chipped and battered children's toy, complete with a motley collection of poisonous lead animals. He'd left her some money too, though not enough to make much difference. The proceeds from the sale of the mews house had gone to his sister, which was something to be grateful for, considering the financial mess her father had left Natasha in, and for a second Bel can't help feeling relieved that at least one of her adoptive parents is dead. Thank goodness she doesn't have Hugo as well as Natasha to contend with this weekend.

The farm is in a box in the loft, along with some old packing cases that her mother hadn't been able to take to France. The loft scores an eight on her worry scale, it smells funny up there and sometimes she thinks she can hear squirrels chewing through the electrics.

But there's no point in worrying about that now, thinks Bel sleepily. At least this weekend she can give herself a break from all that stress, and as she nods off she finds herself wondering, not for the first time, about the birthday cake. Chocolate would be nice, especially if it's covered in that ganache stuff they do on *Bake Off*. Hmm. Bel falls asleep with her stomach gently rumbling.

47

Maisie Arrives at Kittiwake

Maisie can't believe how long it takes to drive to Cornwall. She's flown to Ibiza in half the time, and that's got sandy beaches.

'Cornwall's got sandy beaches,' Bel snaps. Maisie ignores her, it's Bel's fault that the journey is taking so long, she keeps having to stop at every other motorway service station in order to use the ladies.

They have lunch somewhere outside of Bristol. Ed has an Egg McMuffin and seeing him with yolk in his beard makes Maisie's stomach heave. She is going off him; his eyes are too small and she doesn't like his belly button.

It was never meant to be a long-term thing anyway and while it's been great living rent-free in central London, she doesn't fancy him any more.

In fact, the sight of both brothers, pudgy and shapeless, playing some stupid driving game has totally pissed her off. It's not like either of them can even drive. Ed is a boy, she wants a man.

Maisie takes the last of Andrew's wine gums from the glove box. According to the back-seat driver, 'It won't be long now,' and suddenly the prospect of coming face to face with Lance makes her nervous. It seemed like such a hilarious idea three hundred miles ago.

As they reach the brow of a hill, Bel lurches forward in the back seat, points over Maisie's shoulder and screams right next to her ear, 'Look, the sea!' She's right and even though it's what Maisie's been expecting for miles, the sight is oddly surprising, glittering and vast.

She can't remember what lies on the other side of it. Is it a foreign country or the Isle of Man? Her geography teacher tried to touch her up once, what was her name again?

Ed and Jamie, squashed together now for seven hours on the back seat, start pretending they are four years old and talk in babyish voices about building 'thand cathles and wanting an ithe queem', which is quite funny but at the same time annoying because they don't stop, they keep talking in baby voices until without warning Bel erupts like volcano next to them and starts banging on about family honour and everyone being on their best behaviour and not letting her down. Her face is tomato red and she goes on and on about how much this weekend means to her and how hard it is to come to terms with Kittiwake and nobody understanding what the place means to her and then she's like crying and everyone else in the car is silent, until she says in a very quiet voice, 'I'm sorry for that outburst. Andrew, don't forget to take the next left.' Only Andrew does forget to take the next left because obviously the man's a moron, so then Bel starts swearing and the next thing Andrew's driving the car backwards, which, according to Bel, is illegal. Then she wails, 'What if we run into a tractor or someone on horseback? For the love of God, be careful, Andrew!' which makes Ed and Jamie piss themselves laughing.

The road they have turned down is very narrow with tall hedges forming high leafy green barriers on either side, so you can't see anything and every time they round a bend, Bel shrieks 'Slow down, Andrew, anything could be coming round that corner, someone walking a dog, or a child on a bike.'

309

Maisie wonders how anyone can live in a place where there are no shops. Once in a while there's a break in the hedge, and all she can see for miles are fields and trees and occasionally another glimpse of the sea, but no shops, only cows.

Maisie has read that more people are killed by cows in the UK than by terrorist attacks. She'd rather take her chances on a bomb in the West End than run the risk of an encounter with a cow down here, they're fucking massive.

She squints at the sky: the weather is crap. What's the point in paying for a spray tan if you can't show it off? Maisie has had to compromise by wearing skinny jeans with lots of deliberate rips and tears in the denim. Andrew had been aghast, 'Are you telling me you actually paid money for jeans with holes in the knees?'

The man is a freakin' dinosaur.

'Do they have a pool?' she asks. Preferably an indoor one, she thinks, looking at the thickening cloud.

'No,' Bel replies, and launches into a long-winded story about someone Maisie's never heard of who drowned there decades before she was born.

'If you want to swim, there's always the sea,' Andrew reminds her. Maisie doesn't bother to tell him that she's not interested in swimming, she simply wants to wear her new bikini. Anyway, she can't swim – no one taught her, not properly – so she won't be going near any cows and she's not going in the sea either. All she wants is to doss around in a posh house while giving the bloke that owns it either a heart attack or the horn, or both. Because that's another thing she's read in one of her 'real life and celebrity' magazines, that loads of middle-aged men peg out due to sexual arousal; something about not having enough blood supply to feed both the penis and the brain at the same time, which is pretty gross when you think about it.

She is intrigued to see Lance's wife and their kids in the flesh, Freya, Luna and Ludo, and there is a dog too and chickens in the garden. 'All the eggs will be Kittiwake's own,' Bel informed her self-importantly.

Then there's the Natasha woman, Bel's mum, who sounds like a right piece of work. According to Bel, she is very well turned out – 'Like a pineapple upside-down cake,' ventures Andrew, sniggering at his own joke, but everyone ignores him.

'My mother is what they used to call a fashion plate,' Bel sighs.

I'll be the judge of that, thinks Maisie, wondering if the little white fur stole she found in the Clapham attic ever belonged to this Natasha woman. It smells old enough to belong to someone from the past.

Sod it, she's wearing it anyway. The old bat's nearly eighty, so neither her eyesight or her memory will be up to much.

Maisie plans to look amazing for the party. Tomorrow night she's going to be 'Amazing Maisie', like she was that night in the hotel, only this time she's doing it properly. She has a silver beaded dress that fits her like a condom and a blond wig, because sometimes they have more fun – she laughs out loud at this but nobody notices because Bel is suddenly screaming and pointing 'Look! Kittiwake, I can see Kittiwake.'

Maisie follows the line of Bel's finger but all she can see is the top of some chimneys and it's only when Andrew rounds the next corner that the house comes into view and Maisie can physically feel her jaw drop. It's big. Fuck me, she thinks, it's big and it's posh and it's yellow but like a good yellow with a hint of mustard in it. I should buy a handbag in that colour, or shoes . . . yeah, yellow shoes.

48

Back Where She Was Born

Cornwall, Saturday afternoon

Bel has no idea why she cannot fully relax. Apart from the weather, everything at Kittiwake is completely fine, a couple of eggy moments during the gift-opening ceremony earlier, perhaps, and Bel is once again convinced that she'd seen Lance and Freya swapping smirks at the present she'd bought him.

She'd been so proud of it. It had seemed like such a brainwave, commissioning a woman in Dulwich Village who had exhibited at the RA's summer exhibition no less, to paint a small oil landscape for her brother's big birthday. But as the wrapping paper fell away, she'd been engulfed by doubt. Was it her imagination or was the painting rather horrid? An amateurish daub that rather than grace one of Kittiwake's finely rendered walls, would be consigned to the bin as soon as this long bank holiday weekend is over.

Damn Lance. There is something about his face that she has never been able to read. Even as a child he'd had the slight supercilious curl to his lip that still hovers today. She knows it's not his fault but it has always lent him an air of mocking superiority.

Ever since he was born, he's made me feel like some kind of poor relation, she thinks, swigging her Pimm's. Dammit, she hadn't meant to drink till this evening. Oh God, this evening – she already feels exhausted by the prospect of more socialising. It's hard enough dealing with her extended family, including Freya's numerous Norwegian relatives, never mind all these glamorous total strangers.

Bel scans the party-goers playing croquet on the back lawn. So many gorgeous women, so many handsome, tanned, stubble-faced men, so much bohemian jewellery and so many straw hats, despite it not being straw-hat weather.

She herself is wearing her nice new skirt but with a casual red T-shirt as Maisie had suggested, rather than the white blouse, which she will change into for tonight. Freya had looked slightly crestfallen when she and Andrew admitted during the post-fish pie cheese board that they'd bottled out of the fancy-dress option. 'Quite right, too,' her mother had chimed in from the other end of the table, 'such a silly waste of time,' and Bel had watched Freya's face fall even further. Thinking back to this exchange now, Bel is grateful for the realisation that Natasha is capable of pricking some- one else's bubble rather than just her own. 'She's a difficult woman,' she mutters under her breath, simultaneously recalling how taken aback she'd been by her mother's arrival last night. The first thing that had struck her when Natasha walked into the dining room was how old she looked and how small, as if she'd shrunk in the wash like good cashmere.

Bel had immediately gone over to greet her, feeling mountainous beside her. Natasha flinched slightly as she approached, possibly nervous that Bel might tread on her, before offering up a papery cheek to be kissed.

They were halfway through supper when she'd arrived, which was a tad embarrassing but Freya had decided not to delay pro- ceedings because the pie was threatening to dry out and Natasha had swiftly been seated at the table some distance from Bel, which was a relief. Her mother was clearly put out at the fact no one had waited for her and had typically refused to eat anything except a small bunch of black grapes.

Her loss, thinks Bel, that fish pie was amazing. Even Maisie had wolfed it down and she is normally very squeamish about fish, squealing with horror when Bel buys trout for supper and she accidentally touches the blood-smeared plastic bag in the fridge.

Still, she had to admit Madam was toeing the line here at Kittiwake. Bel has never seen Maisie so demure as last night, sitting there in some kind of pretty vintage seventies peasant-style dress, holding her knife and fork correctly for once. Maisie had barely said a word but when she did Bel could tell she was doing her best to sound a little less Croydon than usual. Again, she feels a wave of warmth towards her. Must be the Pimm's, she shouldn't drink any more, she'll only get a headache.

Bel feels increasingly self-conscious, Andrew and the boys are nowhere to be seen and no one is making any real effort to include her in their conversations. New guests keep arriving all the time and the idea of mingling and introducing herself to strangers holds very little appeal. She's already been met with blank incomprehension after telling some woman in an orange straw trilby that she is Lance's sister. 'Older, obviously,' she'd added helpfully in the ensuing silence, only for the woman to blurt, 'Oh, gosh, I didn't even know he had a sister.'

Though they've never met him, all Bel's friends know about Lance, but then Lance appears in glossy magazines, Lance is a player, Lance is a successful businessman, Lance is someone to be proud of, while she is a dumpy middle-aged housewife and mother who lives in a house with too many coats.

Bel shivers in the stiff breeze. Talking of coats, she might go in soon and put on a cardigan. She glances up at Kittiwake. Even when the sun goes in, the house continues to glow. They really have done a remarkable job; there was a time when Kittiwake had looked quite sorry for itself, and it certainly hadn't been at its best in the sixties when Bel was born here.

It's been years since Bel has thought about that ciné film Benedict showed her when she was a troubled teenager, but immediately she is back in her uncle's funny little mews house watching Serena's lovely face loom up in front of her. Bel half closes her eyes and the memory floods back: a beautiful blonde, laughing and dancing in a previous incarnation of the same room that Bel had gorged herself on fish pie in less than twenty-four hours ago. She has to fight back the tears; Serena, her real mother. Serena, with her green eyes and golden earrings. What if she hadn't abandoned her here, what if she had taken her with her when she left, and what if she had never gone to that party?

Without warning, all the 'what if's crowd Bel's imagination until she feels dizzy. She's reminded of a poem she learned at school when she was very young. They'd written it out in class, 'in your best handwriting please, girls'. It was by Samuel Taylor Coleridge and it went:

> What if you slept
> And what if
> In your sleep
> You dreamed
> And what if
> In your dream
> You went to heaven
> And there plucked a strange and beautiful flower
> And what if
> When you awoke
> You had that flower in your hand
> Ah, what then?

They'd been allowed to draw a flower underneath the poem. 'The most beautiful flower you can possibly imagine, girls,' and Bel had used every single coloured pencil in her pencil case. The pencils that were all engraved A. BERRINGTON, even though deep down she knew that once upon a time she could have been someone else.

Bel drags herself back from the past and looks around in vain for a small figure in a well-ironed linen shirt and immaculate pair of white trousers. She feels an unexpected pang of guilt. It's been a while since she has even seen Natasha, let alone spoken to her. She has noticed the woman cuts a rather lonely figure here at Kittiwake, the place seems to dwarf her. And Bel recalls there are ghosts here that her adoptive mother must face too, and for a moment Bel's heart aches for Natasha, for the little girl that lost her brother and the young wife who thought she would never be a mother and for the widow whose life had never been hers to control. It can't be too late to be honest with each other, she resolves, finishing her drink while something of a commotion breaks out over by the tennis court. Children's voices are raised in anger – young children with high-pitched voices. She turns to look and briefly catches sight of a red-faced Luna and Ludo yelling at each other before something hits her, something hard on the side of her head, and it all goes dark.

49

Natasha at the Party

Natasha sits and seethes. She told them she was going upstairs for a rest, but in reality she needs to get away from all those ghastly people for a while. All that talk, yap, yap, yap.

Natasha isn't used to people talking so much. If only there was a volume control that she could turn down, like one of those dimmer switches, only for sound rather than light. It's all too much. The children shriek, the dog barks, strangers mingle with familiar faces, guests and caterers, she doesn't know who is a friend and who is a mere waitress, so she doesn't talk to anyone.

They have put her in a small single room at the side of the house. Last night she had been too tired to be insulted, but now she is furious. No doubt it was Freya's idea.

Lance said she wouldn't recognise the place, but she does, Kittiwake is horribly familiar. You can plaster it and paint it and throw cashmere cushions all over it, thinks Natasha, but she knows exactly where she is sleeping.

This was Blake's room, her father's butler, the man who pressed his mouth against Ivor's lips, then pumped at his chest

317

with his fists. Blake's panic-stricken voice will reverberate off these walls for ever. 'An ambulance, for God's sake, get an ambulance.'

Next to this room was her father's dressing room and next door to that was the master bedroom. It still is, she supposes; it's where Lance and that horse-faced wife of his sleep.

Natasha decides she has never liked Freya and today that feeling has hardened like enamel.

Freya thinks too much of herself, she has got her claws into this house, acting as if it belongs to her. As for her ghastly family, that overbearing mother with her ugly big feet in hideous Birkenstocks, her bossy sister breastfeeding that baby in front of everyone, as if the world wants to see her ugly blue-veined tits, she could at least put a shawl around her or find somewhere private, it's all so unnecessary.

She has barely seen Lance alone since she arrived. She was late, the plane had been delayed, but no one seemed to notice, they were already eating supper. Someone she didn't recognise moved up to make a space for her. She was nowhere near her son, she could only see him from a distance.

The fish pie was too rich, she couldn't possibly eat it. She managed a handful of grapes but had felt bilious all night.

This morning hadn't been any better. She had gone downstairs in a starched navy linen shirt and immaculately pressed white trousers to find the kitchen full of half-dressed strangers and she had sat, ignored, under the clothes pulley, hanging where it always has. So far as she's concerned, keeping that pulley is an affectation, a typical piece of set dressing from her son's wife.

When she was a child they never ate in the kitchen, that was where the staff ate, but Freya has knocked down the wall between the kitchen and what was the old dining room and the resulting space is as big as an aircraft hangar. 'It will be cold in the winter,' she commented to Freya's mother, who merely

318

laughed at her and said, 'Under-floor heating, Nathalie, that's the solution. If you get asked back at Christmas, this place will be as warm as toast.'

If you get asked back – the cheek of the bitch. As for the 'Nathalie' . . .

It's been a long time since anyone has got her name wrong. She hadn't bothered to correct the troll woman; as it happens she has no idea what she is called and she has no intention of finding out.

'There was a wooden table here with a meat mincer clamped to the edge,' she muttered to herself. 'A woman called Brenda came to do the cleaning and we had a governess who became hysterical when Ivor died.'

'Sorry, what's that, Grandma?' One of those ape boys of Bel's had looked at her as if she were completely losing her marbles.

Grandma, what an unlikely role to find herself playing.

'I'm remembering the past,' she told him. His breath was very strong. His mother should make sure he cleaned his teeth properly. He had toast crumbs in his beard and he didn't offer to help her to anything.

Breakfast was done buffet-style: smoked salmon and cream cheese bagels. Such a chewy consistency, the bagel; Natasha longed for the flaky ease of a croissant and seeing her struggle Bel offered to cut hers into small pieces as if she was incapable of doing it herself.

'I'm not quite gaga yet,' she had snapped and that old familiar look of hurt clouded her daughter's eyes.

Bel is fatter than ever, she noticed, but then, Bel has always been greedy. She had two bagels at breakfast, Natasha watched her and counted them. She'd always had to watch what Bel ate, she'd warned her what would happen if she ate too much and now it has.

Natasha eases off her Tod's suede loafers and makes herself as

319

comfortable as possible on the single bed. A single bed – could there be anything more coffin-like?

Deep down it's the watch that has upset her the most. Once everyone had eaten their bagels and Freya and her big-footed yeti mother had cleared the plates, everyone was summoned to the sitting room for the 'opening of the gifts'. A mound of brightly wrapped parcels lay heaped up on a cream leather footstool in front of a vast velvet sofa the deep blue of a Greek sea. Ludo and Luna and those pug-faced Norwegian cousins were leaping around the furniture shrieking. They were overly excited, in Natasha's opinion, and she would have liked to banish them from the room, but she dutifully kept quiet and added her small parcel to the pile.

The children would get their presents later, she decided, when all the fuss had died down. They are still in her suitcase, no doubt those will be wrong, too.

Lance had opened a gift from his old college friend first, a bald man whom Natasha was told she had met several times over the years. Toby someone, who has moved on to wife number two, a wisp of a thing who kept popping outside and coming back in reeking of cigarettes.

Natasha has left her menthols back in France, she could do with one now. She would like to see Freya's face if she filled the little onyx trinket holder on the bedside table with her Marlboro Green cigarette butts.

It was a cricket bat, the gift from Toby and Lucy, but signed by someone famous. Lance seemed delighted and he began batting the abandoned wrapping paper until Freya yelped and said, 'Actually, darling, maybe you should play with that thing outside before you take someone's head off,' and Toby and his new wife had exchanged looks, as if to say 'miserable cow'.

Freya should watch it, thinks Natasha. If Toby, who is fat and bald, can get a younger prettier second wife, then Lance certainly can.

Bel's gift came next. She flushed and sort of preened as she passed it to him, gushing that she had commissioned it specially, 'a woman in Dulwich Village, bit of a reputation'. It was hideous! A viciously garish oil painting of a poppy field. Freya visibly winced, but Lance was kind – he has always been kind to Bel; 'I love it,' he lied.

Then came the children's presents: socks, books, a silk handkerchief, a framed photograph of the pair of them on a beach, followed by a huge Nordic sweater from Freya's mob, which Lance promptly pulled over his head and then thanked each of them individually, even Baby Aksel who at that precise moment chose to puke all over his mother's giant tit – disgusting.

The pile had rapidly diminished until there were only a few parcels left. Freya should have left hers till last, but she lunged forward and handed Lance a box-shaped parcel, and he had ripped the paper off in a pretend frenzy. It was a watch. Of course it was a watch, it was exactly the watch Lance had wanted: 'Wow, Freya – the Bell and Ross BR-X1!' he exclaimed, thrilled, and Natasha felt her heart close as tight as a clam.

She was about to snatch her gift from the footstool, tell him she'd wrapped the wrong thing and that it was a mistake, but her son reached for it before she could.

'And last but not least, from my favourite mother,' he had grinned and kissed her on the head. He smelt of lime and basil and toothpaste – those sons of Bel's should look, sniff and learn.

The Caravelle Sea Hunter with its small black face looked mean in comparison to the watch Freya had given him, a miserable inconsequential thing, exactly like his father had turned out to be, Natasha thinks bitterly.

Naturally, Lance had been very good about it, made room for it on his wrist, strapped it on next to the gleaming titanium thing his wife had bought him with its dials and gadgets and face as big as a camera lens.

'It was your father's,' she had murmured, but he pretended not to hear her and ten minutes later, she saw him take it off.

It will sit in a drawer now, as it had done since Hugo died twenty years ago. May he rot in hell, what a dance that man had led her, all those dreadful things he had made her do . . .

Natasha is distracted from her reverie by a commotion on the lawn beneath her bedroom. Watching from her open window, she gathers that Ludo has thwacked a stone with a tennis racket and it has caught Annabel on the side of the head.

Children need watching, their games can be dangerous, Natasha knows this only too well. Many years ago she was playing a game with her brothers in this very house, a silly game involving a golf club, but Ivor had cheated and she had got angry and she had swung the club hard and the next thing she remembered was her mother screaming.

It was an accident, she hadn't meant any harm, but he shouldn't have cheated, he didn't need to cheat, he was getting everything anyway.

Natasha pulls herself back to the present. Back down on the lawn, Annabel – or Bel, as she likes to call herself these days – seems to be staggering slightly. How much has the woman had to drink, for goodness sake? And then she falls.

Natasha watches as voices are raised and a crowd huddles around her adopted daughter. Eventually a middle-aged man in pink trousers takes charge and he and a tattooed waitress carry Annabel like a sack of potatoes into the house, one pudgy thigh exposed for all to see. How embarrassing.

'She'll be as right as rain in a minute, no need to panic,' she hears the man say, and Natasha lies back on the bed and tries not to think of that Easter holiday when everything went so disastrously wrong and set off a chain of events that kept on going wrong for years to come.

The last thing she remembers before sleep drags her under is that when Ivor died he hadn't finished all his chocolate Easter eggs. Many years later, Benedict told her that the night after they lost their brother he had found the eggs under Ivor's bed, and even though he couldn't stop crying, he had eaten them all until not a single chocolate button was left.

50

The Main Event

Kittiwake, Saturday evening

Freya looks anxiously at the darkening sky. The gathering clouds have turned the colour of tarnished knives and the evening light is a curious metallic yellow.

It might be her imagination, but with the change in the weather, a slight whiff of rotting bladderwrack and dirty clam shells seems to have rolled in from the sea. Even indoors, with a Diptyque candle in every corner, she can smell it.

Freya shudders as a current of foreboding threads across her shoulder blades, but she pulls herself together immediately.

There is nothing to worry about, apart from Bel playing the drama queen and pretending to faint when she got hit on the head by a tiny piece of flying gravel, and Ludo flouncing off in a sulk because his father embarrassed him by telling him off in front of his cousins. Oh, and Natasha being distant and peculiar – but apart from that, things are going well.

People will be talking about this party for months, the juggling cocktail mixologist, the canapés, the hilarious three-legged race on the buttercup lawn.

Freya knocks back a couple of paracetamol and takes one more for luck. She's got an awful headache, but unlike Bel, she can't loll around on the bed, she is the hostess and there is still tonight's hog roast and disco and tomorrow's (fingers crossed) beach breakfast barbie and evening bonfire to get through.

Freya tries to relieve the tension in her neck and shoulders with a few yoga stretches, but every time she moves her head, her neck grinds like an overfilled peppermill.

On Monday she will get someone up to the house to give her a massage, and in a split second of intense resentment she wonders if Lance would ever go to this much effort for her birthday.

But the moment passes and Freya lifts the corners of her mouth as she catches sight of their 'his and hers' fancy-dress costumes laid out on the bed. Tonight Mr and Mrs Berrington will be Poldark and Demelza. What a brainwave that had been, Freya thinks smugly. A friend in London works for a theatrical costumier and the outfits arrived a couple of days ago; she and Lance tried them on, to be on the safe side, but happily, Lance has the calves for breeches and the corset puts Freya's post-breastfeeding bosoms right back where they used to be.

She hadn't imagined anyone else would have had the same brainwave, but right now, as she watches the guests stream in from the yurt field, Freya is infuriated to see a quite a number of Poldark and Demelza doppelgängers, dammit. There is also what looks like a giant Cornish pasty holding hands with a size-sixteen bright green pixie.

She checks her watch, the nannies have sole care of the children now, they are having their own private barbecue on the back lawn. Afterwards there will be ice creams from the van parked by the gates and then cartoons in the playroom. She needn't fret; her mother and Elise have offered back-up should it be needed.

Having her own family here has been a bittersweet experience for Freya. Their physical presence is a reminder of how much she misses them; lapsing back into Norwegian, she finds the words of her mother tongue as comforting and familiar as a warm drink on her lips.

She, Elise and Mari touch each other all the time; her mother strokes her hair and kisses the top of her head, her sister chases her up the stairs.

By contrast, she has noticed how distant Lance and Bel are. They may as well be two polite strangers in a lift, there is no hugging and no teasing.

As for Natasha, her behaviour is grotesque. She ignores Bel, while following Lance around like an adoring but unwanted puppy.

Freya feels sorry for Bel, but at the same time she's infuriated by her. The woman is hopeless. As for that hideous painting she gave to Lance, what had she been thinking? As soon as this weekend is over, it's going to a charity shop. Freya laughs at the thought of it, how can anyone get anything so wrong?

She immediately feels guilty. The watch situation was a bit of a nightmare – Natasha's face had frozen when Lance had opened Freya's gift.

But then turning up with a memento of his father was such an odd thing to do. Lance has airbrushed his father out of his life – the man was, by all accounts, a total shit – so why would Natasha think he needed reminding of him?

Lance has told her that when he was little his father hit his mother and it was only when he died that she stopped wearing sunglasses indoors. He died before they even met, but from the photos she's seen Hugo was a good-looking man in exquisitely cut suits, with a nasty smirk that played around his lips. Much to her horror, she has occasionally seen that exact same smirk on Ludo's face.

Freya checks the time on her phone. She has scheduled the next fifteen minutes on her itinerary as 'changing time' and needs

326

Lance to come upstairs to help her into her costume. It's seven fifteen, the hog roast is timed for eight, with the cutting of the cake an hour later, by which time it should be dark enough in the barn for the candles on the confectionery Kittiwake to be at their most effective. Freya is more delighted by the cake than anything, it's a masterpiece, a perfectly scaled-down sponge-based Kittiwake complete with pale yellow royal icing and tiny fondant climbing roses. It could taste of brick and sawdust inside for all she cares, she can't wait to see the reaction when it gets carried in, all fifty candles flaming.

For a moment Freya allows herself to bask in her own glory. The obstacle course had been a fantastic idea, Lucy had even twisted her ankle, which was an added bonus, Lance loved her present and her little lace-up Demelza boots fit like a dream. Later on there will be champagne and dancing. With any luck, Lance will be drunk enough and happy enough to fuck her.

Down the corridor, Andrew checks up on Bel again, she is fast asleep, snoring like a hedge trimmer. He feels her brow, there is no fever and he googles 'concussion' but he can't get onto the internet because 4G doesn't work around here, and he doesn't want to bother Freya or Lance for the Wi-Fi code.

No doubt Maisie and the boys will have managed to log on by now, he'll ask one of them for help later, but Bel's breathing sounds completely normally, so that's good.

He's also reassured by the fact that she's eaten some of the sandwiches he brought up a couple of hours ago when the caterers served afternoon tea on the terrace. Andrew had enjoyed that, pretty waitresses offering cucumber triangles and tiny bite-sized scones with jam and cream. He'd had quite a heated debate with Freya's mother over which should go first, the cream or the jam, and that had been nice too.

Andrew isn't entirely comfortable amongst the Kittiwake

gathering, there are a lot of very good-looking men around ten years younger than him with thick hair, deep tans and fashionable heavy-rimmed glasses. No one is particularly interested in an NHS statistician from South London, however senior, and even his own mother-in-law has yet to address him. He's not particularly fussed that Natasha doesn't like him. In his opinion, the woman is toxic and he gave up trying with her years ago. As for Lance, they have nothing in common; his brother-in-law is so alpha male that even his handshake hurts.

If it were up to him, he would much rather stay up here with Bel than rejoin the party. Maybe he could nip down, show his face, then smuggle up a couple of beers and a bit of that hog roast? Andrew's mouth waters, the smell wafting round from the back of the house is pretty incredible, and he wonders fleetingly whether today will be one of Maisie's vegan days, or if she will make an exception for roast pig, like she frequently does for chicken, bacon, mince and lamb.

He hasn't seen much of her or the boys since they got here. He wishes his sons could be more at ease in company, introduce themselves, shake hands firmly with strangers, instead of sidling off and disappearing for hours on end. But Andrew understands their reluctance to mingle, because he is shy too and being surrounded by all these overtly confident, good-looking people is nerve-racking and playing havoc with his digestion. Andrew takes a swig of Gaviscon and gives a small burp of relief.

All the women have thin wrists and multi-stranded necklaces, featuring tiny gleaming charms. They all look as though they have spent the summer on some fabulous Greek island and some of them have rings around their toes and pierced noses.

He wishes now that he and Bel had bothered to come up with some sort of fancy-dress plan. In a spasm of desperation he toys with the idea of dragging the bottom sheet off the bed and pretending to be a member of the Ku Klux Klan, but is immediately appalled by the idea.

He will wear the pale blue linen shirt from Marks that Bel packed for him, and he will be friendly and sociable because it's what Bel would want him to be. It's only for a couple more nights, nothing goes on for ever. Also the food is very good.

Natasha is still groggy from her afternoon nap. Much as she dreads the thought of heading back downstairs, she doesn't want to give Freya the satisfaction of labelling her a 'difficult bitch'. So she slips into a simple black silk dress with sheer chiffon blouson sleeves and a pair of gold brocade slipper shoes and fights back a wave of desolation as she takes out her powder compact and runs a coral lipstick around her narrow mouth.

Her mother's face looks back at her in the mirror. How did she get so old? And she watches her mouth twist into the shape that Peggy's made when they told her Ivor was dead, but, unlike her mother's, Natasha's scream is silent.

Maisie has dressed up as a sexy silver siren, part mermaid, part Hollywood starlet, her silver dress is slit to both the navel and the knee and fans out to form a fishtail at the back.

She has sprayed her silver-blond wig with green glitter 'seaweed' streaks and around each wrist and ankle are bracelets threaded with tiny silver shells that make a tinkling noise as she walks.

Once the glue is dry on her double set of false eyelashes, she paints her eyelids bright gold and her lips dark ruby. She is treasure from a sunken chest, she is a long-lost jewel from the bottom of the sea and her heart is beating like Bel's egg whisk when she makes meringues.

He recognised her over the fish pie last night. He had choked and pretended to have a tiny bone stuck in his windpipe and Freya droned on about the fishmonger promising he had been through the salmon with a pair of surgical tweezers and what a drag it would be if he ruined his own birthday by choking to death.

Which was an odd kind of crap joke that made the two foreign women laugh a lot. She found out later they were Freya's mother and sister; Maisie feels sorry for the sister, who looks like Freya crossed with a pug.

So far today they have kept out of each other's way. Maisie has been on her best behaviour, but she's had a line of coke in preparation for tonight and drunk a bottle of prosecco while getting ready. She straps up her silver heels, throws the little white fox shrug around her shoulders and wobbles down the stairs. Fuck knows where Ed and Jamie are. Last time she saw them they were holed up in the twin room she's meant to be sharing with Ed, playing video games on a PS4 they'd hooked up to the TV. If they ever appear and anyone asks what they've dressed up as, she can always reply 'losers'.

It had been Maisie's idea to switch rooms. Last night she'd told them she wasn't feeling well, blaming the long drive, and Bel had backed her up, saying she did look quite feverish. Ed had leapt at the chance of a bit of downtime with his brother – and a break from his demanding girlfriend.

With Maisie off Ed's back and their mother out of the picture, there's no one to give the boys a hard time for not 'mixing' or joining in the dancing, which Maisie loves and Ed doesn't. He and Jamie are quite happy, they've got beer and crisps and a big pile of weird Norwegian sweets. Maybe later Maisie will bring them each a piece of cake wrapped up in a paper napkin.

The barn is pulsing by the time Lance and Freya make their orchestrated entrance. As they walk in hand in hand, accompanied by the *Poldark* theme tune, which Freya has had remixed to sound a bit more clubby, all the guests turn and applaud.

Freya's spirits soar, she doesn't even need a drink, it's all been completely worthwhile – the expense, the headaches, the spreadsheets – and she starts to dance, at first with Lance and then with her sister and Baby Aksel and then with the enormous Cornish pasty, who apologises every time he steps on her little leather Demelza boots.

Andrew sits down slightly self-consciously on one of the hay bales. In another hour or so he will have done his duty and can return to Bel and his pyjamas, but in the meantime he eats his second hog-roast-and-apple-sauce roll and watches Maisie dance with Donald Trump. As she gyrates Andrew hurriedly turns his gaze in another direction; there is something a bit 'dirty old man' about watching your son's girlfriend gyrate.

Next thing he knows, Freya's mother has grabbed him by the wrist and dragged him to the dance area. He shuffles awkwardly from one foot to the other in front of her, neither of them recognise the song that blares from the speakers, and it's all rather excruciating, but fortunately they are both spared any further humiliation by the arrival of the cake.

There is an audible gasp as the creation is carried in by a couple of six-foot waiters. They step carefully, avoiding any breeze that could blow the candles out – fifty of them are studded into Kittiwake's crenellated rooftop, it looks like the place is on fire. The effect is spectacular, as Freya knew it would be, it had cost her over a thousand pounds and in the morning any remnants will be stale, fit only for the birds, but in this moment as the guests clap and cheer, it is worth every penny. The cake is so realistic that she is surprised not to hear the tiny sugar-glazed windowpanes cracking in the heat of the candle flame. People burst into an impromptu 'Happy birthday, dear Lance' and Freya feels her eyes well up. This is it, this is the moment – if only she hadn't left her fucking phone indoors. Dammit, all that money and she can't even Instagram it.

The cake comes to a halt on one of the trestle tables at the back of the barn and a slightly unsteady Lance lurches over to blow the candles out.

He bends over the cake, one hand protectively holding back the ruffles of his potentially flammable shirt, and blows hard and long. 'Happy birthday, dear Laaaance, happy birthday to you.'

The candles are all extinguished and everyone surges towards the cake to inspect its scaled-down perfection. Even the twisted vines around the porch are an identical match, while the front door is so realistic, it looks like you could actually open it and step inside the cake, into a world of marzipan stairs and sugar-spun chandeliers.

A knife is produced, long-handled and sharp. Freya blinks, it's not the knife she had chosen for the job. Its partner, the eBay-sourced decorative silver serving slice, is in situ on the cake board, but the matching knife isn't there. This one looks like someone has hastily wiped down the carving knife from the hog roast. Someone in the crowd shouts, 'How could you?' in mock horror at the idea of slicing into this masterpiece, but another voice shouts 'Cut it' and soon the barn is full of revellers chanting 'Cut it, cut it, cut it!'

Lance brandishes the knife and aims right for the centre of the roof. As he brings the blade down, the entire party whoops and cheers, plates are passed around and people clamour for bits of turret or a slice with 'some of that fondant icing'.

Freya breathes out, they can all relax now and party until they drop. She weaves her way through the throng to have a quick word with the 'mood' technician they have hired for the night, and he turns the music up, dims the lights and begins to project the digitalised ciné film. Seconds later, to everyone's delight, the barn walls come alive with dancing strangers from another century. The space begins to seethe and pump, people laugh and point at the funny old-fashioned people and some of them begin to imitate the Technicolor ciné guests, boogieing sixties-style.

*

Natasha stands apart from the main action, watching the Kittiwake cake crumble and fall apart. There goes Ivor's bedroom window. Now the top of the west turret.

She keeps catching fleeting glimpses of faces she vaguely recognises, though she knows they can't possibly be here. How can Valerie Cooper be dancing the twist, with her auburn hair flying around her shoulders as if she were still twenty, when Natasha knows she has been bed-bound in a nursing home for the past five years?

Natasha is confused, her balance feels off-kilter, she can't remember what she is doing here or how on earth she knows all these oddly dressed people. She wishes she was back in her little house on the Île de Ré with its small courtyard where she can sit in silence and choose what she wants to remember and what she chooses to forget. But here everything is all jumbled up and she feels anxious. Looking for an escape route, she catches sight of a familiar blonde and instantly the blood curdles in her veins. She can't possibly be here. She died. Natasha knows she died, because she was there when it happened, she saw her fall, she saw the dark ring of blood ooze around her silver head. Natasha finds herself moving closer to the girl, close enough for her own shadow to fall across her and block her from view. All of a sudden the illusion makes sense – she should have known, it's a film. Once upon a time, she and Hugo had bought Benedict a ciné camera for his birthday; how silly of her to think it was real.

Surrounded by strangers and images of long-lost friends, Natasha feels herself wilt. Maybe she should go to bed now. She has seen everything there is to see. Tomorrow night there will be a small firework display to finish off the weekend and then her taxi will come and she can fly home and look at her own calm white walls. Serena isn't here, she is an apparition, a piece of celluloid preserved in a metal tin and projected onto the bare barn wall.

Natasha would rather the tin had never been opened, she hadn't wished to see the genie dancing out of her bottle, the nightmares are enough without seeing her magnified like this, those blue eyes boring into her, the way they had that night over half a century ago. She turns to go, she is tired now, the champagne feels acidic in her stomach. Tonight she will sleep in Blake's old room and try not to think of him holding her dead brother in his arms. She will take a sleeping pill – she has needed them for years, her French doctor is very accommodating – and sleep will solve everything. But first she must say goodnight to her fifty-year-old baby. She is his mother, she's allowed to seek him out, to search for him like she had when he was a toddler and went missing for twenty minutes in a Spanish airport.

Oddly enough, she feels the same trepidation as she had all those years ago: Lance seems to have disappeared from his own party. Her heart begins to race as she scans the crowd for a sight of him. She has to keep reminding herself that he is no longer three years old and he is not wearing blue checked shorts and a red T-shirt, he is a fully grown man with children of his own. Eventually she finds him behind a stack of hay bales, a few yards beyond the table where the cake lies in ruins. The wreckage, now missing its roof, reminds her of when she was a little girl coming back to London after the war and seeing the ruined church round the corner from where she lived. The Luftwaffe had bombed it – danger has always been everywhere.

He is dancing, her son is dancing with a girl in a silver dress, his hand is on the small of her back, her white-blond hair spills down past her shoulders. Her son is dancing with Serena. So, the lying bitch *is* here, how like her to come back now. It has to be Serena, she is wearing the same little fox fur shrug that she wore that night in Mayfair, the one she stole from Peggy's wardrobe at Kittiwake. She is the same as she ever was, a thief and a slut.

Maisie sees it before he does, a flash of silver, and she moves faster than him, spinning out of his arms and looking over her shoulder in

334

horror as Natasha pushes the hog roast knife, all covered in cream and icing, into her own son. Then Maisie screams, she screams like a woman in a film would scream, the scream is blood-curdling and oddly contagious.

Maisie screams then Beyoncé screams and Melania Trump screams and then the woman dressed up as a giant pixie screams and eventually someone turns off the music and the lights come up.

Elise takes charge of the situation immediately, ripping Freya's Demelza petticoat to make an impromptu tourniquet, 'It's only a nick,' she tells Lance, who has gone as white as Kittiwake's freshly laundered pillowcases, 'nothing to worry about,' but even though Elise keeps reassuring everyone that it's a superficial flesh wound, there is quite a lot of blood.

The man dressed up as a Cornish pasty gently removes the knife from Natasha's hand and the old woman just stands there looking like a hundred-year-old doll.

'I saw Serena,' she repeats. 'I thought Serena had come back to Kittiwake, I saw her, I saw Serena.'

51

Serena Leaves the Baby

Kittiwake, February 1963

Serena looked at the baby again and tried very hard to feel something, but the space in her chest where she was expecting a warm and fuzzy glow was resolutely empty.

All she felt was distant, as if she were watching herself from far away, on another planet looking down from afar at this girl and her baby.

'My baby,' she whispered to herself, 'you have a baby girl.' It's what Morwenna, the midwife in the hospital, had told her, so it must be true. Morwenna's hands were covered in blood but she kept smiling and said, 'She's perfect.'

Only she isn't, thought Serena, she's a small sallow thing, a bit like a weasel wrapped in a blanket.

Things had been fine while she recovered in the maternity ward. They had looked after her, no one asked any questions and at visiting time when other new mothers had their 'loved ones' crowding around them, a nurse who was about the same age as

Serena came and drew the curtains around her bed and simply said, 'You get yourself some rest now.'

They had taken the baby to a nursery at night and fed her from a bottle. Serena watched a few of the other women breastfeed, but it looked disgusting, like the baby piglets at the farm down the road, snuffling and tugging at their mother's teats. She saw what happened to the mothers' nipples, how they were pulled out of shape, and she heard them cry with the pain of it.

Her baby has never been anything but bottle-fed. The hospital gave her a big tin of powdered formula to start her off, with 'added vitamins for healthy bones' and once she ran out, she got Robbie from the farm to go to the chemist and buy her some more.

Robbie was loyal, he was the one who had taken her to hospital when her waters broke and she panicked. His mother didn't approve of her. Serena hid on Tuesdays when Bren came to clean the house – she took the baby up to the attic and watched through a hole in the floorboards as Bren swept and polished below. If the baby cried, she held the shawl over her mouth, but never too tightly. The baby kept breathing, but sometimes she looked at Serena as if to say, It's you against me.

The baby was stronger than she looked and sometimes Serena was a bit frightened of her.

Robbie said she should go home, back to Southend, and take the baby with her. He swore blind her mum and Nanna would love the 'little 'un' and that Ida would forgive her in the end, but it wasn't Ida who needed to forgive Serena, it was Serena herself. She couldn't get over what she had done, how stupid she'd been in allowing this to happen. She had so wanted to confound all expectations, to surprise everyone, she'd had such big dreams and they didn't include being an unmarried mother.

She refused to take this baby back to Southend, only to hear a trail of whispers behind her back, 'Yes, that's her, the Tipping girl and her little bastard, oh no, no man, on her own, like her mother and her grandmother before her – not much luck with the opposite sex, those Tipping women, silly bitches!'

When she was pregnant, she couldn't think beyond getting the baby out of her. She'd convinced herself that, once the child was born, then the next step would become obvious. But it was nearly three weeks since she had given birth and she was still confused.

Serena looked at the sleeping bundle. The baby was out of her now, detached like a mini spacecraft. She was a separate entity, the cord had been cut, they were no longer physically attached, the baby didn't actually need her any more. When she was a foetus, she'd relied on Serena for blood and food and oxygen, Serena hadn't quite understood the science of it all, but she knew there was a tube attaching her and the baby, and the baby survived because of the tube. Well, the tube business was over and anyone could feed a baby with a bottle as long as they had the powdered stuff.

Serena eyed the tin of Cow & Gate on her windowsill, it contained about another day's supply, but after that she would need to get some more. Robbie had fetched it for her up until now, but he'd gone away for a bit, to work on his uncle's farm over in Zennor, which was miles away – his uncle had broken his leg and needed help with his cows.

A great tide of loneliness engulfed Serena, she couldn't stay here, not by herself, not without Robbie making sure she had what she needed. She shivered, her teeth physically chattering like the comedy wind-up false teeth they used to sell on Southend Pier. The house was so cold and the Aga had run out of oil, so the only way she could keep herself and the baby warm was to go to bed with Peggy's old beaver-fur coat spread over them. Every morning when they woke up, she and the baby stared at each other in disappointment.

Without the Aga, she couldn't dry the nappies she made herself from cutting up towels into napkin-sized squares which she had

338

learned to pin around the baby's skinny legs. At first she threw the shitty ones away, unable to face washing the stains out, chucking them on the fire in the sitting room, and putting her sleeve over her nose until the whiff of burning shit had evaporated, but the fire had gone out and there was no dry wood left in the log store.

Serena seethed, this was all Benedict's fault, he should be home by now, taking care of the situation. She had written to him months ago, telling him she needed to talk to him and that the matter was urgent, but she'd heard nothing back. She realised he went skiing over Christmas – he'd told her how much he loved it – but now it was the beginning of February. God knows she understood that rich people had different rules, she'd spent enough time here at Kittiwake mixing with Benedict's posh mates to know that, but surely you couldn't celebrate the new year for ever. At some point even the largest jeroboam ran dry.

If only she knew for sure who the father was. She eyed the creature suspiciously, willing her to exhibit some resemblance to Benedict, but the child remained resolutely bald and nondescript, like a tiny secret service agent. She could have come from anywhere and anyone.

Her eyes may have been blue but sometimes they looked grey. Today there was yellow gooey stuff coming out of one of them. Serena wiped it clean with the edge of her sleeve. Her mother once told her that when she was a baby she won a bonniest baby competition, she got a little silver cup and some premium bonds. Maybe this ugly baby wasn't even hers, maybe they got her mixed up with Serena's real baby at the hospital and somewhere in another woman's arms was a smiling baby with Serena's blond hair and Benedict's brown eyes. The changeling baby looked at her doubtfully and in that instant Serena made up her mind.

She couldn't stay here, Benedict might never come back, the house would fall down around her ears and she and the baby would starve to death. She was only twenty years old, she had time for another life, she could start again with a different name and forget this chapter ever existed. Maybe one day years from now, when everything had worked out and she had married a rich, successful, handsome businessman/pilot/film star, she would visit her mother and grandmother, pulling up outside the house in a swish car that took up half the street with bags of gifts for Nanna and Mum, bottles of stout and scent and bouquets of flowers, and she would take them out for dinner and eat steaks the size of dinner plates decorated with grilled tomato and little sprigs of parsley.

'We never gave up on you,' her mother would say, 'we always knew you'd come back. I said to Nanna, "You wait, one day that girl will come home, and when she does, she'll have the world at her feet."'

Well, that's not going to happen if I sit around here, decided Serena. I might as well be back on the till at Keddies as rotting away down here.

It was 1963, Helen Shapiro was famous and she was only sixteen, Serena was getting left behind, she needed to catch up, she needed to go to London. If the rainbow started here, then London was where the pot of gold lay. Serena ran up to the attic room where everything that had ever been abandoned at Kittiwake eventually ended up and dug around until she found a large leather Gladstone bag, heavy but capacious. Back in the bedroom she'd adopted as hers months ago, she filled the bag with all her best clothes, plus the little white fox fur shrug plucked from a wardrobe she'd had no right to open.

Benedict had recognised it immediately. 'That was my mother's,' he told her. 'Her name is Peggy. I haven't seen her in years, she lives in America.'

When had he told her that? After they'd had sex or over the dinner table? She couldn't remember. She threw in a silver-backed hairbrush – she might need to sell a few things before she got settled. The bag was still not full, and it occurred to her that she could quite easily fit the baby in there. She picked her up and bundled her in, but the baby immediately started crying. She didn't like it in the bag. Serena lifted her out again; it was a sign.

The cleaner was due the next day, Robbie's mum. The woman was like clockwork: week after week she turned up on the same day at the same time. She would be here first thing in the morning.

The baby was properly crying now. She got louder every day. Brenda would hear her, she would find her. Robbie said she was looking forward to having a grandchild. Well, she could have this one to practise on while she waited for her own.

Serena prepared a fresh bottle for her daughter and fed her until milk spilled out of her tiny mouth. After a perfunctory attempt at winding the infant, Serena changed her nappy – the new one had been cut down from a luxurious lemon-coloured bath-sheet complete with a Harrods label – and then she dressed her in the clothes that Robbie had smuggled up from the farmhouse. Everything the baby wore had been 'borrowed' from the hand-knitted items Robbie's mother was stockpiling for the arrival of his sister's baby in a few months' time. 'Our Sal would go through the roof if she ever found out,' Robbie warned her.

Conscious of how cold it would be for the child without the warmth of her mother's body tonight, Serena swaddled the baby in a brushed-cotton pillowcase and wrapped the bundle in a velvet opera cloak (courtesy of Peggy again) before nestling her securely between the folded piles of blankets in the bottom drawer of the wardrobe.

Absent-mindedly she closed the drawer, before remembering the baby had to be able to breathe. She quickly re-opened it to discover that the baby had fallen asleep. She must have liked it in the drawer. Serena dropped a fleeting kiss on her forehead, then she dragged the beaver-skin coat off the bed and put it on over her Aran jumper and tartan wool trousers. There were some discarded walking boots in the hallway which were near enough her size, so she slipped them on and then, pausing only to fill the deep furry pockets of the coat with anything on the dressing table that might fetch a few bob in a pawnbroker's, she picked up the Gladstone bag, turned her back on her baby and walked out on a future she had never planned in the first place.

52

The Reinvention of Renee Culpepper

Serena slid into London life like a fish. Luck was on her side from the moment she put out her thumb a mile or so from Kittiwake's rusty iron gates and was picked up by a woman in her sixties.

'Call me Gwen, dear' was eager to have someone to chat to on the long drive to Okehampton to see her newly widowed sister.

'Your job is to keep me awake at the wheel,' Gwen instructed Serena, who obediently passed her cups of Thermos-flask coffee at regular intervals and shared Gwen's tinfoil-wrapped sandwiches: 'Corned beef and homemade pickle, or egg mayonnaise, dear?'

Serena felt safe in Gwen's Morris Traveller with its flea-bitten travel rugs and stench of wet dog, and as she said goodbye, she promised the older woman that she wouldn't take any lifts from lorry drivers.

But inevitably she did, she jumped in the first lorry that stopped on the A30 and was mildly surprised that, despite Dave's cab being awash with pornographic magazines and boxes of tissues, he didn't even bother her for a kiss.

He did however eye her up and down as he dropped her, unmolested, on the outskirts of Croydon, and told her about a 'photographer friend' who would probably put her up for a night or two in exchange for a couple of photography sessions, at which point he'd scribbled down an address, tapped his nose and said, 'If you know what I mean?'

Serena didn't but she could guess and a couple of short hitches and a stale cheese roll courtesy of a cab driver in an all-night café later, she found herself knocking on the front door of a shabby Victorian terrace in Camberwell.

A woman in her late sixties answered the door, shadowed by a man in his early forties wearing a plaid dressing gown. If either Margaret or Graham Spencer were surprised to see a total stranger standing on their doorstep at 2.45 a.m., neither of them showed it.

Within half an hour, Serena was ensconced in the spare bedroom with a hot Ribena and a custard cream biscuit, but before she could climb into the small single bed, she had to remove dozens of oversized stuffed toys and knitted gonks that were piled on top of the purple nylon counterpane.

In the morning Graham and his mother explained the house rules. Serena would get free bed and board, dinners not included, in exchange for two three-hour modelling sessions a week. 'You're not shy, dear, are you?' asked Mrs Spencer, her eyes huge and innocent behind her pebble-thick lenses.

The set up was pretty simple: on Tuesday and Thursday mornings, the 'South London Photography Society' met up in what Mrs Spencer insisted on calling the parlour to take photographs – 'Of the glamour persuasion,' breathed Graham. 'We're very keen on appreciating the female form.'

'And I'm always here,' added Margaret, 'supplying refreshments, and making sure everything's kept nice.'

That first Tuesday, as she posed in a borrowed bikini holding a beach ball, Serena was conscious for the first time in her life of the extra roll of soft white flesh around her midriff and the slight pendulous quality of her breasts, but fortunately the participants seemed neither to notice nor care.

The photography club consisted entirely of middle-aged men, some of whom didn't even take their coats off. What little conversation there was revolved mostly around complaining about the poor quality of light, which was entirely due to Graham's mother keeping the front curtains closed so as not to upset the neighbours.

'Some people are very narrow-minded,' Margaret confided in Serena. 'They don't understand that Graham's photography club is a serious amateur photographers' association and not a regular meeting of the dirty old man brigade.'

Despite Mrs Spencer's protestations, Serena suspected some of the men didn't actually have any film in their cameras and these tended to be the ones who breathed most deeply and stood far too close.

This was a temporary measure, Serena persuaded herself daily, this would not last, there was something better round the corner. There had to be, she couldn't have given up her child for this.

Several weeks later, towards the end of an exhausting session involving nightwear, soft toys and a Dralon pouffe, one of the photographers requested her name for the title of a shot he wanted to enter for a competition. 'I'm Renee,' she said, the lie slipping out without her even thinking. Instantly the modelling became easier; she wasn't Serena the runaway mum any more, she was Renee, part-time glamour model, and very soon no one thought to call her anything else.

It didn't take Renee long to realise she couldn't survive in the capital on free bed and breakfast alone, and anyway she hadn't come to London to get stuck in Camberwell. Once she built up the confidence to tackle the city's complicated bus routes, she found herself a part-time bar job in a pub not far from the West End.

The Packhorse in Kennington was situated within the division bell area; according to the landlord, that meant theoretically an MP could leave his pint and be at the Houses of Parliament within eight minutes. 'We get a lot of that type in here,' he added darkly.

It was while working in SE1 that Renee encountered Maureen Leach, a tough port-and-lemon-drinking Irishwoman in her late fifties who 'knew people and organised things'.

Mo was a Packhorse regular, and having taken a shine to Renee, she 'organised things' so that she could escape the clutches of South London's premier photography club and move into a flat in Earls Court with two other 'fun-loving young ladies', Gloria, a short busty redhead, and Patty, a tall black woman with the biggest feet Renee had ever seen.

Serena Tipping was officially Renee Culpepper now. She took the name 'Culpepper' from the label on a jar of dyspepsia salts that had sat on the bathroom windowsill in Southend for as long as she could remember: *Culpepper's Salts for the relief of acid stomach and indigestion.*

Happy in her new postcode with her new identity, as far as Renee was concerned, Serena Tipping was some girl she used to know who dyed her own hair and worked in a supermarket in Southend.

Renee, on the other hand, went to a salon in Chelsea where twinkle toes 'Terry the poof' had given her a silver bouffant that shone like a massive pearl.

Despite the new hairdo, Maureen informed her that she was unsuited to 'proper modelling', being too short and curvy, but not to fret because there was always plenty of work for a pretty girl with bags of personality.

The 'too short and curvy' comment had stung for a while. Renee wasn't as short or as curvy as her flatmate Gloria, who was four foot eleven inches of pure curves and nonetheless exceedingly popular with the gentlemen. As indeed all three of them were. Maureen made sure they were invited to all the right parties, which meant they never had to pay for a drink or dinner. As to how they paid their rent, well, as Maureen said, 'That's none of my beeswax,' adding with a wink, 'See no evil – that's me.'

It took a while for Serena to twig that some of her flatmates' 'gentlemen friends' were actually clients.

Renee got paid by Terry's salon in exchange for having her photo in the window, and for a while she continued to cross the river to work in the pub and 'model' for Graham and his friends. Margaret was always pleased to see her, but after a traumatic incident one Tuesday involving Mrs Spencer cajoling a nude Renee into a see-through rain mac only for one of Graham's photographer pals to masturbate feverishly behind the sofa, she walked out and never went back.

Gloria and Patty laughed themselves silly when she told them. 'Men are so pathetic,' they told her, and gradually it dawned on Renee that although Gloria and Patty regularly slept with their male clients, they also slept together. Mostly in Gloria's fluffy pink boudoir, while Patty's room was more or less exclusively kept for the correction of middle-aged gents who paid great wads of cash to be smacked around by a six-foot Nefertiti in stockings and a suspender belt.

Renee was happy, girls came up to her on the street and said how much they liked her hair and where did she get it done. She started buying better clothes – 'Nothing too out there,' Maureen warned her. 'Men like it simple and sexy. Tits and arse, dear, tits and arse' – and Maureen, it turned out, knew what she was talking about.

Men with wives gave her presents and called her their 'special girl', and she sat on plump pinstriped knees and pretended she didn't mind the thrust of their cocks against her buttocks.

She danced at parties and kissed a boxer and got lots of work at the Olympia Exhibition Centre, where she was paid to perch on the bonnets of shiny new cars or demonstrate new kitchen appliances. Sometimes she even got to dress up as a bride at wedding fayres, and tried not to mind when the job was done and she had to give everything back. Well, almost everything: once she stole a garter.

Maureen was right, there was plenty of work for a girl like her, and although she and her flatmates were busy most nights, they liked to take Sundays off, spending the day sprawling around the flat in pyjamas and face masks and eating beans on toast for supper.

Renee was having fun with no strings attached, until Benedict walked into a coffee bar off Piccadilly where she was eating a breakfast of poached eggs on toast in sunglasses at 3 p.m.

He sidled into the booth next to her so that she couldn't get out and ordered a cappuccino which he dropped three cubes of sugar into. The froth held the cubes for several seconds before they disappeared below the surface.

He didn't say anything, he simply reached into his inside jacket pocket and brought out his wallet. Opening it, he removed a photograph from one of the compartments and slid it in front of her. 'Annabel,' he told her, and suddenly she was looking at her daughter. How she recognised her she couldn't quite explain. The baby was no longer a newborn, she was sitting on a woman's knee, smiling a lopsided smile into the camera.

'My sister and her husband, Hugo Berrington, have adopted her,' Benedict explained. 'It's official, the paperwork is done – you abandoned her so they didn't need your approval. She lives in Barnes in a nice house with a garden and has all the toys a little girl could ask for.'

Renee pushed aside her poached eggs. She was hung-over and vulnerable, the photograph had made her cry and she knew it was all her fault. She had done this, she had made this happen, she could pretend to be Renee Culpepper till the cows came home but underneath the fancy hairdo and the new astrakhan-collared coat, she was a runaway daughter and a runaway mother, she was Serena Tipping and she'd screwed everything up.

He didn't look at her and she didn't look at him. 'One question,' he muttered. 'Do you believe, deep down, she is mine?'

Renee paused, but only for a split second. 'Yes,' she answered, although she couldn't possibly know.

'Only it makes things easier, neater. I'm very fond of her.'

'Could I see her?'

'Oh, no, I shouldn't think so. I don't think Hugo would like it.'

'What about your sister?'

'My sister is quite frail, it's best that nothing upsets her,' he said. 'She's been through a lot, she wanted a baby very badly and you didn't, so don't even think about changing your mind because it's too late. It was your choice, Serena.' And with that, Benedict extinguished his cigarette in the dregs of his coffee cup and walked out of the café.

After that, Renee stopped sleeping at night. Violet shadows appeared beneath her eyes and Maureen told her to cover them with powder. 'No one wants a haggard nineteen-year-old,' she informed Renee, who didn't dare admit that she was already twenty.

When she did sleep, she had nightmares about closing the drawer with the baby in it and opening it to find the child dead, her marble eyes staring glassily, her lips mauve. Sometimes when she opened the drawer the baby had turned into a black rat and other times she had simply disappeared.

She stayed in bed during the day when she should have been out earning money, but the noises coming from Patty's boudoir dungeon kept her awake, the muffled cries of men who left their expensive briefcases and rolled umbrellas in the living room and crawled around Patty's carpet licking her size-nine boots. 'You fucking piece of shit!' she heard Patty cry.

349

One day when she could stand it no more, she picked up the telephone directory and looked up Hugo Berrington. There beside the telephone number, Barnes 7258, was the address where her child now lived: 33 Claverley Avenue, Barnes.

She could visit or she could write.

She decided to write,

Dear Natasha . . .

53

The Letters

July 1963

Hugo Berrington was furious, he had intercepted the letters and read them in private in his office. They were addressed to his wife, but fortunately she hadn't seen them. The post was his concern and in any case Natasha was too distracted in the mornings to notice what came through the letterbox. After all, she had Annabel to sort out and herself to make look vaguely presentable, a process requiring the positioning of a hairpiece, without which his wife's head looked slightly too small.

The letters concerned their adopted child. He didn't recognise the handwriting, which was round and childish with fat letters slanting off the page.

The contents were polite enough, but reeked of trouble.

> *Dear Natasha,*
>   *You don't know me but I was a friend of your brother's,*
> *I was staying at Kittiwake for a while, my baby girl was*
> *born there in January.*

*I don't want to take her away, I promise, I can't give
her anything and I know you can, all I want is to see her,
just once, just to hold her, you can find me at the above
address, please Natasha.*
    Yours
    Serena Tipping

The second letter read,

Dear Natasha,
    *I haven't heard back from you, but I think maybe your
letters have gone astray because at the moment for reasons
which are a bit complicated, I am working under the name
Renee Culpepper, so if you address the letter to Miss R.
Culpepper then I'm sure it will get to me.*
    Best wishes
    Renee Culpepper
    PS Please Natasha, I won't keep bothering you.

But she did.
There was a third letter.

*I am dying here Natasha, you haven't written and it's
doing my nut in, I only want to see that she's ok, I could
come to where you live, but I don't want to cause a scene.
I know that she's yours and I can cope with that, but I
can't cope with never holding her just one more time.*
    *We can meet anywhere, any park in London,
any station, any café, you tell me where and when I
will be there.*
    Here's hoping to hear back soon,
    Renee/Serena

Silly bitch! He could have written back, disguised his handwriting to suggest Natasha's hand was holding the pen, and lured her anywhere. He'd soon send her off with a flea in her ear, never to bother them again. There wasn't a court in the land that would let that woman back into the child's life.

But it wasn't Baby Annabel that was Hugo's main concern. He'd recognised the girl's address, 17C Philbeach Gardens, as the location of the top-floor flat he occasionally visited for a little afternoon delight.

Hugo had certain sexual predilections that he knew better than to ask his wife to indulge; Natasha was too well bred and anyway it wasn't the sort of thing one got up to with one's wife. A man wouldn't marry a girl who willingly partook in the kind of acts he was prepared to pay for. Hugo felt himself stiffening at the thought, aware that his briefcase contained several toys which had no place in a reputable lawyer's office.

Hugo liked threesomes and a little light bondage, he liked to watch girl-on-girl action, he liked watching the black girl fuck the redhead, and then he liked to discipline them both. The black girl had quite a collection of canes, ropes and whips, while the redhead had the biggest tits he had ever got his hands on.

Unfortunately, the trouble with being a sexual deviant, Hugo mused, was that it left one wide open to blackmail – and that was clearly what this little tart had in mind. He didn't buy the whole 'guilty mother' sob story. Girls like Serena Tipping were out for what they could get, and with Natasha's aristocratic connections and his links with the establishment, she probably thought she could collect a small fortune. He shuddered at the thought of the *News of the World* getting their hands on the story: 'Prominent Lawyer in Kinky Sex Romps with Earls Court Slappers', complete with accompanying pictures of the girls looking like whores in their underwear.

Natasha would leave him and he couldn't afford a divorce. He needed to shut this girl up before things got messy.

Hugo had no idea what she looked like, and he wasn't about to ask Benedict. He had heard of the notorious Kittiwake parties but never managed to attend one himself. As for bumping into the girl at Philbeach Gardens, it hadn't happened so far. He was aware of a third flatmate – once, during a particularly noisy session, Gloria had fallen back on the pillows laughing and said, 'I hope we didn't wake Renee!' and during another visit he'd tripped over a small pair of shoes in the living room and been told they were 'bloody Renee's' – but thankfully they had never set eyes on each other, so she wouldn't recognise him.

Hugo decided that he needed to 'accidentally' bump into this Renee Culpepper and if anyone knew where this encounter might casually occur, it was Maureen Leach, Mo knew all the girls. When he called her, she obligingly let slip that Renee was pretty and blond and worked the occasional lunchtime shift in the Packhorse in Kennington. 'The regulars love her,' Maureen added proudly; her girls were like the daughters she'd never had.

Hugo waited until twelve thirty before hailing a cab from outside his office in Holborn and arrived at the Packhorse shortly before one.

His gin and tonic was delivered by the barmaid herself, complete with 'ice and a slice, darling'. Hugo settled himself into a green leather banquette in the corner to watch and wait.

She was good with the customers, friendly and flirty but in a slightly tired and distracted sort of way. She looked a little older than he was hoping, less fresh, but as if to compensate she was wearing a suitably low-cut top to show off a proper pair of well-rounded knockers. Why was it, Hugo wondered, that the working classes had such vastly superior tits to the landed gentry?

He caught her eye a couple of times. Possibly she thought he was an MP or maybe even a spy! Lots of girls liked that sort of thing these days, so he played along, casually removing a newspaper from his briefcase. Everyone knew *The Times* was the newspaper of choice where spies were concerned.

Playing up his secret service alter ego, Hugo spent several minutes looking around shiftily before pulling his hat down low and making a pretend visit to the pay phone by the gents. When he returned to his corner, he caught her eye again and she blushed, immediately looking five years younger. Hugo licked his lips, removed his hat and headed for the bar. She wiggled her way over and asked if he fancied a scotch egg or anything else with his drink. Recognising a come-on when he saw one, Hugo looked at her intently and simply asked what time she would be finishing and if he could take her somewhere nice for a late lunch.

She giggled and flushed deeper, he could feel her eyes taking in his driving gloves and overcoat, calculating whether he was worth the punt. 'The Grosvenor House Hotel has a very nice grill,' he continued, and with that she nodded her pretty little blond head in agreement.

'I'd like that very much' she trilled in her common accent. The temptation to gag her was going to be difficult to resist.

In the taxi up to Park Lane, Renee held 'Peter's' hand. We can all play silly buggers about who we are, thought Hugo, leaning over to kiss her on the neck. Her scent was cloyingly sweet and he could see the pinpricks of much darker hair pushing through the base of her scalp. She wasn't even a real blonde.

54

The Shadowy Man

This is more like it, thought Renee, snuggling up against the handsome stranger as the cab crossed Vauxhall Bridge. She didn't feel as if she was in any danger; he was a gentleman, she could tell by the way he carried himself, the lunchtime tipple of gin and tonic rather than the oik's stout, the imperious flagging down of the taxi, the luxurious feel of his coat, the shine of his shoes.

He was taking her out for lunch too, like a proper date, and for a moment she allowed herself the fantasy that Peter could be the shadowy man who lurked around the edges of her Keddie's happy-ever-after daydreams.

Maybe this would be the fellow who'd one day wait for her at the end of the aisle? Because if Peter ended up falling in love with her, everything would be all right. They could get engaged and she could go back to Southend with her fancy fiancé wearing a fancy engagement ring with a massive emerald in the middle. And once she was married, she could have other children, because she would have a house with gingham curtains in the kitchen and a Pifco hair dryer in the bedroom. She would be respectable, this man could be her knight in shining armour.

He certainly had lovely manners; he tipped the taxi driver with a note and gently steered her by the elbow up the steps to the hotel where a waistcoated flunkey opened the door into a world Renee never wanted to leave.

Play your cards right, girl, and this could be your future, she silently told herself as her heels began to sink into a cream carpet as soft as a cloud.

After the sour beery stench of the Packhorse, the hotel smelled of polished brass fittings and beeswax. Complicated flower arrangements in huge vases on glass tables added to the aroma and she breathed in with a sigh. 'This is the life.'

At lunch, thanks to memories of dining with Benedict and his friends at Kittiwake, she knew what a finger bowl was, how to hold her cutlery and which knife buttered her roll. Renee was determined to make a good impression, to enchant him with her charm and sophistication; she would use the word 'lavatory' rather than 'toilet', she would push her peas against the back of her fork and hold the wine glass by the stem.

He kept filling her glass and his steak arrived very rare, the blood oozing around his green beans and new potatoes. She had the chicken and spilled a tiny bit of gravy on her top. When he went to 'make a couple of calls', she frantically tried to dab the stain off with some water and her napkin. It doesn't matter, she told herself, it barely shows.

When he got back from the phone booth, he asked whether she would like to continue their chat over some brandy somewhere private and she nodded and said, 'What a delightful idea', as if they were off to see the Chelsea Flower Show.

Once more he took her by the elbow and this time he steered her to the lobby, where the lift doors silently glided open.

'I have a room,' he said. 'It overlooks Hyde Park, so you can watch the horses.'

Not knowing what else to do, she giggled. Things were

moving so fast, maybe he truly liked her. But how much sex she should give him?

She could go as far as she liked, she decided, thanks to Gloria, who'd made her buy a cheap gold ring from Woolworths before marching her down to the local surgery where Renee signed up as Mrs R. Culpepper, and was given a six-month supply of the contraceptive pill. 'We don't want you getting in the club,' laughed Gloria, and Renee had laughed too, 'As if!'

But now she found herself worrying about getting undressed in the daylight – what if he noticed the stretch marks on her stomach and guessed she'd had a baby? Serena fretted, she had read an article in a women's magazine about how men liked you to keep them waiting, how you shouldn't go all the way on the first date. Mentally, she quickly undressed herself: today's bra had seen better days and she was wearing a pair of Gloria's knickers because she was behind with her laundry, but at least they were quite fancy, red with frilly bits. Perhaps she could keep her slip on?

The room was plainer than she'd expected and the view looked over a fire escape at the side of the hotel rather than the park. 'But it doesn't matter does it?' he said as he closed the curtains and turned on a side light. 'You're the only view I want,' and she giggled again as she sat on the bed and wondered what would happen next. The sound of someone knocking on the door nearly had her jumping out of her skin.

Peter looked amused. 'Room service, I presume,' he said, then he called, 'Enter,' like an actor, and a boy walked in with a tray that held a bottle and two glasses. He looked at the closed curtains and he looked at Renee perched on the bed and she could swear blind he gave a smirk. Right then she made up her mind that if she did marry Peter and he had as much money as she was beginning to hope, she would have her wedding reception right here in this hotel. That would surely wipe the smirk off the snotty git's face.

They talked like grown-ups for a while over the balloon-shaped brandy glasses. She asked him questions about where he lived and what he liked to do, and he told her 'London, and all sorts of activities.'

'Such as?' she pressed.

'Such as this,' he said, and he sidled over to sit next to her on the bed and he kissed her long and deep and hard. It was a good kiss, she only wished she could have cleaned her teeth first.

But the brandy loosened everything and he undressed her slowly and gently, kissing every new bit of flesh as it was revealed. She was glad the curtains were shut, the side lamp had a cream satin pleated shade and the light that emanated from it was as flattering as a candle.

For a moment she believed she was beautiful, she forgot that she had a small daughter who was now living with complete strangers. She was Renee Culpepper and this could be the start of something special, she didn't even mind if he was a double agent, she wouldn't mind being a spy's wife, she could keep secrets, after all not even Patty or Gloria knew about the baby.

She was down to her bra and Gloria's pants now. Peter was still dressed, she tentatively pulled at his tie, but she tugged the wrong end and momentarily it tightened around his neck. 'Now, now, young lady.' He smiled patiently. And the next thing she knew, he had removed his tie and lashed her wrists together behind her back.

Oh, so he liked it a bit kinky, did he? Renee pouted at him, not sure of the rules, and he smiled and pushed her down on the bed, but oh so gently, and she closed her eyes. It was going to be all right, he kissed like a prince . . .

And then he hit her.

He hit her hard across the face and her eyes flew open. This wasn't how princes behaved. She sat up, panicked, but he knocked her back down, he punched her twice in the face and the second time her jaw cracked like Nanna Tipping eating toffee on bonfire night and she didn't move again.

He was standing up now, he was putting on his coat and gathering up his possessions. Perhaps if she lay very still he might not hit her again. And he didn't. Instead he sat on the end of the bed and in a low reasonable voice, as if he were reading a book to a child, he said,

'Listen, you silly bitch, if you write one more letter to my wife asking to see your bastard baby, I will hurt you so badly you will wish neither you nor that brat had ever been born. I will cut your face to ribbons and no one will ever look at you again, do you understand?'

She nodded, it hurt, then he left. There was blood on the starched white pillowcase and her teeth felt loose in her head. For a while she lay there, grateful for the quiet, then after wriggling her hands free from his tie she fetched a hand towel from the bathroom and allowed her mouth to bleed into that. When it stopped, she searched in her bag unsuccessfully for a couple of aspirin.

If she were brave she would go to the police, but she wasn't and anyway she knew what they would think of her. They would recognise her for what she was: a girl who may not have asked for what she got, but deserved it anyway.

In any case, they might find out who she was and what she had done and then they might send her to prison.

Renee spent the rest of the night dozing in the big double bed at the Grosvenor House Hotel, swigging the brandy when the pain got too much. As dawn broke, she woke up and wondered if she would ever meet the elusive shadow who came home bearing flowers, kissed her on the nose when she took off her pinny and told her, 'Something smells delicious.' Even though the only meals she'd ever made anyone consisted of Spam fritters, chips and Angel Delight.

At midday when the cleaners came knocking, she stuffed the bloodied towel in the wardrobe, slipped Hugo's tie into her bag and walked down the corridor holding onto the wall.

55

Renee Meets Her Fate

When Renee got back to Philbeach Gardens, Patty and Gloria were horrified by the state of her face and they clucked around making cups of heavily sugared tea, 'It's good for the shock,' insisted Gloria, 'it's what they did in the war.' Renee didn't mind, she liked sweet tea.

Her left eye had puffed up so much that she could barely see out of it and Patty was concerned that her jaw might be broken, but Renee insisted that it wasn't, it was a bit hard to chew that's all.

She asked them to tell Maureen that she'd fallen down a flight of stairs and couldn't be seen out in public for a couple of weeks. By then she'd be as right as rain.

Her flatmates took care of her until the swelling and the bruising went down, they fed her soft-boiled eggs and porridge. Patty even went out in the rain to fetch her some Angel Delight, which was lovely, but she bought butterscotch flavour and not strawberry which was Serena's and therefore Renee's absolute favourite.

When the girls were working or out, Renee holed up in her bedroom under an eiderdown and tried not to cry. If only she could see Benedict and explain everything, he would help, she was sure he would. But then she remembered that Hugo was married to Benedict's sister and his loyalties would always lie with her.

Her only option was to forget the baby. Other women had been in her position and managed to get on with their lives. If she went near the child, she had no doubt that Hugo would come after her and scar her for life.

She was twenty years old, her looks wouldn't last for ever, but for the moment they were all she had and already the bloom was fading.

She suspected she took after her mother and that, by the time she turned twenty-five, she would be ordinary.

'I will cut your face to ribbons.' Every time she picked up a knife in the kitchen, she imagined the blade against her cheek and she felt sick.

Renee had lost her appetite, she still couldn't chew without hearing an odd clicking noise below her right ear, and sometimes her entire jaw seemed to slip out of its socket and she had to make strange contorted faces to get it back to where it should be. But at least her massively swollen eye had gone down and all that was left of the injury now was a greenish-yellow circular ring.

'You should be able to cover that up with make-up by Friday, but for God's sake eat something, you're starting to lose your tits,' Gloria told her.

Friday was when Renee needed to get back to business, to show her face. Maureen was getting bored of her excuses. 'I'm offering you a golden opportunity to mingle with society's finest, darling, this is how girls like you get on and I want you, Patty and Gloria all there together, my bevy of beauties, my tasty trio, something for everyone. So don't let me down.'

Individually, the three of them were arresting in their own way, but when they turned up at a venue together they were a knockout combination, and Maureen was counting on them to supply maximum impact.

'It's an important client,' Maureen went on. 'Mayfair, none of your rubbish, all highly respectable, although some of the gentlemen will be attending without their wives, so expect things to get a little lively after midnight.'

Renee went to get her roots done and Terry told her she looked a bit peaky, asked if she fancied pie and mash when she was done. She couldn't think of anything worse, but she thanked him for the offer and watched in awed gratitude as he expertly coifed her hair into an immaculate silver meringue, while simultaneously spilling the beans about his disastrous love life.

'It's the fellas on the Heath that drive me mad: one minute they're sucking you off behind a chestnut tree, the next they're running back to their wives and lying about being kept late in the office. It's easy-peasy for you, darling, you've got luck and the law on your side.'

Renee grinned, only to hear her jaw click ominously and she had to physically manoeuvre it back into place.

'You all right, love?' asked Terry. 'Only for a moment there you looked exactly like my Aunty Violet when she was having a stroke.'

They started getting ready around five o'clock on the Friday evening, lining their stomachs with scrambled eggs, no toast for Renee, feeding the electricity meter with enough change for two hot baths. Patty and Gloria jumped in the first one together and Renee took the second. By the time she got out, there was a tide of leg shavings around the bath, speckles of red, black and gold.

Fresh from their ablutions, the girls sat around in dressing gowns listening to songs from the musical *South Pacific* on the record player while painting each other's nails and deciding what to wear.

'I'm going full-on silver,' Renee announced. She'd got a little sequin shift dress that clung to every dip and curve in her body – not that she had much in the way of curves at the moment, but never mind, the dress was sensational.

She decided to add the little fox-fur shrug she'd swiped from Kittiwake. Not only would it keep her warm, it would disguise the bony sharpness of her shoulder blades and the birdlike fragility of her clavicles. 'I'll be better soon,' she promised herself, fretting over finding the right pair of shoes. Nothing in her wardrobe quite worked with the silver dress, she needed something delicate and strappy. Fortunately, Patty had a pair of silver stilettoes with a diamanté buckle on the ankle strap, and once the toes were stuffed with cotton wool, they sort of fitted.

Patty opted for a purple crushed velvet all-in-one catsuit with a chunky silver zip running from throat to navel; how much flesh would be revealed depended on how far down she or anyone else pulled that zip. Gloria eventually chose a floor-length green satin ballgown that screamed Hollywood va-va-voom.

The girls were giddy, they wore multiple sets of false eyelashes, rouged their cheeks and coated their lips with the colours of summer fruits: raspberry pink, strawberry red, and the richest shade of plum. At eight o'clock they toasted themselves with Cinzano and tumbled out into the night.

The party was being held in Mayfair. Renee, skint from not working, tried to persuade the others to take the Tube straight from Earls Court to Green Park, but Gloria was feeling flush, she had a new fancy man who paid her to visit him in his office and let him fondle her breasts. 'No trouble, doesn't want anything else, I just sit on his knee, pretending to be his secretary, taking notes, while he plays with my tits, talking business while I pretend I know how to do shorthand.'

They laughed all the way to Curzon Place, until Renee realised she was within walking distance of the Grosvenor House Hotel and began to tremble involuntarily. She had thrown away all the clothes she was wearing that day, right down to her tights. Even Gloria's knickers had gone in the bin. She'd wanted to be rid of everything that might remind her of that day, except for the white bag she had with her tonight – she couldn't afford to go chucking out handbags.

As they straightened themselves up on the pavement outside an imposing white stucco terraced house, Patty ran through what they need to know about the host and his friends.

'A thirtieth birthday party, one Charles Gillingham, father loaded but living in Monaco, so Charlie boy has the run of the London pad, does something in the City during the day, likes to party at night, recent broken engagement to someone called Bunny or Kitty or Piggy. Anyway, he's up for grabs, though we all know he's looking for a nice girl from the Home Counties called Lucinda who wears a single strand of pearls and rides ponies, so don't get your hopes up too high, ladies. Oh, and Mo says no fucking on the premises.'

The steps up to the house were wide and shallow with railings on either side. On the top step, flanking the front door, were two matching ornamental trees, trimmed into perfect round green lollypop shapes.

Renee felt like Alice in Wonderland: she had no idea what lay behind the huge glossy black front door. Maybe she would simply fall down a hole.

Patty lifted the door-knocker, a heavy brass ring dangling from a lion's mouth, and she barely had time to drop it before a butler opened the door. For a moment, as the light from an enormous chandelier illuminated the trio on the front step, they froze, confused and blinking, until Gloria broke the silence.

'We're friends of Maureen's,' she gushed.

'And Charlie's,' added Renee. Gloria could be a bit thick sometimes.

Behind the man, there was a hubbub of music and laughter. A kaleidoscope of women in vibrantly coloured evening dresses and men in black tie milled around a wide staircase leading up to a mezzanine floor where a small jazz band were in full swing.

The butler raised a single eyebrow and stood aside to let them in.

Renee took a deep breath. This was the first time she'd been out since the incident, it was time to get back in the saddle. Tonight, she decided, she was going to have the time of her life, and she reached a slightly grubby white satin-gloved hand out for a glass of golden fizz. Behind her she heard Patty mutter 'fuck me' and Renee followed her gaze across the black-and-white tiled entrance hall to where an ornamental fountain spewed jets of frothy crystal water practically as high as the ceiling. 'Like having your very own indoor Trevi,' squealed Gloria, and Renee watched her friends head over to the fountain, presumably to throw coins in for luck. Heads turned like sunflowers to watch them pass and it occurred to her that most of the other women present seemed as colourless as bleached-out photographs in comparison to her friends.

She would catch up with them later: Gloria and Patty always operated as a pair. Renee decided to prowl around on her own and headed for the stairs. Tonight called for drinking and dancing. Food was still a bit of a nightmare with her jaw, which was a shame because the canapés – cherry tomatoes elaborately piped with some kind of fish mousse, tiny squares of French toast slathered in rich liver pâté, and minute mushroom vol-au-vents carried around on silver salvers – looked exquisite.

At the top of the stairs, to the left of the band, was a small ballroom. For a moment, Renee wished Ida and Nanna were here to witness this, even though her nan would never make it up those stairs.

A throng of people were already dancing, girls with elaborately pinned hair in the arms of pink-faced men wearing traditional evening suits with neatly executed bow ties. Couples greeted other couples who looked more or less exactly the same as each other as they circled the floor.

Eton, Harrow, Marlborough, Winchester, intoned Renee silently. She knew the drill, Kittiwake had, in some respects, been a kind of finishing school, a crash course in learning how the other half lived and behaved. That was why she was now able to hover on the fringes without feeling entirely frozen out: she knew how these people operated. She knew that posh girls cried over big noses and being left on the shelf exactly like shop girls did, and she knew that posh boys lived in fear of never amounting to anything, and that everyone was in the same boat.

She danced in the corner, where a slightly more raffish group of guests had congregated. These girls wore shorter skirts and their hair was loose around their shoulders, cigarette smoke hung heavy in the air and champagne was being swigged directly from the bottle. Renee glided in and raised her hands in the air, the music dictating the movement in her hips. Several men tried to catch her eye, but she wasn't ready yet, she might be dancing and she might be smiling but inside she was still cowering at Hugo's shadow as he loomed over the bed that horrible afternoon.

Her fur jacket began to stick to her shoulders, it was too hot, she needed to leave it somewhere safe where she could retrieve it at the end of the night. Renee shimmied out of the scrum and crossed the mezzanine in front of the band, who had paused for a short break. As they watched her pass, one of the musicians put his saxophone to his lips and the instrument wolf-whistled at the pretty girl in the silver dress with the arctic fox stole.

Secretly thrilled, Renee scaled another staircase so that the band couldn't see her blush, and chose a door at random. The house was so extraordinary, heaven only knew what she might find on the other side. For a moment she imagined a small petting zoo, complete with peacocks and miniature zebras, but it was actually a library, dark and panelled, shelves crammed with thousands of leather-bound books that reached from the floor to the ceiling. She peeled off her fur and arranged it across the back of a black leather wing back chair, one of a pair facing a large mahogany desk. On top of the desk sat several Bakelite telephones in different colours, a whisky decanter and a globe. Next to a stack of legal books was an ornate table light in the shape of a naked bronze woman holding a red satin shade above her delicately sculpted head.

Renee shut the door behind her. The room was gloriously cool and quiet and she was relieved to be alone. Giving the globe on the desk a quick spin, Renee noticed the curtains behind the desk move and realised the accompanying breeze was coming from a pair of open French windows which led out onto a small balustraded balcony. The idea of a quick cigarette in the fresh air before she rejoined the throng was irresistibly appealing and Renee, cigarettes at the ready, made her way round the back of the desk and stepped outside onto the balcony.

Natasha had come to the party alone. Hugo was at his parents' place, his father having recently suffered a stroke. Not big enough to kill him, unfortunately – they could have done with the money.

Natasha sighed. Her family had known the Gillinghams for years, they used to attend each other's birthday parties when they were children and somehow the invitations had never stopped – sweet really.

She hadn't seen Charles as yet, but judging by some of the guests, he was evidently running with a rather racy crowd. Natasha had come to the library to escape from it all. Only a few minutes ago she'd watched some young idiot pour washing up liquid into the fountain and the resulting froth caused such hilarity it gave her an instant headache.

I'm too old for all this, she thought. As she perched on the balustrade and looked out at the street below, she felt slightly self-conscious about the little tiara she had worn. No one else was bothering with that sort of thing any more.

Most of all she wished Benedict would hurry up. He'd promised he'd be here by now, it was nearly ten o'clock. She decided to wait another ten minutes and then she'd go home. Annabel woke up so early and in the morning Mrs Phelan would be gone and Natasha would be dealing with the baby on her own – which was absolutely fine. After all, it was what she'd always wanted.

She was about to go inside when a blond woman emerged to join her on the balcony, a cheap white faux leather handbag over her arm and a squashed packet of filter-tipped Embassy Number 6 in her hand. She was pretty, Natasha noticed, in an obvious kind of way. The spaghetti-strapped sequined dress was cut low enough to reveal a deep cleavage while her legs were quite good, albeit with a hint of what Natasha's mother would have called 'bottle' about them – but it was her voice that held her transfixed. Barbara Windsor meets *My Fair Lady*, thought Natasha when the girl asked her for a light. She hid her smirk in her handbag as she dug out her Dunhill lighter and clicked it in the direction of the stranger's cigarette. As the blonde leant forward, Natasha caught a whiff of her scent. She recognised it immediately, it was very sweet, like dolly mixtures. Now where had she smelt that before?

Their eyes met across the flick of the lighter. Renee recognised her as soon as the flame illuminated her face. This was Natasha, this was Benedict's sister – she had seen the photo he kept in his wallet, the one with her daughter sitting on this woman's knee. This was Natasha Berrington née Carmichael, this was the woman who was married to the man who beat up other women, this was the woman who never got to read the letters that she wrote to her, this was the woman who was mothering her child.

Suddenly Renee was overwhelmed by an anger that had been slowly burning inside her since Hugo cracked her jaw and bloodied

369

her nose and blackened her eye, and she hitched herself up on the balcony next to Natasha and said, 'You're Natasha, aren't you?'

The woman nodded suspiciously and Renee kept talking, 'You don't know me, but I know you. See the thing is, my name's Renee, but it used to be something else. I'm from Southend in real life and ... How can I put this, Natasha? Thanks for the light by the way, darling. Lovely house, innit? Well, what I'm trying to say, Natasha – I hope you don't mind me calling you Natasha.'

She realised she wasn't making much sense but the words tumbled out without her having any control over them, she genuinely had no idea what might come out next. And then she said it: 'I know your husband. We had what you might call an encounter.' At this, the words dried up. She had shocked herself, she hadn't known she was going to mention Hugo, but having done so she decided she was going to tell Natasha everything: that the man she was married to was a monster, that she and Annabel might not be safe. She was going to spill the beans about the letters and the lunch and the beating. It was only fair, Natasha needed to know what kind of a man he was. And once she knew, then Renee would walk away, she wouldn't do anything else. But first she leaned down to where her handbag sat at her feet and she pulled out Hugo's tie. 'See, I'm not making it up.'

Natasha recognised the strip of fabric immediately – navy silk with a repeat pattern of interlocking red ellipses – she'd bought the tie for Hugo from Selfridges for Christmas last year, before Baby Annabel came to live with them. Instinctively she reached for it and again she caught the girl's perfume, sweet like sherbet, and instantly the penny dropped, she remembered smelling it on Hugo a couple of weeks ago. He'd come home one evening reeking of it. So this was one of Hugo's little tarts. God knows he probably wasn't even at his father's bedside tonight, he was more likely in some other little scrubber's bed. They were all the same, cheap-smelling and big-titted and happy to suck her husband's cock and do God knows what else for a few quid and the odd diamanté bracelet.

Natasha had always had a temper. When she was a child she was apt to lash out at the smallest provocation, but as an adult she had managed to keep her tantrums under control, helped by the little white pills the doctor prescribed. But she wasn't taking the pills any more, Hugo wouldn't let her, not now she was a mother. She allowed the old familiar fury to wash over her. Who did this silly bitch with her plastic handbag and her dyed hair think she was? Coming up to Natasha and waving her husband's tie in her face like some end of the pier magician playing a rubbish trick.

Later on, she would convince herself she didn't mean it, that the push was playful rather than deadly, that she didn't realise the woman's legs were so short and she was so precariously balanced and anyway it happened so fast, like a speeded-up reel of film that repeated over and over again. Renee showed her the tie and Natasha pushed her – not hard, but she fell, she fell backwards off the balustrade, push, fall, push, fall, push, fall.

As Natasha stepped in from the balcony, downstairs on the ground floor Johnny Montgomery poured an entire bottle of red cochineal food dye into the fountain and the frothing water turned blood red. Everyone laughed, and then somebody screamed.

56

Falling (2)

Mayfair, London, 1963

Renee fell and took Serena with her, they fell head over heels together, the girl with the silver hair and the slightly crooked jaw and the girl who'd left Southend without saying goodbye to her mother or her nan.

As they fell, Serena sensed Renee slipping away. She was never entirely real, but it was fun to play make believe for a while, up to a point, up until that afternoon in the Grosvenor House Hotel.

Goodbye Renee and goodbye Patty and Gloria, Serena would miss them, she hoped Patty would get her shoes back and that Gloria would help herself to Renee's knickers, she hoped that they'd stay happy and safe in the little flat in Earls Court and that they wouldn't be too upset that she lied to them about who she was, but it was too late now to explain.

I'm Serena Tipping, she admitted to herself, falling faster now, and the only thing I regret is leaving the baby. If I had another chance, if I could come back and do things differently – that's the only thing I'd change, I'd pick that baby up and I would take her back to Southend and I would ring the doorbell and I would say . . .

Benedict heard the commotion as he rounded the corner onto Curzon Place and immediately broke into a run. People began streaming out of the house, some seemed to be escaping, others milled about, forming a ragged circle on the pavement. They seemed to be staring at something on the ground; at first it looked like someone had kicked over a tin of silver paint, but as he got closer, he realised the splash of silver was a dress and with every step the picture became clearer, it was a girl, a girl in a silver dress was lying on the ground, a girl with platinum hair, wearing a silver dress, was lying motionless on the ground – and with a horrible certainty, he knew it was Serena.

Benedict pushed his way through the gaggle of panic, the men round-eyed with horror, the women sobbing. 'I know her,' he shouted. 'Let me through, for Christ's sake!' Something in his tone made people stand aside and he knelt down by Serena's lovely head and held her hand and told her that he was there, that she wasn't alone. 'I won't leave you,' he whispered into her ear and he tried not to recoil at the sight of the dark sticky red ring that seeped around her silver hair and he tried to pretend there was still hope even when he knew it was over and he tried to keep her warm even when he knew she could no longer feel the cold and with every second the wail of the siren was getting closer and closer.

Inside the house, guests were grabbing their coats and leaving as fast as they could. Something horrible had happened and it wouldn't do them any good to be associated with it, whatever it was.

Rumours immediately began to spread. She fell, she jumped, she jumped from the roof, like an angel, a shooting silver star, a suicide.

The band stood forlornly on the mezzanine, wondering whether they would get paid if they left. Below them, people stopped dancing in the fountain and, unnoticed, a single discarded man's sock blocked the overflow, sending frothy pink liquid flooding across the hall, eventually finding an escape route out of the open door, down the stone steps and on to the pavement where it pooled around the dead girl's ankles.

This was the moment the ambulance and the police arrived and a blanket was placed over the woman's body before being pulled up over her head. At the sight of this a small red-haired girl in a green satin dress clutched the railings and started screaming and didn't stop until a tall black woman wrapped her in her arms and comforted her as if she were a child, tears streaming down her own face.

Benedict was telling a policeman, 'Her name was Serena Tipping,' and the red-haired girl, hearing this, began to struggle in her friend's arms, trying to contradict Benedict. 'Renee,' she was shouting, 'her name is Renee!' but the black girl silenced her. Then, without another word, the two of them melted away into the darkness.

Natasha exited the house via the kitchen, through the back garden and out of a hastily unlocked wrought-iron gate onto an alleyway to the rear of the house.

The night had turned cold now and she was grateful for the arctic fox fur stole she had around her narrow shoulders. In five minutes she'd be at Bond Street Tube and there were always taxis around the station. Natasha hummed as she walked, the moon was very bright and her heels made a satisfying click-clack, like her mother's used to. She'd be home soon.

In Curzon Place, outside the white stucco house, a female police constable spotted two things in the gutter. One seemed to be a large dead goldfish, the other was a silver high-heeled shoe.

374

She decided to leave the goldfish, but picked up the shoe. There was blood on the diamanté buckle and the toes were stuffed with cotton wool.

Poor Cinderella, sometimes even fairy tales go wrong.

Natasha took a glass of whisky up to bed. Mr Phelan had picked up Mrs Phelan and thankfully Baby Annabel was out for the count in the nursery.

As she dropped the little white fox fur to her bedroom floor, Natasha was struck by the embroidered silver label stitched to the lining. How strange that it should share the same French furrier's name tag that most of her mother's coats sported. Peggy had worn a Mme Paquin white fur stole too. Life was full of coincidences, thought Natasha, and she was still wondering how the cheap little tart had afforded such luxury when the phone started ringing.

For a moment, she thought it might be Hugo. Perhaps his father had passed away and they could forget about their money worries for a while, but it was Benedict.

'Were you at Charlie's party?' he demanded breathlessly. He sounded upset.

'Yes,' she answered coolly. 'And you never showed up.'

'I did,' he panted, as if he'd been running. 'Only you'd gone by the time I got there. There was an accident.'

'I know' she replied. 'It was pandemonium, a girl jumped out of a window or something.'

'It was Serena,' he interrupted, 'the girl from Kittiwake. It was Annabel's mother, she's dead.'

Once Natasha had managed to get rid of a weepy Benedict, she hid the white fur stole at the back of her wardrobe. Silly in some respects; after all, by rights it was hers. It was obvious now that the girl must have taken it from Kittiwake, but she knew she would never wear it again. It would be bad luck.

In the morning the Sunday papers reported the accident in

lurid detail, the dead girl was a Serena Tipping aged twenty from Southend, also known as Renee Culpepper, a society hostess from Earls Court.

There was no mention anywhere that she was ever a mother.

57

After the Party

Kittiwake, August 2018

Freya's mother Mari calls the doctor, but it's ten o'clock on a bank holiday Saturday night and no one is on duty. The recorded message suggests dialling NHS Direct on 111.

The barn is empty. Everyone staying at Kittiwake has drifted back to the house, those sleeping in the yurts have retired to the yurt field, some have gone home early and those who live locally disappeared almost as soon as it happened. It's embarrassing: Lance's mother stabbed her own son.

'She's obviously lost her marbles,' whispers Freya to her husband. Then the whisper turns into a hiss as she adds, 'I'm not having that madwoman under this roof tonight.'

'What am I supposed to do with her?' pleads Lance, 'I can't put her in one of the empty yurts – she's nearly eighty, for Christ's sake.'

Mari reminds him not to shout at his wife and Lance tells her to 'fuck off'.

Freya leaves the room in tears and her sister follows her.

Natasha is sitting quietly by the Aga drinking sweet hot tea.

377

She's had a nasty shock – Serena came back from the grave and she had to fight her off, only it wasn't Serena because even if Serena wasn't dead, she'd be old enough to be Lance's mother, and a mother shouldn't dance with her son like that, it's disgusting, no wonder she had to be stopped.

Natasha is very tired indeed and everyone in the kitchen is upset and talking far too loudly. Her son is sitting on the kitchen table having his wound attended to by that troll creature – poor man, constantly being mauled at by strange women.

For a moment Natasha wonders if she's in a pantomime, the one with the pumpkin and the mice, the man sitting on the table who looks like her son is dressed up like a footman, so he must be Buttons and the pig woman fussing over him must be one of the ugly sisters. In which case Natasha must be Cinderella.

Only that's what they called Serena in the newspapers: 'Death of Party Girl Cinderella' said the headlines. Because she lost a shoe, a shoe with a diamanté buckle, one two buckle my shoe, three, four knock on the door . . .

It's the police, Freya has called them because Elise told her she had to, she didn't have any choice. 'That woman might decide to stab one of the children next.' No one can sleep safely in this house while Natasha is free to roam about, 'Think about all the Sabatier knives in the kitchen, Freya, think about Baby Aksel.'

Even if they did find somewhere, they couldn't keep her locked away – she could end up harming herself.

'If you don't phone them, I will,' threatened Elise in Norwegian.

Freya opens the door to the police and they follow her into the kitchen, two of them, a man and a woman in police uniform, but they have brought a plain-clothes liaison officer with them, someone who can professionally assess Natasha and, if necessary, find her somewhere safe to stay for the night.

She looks very frail, sitting on a stool laughing at the police-men, muttering about Punch and Judy and then shouting, 'Who's got the sausages?'

The liaison officer raises an eyebrow at his colleagues and goes away 'for a minute' to make some phone calls.

A few of the remaining party guests drift in and out of the kitchen to say their goodbyes, a priest says, 'Thank you very much for a wonderful party' and Natasha laughs even harder.

Upstairs, next to the dormitory of sleeping children, Ed and Jamie are still playing video games. Maisie joins them, she has changed into her pyjamas and lies down on the bed Ed slept in last night. She's not sleeping on her own tonight, no way.

She thinks about telling the brothers about what has hap-pened but can't be bothered. They won't interested, not when everything they need is on the screen in front of them: cars smashing into walls and buildings bursting into flames, men machine-gunning other men in the face and brains splattering as they scream in agony.

Some old woman going crazy with a carving knife isn't likely to grab their attention, even if it was their grandmother. Though maybe Bel should be told? Considering it's her mother who has gone berserk.

Maisie would go and tell her but she's too tired to move and anyway she doesn't want to answer any questions about why and how she was dancing with Lance. She allows herself a tiny smirk, the erection she'd felt straining from his breeches was huge, ha!

She imagines they will all drive home tomorrow. No one will want to stay here after what happened tonight. Then on Tuesday, after the bank holiday, she'll start asking around at work, see if anyone's got a room going spare. She's going to have to brace herself for a bit of a come-down in the comfort stakes, she can't imagine she's going to find anywhere with such a big showerhead and under-floor heating in the bathroom. She will miss Bel's home-cooked dinners and Andrew's shit jokes, too. She's going to have to manage her own laundry from now on and get used to cheap hummus and avocados from the market, rather than Marks, dammit.

Andrew has been sitting quietly in the barn for a long time. He had seen the way Maisie danced with Lance and it embarrassed him, what the hell were they both doing? Lance is old enough to know better and Maisie is supposed to be so keen on his eldest son that she has moved into their home. No doubt Bel will be delighted when he tells her, she's never liked the girl, but what if no one else saw what he and Natasha had seen, what if Maisie denies it? Then he'll have stirred up trouble for no reason. And in any case it could have been entirely innocent, although somehow he doubts it.

For a while he helps the hog-roast men pack everything up, apart from the knife, which has been taken away for safekeeping. The men are chatty and tell Andrew that they've been doing festivals around the country for the past five years and they've never seen anything as mad as tonight. In the end they all start laughing about it, which is awful but a sort of relief. Andrew laughs so much that he winds himself and he's a tiny bit sick behind one of the hay bales. He may have drunk more than he thought he had.

Outside the barn the wind has got up and the rain is visibly rolling in from the sea. Without the multi strings of old-fashioned light bulbs which had illuminated the dancing, the inside of the barn is gloomy and getting colder by the minute. Andrew finds a discarded plastic knife and decides to hack a piece of the Kittiwake cake off for Bel. He studies the crumbling edifice and realises he can take her the bedroom where she is sleeping right now – she'll love that, she'll say, 'Oh, Andrew, it's far too good to eat' and he'll show her the photos of how it looked when the candles were blazing. Then, while she's eating the cake, he will gently tell her about her mother.

Crossing the back lawn over to the house, Andrew is caught in a sudden downpour, his linen shirt is instantly drenched and he notices a police car in the drive.

Poor Natasha. He can't help feeling sorry for her, she is obviously terribly confused. This weekend has been too much for her, this house is too much. He never wants to come here again, he'd like to go home tonight but knows he'll have to wait until the morning. Anyway, he can't drive, not when he's pissed.

Avoiding the kitchen, Andrew creeps into the house through a side entrance and makes his way round to the necessary staircase by cutting through the empty sitting room. He takes his shoes off – Freya doesn't need to deal with mud on top of blood – and he climbs the stairs in his stockinged feet carrying the rain-sodden cake carefully on a soggy paper plate.

He might have a bath before bed. Bel will come and sit on the toilet seat like she does at home, and she'll fire lots of questions at him, she will want to know everything, every little detail, she will interrogate him about the food, music, costumes, dancing and what about the boys? He doesn't want to tell her that he hasn't seen them all night. He'll simply say they kept a pretty low profile, but that Maisie seemed to enjoy herself.

He has to put the cake down on the floor to twist the handle on the bedroom door. It's much stiffer than he remembers and he has to push hard to get in. There must be some kind of draught creating an airlock, maybe Bel has opened a window?

Andrew shoves at the door with his shoulder and stumbles over the threshold.

The room is like an ice-box and behind the dressing table the curtains flap wildly. Andrew switches the light on and rushes over to shut the window before turning round to find that Bel is nowhere to be seen, the bed is rumpled but empty. He checks

381

the en suite, feeling a childish sense of panic when he finds that empty too. Leaving the bathroom in a hurry, he bangs his ankle on the open drawer at the bottom of the wardrobe. Damn and blast it, he feels like crying as he hobbles down the corridor to find his wife. 'Bel!' he shouts. 'Bel, it's me, where are you?'

Natasha is sitting in the back of the police car next to the nice man who held her hand as they made their way out of the house. He has a kind face and she finds herself confiding in him about what actually happened at the party, the silly mistake she had made. 'It's a secret,' she tells him and then she whispers in his ear, 'I knew it couldn't be Serena, because I saw her die. She fell, I pushed her and she fell backwards, I think she landed on her head. My brother fell too and he died, he fell forward into water and drowned.'

Natasha is laughing now, laughing and crying, and she tries to hit herself across the face like her husband used to when she got 'silly' in the past. Slap slap, harder and harder, until the nice man decides to give her a pill, a little white pill exactly like the ones that Hugo used to give her all those years ago, and very soon Natasha is asleep with her head on the nice man's shoulder.

Bel isn't in the house. Andrew searches everywhere before he gives up and heads for the kitchen where the remaining adults are drinking a good single malt and rubbing their faces with tiredness. Natasha and the police have disappeared; he feels a bit silly but is tempted to call them back. 'It's Bel,' he tells everyone, 'she's gone missing.' Freya actually laughs, a snickering hysterical laugh, until her mother says something sharp in Norwegian and she falls silent.

At midnight, the men take torches into the grounds. Even Jamie and Ed join in the search. Indoors the women drink tea, 'This is ridiculous,' they keep muttering, they must have found her by now. Maybe she was more concussed than we thought? She may have been confused and wandered off. They should have taken her to hospital when the accident first happened, surely she can't have got far, they will find her, any minute now, they will find her.

58

Found

Andrew finds Bel halfway between the house and the barn. She must have walked the long way round and tripped and fallen on the rough track where Lance had parked his huge black Range Rover. The bulk of the four-wheel drive is masking her from view in the dark. How ridiculous, she was here all the time.

At first, he almost laughs with relief. She is fast asleep and smiling. She looks like someone has cast a spell on her, like a princess who has become middle-aged in her sleep. He needs to get her indoors, where there's a glass of Jameson's and a finely sprung mattress waiting for her. They can get her checked out by a doctor once they get back to London.

Greedy Bel, he should have known she couldn't resist the lure of the birthday cake. She must have come down in search of a slice and tripped. He puts his hands under her arms and tries to lift her, they'll have a good laugh about this in the morning, only it is already the morning and his wife isn't breathing.

A stroke, they said. Nothing to do with the bump on her head. A faulty valve – it could have happened at any time. She didn't suffer, she would have been dead before she hit the ground.

*

Her sons wear shirts and ties at her funeral and they cry like they did when they were small. Andrew looks shell-shocked but he is polite to everyone who shows up and he wears Bel's favourite jacket and makes sure he polishes his glasses because she hated it when his lenses were all smeared.

Natasha doesn't come – she isn't strong enough to leave the hospital – but Lance and Freya turn up without the children in that wretched Range Rover and as Andrew shakes his brother-in-law's hand and lets his sister-in-law kiss his cheek, he knows they will never see each other again. Why should they? The day seems to go on for ever, there are hymns and readings and in amongst the floral tributes is a small bunch of cream roses. The card attached is handwritten:

From Maisie with love xx

Epilogue

Serena Changes Her Mind

Kittiwake, Cornwall, February 1963

Serena looks at the baby. Yellow goo is oozing out of her left eye and she looks like a potato. Maybe when her hair grows, she will be more attractive. She may even grow up to look like Benedict, which would solve a lot of problems, but Serena knows deep down that she won't. Benedict has brown eyes and dark skin, this baby is destined to be fair and freckly and burn in the sun.

'I'm going to have to buy you a sun hat,' she tells the baby, buttoning one of Bren's finest two-ply white woollen bonnets under her tiny chin. 'Yes, I am, a sun hat for holidays by the seaside, only not this seaside, sweetheart, another one, a proper one with donkeys.' At that the baby's eyes widen and she gives her mother a gummy grin.

Serena has never seen her do this before and the sight of her daughter's empty pink gums undoes a knot in her chest and she laughs as she wraps the child in the arctic fox shrug she used to wear for Kittiwake's notorious parties.

It isn't hers and she has no right to take it now, but it will keep

386

the baby warm. Snow is still thick on the ground, but at last it's thawing and the sun is lemonade-bright to the eyes.

Serena opens the Gladstone bag that she found in the attic. She has wiped off all the dust inside and out and lined it with all the clothes she thinks she can manage, plus a couple of spare towelling nappies and an extra bottle for little miss.

Finally, after checking all the contents several times, she pops the baby inside, 'It's time to take you home,' she tells her.

Serena treads carefully in her slightly too big borrowed boots down the icy driveway to the gates, the bag is heavy but she hasn't got much choice. When she reaches the stone pillars at the end of the drive, she looks back at Kittiwake, sparkling in the winter frost, and notices how with its windowsills piped in snow it looks like an iced lemon cake. It's the most beautiful house she has ever stepped foot in and she wonders if she will ever come back.

Probably not. She turns away and rounds the corner and sticks out her thumb.

In Southend, Ida and her mum are sitting on the sofa with a hot-water bottle each under a multi-coloured crocheted blanket. This winter has gone on for ever and bar a glittery robin Christmas card postmarked Cornwall there has been no word from Serena.

Ida worries her mum will die before she sees the girl again, Noreen is very low and can't even be bothered to bite the heads off jelly babies any more, whole bags of them get ignored until they harden and have to be thrown away.

Ida reckons she'll have to give in and buy the old woman a new budgie. The old one fell off its perch a couple of weeks ago and her mum's been in a sulk ever since.

It's not doing Ida much good either, all this stopping in night after night to babysit her own mum.

She even feels guilty about leaving her to go out to work and every time she comes home, she dreads what she might find, but mostly Noreen hasn't moved, she spends hours sitting on the sofa staring at the mantelpiece at that photo of Serena when she won the bonniest baby competition on the pier.

Sometimes, after tea, when it all gets too much, Ida lies about what time it is, she tells her mum it's gone 10 p.m. and she should be getting to bed, even though, in reality, it's only 9 o'clock. Then Ida frogmarches her mother to the lavatory in the hope she'll stay dry through the night, helps her into her nightie and reminds her to drop her teeth into the cup of Steradent on the windowsill. Her mother seems to be shrinking every day.

Once she's settled, Ida goes upstairs and reads her Mills & Boon library book alone under the covers for an hour or so, because anything is better than the suffocating sadness of the two of them trapped in that front room, both silently wishing she'd come back, please come home, Serena.

Every fibre of that room seems to scream unhappiness, they can't forget and they can't move on, it's as if the place has been wallpapered with her face.

Ida yawns theatrically, she is on the verge of pulling the 'Oh my goodness, look at the time' trick, when she hears the doorbell ring.

Her mother doesn't hear it and Ida is tempted not to bother getting off the sofa. It'll be kids, no one ever calls in real life, it's been months since she's had a fellow pop by, once they smell her mother on her they run a mile in the opposite direction, and who can blame them?

Bloody kids playing knock down ginger, no doubt, but then, what if? What if it's the police, what if something's happened to Serena? Ida gets off the sofa in one move, instantly panicked, and with loose legs and what feels like piano hammers beating at her heart, she goes to answer the door.

Seconds later, she is making a noise she has never heard herself make before, 'ahahaeeah ohohaaaee' because she is standing there, her daughter is standing in front of her very eyes, 'ahahaeeah ohohaaaee'.

Serena stands on the doorstep in a great big fur coat smelling of woodsmoke and snow, she is all bundled up with a man's scarf around her neck and carrying a kitten in a leather bag.

Ida can hear it, Serena has bought her nan a kitten. Buggers on your nylons are kittens, but who cares when Serena has come home?

Still unable to form recognisable words, Ida pushes her daughter into the front room and Serena says, 'Hello, Nanna, look who's come home.' And then she opens up the bag and she brings out a big white cat. It's too big to be a kitten, it's a massive thing. But then something very odd happens, out of the white fur comes a baby, it's like a magic trick, like a little bird coming out of a rabbit.

'This is Amanda Karen,' says Serena, and she passes the bundle over to her grandmother, who holds her firmly on her knee and says, 'Hello little Mandy Tipping. Welcome home.'

The baby opens her eyes and immediately closes them again. Baby Mandy Tipping sleeps, because her life has already been quite an adventure, and who knows what the future holds.

Jenny Eclair is the *Sunday Times* top ten bestselling author of four critically acclaimed novels: *Camberwell Beauty*; *Having a Lovely Time*; *Life, Death and Vanilla Slices* and *Moving*. One of the UK's most popular writer/performers, she was the first woman to win the prestigious Perrier Award and has many TV and radio credits to her name. She lives in South-East London.